Tim and Felicity Adams, together with their young daughter, Jennifer, emerged from a well-known London clinic into the sunshine. Blinded by the fiery blast of a bomb during the war, Felicity had recently been experiencing moments of wild hope when blurs of light became visible, and her visit to the eye specialist had given her hope that some form of natural healing was taking place.

Afterwards they had lunch, and Felicity drew a quick breath and stared at her plate.

'Oh joy, there's colour, Tim, colour.'

'Mummy?' said Jennifer, wide eyed.

A waiter came up to enquire if anything was wrong.

Tim look up and smiled.

'Nothing,' he said. 'Everything is fine.'

By Mary Jane Staples

The Adams Books

DOWN LAMBETH WAY
OUR EMILY
KING OF CAMBERWELL
ON MOTHER BROWN'S DOORSTEP
A FAMILY AFFAIR
MISSING PERSON
PRIDE OF WALWORTH
ECHOES OF YESTERDAY
THE YOUNG ONES
THE CAMBERWELL RAID
THE LAST SUMMER
THE FAMILY AT WAR
FIRE OVER LONDON
CHURCHILL'S PEOPLE
BRIGHT DAY, DARK NIGHT
TOMORROW IS ANOTHER DAY
THE WAY AHEAD
YEAR OF VICTORY
THE HOMECOMING
SONS AND DAUGHTERS
APPOINTMENT AT THE PALACE
CHANGING TIMES
SPREADING WINGS

Other titles in order of publication

TWO FOR THREE FARTHINGS
THE LODGER
RISING SUMMER
THE PEARLY QUEEN
SERGEANT JOE
THE TRAP
THE GHOST OF WHITECHAPEL

SPREADING
WINGS

Mary Jane Staples

CORGI BOOKS

SPREADING WINGS
A CORGI BOOK : 0 552 15052 5

First publication in Great Britain

PRINTING HISTORY
Corgi edition published 2003

1 3 5 7 9 10 8 6 4 2

Set in 11/12pt New Baskerville by
Phoenix Typesetting, Burley-in-Wharfedale, West Yorkshire.

Corgi Books are published by Transworld Publishers,
61–63 Uxbridge Road, London W5 5SA,
a division of The Random House Group Ltd,
in Australia by Random House Australia (Pty) Ltd,
20 Alfred Street, Milsons Point, Sydney, NSW 2061, Australia,
in New Zealand by Random House New Zealand Ltd,
18 Poland Road, Glenfield, Auckland 10, New Zealand
and in South Africa by Random House (Pty) Ltd,
Endulini, 5a Jubilee Road, Parktown 2193, South Africa.

Printed and bound in Germany by
Elsnerdruck, Berlin.

To
Janet, the Irrepressible and Chris the Logger, and
their all-star triumvirate of Justin, Giles and Ben.

THE ADAMS FAMILY

Daniel Adams = Maisie Gibbs = Edwin Finch
b.1873 (d)   b.1876   (2)   b.1873

Emily = Robert (Boots)   Lizzy = Ned Somers
b.1898 (d)   (2) Simms   b.1898   b.1895
             b.1896

Tommy = Violet Coles   Sammy = Susie Brown
b.1900   b.1900   b.1902   b.1904

Gemma   James
b.1941   b.1941

Eloise = William (Luke) Lucas
b.1917 (B)   b.1910

Tim = Felicity Jessop
b.1921   b.1921

Alice   Kate = David Trimble
b.1925   b.1925   b.1926

Paul
b.1930

See Brown family tree

Annabelle = Nicholas Harrison
b.1916   b.1912

Edward = Leah Goodman
b.1924   b.1927

Bobby = Helene Aarlberg
b.1920   b.1921

Emma = Jonathan Hardy
b.1922   b.1919

Eliza
b.1948

Matthew = Rosie Chapman
b.1915 (A)   b.1911

Jennifer   Pandora
b.1945   b.1951

Philip   Linda
b.1936   b.1938

Charles
b.1947

Estelle   Robert
b.1946   b.1948

Jessie
b.1946

Giles   Emily
b.1942   b.1943

(A) – adopted   (B) – by Cecile Lacoste   b. – born   (d) – deceased

THE BROWN FAMILY

Jim Brown = Bessie Webb
b.1882   b.1884

Susie = Sammy Adams
b.1904   b.1902

Will = Annie Ford
b.1906   b.1908

Sally = Horace Cooper
b.1912   b.1910

Freddy = Cassie Ford
b.1914   b.1915

Daniel = Patsy Kirk
b.1927   b.1927

Bess = Jeremy Passmore
b.1928   b.1921

Jimmy
b.1930

Paula
b.1935

Phoebe
b.1937
(A)

Billy
b.1929

Harry
b.1931

William
b.1936

Donald
b.1939

Maureen
b.1938

Lewis
b.1940

Arabella
b.1948

Andrew
b.1950

Chapter One

An evening in early September, 1953.

Paul, younger son of Tommy and Vi Adams, and a confirmed Labour voter, knocked on the door of a flat in Kennington.

It was opened, although only a little way, by Miss Lulu Saunders, dedicated Socialist in favour of equal rights for women – and more equal in some cases – and daughter of Honest John Saunders, Labour MP.

'Is that you, Lulu?' asked Paul, seeing only part of her face and only one lens of her spectacles.

'You can't come in,' said Lulu.

'But I said I'd call,' protested Paul.

'You're too early, go away,' said Lulu.

'But I've got some happy news,' said Paul.

'Later,' said Lulu, 'later. You can't come in just yet.'

'Look, if you're having a bath –'

'Having a bath? D'you think I'm standing in it, then?'

'How do I know? I can only see your face, and only half of it at that. What's the other half like?'

'Oh, very witty,' said Lulu. 'I'm not dressed, that's all.'

'You mean you're not wearing anything?' said Paul.

'I mean I'm not fully dressed – oh, all right, then.' She opened the door wider. Paul stepped in and discovered she was wearing an old woollen dressing gown.

'Looks kind of loose and comfy,' he said.

'Go in the kitchen, not the living room,' she said.

'Why, what's in the living room?' asked Paul.

'If you must know, it's my wedding dress,' said Lulu. They were getting married this coming Saturday, and she'd been inspecting the gown, thinking about what it meant, and wondering if she was really doing the right thing. She wanted to live with Paul, she wanted to make sure she had him before some other woman entered his life, but did she want all that marriage entailed for a wife? For one thing, it would mean losing some of her freedom and independence. And for another, it might mean children, which would really tie her down. Even so, she still wanted Paul. He stimulated her, challenged her and brought about lively discussion and argument, all of which she enjoyed.

'I don't suppose you'll allow me a glimpse of the creation,' said Paul.

'Well, I'm falling in line with that old-fashioned custom of not letting you see it until I arrive at the church,' said Lulu, who had days when she was all for making him sign an agreement that would guarantee her standing as an equal marriage partner. Then the next day she would wonder if he'd like her to knit him a thick, winter woollen sweater, when she'd never knitted anything in her life. 'Paul, go in the kitchen, and you can tell me your happy news there.'

In he went, and she followed him. There he told her that purchase of the house in Brixton had been completed. It was all theirs, a house they'd made an offer for three months ago. Lulu said she couldn't think of a better wedding present, as long as they didn't go in for middle-class lace curtains. Middle-class lace curtains would make their Socialist friends suspicious of their true politics.

'You can choose the curtains,' said Paul, 'you'd know the kind that would show our friends we're still Labour voters. But listen, any that are made from a set of Red Flags are out. Out.'

'I hear you,' said Lulu. 'Put the kettle on and make some tea while I go and put a dress on.'

She departed for her bedroom, leaving Paul whistling cheerfully as he filled the kettle. He didn't suffer reservations himself. He was all for making Lulu his little woman, even if he knew she'd fight that.

Friday.

Tim and Felicity Adams, together with their young daughter, Jennifer, emerged from a well-known London clinic. Felicity's visit to the famous ophthalmic surgeon, Sir Charles Morgan, was the third since June. Blinded by the fiery blast of a bomb during the Second World War, her unsightly eye scars had gradually healed, but the world still remained a blank to her. However, since May she had experienced recurring moments of wild hope when blurs of light became visible, and even a faint glimmer of colour. In June, Tim had taken her to consult this London specialist, then again in late July, and now in early September.

Sir Charles Morgan had previously advanced a diagnosis based on the possibility of a natural healing process, something that was not unknown. He had just confirmed this opinion. He could not, he said, perform any kind of operation for Felicity's condition. She should exercise patience in the hope that nature would finish the work it had begun. The healing process that had eliminated the scars and was now producing blurs of light, pale images and very faint recognition of colours, was extraordinary. It had to relate, quite definitely, to nature lending a hand, particularly in view of the fact that these moments were happening more frequently. This could mean she was on the way to recovering her sight, even if only partially. Although he could not say for certain that this would be the case, nevertheless hope was very much in order. On bright days, she should guard her eyes with recommended sunglasses, and use an approved eyewash last thing every night.

So out from the clinic into the light of London on this bright day, stepped Felicity, arm in arm with Tim and hand in hand with eight-year-old Jennifer, still on summer holiday from school. Felicity's expression mirrored the message of hope, even if at the moment her eyes, shaded by her dark glasses, were quite blind.

'Mummy, it's lovely,' said Jennifer. 'Imagine nature being ever so kind to you.'

She and her father had been present with her

mother when Sir Charles was giving his diagnosis after his usual examination.

'My imagination is on a high,' said Tim. 'How's yours, Puss?'

'Mine is riotous,' said Felicity, alive with optimism.

'Come on,' said Tim, who was taking the day off from his office, 'let's find a palatial restaurant and celebrate with a palatial lunch.'

'Crumbs, I've never had a palatial lunch,' said Jennifer. 'Have I, Daddy?'

'You'll get one today, Little Puss,' said Tim. He gave Felicity's arm a gentle squeeze and glanced at her. There was, he thought, a faint flush of excitement on her face. God, he said to himself, I hope Morgan is right.

He decided on Simpson's in the Strand for lunch. There, in the main restaurant, the staff overwhelmed Jennifer with fuss and attention, and treated Felicity like a peeress.

They lunched, after an appetizing starter, on roast sirloin of English beef that was so deliciously pink and tender it inspired Jennifer to whisper, 'Daddy, it's ever so palatial.'

At this point, Felicity drew a quick breath and removed her sunglasses. She stared at her plate.

'Oh, joy,' she breathed, 'there's colour, Tim, colour.'

'Mummy?' said Jennifer, wide-eyed.

'Felicity, dear girl, how much colour?' asked Tim, touched to the quick and thinking how unbelievable it was that this was happening so soon after the consultation with Sir Charles Morgan. He

13

had thought the eye surgeon had only been able to advance possibilities and theories, not a specific diagnosis. 'Felicity?'

'Oh, it's faint,' breathed Felicity, 'but is it green, is it?'

'As green as broccoli can be,' said Tim.

'Mummy?' said Jennifer again, face and eyes animated.

'Darlings,' whispered Felicity, 'I think sweet nature is dining with us.'

Jennifer looked at her mother, at her expression of wonder and her staring eyes, and so did Tim, both caught up in this moment that was a repeat of others. Knives and forks were still.

Up came a concerned waiter.

'Sir, is anything wrong?'

Tim looked up. He smiled.

'Nothing,' he said, 'everything is fine.'

'And madam?'

Felicity, replacing her sunglasses as the image faded, said, 'Everything is marvellous.'

A fading image was still one more step on the road to recovery, wasn't it?

This one had been due, for they were happening every two or three days now, and the last one had been Tuesday. Sometimes they lasted for as long as a minute, sometimes for only a few moments. Sometimes the image was more definite, such as this last one, although none had ever been sharp and clear.

All the same, Felicity told herself that she now knew exactly what was meant by hope springs eternal.

Perhaps, perhaps one day I might actually see my cherished daughter. And Tim again.

14

*　*　*

Cadet Philip Harrison of the RAF, son of Annabelle and Nick Harrison, was on the phone to Phoebe, adopted daughter of Sammy and Susie Adams, trying to have a cosy chat with her.

'Yes, like I've already mentioned, it really is nice of you to ring,' said Phoebe, sixteen and a recent school-leaver, 'but I can't talk for long. I'm busy helping my sister. That's Paula, you know.'

'Yes, I know Paula, and I also know she's getting married tomorrow,' said Philip. 'To an Italian haymaker.'

'Enrico's nice,' said Phoebe. 'Anyway, because of that, I'm having to do all kinds of things for Paula. And then my mother keeps wanting to make sure I look fab in my bridesmaid's dress, but not quite as fab as the bride.'

'Phoebe, I'm sure you'll look a dream.'

'But it wouldn't do for me to outshine the bride, especially as she's my sister,' said Phoebe. 'It's all very exciting, of course, but a bit too much for Daddy. He's at his offices as usual, and when he left this morning he said he'd probably not be home until midnight. He said he didn't want to get caught up in all this pre-wedding-day racket, and my mother said if he wasn't home at his usual time to take some of the worries off her hands, he needn't come home at all.'

'I feel for all of you,' said Philip, 'but at least the worries are kind of happy ones, aren't they?'

'There's a hundred and more guests coming, because it's a double wedding,' said Phoebe.

'Yes, I know,' said Philip, 'cousin Paul is marrying Lulu Saunders. I've never met her—'

'You will tomorrow,' said Phoebe. 'She's ever so ambitious, she wants to be a Labour MP and do wonders for the workers, which Daddy says is all right for her, but not what he wants for female girls like Paula or me, though I'm sure I never know what he means by female girls. Philip, don't keep me talking, we're all far too busy for that.'

'I only phoned to let you know I'm hoping to hitch-hike home early this evening,' said Philip, 'and that I'll see you tomorrow when you arrive at the church in your bridesmaid's frills.'

'Why didn't you say so at first instead of doing all this talking?' said Phoebe.

'If I'd had the chance—'

'Anyway, it's nice you did phone,' said Phoebe, 'but I have to say goodbye now.'

'So long, Pussycat, stay with it,' said Philip.

Sammy, busy at his office desk, found time to phone his old friend, Mr Eli Greenberg. Mr Greenberg had suffered a hairline skull fracture three months ago, but the old rag-and-bone merchant proved he was as tough as an army boot, 1914 vintage, by recovering in remarkably quick time. He was supposed to be in retirement, but was still at his Camberwell yard, attending to the books, the phone and enquiries, while his sturdy stepsons, Michal and Jacob, looked after all the heavy work, including house clearances.

'Sammy, that's you?' he said when the call came through.

'Yes, it's me, Eli old cock,' said Sammy, 'just wanting to know how you are.'

'Sammy, I'm right as a fiddle, ain't I?'

'Pleased to hear it,' said Sammy, 'and to know you'll be able to do your stuff in collecting tomorrow's brides and their dads in your old pony and cart and driving them to the church. One of the dads is yours truly.'

'Vhy, Sammy, vould I let you down in such a matter?' said Mr Greenberg, who still spoke his own kind of English. 'Ain't I had the pleasure of doing same for so many Adams brides since I first carted Emily to her vedding with Boots?'

'Well, that started the custom,' said Sammy. 'Is the pony up to it?'

'Sammy, it ain't the same vun that did the honours for Emily, but it'll pull the cart in the same vay, von't it?'

'Enough said, Eli old mate. See you tomorrow then, eh?'

'Vell, I ain't going to disappear, Sammy, vhich you can bet your last farthing on.'

Chapter Two

Saturday afternoon.

The double wedding in the church on Denmark Hill was over, and a host of relatives and guests were assembled on the forecourt, with both brides and their grooms posing for photographs, although Lulu was doing so with a feeling that she was caught up in a middle-class affair of flowery pomp.

Chinese Lady and Sir Edwin looked on, Chinese Lady thinking the service had been very moving and proper, except for one thing. While Paula had happily promised to 'love, honour and obey' her handsome Italian bridegroom, Lulu had omitted the word 'obey'. Sir Edwin had whispered that Lulu was the kind of modern woman who probably felt the word put her on a par with a chattel. It caused Chinese Lady to raise her eyebrows. She wasn't in favour of sacred vows being mucked about. Obey didn't mean a wife had to take orders from her husband and let him turn himself into her lord and master. It simply meant humouring him and helping him to be what he should be, her provider and protector.

Lizzy had done that very well with Ned, and so

had Vi with Tommy, and Susie with Sammy, and without their men hardly noticing. Of course, Boots had made it different, first for poor Emily and then with Polly. There just wasn't any way a wife could keep up with his airy-fairy side.

Still, even if Lulu hadn't said 'obey', she had looked a proper bride in her white gown, and Paula had looked lovely.

Now, outside the church, all photographs had been taken, and at the kerbside stood a polished green cart with Mr Greenberg, in topper and grey suit, up at the reins, and his pony patiently standing. Forward went the brides and grooms to be showered with colourful confetti once they reached the pavement, Paula shrieking with laughter and happiness, Lulu smiling, her gold-rimmed spectacles reflecting the brightness of deeper feelings, the feelings of a woman who had the man she wanted as a permanent companion and stimulation.

Honest John Saunders, her dad, looked on as she and Paul climbed aboard the cart.

'Proud of you, Lulu,' he said, then whispered in her ear, 'but mind you don't play up.'

'I didn't hear that,' she said.

Once the brides and grooms were seated, Mr Greenberg turned his head and said, 'Vell now, ain't I seeing double, and vhat a handsome double, ain't it? Shall ve go?'

'Please to drive on,' said Enrico, an enraptured Italian.

'Go, go, Mr Greenberg,' said Paul, and away the pony and cart went, at a slow amble, with young people still showering confetti.

*   *   *

Late afternoon.

In the reception complex on the first floor of the Denmark Hill pub, the Fox and Hounds, the festivities were reaching their end. The wedding breakfast had been provided by caterers at the uppish price of ten and six a head, with drinks extra, the total cost to be shared by Sammy and Lulu's dad. The speeches had been made. Boots, as best man to Paul, had excelled himself without delivering jokes too near the edge for older people, and his nephew David, as best man to Enrico, had followed suit. Paul devoted the better part of his speech to how lucky he was in having super parents, and to his good fortune in acquiring a wife as go-ahead as Lulu who, he was proud to declare, had turned out to be a rattling good cook.

'What else can she do that you like, Paul?' called some wit.

'Write uplifting slogans for Labour voters,' said Paul, which aroused groans in various capitalist-minded guests.

Enrico's speech was brief but fervent. He had said he was very happy, not half, to have an English wife as lovely as Paula, which he hoped would help him to become English himself and one of the family, not half. Also, he was touched, you bet, at how kind everyone had been since he arrived in England and helped him to speak fine English.

The family members were present in force, and included Eloise and Colonel Lucas, and Bess and Jeremy Passmore, as well as a member-to-be in Clare Roper, now engaged to Sammy and Susie's younger son Jimmy. Their elder son Daniel and his wife Patsy were presently in America with their children. It bewildered Chinese Lady, the fact that people could fly to America in an aeroplane and be there the same day. It also alarmed her, for she could picture the children opening a window and falling out. Sir Edwin assured her that aeroplane windows could not be opened, so of course, Chinese Lady said she didn't know what windows were for if they couldn't be opened on a hot day to let some air in.

Polly, in company with Boots, Rosie and Matthew Chapman, looked around at the galaxy of guests and relatives. She noted a predominance of younger generations.

'Boots old bean,' she said, 'you and I are being swamped by the young.'

'Well, if we can keep our heads above water, I think we can live as part of a minority,' said Boots.

'Don't let that worry you two,' said Rosie, 'it's an exclusive minority.'

'There's an old Dorset saying,' said Matthew, born in that county. ' "There's some as know the Dorset land, 'twas they that shaped it with their hand, and when the time comes for the young, 'tis more that's wanted than their tongue." '

'That's not old Dorset, that's old Farmer Chapman,' said Rosie. 'Still, treat it kindly, Polly.'

'Hello, hello,' said Matthew, 'it looks as if the happy couples are departing.'

Enrico and Paula, Paul and Lulu, having changed into going-away outfits, had rejoined the multitude to say their goodbyes. The brides, as per custom, tossed their wedding bouquets high. Hands reached to catch them. Fifteen-year-old Linda, daughter of

Annabelle and Nick Harrison, caught one, and sixteen-year-old Phoebe caught the other, all amid yells and shrieks from crowding young people.

'Crikey,' said Linda to nearby cousin Jimmy Adams, 'look at what I've got.'

'Suits you, especially as you're growing,' said Jimmy, giving her a wink.

Linda laughed. Her personal development provided a topic she secretly shared with cousin Jimmy. After years of being painfully thin, she was now shaping up.

Phoebe, clutching the other bouquet, said to Philip, 'Well, what could this mean, I wonder?'

'That you've now got something to think about,' said Philip.

'I've already got lots to think about,' said Phoebe, 'including the job I'm starting at Daddy's offices now I've left school. I'm much too young to think of what you're thinking of, anyway.'

'Well, look here,' said Philip, 'isn't there a lonely widow among all these people you could give the bouquet to?'

'Oh, brilliant, I must say,' said Phoebe, 'I'm not going round looking for a lonely widow, I'm going to see the brides and grooms go off on their honeymoons. Come on, slowcoach.'

Away she went to join the throngs following the newly-weds out, Philip at her heels in case some other feller decided to muscle in. There were Young Socialists present, friends of Paul and Lulu, and the males looked a competitive lot.

Paula and Enrico were going to the Cotswolds, Lulu and Paul to the Lake District. Sammy was driving Paula and Enrico to Paddington station, and Tommy was driving Paul and Lulu to St Pancras.

Outside, everyone swarmed. Honeymoon luggage was loaded into the cars, and more confetti was showered as the newly-weds said goodbye to their nearest and dearest, Lulu to her dad and step-mother, Paul to Vi, brother David and sister Alice. Alice, still studious and now a university tutor, was up from Bristol. Paula and Enrico said goodbye to Susie, Phoebe, Bess, Daniel and Jimmy. Unhappily for Enrico, his parents were now dead, worn out by long years of farm labouring.

Away went the cars, old boots hanging, and some ribald comments following them.

'Well, I think I'll now go home and relax,' said Susie after all the clamour had died down. And she did, Mr Greenberg driving her in his pony and cart. Up with her, by invitation, went Boots, Polly, Vi and Lizzy. Chinese Lady and Sir Edwin followed on in his ancient car, with Ned and slightly decrepit old Aunt Victoria, mother of Vi. Chinese Lady was wondering if her already extensive family was ever going to stop growing. The double wedding had added one more granddaughter-in-law, and one more grandson-in-law, an Italian one, would you believe. Still, it wasn't anything to grumble about, not when there were already American and French connections in the family. Lord, she thought, when all the young ones like Boots's twins grow up, the family might get connected to all kinds, seeing some people are going on foreign holidays these days. I don't know what's wrong with Margate and Brighton that they don't go there.

Susie and Sammy's house was crowded that

evening in celebration of the happy day, Sammy playing the genial host like a man who had cheerfully put aside thoughts of what his share of expenses was going to cost him.

In a ground-floor Bloomsbury flat, its occupant, a businesswoman, a Miss Stella Peebles, was sitting at a table in her living room, typing a letter while keeping company with a glass of gin and tonic. At one point, she wrinkled her nose, and not for the first time in recent days.

She was sure there was a smell emanating from somewhere, a faint smell, but enough to offend her fine nose now and again. She'd sniffed around a couple of times, but hadn't been able to locate its source.

She drank more gin and tonic, and resumed her typing.

Chapter Three

It was late that night when Mrs Paula Cellino sighed and murmured, 'Rico . . . did I dream that?'

'Ah, me too, I feel like that, don't I?' whispered Enrico.

'Mmmm . . .' It was no more than another sigh from Paula, but it conveyed a happy message to the effect that they had made a heavenly start to their honeymoon. Well, a bride at this moment could think in heavenly terms. After all, there'd been some qualms. Not about accepting the embrace of love, but about how she would react. She needn't have worried. She was a very healthy young woman, and Enrico a very understanding Italian. He took his time. His blushing bride stopped blushing and participated with natural ardour.

'For me, wonderful, not half,' whispered Enrico. Warm, vibrant and very glad there had been no embarrassing moments for either of them, Paula snuggled up. 'You were lovely, Paula, yes.'

'Oh, I'm relieved to know that,' she said, and because of her happy feelings, her sense of humour made an entrance. 'Well, it's the first time I've ever been in bed with a man.'

At which, they both let soft, contented laughter escape.

In a Windermere hotel bedroom, Paul slowly slid from Lulu's stiff body.

'I'm sorry,' she said guiltily.

'You don't want to make love?' said Paul, frustrated and disappointed.

'I'm sorry,' said Lulu again, 'but I can't.'

'You could if you'd relax,' said Paul.

'I tried to,' said Lulu.

'Perhaps it was my fault,' said Paul.

'No. No. I'm the problem,' said Lulu. 'I know that.'

'Well, I did think you were too tense, but if I didn't excite you, then it was partly my fault,' said Paul, mentally wincing at his failure to arouse her.

'No, don't take any blame,' said Lulu. 'Disappointments happen. In any case, I've always thought our kind of marriage could be one of friendship, companionship and active minds. And simply being together. So don't be upset.'

'Now listen,' said Paul, considerably upset, 'are you talking about a platonic marriage? There's no such thing. Didn't you reckon on making love?'

'Yes, of course I did,' said Lulu, 'but without thinking it might not be to my liking. I've only just discovered it isn't.'

'Perhaps only because it's your first time,' said Paul. 'I've heard that's how it is for some women.'

'Paul, we're adults, intelligent adults. We can take our time to work on this little problem, can't we? I do care for you, even if –'

'Even if tonight's been a disappointment to you?'

'Paul, we've got such a lot in common. Our minds, our interests and our politics.'

'And that's what you'd prefer, a marriage of our minds and our political interests?' said Paul, male ego at rock-bottom.

'If you want,' said Lulu, 'we can try making love again tomorrow night.'

'Yes, let's forget this conversation,' said Paul, 'it's knocking holes in my head. Tomorrow we'll go out and see something of Windermere, we'll soak up the atmosphere and take in gallons of fresh air, and find out what all that will do for us.'

'I'd like that, I really would,' said Lulu.

'Goodnight, then,' said Paul, and turned on his side. He lay with his back to her.

They both took a long time to get to sleep. Paul felt sick, even humiliated. Lulu felt she should have taken her reservations more seriously, except that she really did want to live with Paul. She was a puzzle to herself as well as Paul at this moment.

Paul wondered, in shock, if she was the kind of woman who became frigid as a wife.

They did go out the next day, after a somewhat quiet breakfast. They boated on Lake Windermere, they explored the adjacent countryside, had lunch at a pub, and did some more hiking. Lulu talked of what they could do as partners whose main interests lay with helping a return to office of a Labour government. Perhaps they could aim for a time, say in four or five years, when they might both be selected as candidates in a future election.

Paul, resolutely keeping his peace about what

was mostly on his mind, said he hoped he'd be able to live with that kind of ambition, since he knew he wasn't as devoted to the prospect as she was. Lulu said she'd be on the spot all the time, to help him recharge his political batteries whenever necessary.

When they got back to their hotel, they had a bath, though not together, and then a good dinner. Finally, of course, after a relaxing time in the hotel lounge, they went up to their room, where the crunch arrived.

'Well?' said Paul.

'How do I feel, you mean?' said Lulu. 'Fine from our day out.'

'No, I didn't mean that,' said Paul.

'I see,' said Lulu. 'Well, let's go to bed and do what we agreed. Try for success.'

It didn't work. She was so stiff and tense that Paul made no real attempt to join forces with her.

'Sometime or other, just let me know if you feel a natural urge,' he said. 'As it is, it's no fun for either of us.'

'Paul, I'm sorry.'

'So am I. Well, as we can't enjoy each other, let's spend our time enjoying the English Lakes.'

Paul was a shaken young man.

He felt frozen out.

They returned home after a week to live in Lulu's flat while spending the second week of their honeymoon furnishing their house in Brixton. In the flat they slept together without attempting that which Lulu found not to her liking. In their future abode one day, Paul said perhaps it would be better to have separate bedrooms.

Shocked, Lulu said, 'Paul, that's ridiculous, I like sleeping with you.'

'It's a trial to me,' said Paul, 'it tempts my instincts, and I don't think my instincts are unnatural. I can't play the role of being your hot-water bottle. Let's have separate bedrooms until such time as you feel you want to make love.'

'But what will our friends and relatives think?' asked Lulu.

'I've always had the impression that, as a woman of independent spirit, you've never been bothered about what people think,' said Paul.

'If you're trying to quarrel with me, I won't let you,' said Lulu.

'Oh, well, san fairy,' said Paul, 'let's be friends if we can't be lovers. Let's agree that separate bedrooms are the best bet for friends.' That arrangement, he thought, would save him from having to repress himself when in bed with her.

Lulu protested, but Paul was adamant, and although she considered it quite against her idea of a companionable day and night marriage, she agreed in the end.

Her dad dropped in at the Brixton house one day. Lulu was out buying curtain runners.

'Hello,' said Paul, in his shirtsleeves. He'd been moving furniture about. 'What brings you to our Brixton homestead?'

'Just thought I'd look in while passing,' said Honest John, an MP well known for his frankness and plain speaking in the House, never mind that it sometimes put a Labour whip on his tail. 'How's it working out?'

'We're halfway there,' said Paul. 'We'll be able to move in this weekend and finish setting ourselves up in style by next weekend.'

'Sounds satisfactory, Paul. Where's Lulu?'

'Out shopping for odds and ends,' said Paul.

'How is she?'

'Committed,' said Paul.

'Committed to what?'

'In time, a seat in Parliament,' said Paul.

'That's still her priority?' said Honest John.

'It's number one,' said Paul.

'You don't look too pleased about it.'

'Well,' said Paul, 'not all my ideas coincide with hers.'

'Is that girl of mine playing up?'

'Oh, anything like that is just between her and me,' said Paul lightly.

'I like that kind of loyalty,' said Honest John, 'but if there's something worrying you, well, I know Lulu through and through, and I might be able to help.'

'Come and have a beer,' said Paul, 'I've got a bottle or two somewhere.'

'You're on,' said Honest John, a stalwart.

Paul found a bottle under a kitchen chair. He also found two glasses under a heap of new tea towels. He and Lulu's dad began to enjoy the beer in the living room, now fully furnished. Lulu wasn't fussy or demanding about placements. 'Yes, that'll do,' she'd say. 'Yes, that's all right there.' 'Yes, anywhere will do for that vase. I always forget to clear dead flowers out, anyway.' And so on. Lulu let it be known there were more important things than fiddling about with furniture-arranging.

With her dad settled into an armchair, Paul said, 'Since you're bound to find out eventually, I might as well tell you we've got separate bedrooms.'

'Good God,' said Honest John.

'You're a man of the world,' said Paul, 'so I don't suppose you need to ask why.'

'No, not my place to ask questions, even if I am Lulu's dad,' said Honest John, 'but if the problem's what I think it might be, let me tell you that in the first months of my first marriage, her late mother would hardly let me touch her. Had a conviction that the job of a wife was to cook, tidy up, make the bed and put the cat out at night. Sex was the dark unknown to her. Get me?'

'It frightened her?' said Paul.

'Talk about scared and innocent. At nineteen, she didn't even know how babies came about. Fact, y'know.'

'What did it do to you?' asked Paul.

'Made me blow my top in the end,' said Lulu's dad, though a sly grin creased his honest countenance. 'Told her I needed a woman, and that there was one ready and willing who worked in the constituency offices, as I did myself at the time, long before I became an MP. Lily – the wife – surprised me then. Don't do it, don't go with another woman, she said. Like to know what she said next?'

'That she'd divorce you?' suggested Paul.

'Not much, Paul. She said she was ready and willing herself, that she'd been given advice and information by a friendly neighbour, and that she knew why she'd been feeling broody lately. Broody, I ask you.' Honest John chuckled. 'It must've been old Mrs Price she'd been listening to. Mrs Price knew every old wives' tale going. Well, that did it. Lily was over being frightened of sex, and from then on we never looked back.'

'And you think Lulu's got the same problem?' said Paul.

'Well, from some of the things she used to say about men and marriage, I did have a suspicion. It surprised me that she married at all, but it pleased me that it was you. I spoke to her on the wedding day, and told her not to play you up. Paul, you'll have to give her time.'

'I'm doing that,' said Paul, 'by having separate bedrooms.'

'Well, let's hope she gets to feel lonely and then neglected,' said Honest John. 'When a wife starts to feel neglected, me lad, she also starts to feel a need. So hang on and wait.'

Lulu arrived back at that point, carrying a parcel.

'Hello, Dad,' she said. 'Looks like you've dropped in for a beer.'

'And a bit of a chat,' said her dad. 'I like the way you and Paul are furnishing your house. It'll end up as a cosy nest for two, eh?'

'It'll be our citadel of thought, theory and enterprise,' said Lulu. 'From which we'll march forth as valiant soldiers of a Socialist army.'

'Lulu, I'm going to start praying for you,' said Honest John. 'You still don't know the British people don't go for that fiery stuff. They're conservative with a small "c". What you describe as a Socialist army would be a barmy army to them.

Talk to her, Paul, and smack her bottom if you have to. I'm off now.' He finished his beer and stood up. 'I'm taking your stepma to the theatre tonight, Lulu. While the House is still in summer recess, she's making sure I don't spend all my time listening to complaints from my constituents. Thanks for the beer, Paul.'

'You're welcome,' said Paul, and saw his father-in-law out. Honest John's parting delivery was advisory.

'Get her off Karl Marx, old chap.'

When Paul rejoined Lulu, she said, 'Dad's forgetting his Socialist roots.'

'Not according to what the Tories say about him,' said Paul. 'And look here, don't count on me to join your Socialist army. Your dad's right, the people won't go for it, they'll equate it with Communism. Now, did you get what you wanted at the shop?'

'Yes, everything,' said Lulu. 'And I do count on you to be with me all the way politically.'

'I've got a good job,' said Paul, 'and my first priority is to make a success of it. Uncle Sammy favours success, and he'll reward me for it. And he won't hold it against me that I'll still remain a Labour voter. But I'm not going to join you every time you go over the top.'

'Over the top?' Lulu looked hurt. 'Paul, you're not losing faith in me, are you?'

'No, just my patience now and again,' said Paul. 'Now, I'll just finish putting the kitchen to rights so that we can use it without falling over unpacked equipment, while you do what you have to do with the parlour curtains.'

'Paul—'

'Lulu, our priority right now is putting this house in order,' said Paul, and off he went to the kitchen.

Lulu stood frowning and fidgety. She was having perverse moments, when political ambitions receded into a kind of foggy background and marital companionship with Paul was a bright and clear fact. She really ought to overcome her feelings of reluctance. That reluctance, of course, was brought about by her belief that the ultimate act represented a man's domination of a woman, which she was totally against.

Paul's own belief at the moment was that Lulu wasn't equipped for a conventional marriage, that he had made a mistake in pressing her to take the plunge. He simply had to live with his mistake.

By Saturday evening, the house was ready for occupation, even if there were a few more jobs to do. So when they returned to Lulu's Kennington flat, it was for the last time. On Sunday they would transfer a few final items to Brixton, then leave the flat to the landlord. As a furnished unit, everything belonged to him, anyway.

They were tired when they went to bed, and fell asleep almost at once, Paul on his side at a distance from Lulu. The fact that it was the last time they would sleep together hurt her. But tiredness claimed her and she slept the night through.

On Sunday they moved into the house. They spent the day wallpapering the spare bedroom, snatching quick cold meals. That night they quarrelled about sleeping separately. Paul said that as far as he was concerned, it was the best thing to do.

Lulu mentioned their friends again, saying that if they found out, they'd think she and Paul were odd.

'Well, we are,' said Paul.

'You mean I am.'

Paul sighed.

'I'm giving you time,' he said.

'Look, I went for marriage, didn't I, after always thinking it wasn't necessary?'

'I think we've both made a mistake.'

'I will have done when I come to hate you.'

'Goodnight,' said Paul, and went up to his own bedroom, wondering why she was kicking against the arrangement. Seeing she had a thing about keeping him at a distance, she ought to be well in favour of separate beds. He couldn't believe she really cared about what their friends might think. For the first time in his life he said what many other men had said in a bemused moment.

'Women.'

What women in their own moments had said about men had filled a book. It wasn't, however, a book that Paul had yet read. His Uncle Sammy would have told him he'd get to it in time.

On Monday, they returned to their places of work, and they spent the evenings being cool and civilized to each other. They also continued to sleep in their own bedrooms, which began to give Lulu a feeling that something was radically wrong with her night life, something that was nothing to do with companionship. Strange stirrings disturbed her.

On Sunday night, she woke up after a few hours' sleep. She felt an urgent need to be with Paul, a need that had been creeping up on her, a need to be in bed with him, and as close as she could get. It became so demanding that she slipped out of her bed and went to his room. In the darkness he was a dim hump beneath his bedclothes. Compulsively, she eased herself in beside him, her body made contact, and she sighed as she snuggled close.

Paul, of course, woke up, conscious of physical reactions. Lulu was right up against him.

'What's going on?'

'Paul, it isn't right, not being together.'

'You're a funny old lot, Lulu, with your wonky ideas about marriage, but listen –'

'Paul?' Her voice was a potent whisper.

'Look, you know what this does to me, so lay off. But don't worry about me too much, I could always look around for an obliging woman.' That was an echo of her dad's words.

'What? What did you say?'

'Just something to remind you I've got natural urges.'

'Well, so have I,' said Lulu.

'But they're not the same as mine, are they?'

She put her face in his shoulder and whispered muffledly, 'Try me.' Her body had come alive at last.

'Not if you don't mean it, not if it's only a peace-making offer.'

'Stop it,' said Lulu, pushing and quivering. 'Be nice to me. Love me.'

'Well, I tell you, Lulu, if we continue the way we have, I will find a woman who'd be willing. I'd have to. I'm human.'

'You'll be signing your death warrant if you

36

even look at another woman. You hear me?'

Shades of her dad and her late mum, thought Paul, and wound his arms around her, his physical being as good as on fire.

'Lulu, you sure? You sure you're sure?'

'Yes . . . yes . . .'

So Paul made love to her, and she was neither tense nor teeth-gritted. She accepted him like a newborn woman, and came out of it in wonder and even exaltation. Some unspoken worries had disappeared. She was normal. She had just been too nervous, that was all, and as for being dominated, that had turned out to be utterly acceptable.

'Well?' murmured Paul, delighted with her.

'Oh, who cares about Socialist banners now?' said Lulu, which was on a par with revolutionary red turning into royal blue. (Not that it was likely to last.) 'Why didn't you tell me it was going to be great?'

'I didn't know, did I?' said Paul. 'This was my first time with you.'

'Well, now we've both found out.'

'No separate bedrooms, Lulu?'

'Paul, I've made the point before, what kind of a marriage would that be?'

'I thought your kind.'

'Well, I was wrong and so were you. Cuddle me.'

Paul wanted to laugh. Lulu, the most modern of modern women, asking for a cuddle? The skies had fallen.

He cuddled her, and they talked in happy whispers about what their priorities were now. Paul said he supposed hers were an apron and the kitchen sink, and his the old-fashioned custom of bringing home his wages and handing them to her.

In the warmth of the bed and their cosy new-found togetherness, a muffled gurgle was heard.

A newborn Lulu was smothering laughter. From somewhere, she had found a sense of humour.

Chapter Four

A visitor arrived at a military hospital near Farnham in Surrey, a hospital given over to the care of army personnel still suffering disablement from crippling war wounds. The receptionist glanced up to see a woman of classically oval features and clear blue eyes, dressed in a grey costume and a brimmed black hat. Beneath the brim looped strands of golden hair were visible. She looked to be in her early thirties.

'Oh, good morning, madam,' said the receptionist, 'what can I do for you?'

'I wish to trace a lady who was a patient here during the war,' said the blonde woman, her voice carrying the lightest of foreign accents.

'I'm afraid I wasn't here during the war.'

A nurse wheeling an inmate passed by, the inmate a man without legs. The visitor winced a little.

'But would your records contain her details?' she asked. 'I can give you her name. Lieutenant Felicity Adams.'

'Well, we did have some ATS patients here, mainly casualties of air raids, I do know that,' said the receptionist. 'I'll talk to our Records Officer, Mr Sylvester. May I have your name?'

'Miss Bruck.'

'Miss Brook, yes, just a moment.' The receptionist used the phone to talk to the Records Officer. Putting the receiver down, she smiled and said, 'Yes, Mr Sylvester will see you. I'll take you to his office.' She came to her feet.

Anneliese Bruck of Berlin followed her along a corridor. The receptionist knocked on a door.

'Come.'

The receptionist opened the door and said, 'Miss Brook.'

'Right, let her come in.'

The receptionist moved aside and Anneliese Bruck entered. The Records Officer, a friendly-looking man in his forties, stood up, and the receptionist closed the door and went back to her desk.

'Good morning,' said Anneliese.

'Good morning,' said Mr Sylvester, 'and how can I help you, Miss Brook?'

'It's Bruck.' Anneliese pronounced her name with a guttural emphasis, and spelled it. 'I am German, Mr Sylvester, and was once a nurse with the German army.'

Mr Sylvester, already taken with her looks, regarded her with great interest.

'Well, I don't meet German ladies every day,' he said. 'Please sit down, Miss Bruck.' Anneliese, hitching her skirt, seated herself. 'Now, what brings you here? That is, what help do you want?'

Anneliese, calm and controlled, said that as a German army nurse she had served in North Africa during the desert war, and subsequently on the

Russian Front. On the Russian Front, the war was cruel and hideous, she said. In North Africa, the war between the Afrika Korps and the British Eighth Army was, by comparison, humane and almost civilized, especially in the way wounded prisoners on both sides were treated. In the German-run hospital at Benghazi she experienced the privilege of nursing a wounded British officer, a captured commando.

'That was a privilege?' said the Records Officer, reseating himself at his desk.

'For me, yes. He was a soldier of the bravest kind. His major wound was his sternum, his chestbone, fractured by two bullets, but always he was cheerful. And sometimes –' A little smile flickered. 'Sometimes even impertinent.'

'That happens when a patient begins to make advances to a nurse,' said Mr Sylvester, with a smile of his own. 'May I ask how you came to speak such perfect English?'

'My grandmother was English, born in your city of Bath, and she helped to bring up my sister and myself. Mr Sylvester, I wish to trace the wife of this British officer. She was an officer herself. I knew her as Lieutenant Felicity Adams.'

'You met her?'

'No. I should have said I knew of her. Although it was forbidden, I arranged for her husband, Lieutenant Tim Adams, my British patient, to send her a prisoner-of-war card.' Anneliese, speaking calmly and precisely, went on to say she noted the name, and that the card was addressed care of this hospital. She had a particular reason for wishing to

41

get in touch with the British officer, but could only do so through his wife, if her present address was known.

Mr Sylvester said this kind of request was unusual, but its purpose was acceptable. He himself had only been working here for six years, and therefore he had no knowledge of wartime patients.

'However –'

'You have wartime records?' said Anneliese.

'Yes. What happened to your wounded prisoner of war, by the way?'

'He escaped at a time when we were evacuating the hospital because the British were about to take Benghazi.' Again a little smile flickered. 'He was that kind of man.' A new expression arrived, a look of disgust. 'If our lunatic fuehrer, Hitler, had had his way, Lieutenant Adams, as a commando, would have been executed. Splendidly, General Rommel refused to obey the order to shoot all captured commandos.'

'If Lieutenant Adams escaped,' said Mr Sylvester, 'if he rejoined the fight as a commando, he may not have survived the war.'

'Some men deserve good fortune, some do not,' said Anneliese. 'If I can trace his wife, she will let me know if her husband survived.'

'What was her name again?'

'Lieutenant Felicity Adams.'

'I must tell you, Miss Bruck, that this hospital deals only with serious casualties of war and, where necessary, with their rehabilitation.'

'You are trying to tell me that Lieutenant Felicity Adams might not have recovered as a casualty? I hope that isn't so.'

'Let's see if her medical file still exists,' said Mr Sylvester. 'I know that we still have the records of most wartime patients.' He came to his feet, crossed to a filing cabinet, pulled open a lower drawer, and began flipping through a long row of files. Not finding the one he was looking for, he closed the drawer and opened the one beneath. Again he went through files under the hopeful gaze of his visitor. He muttered, and with a slower touch he re-examined the files in both drawers. Then he shook his head. 'I'm sorry, Miss Bruck, but the file in question isn't here, it simply isn't.'

Had he known, or had his visitor been able to tell him, that the patient had been admitted under her maiden name of Jessop, his search would have been successful.

'Would that mean she might have died?' asked Anneliese.

'That's very possible.'

'Or might it mean she was on the staff here, as an army nurse?'

'I can soon check that,' said Mr Sylvester, and moved to another filing cabinet. He made his search. 'Again I'm sorry, Miss Bruck, but no, no-one of that name worked here.'

'Well, I must accept this result,' said Anneliese, 'but thank you for giving me so much of your time.'

'I'm disappointed that I haven't been able to help you,' said Mr Sylvester, and saw her out.

Leaving the hospital, she walked down the drive to the main gate, and then made her way to the bus stop. There, she caught a bus to Farnham. On the way her thoughts turned inwards to memories of Benghazi and the young British commando, a badly wounded prisoner of war. He endured initial periods of pain without complaint, and on the road to recovery his engaging personality revealed itself. Extrovert and amusing, he was definitely impertinent at times. Yes, he had escaped while the German-run hospital was being evacuated, and some inner compulsion had prevented her from calling for German military police to take him into custody. She had glimpsed him trying to hide himself, but had taken no action. Had he known that? What he must have known was that he left his commando beret behind, an item, she knew, precious to every commando. Had he survived the rest of the war, was he still alive? It could be that his wife hadn't.

She thought of the defeat of the valiant men of the Afrika Korps, and of the fact that she and other medical personnel had been evacuated from North Africa before the Germans there accepted defeat. She thought of her time in Italy and her eventual transfer to the Russian Front. There, she became aware of war at its most bloodthirsty and disgusting, and of her complete disillusionment with Hitler, Himmler and the SS. As a nurse, the barbaric excesses of the SS, and of the Russian hordes too, sickened her. There came the time in 1945 when Stalin's armies were at the gates of Berlin itself, and she and other nurses only just escaped being taken. What the Russians could do and did do to German army nurses was unspeakable.

The end of the catastrophic war arrived, and her time in shattered West Berlin began. Life was one of hunger, privation and the winter misery of unheated houses. But worst of all was the contempt the occupying American and British troops visibly showed for every German, for a people who had allowed the existence of concentration camps and the extermination of millions of Jews. Protestations of innocence or ignorance were not believed. It was bitter almost beyond endurance to realize Himmler and his SS had given the world cause to despise Germany and its people. She shed her injured pride one day by applying to the welfare office for a little more sustenance for her ailing mother. A British officer in charge himself brought a loaf of bread, a can of evaporated milk and a can of dried egg to her. Handing them to her, he said, 'Fraulein, how much bread did you and your mother give to a starving Jew?'

That shattered what was left of her pride.

It was with her ailing mother that she and her sister lived, in the family house on the outskirts of West Berlin. It had miraculously escaped air-raid destruction. Their father, an army surgeon, had been killed in Russia during the early stages of the German retreat, and their widowed English grandmother had died in a bombing raid by her erstwhile countrymen, those of the RAF.

The whole family, including her English grandmother, had been ardent devotees of Hitler and his Nazi Party. Her sister had willingly served with the German Women's Army Corps. Hitler allowed some women to enlist in the armed forces. All others were expected to stay home and have countless children. Whenever Anneliese looked back at that, she supposed Hitler had unending streams of future cannon fodder in mind. No man could have won more devotion from a nation than he had, and no man, in the end, could have deserved it less. He had destroyed that nation and shamed its people.

A cloud lifted from her grey life during the Soviet blockade of West Berlin in 1948, for the Americans and British then showed a remarkable kindness towards the beleaguered city's people. They organized an airlift that brought supplies of food and other necessities to the starving population. Day after day, and even hour after hour, their laden planes swarmed in, and the British even used seaplanes that landed on the inland waters of Berlin. The airlift lasted ten months before Stalin ended the blockade, and such a sustained effort by the Americans and British captured the admiration and gratitude of the Berliners.

While the airlift was still operating, Anneliese stopped an officer of the RAF one day, and asked in English if he would accept her thanks for giving Berliners a lifeline.

'Well, don't you know, dear lady,' he said, 'it's a hell of a pleasure to give old Joe Stalin one in the eye. He'll never make a cricketer.'

From her English grandmother, Anneliese knew what that phrase meant, and the officer's friendly attitude made her feel the British were perhaps beginning to forgive her and her people, if not Himmler and his SS.

In 1949, her sister Brigid, two years younger, had the immense good fortune to meet a British army officer who fell immediately in love with her. She too was bitter and disillusioned, and the attentions of Major John Gibbs offered a wildly glad hope of exchanging the distorted nature of post-war Germany for the stability of Britain, whose people had no great guilt on their consciences. Brigid was overjoyed when Major Gibbs proposed, not because she was madly in love with him, but because he was kind, understanding and her guarantee of escape. They were married within a few weeks of meeting, and departed for England as soon as his duties in West Berlin came to an end two months later.

Anneliese was left in sole care of her ailing and unhappy mother. When she died a month ago, Anneliese at once made plans to visit her sister in England. The United Kingdom drew her, perhaps because of her quota of English blood, or perhaps because, like Brigid, she longed to release herself from everything that reminded her of all she wanted to forget. Was it possible to secure a work permit? She applied, and was refused. Britain, now allowing the entry of West Indians to take up low-paid jobs, did not need foreign workers other than specialists. Specialists? She pressed her request, emphasizing in detail her nursing qualifications and her experience, and much to her delight, a work permit was granted.

It then occurred to her that there was something she must do soon after arriving, something that immediately became a compulsive wish, even if an absurd one.

It was her first visit to Britain, and she crossed on the ferry from Calais to Dover. She could not believe her eyes when she actually saw that which Berlin's cabaret stars had parodied in song during the war, the famous white cliffs clear and bright on a day of sunshine. They marked the southernmost part of the island that Hitler had planned to invade and conquer. He was, of course, already mad by then in his dreams of turning his armies on Russia, but no-one knew it or hinted at it. Lieutenant Tim Adams, her patient at the Benghazi hospital, had been one with the British people who, under the inspiration of Churchill, the arch-enemy of Hitler, had played their part in the defeat of Germany, which had begun with the defeat of the Afrika Korps. Anneliese fervently hoped Tim Adams had survived, despite the pessimistic opinion of that Records Officer.

She came to then. The bus had arrived in Farnham.

Chapter Five

In Farnham, Anneliese did some shopping, then journeyed by another bus to the southern outskirts of Aldershot. Alighting, she walked to a very pleasant house in a tree-lined avenue.

Her sister, Brigid, opened the door to her.

'Good, you've survived the journey,' she said, her English as excellent as Anneliese's. 'Did my instructions get you there, did you find what you wanted?'

'I found the hospital, yes,' said Anneliese, stepping in. 'But nothing else. There was no file on the wife of Lieutenant Tim Adams.' She entered the lounge with Brigid.

Her sister, now thirty-two, was still a very attractive woman, fair and blue-eyed like herself, but fuller of figure. She was the mother of two-year-old Irena, and a good English housewife, for she now owned a British passport.

'Anneliese, you're crazy, you know, looking for this man, and you won't even say why.'

'It's something between him and me alone,' said Anneliese, removing her black hat, worn with her grey costume as a gesture of mourning for their dead mother, an anguished woman because of all the Nuremberg revelations. 'But as my enquiries came to nothing, I must let the matter rest. In any case, his chances of survival as a commando were always very slim. Also, if I had been able to meet him again, I wonder how he would have regarded me, since he knew me as a proud follower of Hitler and our Third Reich. My God, what we did, what we did to the Jews and our slave labourers.'

'But, Anneliese, we knew nothing of the extermination camps, nothing until the last months of the war,' said Brigid.

'We tolerated what was happening to the Jews well before the war began,' said Anneliese. 'We convinced ourselves that the concentration camps were only detention centres, although we knew just how Himmler and his SS regarded the Jews, and that Hitler had a fanatical hatred of them. Brigid, I feel so dreadfully guilty sometimes.'

'Well, since you're now unable to find this Englishman you nursed, you won't have to carry your guilt to him,' said Brigid. 'Anneliese, must you and I take on this guilt? It belongs to Himmler. Let the ghosts of the dead walk over his bones and keep him forever in unrest. You know I feel as you do, that his SS destroyed Germany as a civilized nation, and I shall never forgive them. But John tells me I must at least forget. I never will, although I'm at peace here and love my English countryside.'

'And do you love John?' asked Anneliese, who knew her sister had married her British army officer primarily to escape Berlin and grey Germany.

'I like him very much, yes, enough to say I'd never let him down or be unfaithful to him,' declared Brigid. 'He's a very tolerant and understanding man, although not too imaginative. But it's the imaginative who disturb us with their absurd fantasies. Or images of concentration camps. John insists the camps are evils of the past, not the present. The present and the future, he says, are for us and Irena.'

'One can't call that unimaginative,' said Anneliese.

'Anneliese, you have a work permit,' said Brigid, 'so stay and make a new life for yourself.'

'I intend to stay, oh, yes,' said Anneliese. 'I intend to keep the dreadful Russianized East Germans at a blissful distance.'

A little cry interrupted them.

'Oh, that's Irena,' said Brigid. 'I must see to her, and start the lunch, a late lunch.'

She left Anneliese to her thoughts, to muse on the fact that her search for Lieutenant Tim Adams had ended at its beginning.

In one of Aldershot's many army training camps, a company of conscripted National Servicemen was in the throes of a passing-out parade on the square, a customary tradition at the end of months of training.

This one was taking place under the critical eyes of the camp's commanding officer, Colonel Lucas. He had lost an arm during the war, but was still heart and soul an army man. He took the salute as the recruits passed by, concentrating their efforts on not losing step. One man did, however, and Colonel Lucas's eyes showed a glint.

'Black mark?' murmured his deputy, Major John Gibbs, forty and, like Colonel Lucas, a regular.

'I'll let it go,' said Colonel Lucas, 'there's always one old woman among these conscripts.'

'These aren't a bad lot,' said Major Gibbs, as the salute ended. 'I've seen worse, although I'll pray for 'em if they're sent to Malaya to deal with those bloodthirsty Communist terrorists.'

The camp sergeant major brought the parade to a halt, and the company was dismissed. All the same, the recruits marched off the square in good order, knowing the colonel would delay their leave if they turned into a scudding rabble.

'One more intake knocked into shape, another to come,' he said.

'Home to their mothers now for a week,' said Major Gibbs.

'Wait till their mothers find out they've developed chests and muscles,' said Colonel Lucas, 'then it'll be a question of pride fighting shock. Are you lunching in the mess, John?'

'No, I'm going home for that,' said Major Gibbs. 'What about you?'

'I'm lunching at home too,' said Colonel Lucas. Neither of them lived in the officers' quarters. They enjoyed the privilege of home life when off duty, Colonel Lucas on the western outskirts of Aldershot, Major Gibbs on the southern outskirts. 'And I've promised Eloise to take her to the Farnham theatre this evening.'

'And I've promised Brigid to be exceptionally nice to her sister Anneliese, who's staying with us for a fortnight,' said Major Gibbs.

'So you mentioned yesterday,' said Colonel Lucas, as they left the parade ground at a leisurely pace. 'Tell me, how do you find her?'

'A cool lady who looks even more like one of Hitler's Aryans than Brigid does,' said Major Gibbs, matured by his years and his war service. He was limited in what postings he might hope for, since a war wound had left him with a gammy leg, just as it had left Colonel Lucas missing an arm. In common with his commanding officer, Major Gibbs knew only the army and could not contemplate a civilian job. 'I met Anneliese in West Berlin after meeting Brigid, and I think she's guarding her pride. She was a German army nurse, y'know, and God knows what she came up against on the Russian Front.'

'Christ,' said Colonel Lucas, 'you don't suspect she was raped, do you? Hundreds of German women were when the Russians began to overrun Eastern Germany, and when they took Berlin.'

'No, I don't honestly suspect that,' said Major Gibbs. 'I think her the kind of woman who'd have killed herself if she'd been outraged in that frightful way. Come and meet her sometime. Bring Eloise with you.'

'I will,' said Colonel Lucas, and they parted for the weekend.

When Major Gibbs arrived home, he found lunch ready and also discovered his sister-in-law was back from a quest to the military hospital near Farnham. He knew about the quest, a search for the wife of a British officer she had nursed. Over lunch he learned of the precipitate end to her endeavours.

'Well, that's a damned disappointment for you, Anne,' he said. He found 'Anneliese' too much of a mouthful.

53

'Yes, John, it is,' she said.

'On the other hand, if you had managed to locate the wife, only to find her husband hadn't survived, that would have been more of a disappointment, eh? The fact is, commandos took on every kind of hazardous commitment during the war and their casualties were high.'

'Yes, I know,' said Anneliese, 'but I've always felt this one deserved to survive.' A little irony surfaced then. 'Even in Hitler's Germany, it wasn't *verboten* for men of the Wehrmacht, the regular army, to admire or respect certain of our enemies.' She smiled at little Irena, who was gazing at her in apparent fascination, and neglecting her food. 'As it is, I shall use my work permit and try to re-enter my profession.'

'You're set on staying?' said Major Gibbs.

'She is, yes, she's been talking to me about it,' said Brigid. 'Irena, use your spoon.'

'Yes, a'right, Mummy love,' lisped the child.

'Well, did you hear that?' said Brigid. 'Mummy love? Where did she get that from?'

'From the milkman's daughter, probably,' said Major Gibbs. 'You're a sweet pickle, aren't you, you little darling.'

The child giggled.

'Yes, I'm going to stay,' said Anneliese.

'With us?' asked Major Gibbs.

'No, no, do you think I would ask that of you?' said Anneliese. 'But you and Brigid and Irena are the only family I have, and in England I could visit you. Berlin is a lonely place for me, and I hate the people who come crawling out of their holes to deny they were Nazis. I can't deny that myself, I was one with Hitler and his ambitions for a Greater Germany. Those feelings are now dead. Dead. John, do you believe and understand?'

'Yes, Anne, of course,' said Major Gibbs, 'but stop trying to take on the guilt of the whole of Germany.' He shook his head. 'Not necessary, no, not a bit. Can't have a female Jeremiah in the family, eh, Brigid? Eh, little pickle?'

Irena, guiding a spoonful of sweetcorn to her mouth, missed her target and some went up her nose.

'Oh, dear,' said Brigid, and used a napkin to clean the child's face. 'There, that's better.'

Anneliese smiled. Brigid was very much a contented 'hausfrau' in an English way.

'I shall find a place near London in which to live and work,' she said. 'And I shall enjoy London's theatres.' She was not short of funds. She and Brigid had inherited a great deal of money. It was not a salary she was after as a nurse, but the challenge of the profession and the opportunity it would give her to become a permanent resident. 'Yes, I shall do that.'

'Fair enough,' said Major Gibbs, and glanced at Brigid. She smiled resignedly and gave a little shrug. One could never change Anneliese once she had made up her mind.

After lunch with Eloise, his French-born wife, and their children, Charles and Pandora, Colonel Lucas said, 'It seems that John Gibbs has his wife's sister staying with them.'

'Alas, poor John,' said Eloise.

'Say that again,' said Colonel Lucas, known as Luke to his wife and friends. He was always inclined to be amused by Eloise's tendency to dramatize.

'Poor John,' said Eloise. They were relaxing in garden chairs, watching the children at play. Luke's batman was clearing up in the kitchen, taking that chore off Eloise's hands, as he did with other domestic jobs. Eloise thought army batmen an excellent invention. 'Luke, one German woman as a wife is surely enough for any man. To also have a German sister-in-law in his house should be forbidden.'

'Come, that's a bit hard, Eloise. To begin with, Brigid's a charming woman.'

'Oh, yes, very charming,' said Eloise, now thirty-six and owning the kind of French flair that befitted what she was known as in some Aldershot circles, 'the colonel's wife'. 'But still German.'

'Who once threw her arms around Hitler?' suggested Luke.

'Has she said so?' asked Eloise, who could not forgive the Germans for turning France into a puppet state of slavish obedience until the Allies liberated it. 'Yes, has she said so?'

'No, but I think you feel she might have done,' said Luke. 'My own feelings are, from all she's told us, that in the end she was damned glad to be able to turn her back on everything associated with Hitler, Himmler and the blistering sadists of the SS.'

'And is her sister glad too that she was able to come here?' asked Eloise.

'Damned if I know,' said Luke. 'I haven't met the

lady. However, I understand she's only staying with John and Brigid for two weeks.'

'Then that means poor John isn't so poor,' said Eloise, and laughed.

'Wicked woman,' said Luke.

Chapter Six

Sammy's son and daughter-in-law, Daniel and Patsy, with their children, were enjoying their time in New England. They were staying with Patsy's pa and stepmother, Meredith and Francesca Kirk, in East Braintree, an attractive suburb of Boston. The welcome had been great, Pa Kirk delighted to see his irrepressible daughter again, and Daniel too, for that matter. Daniel, he reckoned, was the only guy who could keep Patsy from jumping over the moon in her boundless pursuit of life. As for his young grandchildren, Arabella and Andrew, Pa Kirk saw them as the cutest kids any marriage could produce.

He and Francesca were prominent in the media. He had a news spot on radio and television, Francesca a twice-weekly column on the *Globe* newspaper, and occasional airtime on a radio station. She took up women's causes. Her Italian ancestry made her a voluble woman, so much so that Pa Kirk sometimes handed her an old book on social etiquette and told her to bury her nose in Chapter Three, which dealt with situations when it was preferable to be seen and not heard. Francesca would laugh and throw the book back at him.

They had adjusted their working schedules to

take their Anglo-American family out and about, and that included a trip to Cape Cod during the first weekend of the visit. There, at Chatham, they had what Pa Kirk called a log cabin. It turned out to be a very attractive cottage, so Daniel asked why it was called a log cabin. Pa Kirk pointed to piles of logs on each side of the enormous fireplace. 'There you are, Daniel,' he said, 'logs by the hundred, and all for building a roasting fire when evenings turn chilly, as they do around Cape Cod.'

Patsy helped Daniel and the children to discover the old-world charm of the area, with its white-painted clapboard houses and churches, and the culinary delights of its famous broiled lobsters and creamy clam chowder. No-one asked to see a live clam, not after Pa Kirk described the species.

Today, Patsy, Daniel and the children were by themselves in the old quarters of Boston, enjoying a round of sightseeing. Patsy thought her English family ought to see all the interesting aspects of her home town that had such a treasured history, although her pa had said not to overdo it, or it would get too much like a know-all Brit giving French tourists a guided tour around the battlefield of Waterloo in Belgium.

Daniel thought the architecture of terraced rows of houses reminiscent of parts of London, and Patsy said well, of course, Old Boston was built by English settlers, and became the cradle of the Revolution.

'One in the eye for the ghosts of the English settlers,' said Daniel. Patsy, still intent on showing him and the children various historical sites relating to the uprising of the colonists, took them to the house of Paul Revere, famous, she said, for his ride to warn the rebel militia at Lexington that the Redcoats were coming.

'What's the Redcoats?' asked Arabella, five and a half, pretty as a poppet in her parents' eyes, but a tyrant for asking questions. 'Yes, what's the Redcoats?'

'British soldiers,' said Patsy.

'Like those at Buckingham Palace?' asked Arabella, who had seen the Changing of the Guard.

'Yes, like those,' said Daniel, 'except they were here at the time, not at the Palace.'

'What for?' asked Arabella.

'Well, they had a mob of pirates to deal with, like Captain Hook's pirates in *Peter Pan*,' said Daniel.

'Pirates my eye,' said Patsy.

'Crikey,' said Andrew, three years old and sturdy, much like his Uncle Tommy had been at the same age, 'did they capture them, Daddy?'

'No, they got licked,' said Patsy, and laughed.

She took them to see the statue of Sam Adams, a fiery old agitator who organized the mobs that went about tarring and feathering Loyalists. She didn't mention that, knowing it would give Arabella cause to ask a hundred questions, she simply said he played a prominent part in fostering the Revolution. That didn't stop Arabella, who was in her first year at school and already busting to soak up information.

'Mummy, what's fostering?'

'In this case, making a nuisance of himself,' said her dad.

'What for?'

'He was born that way,' said Daniel.

'Hey, how d'you know that?' asked Patsy.

'Well, look at his face,' said Daniel. 'It's got nuisance written all over it.'

'Where?' asked Arabella. 'I can't see it.'

'Look at his nose,' said Daniel. 'It's the kind known as a nuisance hooter.'

'What's a—'

'Catch that taxi, Daniel,' said Patsy, 'and we'll ride up to Bunker Hill and its monument.'

So off they went to see the monument, erected, said Patsy, to commemorate one of the first battles against the British, when General Howes's regiment of Redcoats attempted to storm the hill and were shot to pieces by bullets or rusty nails exploding from muskets.

'Rusty nails?' said Daniel.

'It was the only ammunition some of the defenders had,' said Patsy.

'Well, I don't call that cricket,' said Daniel. 'Rusty nails are wicked.'

'What do they do, Daddy?' asked Arabella, not as taken with monuments as she was with American ice cream.

'Tear nasty holes in you,' said Daniel, 'and give you gangrene.'

'What's gangrene?' asked Arabella.

'Very nasty,' said Daniel.

'We won't catch it, will we?' said Arabella.

'No, little lady, we'll catch an ice cream instead in a few minutes.'

Ice cream was available in a huge variety of different flavours, including peanut butter. The elite of Boston's college girls could often be seen sitting on high stools in an ice cream parlour, sipping milk shakes through straws, and dressed in the outfits of the day, skirts, sweaters, sandals and round feathered hats.

When the Anglo-American family arrived in one of these places to give Arabella and Andrew their treat, a bevy of such girls stopped sipping to regard them with interest.

'Gee whiz, he's a cutie,' said one girl to another. They were both eyeing Daniel. As tall as his namesake, long-gone Grandfather Corporal Daniel Adams, Chinese Lady's first husband, and just as personable, he was not far short of being rated tops with any all-American girl. When these two examples of the species heard him ordering the ice creams, interest jumped several rungs.

'He's English!'

The bevy of girls slipped from their stools and swarmed.

'Hi there, are all you folks English?'

'I am,' said Daniel. 'Patsy's American, and our kids are half and half.'

'Hi, Patsy, can your guy come to our college and join us in a seminar on Shakespeare?'

'Only over my dead body,' said Patsy. 'I'm against him disappearing for ever. Find a fat guy who won't mind being cooked and eaten.'

'Oh, c'm on, Patsy.'

'Nothing doing,' said Patsy, as Daniel picked up a tray of bowls piled high with ice cream, 'so back off.' What was legally hers, in the shape of her English fun guy, was hers for keeps.

'Listen, where'd you find him?

'Walking up a hill in South London.'

'Is that a place full of other guys like him?'

'There aren't any like him anywhere,' said Patsy,

'he's a one-off souvenir of Winston Churchill's time.' And she went to join Daniel and the children at a table. 'Hi there, souvenir,' she said, and sat down, her quick-moving eyes alight with mirth.

'Souvenir?' said Daniel.

'Sure, you're kind of special, like a piece of Plymouth Rock under a glass case in a New York museum,' said Patsy.

'What's Plymouth Rock?' asked Arabella, digging her spoon into a little mountain of strawberry ice cream that was nestling close to a chocolate-flavoured helping of similar size.

'It's where the Pilgrim Fathers landed way back in 1620,' said Patsy.

'What's them?'

'Pilgrims who came over from Plymouth, England, in a ship called the *Mayflower*,' said Patsy.

'But why's Daddy like a piece—'

'Eat your ice cream,' said Daniel.

'Mine's ever such a lot,' said Andrew.

'Well, the fact is, young 'un,' said Daniel, 'we're finding out nothing small or even medium is allowed to see the light of day in American restaurants or ice-cream parlours.'

'Soda fountains,' said Patsy, looking slightly cross.

Andrew, licking his spoon, said, 'What's a—'

'Same as an ice-cream parlour,' said Daniel.

'Daniel,' said Patsy, 'regarding nothing small or even medium. Don't make sneaky remarks about America being a land of plenty.'

'Believe me, Patsy,' said Daniel, 'I'm totally in favour.'

'Is that an honest statement?' asked Patsy.

63

'Sure is, partner,' said Daniel.

'Daniel, I've told you more times than I can remember, don't talk like a cowboy,' said Patsy, 'it's not you.'

'What are you, then, Daddy?' asked Arabella.

'Goofy,' said Patsy.

'What's—'

'Touched in the head,' said Patsy, and laughed. 'Come on, family, let's go to the harbour.'

Another cab carried them there, where they enjoyed the sea breezes and Patsy described the famous Boston Tea Party, when a body of citizens, disguised as Red Indians, threw the whole cargo of tea overboard from three ships on account of it being taxed by the British government.

'Well,' said Daniel, 'I'll say this much, Patsy, you're proud of your Revolution and its Tea Party, although I don't know what tea tastes like made with salt water and no milk. Also, it's been a long morning and I've a feeling that the kids are getting tired.'

'I'm not,' said Arabella.

'I'm hungry,' said young Andrew.

'After all that ice cream?' said Daniel.

'Daddy, that was an hour ago,' said Arabella.

'Well, I suppose at Andrew's age, an hour can be as much as a lifetime,' said Daniel.

'OK, you guys,' said Patsy, heeding her pa's warning, 'the sightseeing's over. We'll catch another cab and go to Quincy Market, where we can take time to have lunch and then shop around for gifts we can take home.'

'Grandpa's home, Mummy?' said Arabella.

'No, our home, sweetie,' said Patsy, 'yours and

Andrew's and Daddy's and mine. It's in little old England. Isn't it great that Hitler didn't sink it?'

'Who's he, Mummy?'

'Ask Daddy,' said Patsy. 'Call up a cab, Daniel.'

The following evening, Pa Kirk and Francesca, free of work commitments, took Patsy and her family for a drive out of town in their roomy Buick auto.

'Where we going?' asked Arabella.

'It's a surprise,' said Francesca, a middle-aged brunette who dressed in style and was full of nervous energy.

'Oh, good, go get 'em, Grandpa,' said Arabella. Pa Kirk was at the wheel.

'What was that you said, monkey?' asked Daniel.

'Daddy, I keep hearing it on the television,' said Arabella. She liked the American cartoon programmes for the young. 'Go get 'em.'

'Hi-ho, Geronimo,' said Daniel.

Arabella giggled.

The car ate up the straight road. Daniel was coming to the conclusion that all out-of-town roads in America were like that, going straight from point A to wherever point B was.

'Surprise coming up right now, Arabella,' said Pa Kirk, and the car slowed and turned into a vast car park facing a large building bearing the sign 'SUPERSHOPPER'.

'What, may I ask, is that?' enquired Daniel.

'A hypermarket,' smiled Patsy. It was no surprise to her.

It turned out to be an eye-opener for Daniel and the kids. The Americans, as ever, were way ahead of the rest of the world where innovations were concerned, and Francesca enjoyed the pleasure of taking Arabella and Andrew in hand to lead the way around.

The store stocked everything from a pair of socks to a suite of furniture, and a can of beans to a large sack of potatoes. The place was vast, the variety of goods breathtaking to any Briton who'd known rationing all through the war, and limited foods and consumer goods during the post-war years of austerity. American housewives used the food department of these hypermarkets to buy all that was necessary for their families for a week, since most of it would keep fresh in fridges or freezers. And customers helped themselves, choosing what they wanted from stacked shelves or display areas, placing their purchases in a trolley, and paying for them at a checkout point, where assistants packed them in commodious bags. Large items were ordered and delivered.

'I don't believe this,' said Daniel.

Arabella and Andrew were gaping. Patsy was smiling. She'd talked to Daniel about these American self-service stores, but not until now did her English fun guy realize exactly what one was like.

'Well, Daniel?'

'Aladdin's cave,' said Daniel.

'Yup, help yourself, Daniel,' said Pa Kirk.

'Grandpa, is all these things free?' asked Arabella.

'Some are,' smiled Pa Kirk.

'Sure, some that appeal to little girl guys,' said Francesca, which was an invitation to Arabella to help herself to a box of candy and maybe a cute doll fully dressed, and for Andrew to pick out a toy or two. Pa Kirk would pay by way of another inno-vation, a credit card.

Francesca herself shopped for groceries, while Daniel, following on with Patsy and her pa, took in the incredible range of food products.

'Say something, honey,' said Patsy.

'Believe me, Patsy,' said Daniel, 'if my good old dad ever took a look at this place, his electricity would short-circuit, but as soon as he'd been repaired he'd be looking for a site on which to build a hyperwhopper store in Camberwell.'

'Hypermarket,' said Patsy.

'It's still a whopper,' said Daniel.

'A genuine surprise, Daniel?' said Pa Kirk.

'You can say that twice over,' said Daniel.

'We'll take a cab tomorrow,' said Patsy, 'and I'll show you and the children a Boston supermarket. Supermarkets mainly sell food and kitchen gadgets. Your dad should start with a supermarket.'

'Before that,' said Daniel, 'I'll put him on a plane so that he can come over here and see for himself how to revolutionize shopping.'

'You do that,' said Pa Kirk, 'and while he's in Boston, I'll take him to a baseball match.'

'Daniel, let's see if we can buy some more gifts here to add to those we bought in Quincy Market,' said Patsy.

'To take home to little old England?' said Daniel.

'Sure thing,' said Patsy.

'Daniel,' said Pa Kirk, while his wife stacked goodies in a trolley under the fascinated eyes of Arabella and Andrew, 'let your family know how much I admire them for helping to keep your island afloat.'

'Your guys helped too,' said Daniel, 'and so did Patsy.'

'Hi-ho, Geronimo,' said Patsy.

In little old England, the businesswoman renting the ground-floor flat in Bloomsbury was certain the unpleasant smell was getting worse. She suspected the unusual, that the drain ran under the house. She also suspected it had sprung a leak.

She sent a note to the landlord.

Chapter Seven

Friday evening.

Eloise and Colonel Lucas were being entertained to dinner by Major Gibbs and his wife Brigid. Children were absent, Brigid's little girl being in bed, and Eloise's son and daughter in the care of her husband's domesticated batman at home.

Brigid, in the kitchen, was attending to last-minute preparations for serving the meal. Colonel Lucas and Eloise were in the garden, Luke getting to know Brigid's striking sister, Anneliese Bruck. Eloise, seated at the garden table with Major Gibbs, was talking to him while keeping an intrigued eye on her husband.

Luke was finding Anneliese immensely interesting in her startling and revealing account of her nursing experiences on the Russian Front. If the account had a nightmarish aspect, it was nevertheless believable. During the last bitter weeks of the war, all kinds of information concerning the behaviour of the swarming Russians had filtered through to the American and British troops.

'That kind of hell, I imagine, has left you with no love for the Russians,' said Luke.

'In war, they are barbarians,' said Anneliese.

'Well, I'll ask you a frank question,' said Luke, 'were they any worse than Himmler's SS or the Waffen-SS?'

'For the rest of my life I feel people will ask me that question,' said Anneliese, and Luke thought her fine blue eyes were dark with pain and sadness. That kind of hurt, he also thought, was a reflection of the natural feelings of a nurse whose vocation was guided by compassion. He had had his own time in hospital by reason of the amputation of his arm, and the caring attention given him by nurses of the QARANC was something he was not likely to forget. He listened as Anneliese went on. 'How can I ever answer that question except to say the Nuremberg trials revealed to the world the extent of the terrible crimes committed by Himmler and all the SS? And that only a handful of German people ever opposed Hitler, a man who asked terrible sacrifices of millions of German soldiers, but in the end proved himself a coward by committing suicide to avoid answering for the hell he created. I shall never stop feeling guilty.'

'Since you were an army nurse, you're a little hard on yourself, aren't you?' said Luke.

'John, Brigid's husband, tells me that too,' said Anneliese, 'but I was also a committed Nazi.'

'Here in this country, we had our own kind,' said Luke. 'Have you heard of Oswald Mosley and his Blackshirts?'

'Yes, and I know the British disowned them,' said Anneliese. 'How I wish I could say the same about myself and all German people.' She paused, feeling

70

she had spoken of all these things far too much since arriving at her sister's home. Everything was becoming exhaustively repetitive to herself and perhaps tiresome to her listeners. 'Colonel Lucas, could we talk of other things?'

'We can talk about the fact that you have a work permit,' said Luke, 'which means, I assume, that you intend to settle here.'

'You have no idea how glad I am that I can begin a new life in your country,' said Anneliese, and Luke took note of her frankness and candour. He was beginning to like her. 'It's partly my own country through my English grandmother.'

'So how will you use your work permit?' he asked.

'By returning to my profession of nursing.'

Luke smiled, and Anneliese liked the way it tempered his rugged, weatherbeaten looks. She had made no comment so far on his loss of an arm. She felt she did not need to, since he was obviously one more war casualty. In Germany, there were thousands of them, crippled for life. Yet some were still impossibly pro-Hitler.

'You've come at the right time,' said Luke. 'As I understand it, our National Health Service seems permanently in need of extra nursing staff.'

'Ah, so?' said Anneliese.

'It's recruiting immigrant nurses,' said Luke. 'I rather fancy that as health treatment is free, people have decided to fall ill more frequently.'

'Excuse me?' said Anneliese.

'Let me put it this way,' said Luke with a dry smile. 'When supplies of lamb chops are free, people eat a lot more lamb, whether they need it or not.'

'Ah, now I see, yes.' Anneliese smiled. 'Are London hospitals wanting extra nursing staff?'

'You favour London?'

'Of course. Who would not choose to have London theatres available? I'm mad about theatres, about Noel Coward and Shakespeare. To see *Hamlet* or *Macbeth* performed on a London stage, who could resist?'

'In that case,' said Luke, 'I'll give you a list of London hospitals, and you can apply to any of them.'

'Colonel Lucas, that is so kind of you.'

'Every thinking soldier knows what he owes the nurses of any army,' said Luke soberly. 'I've a relative – my wife's brother, in fact – who owes much to a German army nurse.'

'Nurses don't discriminate against wounded enemies, Colonel Lucas. I think you must know that.'

Luke thought, as others did, how well she and her sister spoke English, with only the slightest of accents. By reason of her English grandmother, no doubt.

Brigid appeared.

'Dinner, please. I'm about to serve it. John, will you come and see to the wine?'

The dinner proved agreeable, both in content and atmosphere, the atmosphere created by what was like a gathering of friends, not former adversaries, even if Eloise did have unspoken thoughts about the German sisters. Like Bobby's wife Helene, she still found it hard to forgive Germany's humiliation of France. For that matter, also like Helene, she hated the way Marshal Pétain and his collaborators had bowed the knee so disgracefully to Hitler.

However, no-one spoke of those things, no-one referred to the war in any way. Anneliese wanted to know all about London's theatres, and everyone, including Brigid, was able to enlighten her. Brigid had persuaded her husband to take her frequently to enjoy the post-war revival of London's night life.

The subject having been raised, discussion went on in light-hearted fashion, although there was some argument about whether Noel Coward was quite as witty as Oscar Wilde.

'Oh, Noel Coward and Oscar Wilde are equally witty in any language,' said Brigid.

'No, Wilde has the edge,' said Major Gibbs.

'What do you think, Colonel Lucas?' asked Anneliese.

'Count me out,' said Luke, 'I prefer blood-and-thunder melodrama.'

'Well, damned hard luck, Luke,' said Major Gibbs, 'blood-and-thunder melodrama went out with Queen Victoria.'

'Not quite,' said Luke. 'Tod Slaughter's still going strong, still playing hairy villains. I last saw him in the early Thirties, *Sweeney Todd, the Demon Barber of Fleet Street*, at the old Elephant and Castle Theatre, noted most of all for its annual revival of *Maria Marten: The Murder in the Red Barn*. Tod Slaughter—'

'Wait, wait,' cried Anneliese. 'Who is Tod Slaughter and where is the Elephant and Castle, and why is it called that?'

'Ah, I'm now knowledgeable enough about many English things to guess it's the name of an English pub,' said Brigid, with a triumphant flourish of her fork.

'An English pub is used as a theatre?' said Anneliese.

'We're a very eccentric people, we English,' said Eloise, 'but of course, so are we French, if more sophisticated.'

'English? French? I'm losing the plot,' said Anneliese.

'My wife was born of a French mother and an English father,' said Luke, 'and accordingly is eccentric on two counts.'

'It's true I'm not an ordinary woman,' said Eloise, 'any more than my father is an ordinary man.'

'I won't argue,' said Luke, amused as always by her funny little conceits.

'But this theatre and the actor – what was his name?' asked Anneliese.

'Tod Slaughter,' said Luke.

'A ham, Luke, and you know it,' said Major Gibbs.

'A ham?' said Anneliese.

'An actor who overacts,' said Luke.

'But where is this Elephant and Castle?' asked Anneliese. 'And is it a pub used as a theatre?'

'It's in South London, not far from Waterloo Bridge,' said Major Gibbs, 'and it's not a pub, it's an old theatre.'

'Well, why haven't you taken me there?' asked Brigid, her mood playful.

'I would like to see it,' said Anneliese, 'also –' She smiled at Luke. 'Also your blood-and-thunder Victorian melodrama.'

'Well, that calls for some kind of action, I

suppose,' said Major Gibbs. 'What about it, shall we all take a trip to London?'

'When does the new intake arrive, John?' asked Luke.

'Next Tuesday,' said Major Gibbs. 'We could make the trip this coming Saturday to find out if the old Elephant and Castle Theatre still exists.'

'Not a hope in hell,' said Luke. 'The whole area was practically demolished during the Blitz.'

'Oh, I'm sorry,' said Anneliese.

'Not your fault,' said Luke. 'Fortunes of war. But we could still go. The Old Vic isn't far from the Elephant and Castle.'

'I've heard of the Old Vic,' said Brigid.

'It's famous,' said Eloise.

'What is it?' asked Anneliese.

'A theatre that specializes in producing Shakespeare's plays at seat prices affordable to all,' said Luke.

'Could we see it, please?' asked Anneliese.

'It's another theatre I haven't been taken to,' said Brigid, and this time she shook her fork accusingly at her husband.

'I can't recall anyone's ever taken me, either,' he said.

'That's no excuse,' said Brigid.

'Why is it called the Old Vic?' asked Anneliese.

'I fancy it was originally called the Victoria Theatre,' said Luke. 'After the old Queen, of course.'

'Victoria, oh, yes, one could say that during her reign she was the Queen of Europe,' said Anneliese.

'Here one can't get away from her,' smiled

Eloise. 'And in France, one can't get away from Napoleon.'

'I'm fascinated,' said Anneliese. 'Yes, I would very much like to see the Old Vic.'

'Saturday, then?' said Major Gibbs.

'We shall go,' said Eloise, and of course, as 'the colonel's wife', hers was the definitive decision.

Back home later, she said to Luke, 'So, what did you think of Brigid's sister?'

'Frankly, I liked her,' said Luke.

'Very well, you may do that, you may like her,' said Eloise, 'but only as you like old Mrs Cheetham from down the road.'

'Old Mrs Cheetham from down the road is a complaining old biddy who's hard to like,' said Luke.

'Yes, that's what I mean,' said Eloise.

'Suffering polar bears, you shocker,' said Luke. 'Come here.'

'Certainly not,' said Eloise, 'wait till bedtime.'

'I wonder, could we afford a television set?' mused Paul.

'We don't need one,' said Lulu. The evening was grey with twilight. They were in the parlour, sitting on the settee, and she was scribbling on a notepad.

'I could point out we don't need two brooms, but we've got two,' said Paul.

'That's different,' said Lulu, 'one broom is for me, the other's for you. You did agree to equal work rights. Listen, what d'you think of this for an election slogan?' She recited.

> *'Vote the Labour Party in,*
> *Make sure they win,*
> *Get the Tories out*
> *Make it a rout.'*

'Corny,' said Paul.

'Well, what about "Workers unite, Fight the fight, Vote for Labour, Put the Tories to flight"?'

'I'm not sure the workers care much for poetry outside "The Charge of the Light Brigade",' said Paul. 'Now that's rousing stuff. Try adapting your effort to something like "The Charge of the Gas Meters".'

'Gas meters?' said Lulu.

'Gas meters charge the workers many a hard-earned penny,' said Paul.

'You serious?' said Lulu, taking her glasses off to peer suspiciously at him. It only made Paul feel she was turning into a very pretty Socialist, and he didn't think there were a lot of that kind about. Socialist women, somehow, always looked aggressive. Attractive women mostly seemed to be Conservative voters. Well, if you talked to one such lady at her Brixton front door, the moment you mentioned the Labour Party, she'd tell you to depart from her doorstep at once or she'd set her dog on you. 'Paul, I asked, are you serious?' said Lulu.

'What's more serious than the workers' hard-earned pennies slipping into their gas meters day after day?' he asked. 'Try starting off with "Charging to the right of them, charging to the left of them, every meter volleyed and thundered, but on the brave workers rode, into the valley of debt they rode –" Let's see, what rhymes with thundered? Can't have blundered, can't have workers blundering. Keep that for Tory voters – say when they've blundered into a gasworks yard and the workers are galloping over them – hey, holdup, Lulu, what's going on?'

Lulu, shrieking with laughter, was whacking him with her notepad.

'I've married a half-wit!' she cried.

'Steady, Lulu,' said Paul, ducking, 'this is only a semi-detached, and if our neighbours next door hear this carry-on, they'll think we're heading for divorce already – ouch! Lulu, d'you want a smacked bum?'

'Don't be vulgar,' said Lulu, and hit him again. 'Or barmy. Charge of the gas meters? I've never heard such a load of rhubarb. My old granny could do better than that from under her marble slab in Tooting Cemetery.'

Paul grabbed the notepad and chucked it away.

'Was your old granny a Socialist?' he asked.

'No, a flower girl at Piccadilly Circus.'

'Oh, right,' said Paul, 'next time I'm in Tooting I'll put a posy of violets on her marble slab.'

Lulu fell about.

'I'm getting to like living with you,' she said, 'even if I do feel a semi-detached is a bit middle class.'

'You'll get used to it,' said Paul, 'you'll wake up one day and find it doesn't actually hurt.'

'It could undermine my natural affinity with the proletariat,' said Lulu.

'Now that could hurt,' said Paul. 'Try not to think about it.'

'I can't be a traitor,' said Lulu.

'All right,' said Paul, 'give us a kiss, and then let's do some serious work on the charge of the gas meters.'

'The way you're going on lately, it wouldn't surprise me if you ended up completely brainless,' said Lulu.

'Oh, well, let's hope I'll turn the corner in time,' said Paul.

Which so tickled Lulu that she engaged with him in a bit of lovey-dovey.

At her home, Phoebe was talking with Philip on the phone.

'This has got to stop,' she said.

'What has?' asked Philip, not far short of going a bit barmy about Uncle Sammy's adopted daughter. Talk about pretty, pert and peachy, she was all that. 'Yes, what's got to stop?'

'All these phone calls,' said Phoebe. 'Goodness knows how much they'll cost Daddy when he comes to pay the bill.'

'Might I point out I make the calls, the trunk calls, and accordingly pay for them myself, at a bob a time from this call box?' said Philip.

'Oh, I'm no good at understanding telephone engineering,' said Phoebe.

'It's nothing to do with—'

'And I don't know you should throw your money about at a bob a time,' said Phoebe. 'What makes you do it?'

'You do,' said Philip.

'Me?' said Phoebe.

'Not half,' said Philip. 'Listen, could you send me a signed photograph of yourself in a swimsuit?'

'What?'

'There's quite a few other cadets here who've got pin-ups of their girlfriends,' said Philip.

'Well, I'm not going to be anyone's pin-up, it's common, and my mum wouldn't allow it,' said Phoebe. 'Did you say in a swimsuit?'

'Well, you've got a very nice figure and legs,' said Philip.

'Cheeky devil, how do you know?' demanded Phoebe.

'Well,' said Philip, enjoying a good bobsworth of the public telephone, 'when you've been jiving with me in a sweater and skirt—'

'Stop,' said Phoebe.

'Again?' said Philip.

'You're making me blush,' said Phoebe. 'What sweater and which skirt?'

'Your orange sweater and your blue skirt.'

'What, those old things?' said Phoebe.

'They don't look old to me,' said Philip, 'they look just the job, you pretty pussycat.'

'I think you're falling over your tongue,' said Phoebe. 'You ought to get it seen to. Listen, when are you going to take me dancing again?'

'I'll be home next weekend.'

'I can hardly wait,' said Phoebe. 'All right, bring your camera, and I'll wear my old orange sweater and blue skirt.'

'What about a swimsuit?' asked Philip.

'I'm not posing in any swimsuit,' said Phoebe. 'It's sweater and skirt or nothing.'

'Nothing?' said Philip. 'Phoebe, d'you know what you're saying?'

'Oh, help,' said Phoebe, 'I wasn't thinking. It's

your fault, you're confusing me. Now I am blushing.'

'So am I,' said Philip. The pips sounded then, and he had to ring off.

Phoebe giggled.

Chapter Eight

Paul said, 'It's only nine o'clock, so what do we do now?'

'You'll think of something,' said Lulu, snuggling up to him on the settee.

'I'll work on that,' said Paul, discovering daily that his Lulu had hidden depths he hadn't dreamt possible and she herself, probably, hadn't suspected. Who'd have thought, during the weeks when their marriage could have been likened to a disaster area, that she'd become addicted to cuddling up and snuggling up like a contented kitten? Perhaps other modern women also fell off their soapboxes on certain occasions. Aunt Polly was a modern woman. Aunt Polly had been the modern woman of every era she had lived through. Uncle Boots had said so, with his telling smile. But all the same, she didn't mount platforms. A feller could tell Aunt Polly was a woman first and foremost. Wow, thought Paul, I wonder if she and Uncle Boots still – ? Well, do they, I wonder?

'This is cosy,' murmured Lulu, snuggling closer.

'Tell you what,' said Paul, 'as it's only nine o'clock, let's go for a walk down to the pub.'

'Do what?' said Lulu.

'Well, look at it this way,' said Paul, 'a walk down to Brixton's bright lights and a drink at a pub means we can look forward to bedtime at about eleven, say.'

Lulu came to.

'I know what's going on in your mind,' she said. 'Nothing doing. Let's have a walk and a drink at the pub.'

'That's what I said,' remarked Paul

'Oh, did you?' queried Lulu. 'I thought you said it was bedtime. It's only nine o'clock.'

'Yes, I said that as well.'

'Stop confusing me. What'll you have at the pub?'

'A Guinness,' said Paul.

'What for a Guinness?'

'To set me up for an eleven o'clock bedtime,' said Paul.

'Silly me for asking a daft question,' said Lulu.

They enjoyed a brisk walk through the evening air that was just touched with the sharpness of autumn. The lights of Brixton illuminated roads, pavements and the places of entertainment. They noticed a few West Indian immigrants here and there. Two stood outside the main door of Paul and Lulu's local pub. One ventured to speak to Paul.

'Mista? Mista?'

'Hello,' said Paul, 'something I can do for you?'

'Mista, it's like this.' The man, his resonant voice broad with the musical accent of the West Indies, went on to say he and his friend Josiah wished to buy a bottle of Jamaica rum.

'You can get one in this pub,' said Paul.

'Mista, Ah can't get served.'

'Well, damn that,' said Paul, and Lulu said a naughty word under her breath. They had both heard there was resistance to the trickling influx of coloured immigrants.

'Stay there, don't go away,' said Lulu to the West Indians, who were wrapped up in overcoats and hats. She pushed the door open and marched in, while Paul, knowing what she was about, stayed to chat with the immigrants and to ask how they were doing. They said they'd got work, as garbage collectors, and lodgings too, but it had been mighty hard going.

'Mista, don't they want us here?'

'Listen,' said Paul, 'since you are here, stick at it. We're a reserved lot, and it takes us a while to get used to new faces. But it'll work out, so give yourselves time.'

Lulu reappeared, a bottle of Captain Morgan's Jamaica rum in her hand.

'There, take it home,' she said to the overcoated black men, 'and get yourselves warmed up.'

'Lady, that's mighty friendly of you, yes, ma'am. Lady, how much?'

'It's on me,' said Lulu.

'Lady?'

'Have it as a present from my wife,' said Paul.

'Mista, that ain't right. Josiah and me, we don't wanna look like we is begging. No, it ain't right, thanking your lady wife all the same.'

'Look, take it as a gift of welcome,' said Lulu, 'and when you get entitled to a vote, use it for the Labour Party.'

'Ma'am?'

'The Labour Party supports equality for everyone,' said Lulu, 'which includes you gentlemen. Take no notice of what the Tories might promise you. It's all codswallop and middle-class flannel. What a Labour government will promise you, you can rely on.'

'I don't know I get you, lady.'

'You will, when you've been here a year or so,' said Lulu. 'The Labour Party represents the interests of the workers— Hey, wait a minute, Paul.'

Paul, having pushed open the pub door, dragged her in, and the door swung shut.

'That's a mighty fine lady,' said one West Indian to the other.

'Mind, I ain't sure I like charity,' said the other.

'What you moaning about, Josiah Caravel? Didn't you hear her say it was a gift of welcome, and we both need the rum, don't we?'

'Sure do.'

'And our old ladies, they don't know, do they?'

'I sure hope not.'

'Come on, then.'

Off they went to their lodgings, one man carrying the bottle as if it were as precious as a baby.

In the pub, Lulu asked Paul what he meant by dragging her in like a bundle of washing that needed a drink.

'To get you off your soapbox,' said Paul.

'I was only—'

'Yes, you're a good girl, Lulu, but I had a feeling you were going to try out your charge of the gas meters on those innocent blokes from the West Indies.'

'That's not my piece of doggerel, it's yours – oh, sorry.' Lulu had bumped into a bloke. He turned, looked at her and her sweater.

'Help yourself, gal, I ain't offended,' he said.

Lulu smiled, sidling past him in a blind kind of way.

'Is there a problem?' asked Paul.

'Yes, my glasses have steamed up,' said Lulu. The crowded pub exuded heat.

'All right, Lulu lovey,' said Paul, 'take 'em off, wipe them and go grab that table over there. I'll get your gin and tonic and my Guinness.'

'While you're ordering,' said Lulu, 'give the proprietor your opinion of him for refusing to serve immigrants.'

'Didn't you give him yours?'

'I didn't get the chance. I was served by a barmaid too busy to talk to.'

'Right,' said Paul, and pushed his way through to the bar, where he came face to face with the proprietor.

'Evening,' said Paul.

'Evening, me lord.' The man was portly, red-faced and amiable. 'What's yer fancy?'

'It used to be Ava Gardner,' said Paul, 'but then I met a Lulu. Gin and tonic, please, with ice and lemon, and a half of Guinness.'

'Coming up.' The proprietor squirted gin into a glass, followed with some tonic, ice and a slice of lemon. 'Guinness for you, sir?' He grinned. 'Or yer Lulu?'

'For both of us in a way,' said Paul. 'Listen, d'you serve customers irrespective?'

'Can't say I know any customers name of

86

Irrespective, but I'd still serve 'em. Rule of the house, yer know. There y'ar, one gin and tonic, one Guinness. Two and fourpence.'

'Ta muchly,' said Paul. 'There's a couple of immigrants outside who told me they couldn't get served.'

'Eh?'

'Fact,' said Paul.

The proprietor scratched his chin, then grinned.

'Oh, them,' he said, 'Elijah and Josiah. Well, I tell yer why they couldn't get served. See them two handsome chocolate ladies over there?'

Paul took a look at two buxom black women at a table, beaming at each other over their drinks.

'So?' he said.

'That's their wives. They started hollering as soon as Elijah and Josiah made an entrance, which sent 'em back out like a couple of tramps with a shotgun aiming at their backsides. Seems they're a bit too fond of rum, which don't happen to please their wives. Now, how about two and fourpence?'

Paul paid up and carried the drinks to the table at which Lulu had seated herself. There he told her what the proprietor had told him. Lulu turned her head and searched for the whereabouts of the two buxom ladies from the West Indies. She spotted them. They were still beaming, white teeth flashing.

'Now I get it,' she said, 'they're twice as big as their men.'

'Lulu, what have you done? You've sent Elijah and Josiah home with a full bottle of rum. They'll be legless when their wives walk in.'

'Oh, well, luck of the game,' said Lulu, 'and that

reminds me. You owe me fifteen bob and sixpence.'

'What for?'

'The rum.'

'I'm to pay for what turned out to be your misguided act of love thy neighbour?'

'It's your privilege, paying up,' said Lulu, 'and besides, your wages are more than mine.'

'But out of my wages—'

'Don't argue,' said Lulu, 'I'm a worker on the poverty line, so hand over the lolly.'

'I give up,' said Paul, and dug into his pocket. He gave her the necessary amount of silver coins. 'But wait till I get you home.'

'Don't get ideas,' said Lulu. 'Bottoms up, mister.' Down went a mouthful of gin and tonic.

'Down the hatch, missus.' Paul took a long swallow of the dark Guinness. 'Oh, and here's to bedtime.' Another swallow.

'You and your Guinness, it's a plot,' said Lulu.

'Honest intentions,' said Paul.

'Oh, well, cheerio, old sport,' said Lulu, coming to terms with a bit of middle-class lingo over her gin and tonic.

Miss Stella Peebles, the businesswoman who occupied the ground-floor flat of a house in Bloomsbury, arrived home from an evening out with a gentleman friend. She was a handsome woman in her thirties, he a studious-looking City broker in his early forties. She took him into the living room.

'There, can you smell it?' she asked.

'Unfortunately, yes,' he said, his nose twitching. 'Not at all pleasant.'

'It's worse each day,' she said.

'Well, you shouldn't have to live with it. Have you heard from the landlord?'

'Fisher? Yes, I sent him a note and he rang today.' She'd had a phone installed. 'He's sending a plumber round on Monday.'

'That won't be a day too soon. Are your other rooms affected?'

'No, only here,' she said.

'D'you mind, then, if we enjoy the nightcap elsewhere?'

'The bedroom?' she suggested, as they left the living room and closed the door behind them.

'That sounds friendly, Stella.'

'You're welcome, Charles.'

'Should I have brought pyjamas?'

'Are pyjamas necessary?'

'Not as far as I'm concerned.'

'Shall we have the nightcap first?' she asked.

'It should make a stimulating beginning,' he said.

Chapter Nine

Saturday morning.

The phone rang at the poultry farm by Woldingham village in Surrey.

Rosie answered.

'Hello?'

'Greetings, fair cousin,' said David, elder son of Tommy and Vi Adams.

'You're after something,' said Rosie. 'A dressed chicken, perhaps, for your Sunday lunch? Well, you'll have to come and get it.'

'Kind of you, Rosie,' said David, 'but I'm not after a chicken, dressed or undressed. I'm after passing on some unwelcome news.'

'Not about Kate?' said Rosie quickly. David's wife Kate was pregnant with her first child.

'No, she's fine, thanks,' said David. 'The fact is we've lost our chance of buying John Fairall's farm.' Elderly John Fairall was the owner of the farm adjacent to that run by David and Kate. 'His son and daughter-in-law, and their two sons, are coming back from Yorkshire to take it over rather than have their father sell it. He's just been on the phone to let me know.'

'That's a blow, David,' said Rosie. For quite some

time, she and Matthew, together with Emma and Jonathan, their partners, had planned to team up with David and Kate to run a combined poultry and dairy farm, with enough land to include a flock of sheep. They had been waiting for John Fairall to sell. His acreage was twice that of David and Kate's, and a merger would have given them more than five thousand acres. 'Well, we'll have to grin and bear it. But listen.' Rosie went on to say that Emma and Jonathan had come to a decision only yesterday about giving up poultry farming. Emma wanted to go back to their home near the rest of the family, and Jonathan had the offer of a job with his old firm of accountants and auditors at Camberwell Green, and at a salary far more than the poultry farm could afford to match. 'To be fair, David, Matthew and I can see Emma's point of view. She and Jonathan work all hours here.'

'How will that leave you and Matthew?' asked David.

'Thinking,' said Rosie.

'About what?'

'About what we'll do without Emma and Jonathan,' said Rosie. 'I love those two, and their little Jessie, and Matt's going to miss Jonathan. They're buddies.'

'If you had to, you wouldn't mind saying goodbye to the chickens?' said David.

'That depends on what an alternative offers,' said Rosie.

'Well, if you and Matt do your thinking head to head,' said David, 'I'm sure you'll come up with something promising. Have a go, Rosie. Chickens are only grown-up chicklets.'

'Chicks,' said Rosie. 'And let me remind you that foxes might only be grown-up little demons, but they're big demons. David, how's Paula?'

'Living it up with Rico,' said David, 'and learning how to handle cows and the milking machinery. She's great. The farm's paying, Rosie, we're getting better prices for our beef and dairy products.'

'Happy for you, David, old sport,' said Rosie, 'and I'll talk to you again some other time.'

'So long, Rosie, best of luck.'

'So long, David,' said Rosie.

She left the house to look for Matthew. Her children, Giles and Emily, together with Emma's daughter Jessie, were at play far up the field, and Emma and Jonathan were out on delivery runs. She found Matthew setting a new trap for the ubiquitous and crafty foxes, whose ability to get into the field was a wild and wondrous example of the animals' versatility.

'Rosie?' Matthew, in breeches and an old khaki shirt, looked a man of the great outdoors. Dark, tanned and sinewy, he was at forty-two as physically robust as when Rosie first met him twelve years ago in his native county of Dorset. Then he had been the owner of a garage, a garage that was losing money because of the limiting circumstances of war. He was philosophical about it, and more concerned that a gammy ankle, which gave him a pronounced limp, made him ineligible for call-up, although he was subsequently admitted as a highly qualified motor engineer. He had an easy-going nature that reminded Rosie of Boots, and that had been the first thing to appeal to her.

'Gloomy news, old soldier,' said Rosie.

'Oh?' said Matt, and Rosie told him how the proposed farm merger had cracked like a bad egg. Matt said bad eggs were always sitting around waiting to spoil an omelette. 'What with that and losing Emma and Jonathan, we'll need to do some serious thinking,' he said. Rosie mentioned she had told David that, and David had recommended that they put their heads together. Matt laughed. 'That'll rattle our brains,' he said.

'Or get rid of our chicken feathers,' said Rosie. Chicken feathers followed them about, stuck to their clothes and became attached to their hair.

'Ah, well, since we're going to lose Emma and Jonathan, perhaps the great god of change is knocking on our door,' said Matt.

'The great god of change is an interfering old busybody,' said Rosie. 'Let him knock on someone else's door.'

'Rosie, you'd prefer us to stick to what we have?' said Matt.

'What we have we've worked hard for,' said Rosie. 'I'm suddenly realizing I don't want to give it up. I like what we have. Further, old partner, Giles and Emily love it here.'

'That goes for me too,' said Matt.

'You'd never settle for an office job,' said Rosie.

'I've never kept company with a desk,' said Matt, 'and it's too late for me to start now. Rosie, all we need to keep going are two people to take the place of Emma and Jonathan.'

'The trouble is, we can only offer limited wages,' said Rosie. They'd employed extra help, a quite useful bloke, but only for a few months, when he'd transferred his talents to a pig farm. Pig farming was a growing industry in the UK. It helped to combat the still existing meat shortage in a country whose people had a fondness for pork chops and ham.

'Well, I'll drive to Croydon one day next week,' said Matt, 'and ask at the labour exchange if they've got two people looking for outdoor work who will settle for limited wages.'

'And won't mind living with chicken feathers,' said Rosie.

Lieutenant General Kersch of the Russian KGB was presently acting head of the Soviet Press Bureau in London. British Intelligence saw the Bureau as a front for the KGB, but then they used their own agents in a similar way in Moscow, as did America's CIA. Ostensibly, such agents were journalists, gathering news for broadcasts back home while in secret contact with double agents – moles – who had information to impart.

At this moment, Kersch was in trouble with Moscow. Three members of the Bureau, including two top men, Colonel Bukov and Lieutenant Colonel Alexandrov, had gone missing months ago. Moscow had despatched Kersch, renowned KGB investigator, to find them. He had failed, although he had used a team of first-class agents from the Bureau.

He was now a frustrated man, short of leads and short of temper, particularly because he had also failed to find a Polish woman, Katje Galicia, attached to the KGB, and a person called Finch. Bukov and Alexandrov had apparently been 'in business', with these two people. Their present location was as much of a mystery as that of Bukov,

Alexandrov and the third agent. The only lead Kersch had been given when he began the investigation was the fact that the Polish woman had occupied a Bloomsbury apartment up to the time of her disappearance. And nothing was known at all of the person called Finch.

Kersch had been staring at the proverbial blank wall for many weeks, and signals from Moscow were indicating that his negative reports were beginning to be unacceptable. If he suspected British Intelligence had eliminated the missing men, diplomatic inquiries at the Foreign Office were met with assurances that no action had ever been taken against the three named members of the Soviet Press Bureau. Did the Soviet Embassy know of any reason why there should have been? The men were accredited Russian journalists, weren't they?

The Foreign Office man authorized to deal with these inquiries was Bobby Somers, elder son of Lizzy and Ned Somers. His record as an agent for the SOE(French) during the war was such that the Foreign Office gladly welcomed him as a member of the top-level echelon.

The Foreign Office and British Intelligence had no inkling that the so-called Soviet Press Bureau was interested in a person called Finch. Had they known, British Intelligence might have been reminded that Bobby Somers was the step-grandson of Sir Edwin Finch, once an invaluable and outstanding member of their shadowy profession.

As it was, Lieutenant General Kersch was still trying to breach the blank wall head first, in a manner of speaking, with no results except a phantom headache.

Chapter Ten

That afternoon, a car driven by Colonel Lucas was approaching Dulwich. Beside him was Eloise. In the back were Major Gibbs, Brigid and Anneliese. They were on their promised sightseeing trip to the Elephant and Castle, and the Old Vic, mainly for Anneliese's benefit, but a not unwelcome change of routine for the others. Colonel Lucas and Major Gibbs were in civvies.

During the ride from Aldershot through the peaceful countryside and quiet villages of Surrey, Anneliese had experienced a feeling of untroubled calm such as she was unable to find in West Germany. There were too many unhappy memories of lovely areas given over to camps for Hitler Youth. Militarized camps and militarized exercises. By 1944 she had come to realize this, to understand that during the Thirties those young people of Hitler's Germany had been trained to accept and to participate in a coming war of expansion.

How distressed her English grandmother had been on the day when Britain declared war on Germany. But because she believed in the Nazi Party and in Hitler with as much enthusiasm as the rest of the family, she went along with the fuehrer and his ambitions until, disillusioned at last, she died in an Allied air raid.

Anneliese was asking herself how long she was going to live with these wretched memories when Eloise broke into excited speech.

'Luke, this is Herne Hill!'

They had travelled down Norwood Road to head for Camberwell and Walworth, and were now close to Herne Hill railway station.

'So it's Herne Hill,' said Luke. 'Is that significant?'

'Yes, you know my father lives near here,' said Eloise. 'We can call on him. Everyone must meet him.'

'Exceptional though your father is, Eloise, we must deny ourselves the pleasure,' said Luke. 'I'm certainly not going to land all of us on his doorstep without letting him know in advance.'

'Oh, you beast,' said Eloise, 'I haven't seen Papa for ages.' Had she known the route Luke had worked out for the journey, she would have insisted on phoning Boots to ask him if they could call. 'It would only take a few minutes, and we aren't pressed for time.'

'Damn it, very well,' said Luke, and turned into Half Moon Lane. 'But only for you to say hello to him. Do you mind?' he asked his passengers.

'Not a bit,' said Major Gibbs.

'One should not pass one's father by,' said Brigid.

'I'm happy about whatever we do,' said Anneliese.

'Don't say things like that, Anneliese,' said Luke, 'not in front of Eloise, or we'll end up at the North Pole.'

'Luke's an absurd man,' said Eloise.

'Oh, I'm fond of absurd men,' said Anneliese, 'they're so human compared to intense men.'

I must keep my eye on Anneliese, thought Eloise.

Luke, having turned into East Dulwich Grove, pulled up outside an imposing house.

'Luke, you should have parked in the drive,' said Eloise.

'That would have given the impression we've come to stay a while,' said Luke. 'Hop out and say your hello. No more than that. We'll wait.'

'Really, you're very absurd,' said Eloise, but she eased herself out of the car and walked up the drive. She knocked on the front door. It opened after a moment or so, and Boots appeared. Watching from the car, Anneliese and Brigid saw a tall man of distinguished looks that weren't diminished by the fact that he was casually attired in sweater and slacks.

'Well, hello, my French chicken,' said Boots, 'to what do I owe this welcome pleasure?'

'Papa, how nice to see you,' said Eloise. She embraced him and kissed him, her grey eyes, so like her father's, alight with affection. She explained how her arrival on his doorstep had come about.

'Well, Polly and the twins are with her parents at the moment,' said Boots, 'and I'm due to pick them up in ten minutes, but bring Luke and your friends in.'

'Oh, Luke is being absurd,' said Eloise. 'He says he's determined not to intrude.'

'Then I'll come and say hello to him,' said Boots, and walked with Eloise to the car. Luke wound his window down. Boots leaned. 'How's life, Luke?'

'Sorry about disturbing you, Boots,' said Luke, who always thought of Eloise's paternal parent as a friend, rather than as his father-in-law. 'But Eloise insisted on saying hello to you.'

Boots, noting the passengers, and having had Eloise tell him that the two blonde women were German, said, 'There's time to introduce your friends, Luke.'

Luke turned.

'Meet Eloise's father,' he said, 'once a staff officer with Montgomery's 30 Corps. Boots, here's Major Gibbs, my second-in-command, his wife Brigid and his sister-in-law, Miss Anneliese Bruck.'

'How d'you do?' said Major Gibbs.

'Hello,' smiled Brigid, impressed by the masculine appeal of Eloise's father.

Anneliese saw a man with the finest of looks, wide grey eyes with the left one oddly a little darker than the right, and such a firm, generous mouth. His smile entranced her, and there was a strange little feeling that he wasn't unknown to her. Yet she was sure she had never met him. Unless in Berlin, perhaps, in the British zone? No, she would have remembered the time and place of a meeting with such a fascinating man. Yet the strange feeling persisted.

'Hello,' she said, smiling.

'A pleasure,' said Boots. 'I'd invite you all in, but I'm committed to picking up my wife and children in a few minutes.'

'Well, I love Polly and the twins, Papa,' said Eloise, 'but they're a disappointment to me for not being here.'

'Count it as hard luck,' said Boots, and went

99

round the car to open the passenger door for his inimitable French daughter.

Brigid spoke up.

'No, no, Eloise, you should not say such things when we are being a nuisance.'

'No nuisance,' smiled Boots, 'and I'm only sorry I can't entertain you.'

His voice, a mellow baritone, further entranced Anneliese.

'Eloise,' said Luke firmly, 'get in.'

Eloise slid in, and they all said goodbye to Boots.

'Some other time, perhaps?' he said as he closed the door.

'Any time is a good time for Eloise and me,' said Luke, and drove away. Anneliese turned her head to look through the rear window at Eloise's father, who lifted his hand in a gesture of goodbye.

'Luke, you should have said any time for all of us,' murmured Brigid. 'Such a lovely man.'

'What does that do for me?' queried her husband.

'Oh, you are lovely too, yes,' said Brigid.

'What did you think of my father, Anneliese?' asked Eloise.

'I have a strange feeling I've seen him before,' said Anneliese, 'but no, it's impossible.'

'Certainly, he was never in Berlin,' said Luke, 'he returned home from Hamburg some months after the war ended.'

'And I was never in Hamburg,' said Anneliese.

Later, they were travelling along Camberwell Road. Anneliese, absorbed, noted the scenes. There were shops interspersed with dwellings on either side of the road. And there were people, many of them.

The shops were practical rather than smart, and as for the people, the men were hardly stylish, the women hardly elegant. But no-one could have said they looked grim and suffering, or that the locality had a run-down look. Far from it. There was an air of liveliness, of bustling movement, and an atmosphere one could relate to a city now cheerfully recovering from the destruction of war. Anneliese supposed the people to be working-class, but not of a poverty-stricken kind.

The scenes were similar as they travelled down Walworth Road to the Elephant and Castle, which turned out to be a disappointment to Luke. It was now a vast roundabout, with excessive development still in progress on all sides, including a large block of offices for the Ministry of Education, something that Luke saw as a bureaucratic intrusion on an area that belonged solely to the people of Walworth.

He slowly circled the roundabout.

'Damn everything, it's gone,' he said. 'Well, I did say the air raids—'

'What's gone?' asked Eloise.

'The old Elephant and Castle Theatre, the Trocadero Cinema and everything else that made the place what it was pre-war,' said Luke. 'Anneliese, there's nothing of character to show you.'

'Oh, but there's a wonderful look of space,' said Anneliese.

'Bugger space,' said Luke, but under his breath.

'Excuse me?' said Anneliese.

'Don't get him to repeat it,' said Major Gibbs, guessing Luke had expressed himself in army terms.

Luke circled the roundabout twice.

'Well, let's try the Old Vic Theatre,' he said, 'and if that's being turned into a block of offices, I'll shoot the developers.'

The Old Vic, however, not only still existed, its Victorian frontage was still unchanged. Anneliese was newly fascinated, for the theatre stood in what she could only think of as a back street, not an imposing thoroughfare. Further, placards announced that there was an evening performance of *The Merchant of Venice*.

Excitement coursed through her. It showed in her face and expression. Luke noted it.

'Well, what d'you say, all of you, shall we find out if there are seats available?' he asked.

'I don't fancy we've come all this way just to look at the place and its placards,' said Major Gibbs.

'But, my dear Luke,' said Brigid, 'will the pound of flesh be enough blood and thunder for you?'

'I'm willing to settle for the pound of flesh,' said Luke.

'Oh, I should love to see the play myself,' said Anneliese. 'Can we get seats, do you think, John?'

'I'll find out,' said Major Gibbs.

They all left the car and entered the foyer, spacious and carpeted. Luke and Major Gibbs enquired at the box office for seats this evening.

'Stalls?' said the box-office lady.

'Five?' said Major Gibbs.

'Tenth row, sir? That's all we can offer.'

'Fine,' said Luke.

'Five shillings each – twenty-five shillings in all. Thank you, sir.'

Luke paid.

Eloise, Brigid and Anneliese were all delighted,

the more so when Luke said he'd now drive everyone into the West End, where the ladies could do
some window-shopping before they all enjoyed a
pre-theatre dinner.

How civilized everyone is, thought Anneliese,
how very much easier it is for a victorious nation to
recover than a defeated one. In some German
cities, like those in the East, some people still
behaved like hungry wolves despite improving
conditions.

Eloise's father, she thought, as the car crossed
Waterloo Bridge, is my idea of a civilized man, even
though he was only at the car for a couple of minutes, which is hardly enough time for any sensible
person to form a correct impression.

How strange that I still feel I've seen him before.

That night, as Anneliese lay in bed, her mind was
occupied by thoughts of the day and the evening, of
the ride from Aldershot, the brief but fascinating
meeting with Eloise's father, the bustling atmosphere of South London, the grandeur of Trafalgar
Square, the stylish shops of Regent Street, the very
satisfying dinner in the Edwardian atmosphere of a
West End restaurant, and finally the wonderful Old
Vic production of *The Merchant of Venice*.

Yes, London was where she would work and live,
if luck was with her. Colonel Lucas had given her a
list of London hospitals, and next week she would
look for an apartment, from where she could apply
for a post. That could mean living among London's
cockneys, but her English grandmother had always
referred to them as a hardy and resilient people.

One day, perhaps, she would go to Bath and find

out if any distant relatives of her grandmother lived there. She could not look anywhere for Lieutenant Tim Adams. She did not have his address, and nor did she have any information as to whether he was alive or dead. He had to remain a memory.

Felicity lay awake in bed, next to the warmth of Tim, her thoughts clouded with depression. For ten days now there had been no signs of a healing process. Up to that time, the blurs of light had happened regularly. Since then, nothing except the blankness she had lived with for years. Was she to say goodbye to hope? If there were still no signs for another week, then perhaps she must.

She turned, put herself close to Tim and slowly lapsed into sleep, a sleep in which there were no bright dreams.

Chapter Eleven

Sunday morning.

Breakfast at Sammy and Susie's home was like a scene from a play.

Phoebe. 'Mum, I've been thinking.'

Jimmy. 'Good. It's an encouraging sign, Dad, seeing she's starting work at your offices tomorrow.'

Sammy. 'We've already got two prime thinkers, me and your Uncle Boots. All we want from Phoebe is some daily work in our bookkeeping department.'

Phoebe. 'Excuse me, but I was speaking to Mum.'

Susie. 'And what d'you want to say, Phoebe love?'

Phoebe. 'Only that I think I need a new swimsuit.'

Susie. 'A new swimsuit?'

Phoebe. 'My old one's out of date.'

Jimmy. 'Get ready for a shock, Mum. I think Phoebe's got a bikini in mind.'

Sammy. 'A bikini? That's about as much as three fig leaves, and I ain't in favour.' Bikinis were the new swimsuit fashion, named after an atoll in the Pacific, scene of atom-bomb experiments. Female celebrities wore bikinis in the South of France, and some had been known to lose the tops when photographers were about. Sammy supposed some bikini tops were insecure. Susie knew better where certain female celebrities were concerned, those with highly photogenic bosoms.

Phoebe. 'Did I say a bikini, did I, Mum?'

Susie. 'Well, I think they're only suitable for the young, and at your age, lovey, you're just right for looking sweet in one.'

Sammy. 'Susie, I ain't in favour, and that's my last word.'

Jimmy. 'Your mind's made up, Dad?'

Sammy, loudly. 'Final and definite. I'm like iron on the matter.'

Susie. 'Yes, we know about your iron will, Sammy, you've given it an airing before, but don't shout, there's a good boy. If Phoebe really would like a bikini, we don't have to throw the furniture about.'

Sammy. 'Never mind the furniture, watch the house getting blown up if I catch Phoebe walking around the garden in three fig leaves. My permission's in the negative. And you can take that as positive.'

Jimmy. 'I could point out, Phoebe, that we've had our seaside holiday, and autumn's coming up. I don't think bikinis and autumn go together. And Dad's like iron, anyway.'

Phoebe. 'I don't know why everyone's going on about bikinis. All I said was that I think I need a new swimsuit.'

Susie. 'Still, your dad's Brixton shop stocks bikinis, Phoebe, and you and I could go there next Saturday for a trial fitting.'

Sammy, bawling. 'I'll shut the shop, you hear me, Susie?'

Jimmy, grinning. 'I'll shut my eyes if Mum and Phoebe both come back from Brixton in bikinis.'

Sammy, hoarsely. 'That's it, put 'em on top of a Brixton bus in fig leaves. Don't mind me, I'm only the window-cleaner.'

Susie. 'Eat your toast up, Sammy.'

Phoebe. 'I'd just like a smart one-piece swimsuit in sapphire blue, if that's all right with everyone.'

Jimmy. 'But you won't need it till next summer.'

Phoebe. 'Oh, well, time flies, Jimmy.'

Sammy to Susie. 'Is Phoebe talking sense now?'

Susie. 'Yes, Sammy, it looks like your iron will has won.'

Jimmy. 'Crisis over, Dad, you've come out on top.'

Sammy. 'That's a relief, I can now enjoy me toast and marmalade.'

Susie, murmuring. 'Still, I wonder if I could get away with a bikini myself?'

Collapse of Sammy, and not for the first time in his years with Susie.

Breakfast at the home of Tommy and Vi. They were talking about Vi's mum.

'It's time we had her with us, Vi,' said Tommy.

'You really wouldn't mind?' said Vi. Her ageing mum was known as Aunt Victoria to all the families. She was a widow: her husband, bluff Uncle Tom, had died not long ago. 'You'd like us to have her?' said Vi.

'Well, the old lady's seventy-five and not what she was,' said Tommy. 'I don't like her living alone in that old house, with all the stairs. Suppose she had a fall with no-one there?'

'I worry a bit about those stairs,' said Vi, soft-eyed and caring.

'She's a game old girl,' said Tommy. 'She don't complain about being alone. But it's time she had someone to keep an eye on her, and that's us, Vi. We'll pop round this morning and talk to her about moving in.'

'Tommy, you're a love,' said Vi.

'We've got plenty of room,' said Tommy, 'and come to that, she'll be a bit of company for you while I'm at work.' Their sons, David and Paul, were both married now, and their daughter Alice was now a tutor at Bristol University. 'She can have two rooms, one as a bedroom, one as her own living room.'

'Tommy, yes,' said Vi, 'let's encourage her to have her own living room, and buy her a wireless and television.'

Tommy smiled.

'See what you mean, Vi,' he said. 'It could turn out to be a bit of a headache if she got into the way of keeping you company all day every day.'

'Mind, she might like her own living room, seeing she's always prided herself on being a bit independent,' said Vi.

'That'll help,' said Tommy. 'Alice takes after her, y'know. She's independent, but a bit too much, in my opinion. We hardly ever see her, except for a few days at holiday times, and it don't look as if she'll ever get married.'

'Some women don't feel they need to,' said Vi.

'They wouldn't be alive if their parents hadn't got married,' said Tommy. 'Being born means you're obligated to keep things going by getting married and doing a bit of performing yourself.'

'Performing?' said Vi.

'Unless you're short of equipment or what you have don't work,' said Tommy.

'Tommy!''

'Did I say something?' asked Tommy.

'Yes, something you'd better not repeat when Mum comes to stay,' said Vi.

'Oh, your mum's got over being a bit prim,' said Tommy. 'She'd appreciate what I'm getting at.'

Vi smiled. Tommy was always frank and forthright, a plain-speaking and simple man compared to Boots, who was sophisticated, and Sammy, a live wire who could outdo spivs.

'Wasn't it a pity, Tommy, that Alice never took up serious with that nice Scotsman, Fergus MacAllister?' said Vi.

'Contrary about him, that's what she was,' said Tommy. 'I told her years ago that if she didn't act sensible, she'd end up getting married to her books. And that's what she's done. How old is she now?'

'Twenty-eight,' said Vi.

'Stone the crows, she's past it,' said Tommy, 'and that's put me off me breakfast.'

'You've eaten your breakfast,' smiled Vi.

'Have I?' said Tommy. 'Oh, well, give us another cup of tea, Vi, and then we'll go and see your mum.'

Old Aunt Victoria, still living in the Camberwell house that Tommy and Vi had purchased for her and Uncle Tom long years ago, listened as they told her what they had in mind for her.

Thin and angular now, her grey hair sprinkled with white, she was visibly touched. A little cough covered up her emotions.

'Well, I must say it's very nice of you two,' she said.

Born a cockney, she had decided to improve herself by taking on what she considered a respectable way of talking. This caused her to avoid dropping aitches, but it also caused her to add some, so that she often turned a word like 'airy' into 'hairy', which gave it a completely different meaning. 'But I wouldn't want to be a burden to you.'

'Mum, you've never been a burden to anyone all your life,' said Tommy, although he knew Uncle Tom had sometimes let drop a hint that his old lady was occasionally a bit of a heavy cross to bear. 'And you're not going to start now. No, Vi and me, we've made up our minds it's best if you come and live with us.'

'I just don't know I ought to give you the worry of looking after me,' said Aunt Victoria.

'Mum, as things are, we already worry about you being alone, with all your stairs to climb,' said Vi.

'Oh, it's coming down them that's a problem for my limbs,' said Aunt Victoria, who, like Chinese Lady, owned a Victorian reluctance to use the word 'legs' when it related to a woman.

'It's a problem because you're on your own,' said Tommy.

'Yes, I mean, suppose you had a fall with no-one here,' said Vi. 'Mum, me and Tommy want to have you.'

'With your own bedroom and living room,' said Tommy.

'And a wireless and television,' said Vi.

'Goodness, you're giving me a turn with all this kindness,' said Aunt Victoria, fluttering a bit.

'And when you sell this house,' said Tommy,

'you'll have a bit of a useful nest egg, which'll help you keep a lot of your independence.'

'That's right, Mum,' said Vi.

'Well, with my State pension and the pension I get from the Gas Board as your dad's widow, I shouldn't have to ask for any money,' said Aunt Victoria. 'I could give you and Tommy a bit of rent, I'm sure.'

'We don't need any rent,' said Tommy, 'and wouldn't take it, anyway.'

'I just don't know what to say, Tommy.'

'Mum, you don't have to say anything,' said Vi. 'It's settled, and you can move in with us as soon as you like.'

'Well, if you insist,' said Aunt Victoria. In her emotion, she added an aitch to 'insist'. 'Mind, I don't know what I'm going to do with all me— all my furniture.'

'Tommy will bring any little bits and pieces special to you,' said Vi.

'And I know who'll clear out your furniture and pay you a fair price for it,' said Tommy. 'Eli Greenberg. His sons will collect it. His yard isn't far from here.'

'Well, I won't say no to that,' said Aunt Victoria, lace blouse fastened at the neck with a filigree silver brooch. She paused for thought. 'I suppose his sons dress respectable?'

'They won't give your neighbours reason to turn their noses up,' said Tommy with a little grin. 'I'll have a word with Mr Greenberg about the date of collection, and let you know.'

'Well, me moving to Denmark Hill, I won't know

if I'm coming or going,' said Aunt Victoria. 'Vi, I think I'll buy some new hats.'

'You don't have to,' said Vi.

'No, I'd best do that,' said Aunt Victoria, who considered Denmark Hill a place where the tone of a lady's hat governed her respectability and social standing. (Chinese Lady thought only in terms of respectability where hats were concerned. Social standing didn't bother her.) 'My, we'll be able to enjoy talking together, Vi.'

'Yes, you and Vi can do that,' said Tommy. 'Sometimes,' he added, and winked at Vi.

'Tommy, have you got something in your eye?' asked Aunt Victoria.

'Only a wish,' said Tommy.

'A wish?'

'For a cup of coffee,' said Tommy.

'Oh, I'm forgetting me manners,' said Aunt Victoria.

Sunday afternoon.

Jimmy and his fiancée, Clare Roper, were walking in Victoria Park, near her home in Bow. Jimmy, as extrovert and entertaining as his brother Daniel, was considered by Clare to be the best bloke any girl could ever hope for. Clare, auburn-haired, sprightly and a stunner, was considered by Jimmy to be an absolute darling. Therefore, they were made for each other, and Clare could hardly wait for their Easter wedding. Her bottom drawer was already filling up, and the items included some underwear that she thought Jimmy might find a bit too much for his eyesight. But since she had an excellent dress sense, it was unlikely that Jimmy would find fault with anything in her bottom drawer.

Clare, wearing a warm sweater, a swinging skirt, and a round hat with a curled brim, was hand in hand with Jimmy and talking to him about her granddad's allotment, and how he'd provided a harvest of fresh veg.

'I've been helping him a lot,' she said. 'Well, I want to be a help to you when we're married.'

'On an allotment?' said Jimmy.

'Jimmy, we're going to have an allotment as well as a garden?'

'Didn't you mean that?' said Jimmy.

'No, course not, silly, I meant helping you in our garden, if we get a house with one.'

'We're not going to have any house without a garden,' said Jimmy.

'Oh, ain't that me dream?' said Clare, cockney ebullience surfacing.

'And what kind of a bathroom would you like, large or small?' asked Jimmy.

'Jimmy, a small one wouldn't be no good,' said Clare, 'you'd never get in any small bath. Well, look at you, you're as long as a lamppost.'

'A short lamppost,' said Jimmy. 'A normal one's over twelve feet. What's your opinion of lampposts, by the way?'

'Me opinion of lampposts?'

'Yes, d'you think they're ornamental?'

'Well, yes, sort of,' said Clare.

'Right, you gorgeous girl,' said Jimmy, 'when we start looking for a house, let's try to find one with a lamppost outside. Would you go for that?'

'Jimmy, d'you know you talk a bit barmy some-times?'

'What's barmy about an ornamental lamppost outside our front door?'

'Well, it sounded barmy the way you said it.'

They approached an elderly couple sitting on a bench. Clare stopped.

'Oh, hello,' she said.

'Look, it's Clare Roper,' said the old lady to her old man.

'So it is,' he said, but neither of them seemed happy.

'Jimmy, this is Mr and Mrs Cooper that used to be me mum and dad's neighbours before they moved,' said Clare. 'They're the grandparents of Sally at the fact'ry office.'

'How d'you do?' said Jimmy.

'So-so,' said Mr Cooper.

'This is me fiancé, Jimmy Adams,' said Clare.

'Yes, we heard, didn't we?' said Mrs Cooper.

'That's right, we heard,' said Mr Cooper.

Jimmy thought them a bit stiff, so he made an effort to unbend them.

'Could I ask you a question?' he enquired.

'Go ahead,' said Mr Cooper, 'but I dunno about any answers. I ain't as sharp on answers as I was.'

'It's not complicated,' said Jimmy. Clare quivered, sure he was going to try for a laugh, and just as sure he wasn't going to get one. She wished she hadn't stopped to say hello. 'I just want to ask if you think lampposts are ornamental,' said Jimmy.

'Beg pardon?' said Mrs Cooper, putting a hand to her ear.

'He wants to know about lampposts being ornamental,' said Mr Cooper. 'I like 'em meself, I've seen a lot of 'em lining the Embankment. 'Ighly ornamental, they are.'

'Would you like one outside your front door?' asked Jimmy.

'We ain't got no front door,' said Mrs Cooper.

'Well, not a proper one,' said Mr Cooper, 'seeing we live on the third floor of one of them new blocks of flats.'

'What's me old man saying?' asked Mrs Cooper of Jimmy.

'I'm saying there ain't no room outside our flat for a lamppost,' said Mr Cooper loudly.

'Tell the young man we only got room to fall off the balcony one day,' said Mrs Cooper.

'There y'ar, sonny,' said the other half, 'now yer know.'

'Yup, rotten hard luck,' said Jimmy. 'Never mind, nice to have met you.'

'Goodbye,' said Clare, and she and Jimmy went on their way.

'I've met happier people,' said Jimmy.

'Oh, they're a funny couple,' said Clare.

'Not funny ha-ha, that's for sure,' said Jimmy. 'Still, no-one's perfect. Listen, how's the switch-board job suiting you these days?'

'It's no problem,' said Clare. But there was a difference of attitude among the general office girls. Ever since her engagement to Jimmy, the son of Mister Sammy, the overall boss, the girls had stopped being friendly. They were making the atmosphere unpleasant for her. Of course, the trouble was they all fancied Jimmy themselves, especially Sally Cooper, whose grandparents had obviously been given some kind of unfriendly story. Clare had bumped into them a week ago, and received a cold shoulder, but she had no intention of telling Jimmy about such silliness. She was happy to say, 'Anyway, when we're married I'll be leaving me job and keeping house for you, won't I?'

'Well, the family's an old-fashioned lot,' said Jimmy, admiring one of the park's herbaceous borders, 'and we're not allowed to let our wives go out to work.'

'Not allowed?' said Clare.

'Yes, not allowed by Grandma Finch,' said Jimmy, following in the footsteps of cousins who'd had to let their girlfriends know that Grandma Finch laid down family law. 'She's been giving my cousin Paul a few earfuls for being out of line.'

'D'you mean – ?'

'Yes, he sends his wife out to work,' said Jimmy. 'At least, that's how Grandma puts it. So I won't be sending you out to any job, Clare, or she'll come round with a broom handle and do me some inconvenient injuries. As I'll be a newly married man at the time, the last thing I'll need is an inconvenient injury where it most hurts.'

Clare laughed and hugged his arm.

'Jimmy, I wouldn't want to have to bandage you up,' she said.

'I'm glad you said that, Clare. I can't think of anything more embarrassing than being bandaged up where it most hurts.'

Clare shrieked. Other people in the park looked.

'Jimmy, you shocker,' she gasped.

'You want to have second thoughts about bandages?' said Jimmy.

'No, I want to ask your mum when it was that they let you out of your monkey cage,' said Clare.

'What a lovely girl you are,' said Jimmy. 'I can't wait to see more of you.'

Clare laughed again, happily sure she could live with the envy and jealousy of the general office girls until Easter.

Chapter Twelve

Monday morning.

The overnight flight from Boston, USA, landed at London Airport on time, 7.10 a.m. The passengers disembarked. Among them were Patsy, Daniel, Arabella and Andrew. The sky was clear, but the morning was lightly touched with the freshness of autumn. It was the last Monday in September, and the Indian summer had gone back to wherever it had come from.

They waited in the baggage hall for their luggage to come through.

'Are we home?' asked Andrew.

'We will be when your grandpa gets us there,' said Daniel.

'Will my bed be made?' asked Andrew.

'Crumbs,' said Arabella, 'you're not thinking of getting into it, are you?'

'Yes,' said Andrew. He was tired out after the twelve-hour flight. He'd only had catnaps. So had everyone else.

'OK, little man,' said Patsy, 'we'll get you tucked up.'

'I'll be thinking about going to school tomorrow,' said Arabella.

'Well, they let you have over a week's extra holiday,' said Daniel. Arabella was attending a private school. Patsy had insisted, on the grounds that she considered the local State primary school wasn't quite up to standard.

Their luggage came through, and after a Customs officer had excused them of any payment of duty on the gifts they declared, they made their way to the exit. And there was Sammy, who'd risen at the crack of dawn to keep his promise to meet them and drive them home.

The children's reunion with their grandpa was joyful, and all the way home, Arabella poured out excited details of what they had seen, what they had done and what American ice cream was like.

'Just the tops,' she said.

'Kind of moreish?' smiled Sammy.

'It sure was,' said Arabella.

'Hello, what have we got here, a little American girl?' said Sammy.

'You sure have, Pa,' said Daniel.

'I'm going to do something about you two cowboys,' said Patsy.

'We didn't see any cowboys or Red Indians,' said Arabella.

'That'll be a relief to your grandma,' said Sammy, 'she thought you might bring a Red Indian chief home as a present for her. And I thought I'd have to build a wigwam for him in our garden.'

Arabella giggled.

'Grandpa, you're awful cute,' she said. 'Gee whiz, look at Andrew, he's asleep.'

Sammy smiled and motored on, while Daniel

talked about the phenomenon of supermarkets and hypermarkets.

'Never heard of 'em,' said Sammy.

'Oh, they fascinated Daniel,' said Patsy, 'and he's brought home some photographs of a Boston supermarket to show you.'

'Come to dinner next Sunday,' said Sammy, 'and bring 'em with you.'

'You can have first look, Pa,' said Daniel, 'I'll show them to you at the office tomorrow.'

'That's it, catch me when I've got five minutes to spare,' said Sammy.

He dropped the family off at their home, said it was a great pleasure to see them back, then excused himself to drive on to his offices.

Miss Stella Peebles received the plumber and his bag of tools at her Bloomsbury flat at nine. He was a burly bloke in a boiler suit, wearing a good-natured smile under his bowler hat.

'Morning to you, lady,' he said, 'I've come about your smell.'

'Good morning,' she said. 'It's not my smell, it's the drain, I suspect, and I hope you won't take long to put it right. I don't want to be absent from my office all day.'

'I take note according, missus –'

'Miss. Miss Peebles.'

'That's funny, I've got a Scottish aunt name of Peebles. Amy Peebles. Lives in Tottenham. I'm Larry Hopkins meself, registered plumber. Now, might I ask you to lead me to this here smell that Mr Fisher says is bothering you?'

'This way,' said Miss Peebles, and took him into

her living room. Mr Hopkins indulged in a hearty and professional sniff.

'Well, we've got a smell all right, missus –'

'Miss.'

'Yes, how d'yerdo, miss.' Mr Hopkins helped himself to another sniff. 'Well, I can't say we don't have a smell, because we do, and I'd be telling a lie if I said we didn't.'

'I'm all too aware of it, but I'm not asking you to share it with me,' said Miss Peebles. 'It's a bad drain smell, and I'm asking you to kindly find out what's causing it, and to do away with it. I'll be in my bedroom, I've some accounts to check.'

'Right you are, miss,' said Mr Hopkins, oozing breezy optimism. 'You leave it to me, I'll get after it. Bit of a stink, I'd call it.'

Miss Peebles retired to her bedroom, taking a sheaf of accounts with her, as well as a notepad. Mr Hopkins soon began to make himself heard in the kitchen, banging away at something.

'Drain's all right, miss,' he called after a while, 'your tap water's running away as good as gold. We don't have what you might call an interior drain blockage.'

'Then something else is the problem,' said Miss Peebles, presenting her handsome self at the open kitchen door. 'Kindly find it. What's that?'

'That? Oh, tools of me trade, miss,' said Mr Hopkins.

'They're all over the floor.'

'Just spread out a bit tidy, miss.'

'I think you mean untidy,' said Miss Peebles, and returned to her bedroom.

Mr Hopkins resumed his work, this time in the

bathroom, from where, after ten minutes or so, he transferred his experienced self to the living room. Miss Peebles heard furniture being moved about. There was silence for a little while, after which came the sound of floorboards being lifted. A minute later, another silence ensued, a strangely eerie one. Then she heard the plumber explode into frightening words.

'Jesus Christ and Godalmighty!'

Miss Peebles rushed in. Mr Hopkins was standing and staring, his face white. She saw a heap of dislodged floorboards and what lay between uncovered joists. Three dead men dressed in grey suits, each man's face in a state of repellent decomposition, lips shrunken, teeth glaring, closed eyes like dirty grey sockets, flesh ravaged by rat bites.

'Oh, my God!'

Miss Peebles sagged. Mr Hopkins caught her.

'Hello, that you, Eli old cock?' said Sammy over the phone.

'It's me, Sammy, and vhy not?'

'You're still in your office, then, partially retired?' said Sammy.

'Vell, I'm partial you might say, Sammy, being only here to look after the phone and to see the paper money don't blow avay, ain't I?'

'Sit on it,' said Sammy. 'Listen, I want an old-fashioned wall barometer, walnut-framed. It's for Susie. She wants to hang it in our hall. Then she can see what kind of weather to expect on her way out to the shops.'

'Ah, Susie,' sighed Mr Greenberg, 'ain't she always been a queen, Sammy?'

'Granted,' said Sammy, 'but I'm not letting her wear a crown or she'll be after a royal footstool instead of a barometer. Would you have a barometer, Eli?'

'Vell, I'll get Michal to take a look, Sammy, but if ve don't have vun, I know two or three people in the business, don't I? Except it might take longer than today, vhich I hope von't be inconvenient to Susie.'

'No hurry, Eli,' said Sammy. 'I'm asking for your valuable help on account of being too busy to go looking meself, especially in Bond Street antique shops. I'll get skinned alive, like Boots did when he bought Polly a mink vase for her birthday.'

'Ming, Sammy?'

'Something like that. I tell you, Eli, Boots of all people getting skinned. Just shows you that a good education doesn't always save a bloke from losing his marbles in a Bond Street emporium.'

'Sad, Sammy, sad,' said Mr Greenberg. 'But vasn't it a pleasure to hear from Tommy this morning about a house clearance for Vi's old mother?'

'Tommy's told you our Aunt Victoria's moving in with him and Vi?' said Sammy.

'Vhat a kind gesture, ain't it?' said Mr Greenberg. 'And a happy house-clearance job for Michal and Jacob. Might I ask vhat the furniture is like?'

'Old-fashioned,' said Sammy, 'but still wearing well.'

'Ah, and ain't that kind of furniture vell made, Sammy?' said Mr Greenberg. 'Modern furniture ain't so hot, some of it. It von't last. Mind, I ain't saying there'll be fifty customers a day coming to look at your Aunt Victoria's stuff, but some might have an eye for special bits and pieces, like, say, a mahogany hallstand, or a set of handsome fire irons or a glass-fronted china cabinet.'

'You've got grounds for hope,' said Sammy.

'Vell, a house clearance can be full of happy surprises,' said Mr Greenberg, 'and I von't let Michal and Jacob offer vhat vouldn't be a fair price. Ain't Tommy's family as dear to me as your own, Sammy.'

'Leave it to you, Eli old cock,' said Sammy. 'Don't forget about Susie's barometer.'

He went to Boots's office after putting the phone down. Rachel was there, talking to Boots.

'Good morning, Sammy,' smiled Rachel, and Sammy thought she was getting more well preserved each day. What a pleasure that some female women could grow younger. No wonder Rachel was on the receiving end of marriage offers.

'I know I'm late,' he said. 'All due, y'know, to picking up Patsy and Daniel, and their kids, at London Airport.'

'Yes, so Boots told me,' said Rachel. 'My life, all the way from America on a plane. Soon people will be hopping over to Paris for lunch, and getting back here for tea. We should marvel at that?'

'Tea back home's all right,' said Sammy, 'but I ain't sure I'd go a bundle on a French lunch of snails and garlic. Me stomach ain't too receptive to that kind of marvel. Anyway, nice to see you looking handsome, Rachel.'

'Thank you, Sammy,' said Rachel.

'Rachel's been talking to me about a site for some kind of development,' said Boots. 'Rachel, expound to Sammy.'

'Excuse me if I ain't familiar with expound,' said

Sammy. 'My education was a bit feeble. Still, I daresay Rachel could put me wise.'

'Simply, Sammy, it's like this,' said Rachel, and expounded to the effect that a Camberwell garage had been blown up during an air raid. What the bomb did to it was bad enough, and what the resultant explosion of fire did to it was destroy it completely. The site was still a flattened mess.

'That's expounding?' said Sammy. 'Rachel, I know that site. We made an offer for it two years ago, but the owner said he was after developing it himself.'

'Yes, Sammy, I know,' said Rachel, 'but he can't raise the capital without selling some of his other assets. So he's now considering accepting the right kind of offer.'

'Eh?' said Sammy. 'Where'd you get that information from?'

'From my daddy,' smiled Rachel. 'He knows the owner, Joseph Symons.'

'There we are, Sammy,' said Boots. 'What can one say about Rachel's respected father except that he knows more useful people than even you do?'

'I concur,' said Sammy. He grinned. 'If I don't know about expounding, I'm familiar with concurring. I ask you, haven't I spent me business years concurring or digging me heels in over contracts?'

'You have, Sammy,' smiled Boots, and Sammy thought that if Rachel was well preserved, so was his elder brother. Blind O'Reilly, he thought, if me and Tommy don't start using a monkey-gland ointment or something, we're going to be all over wrinkles while Boots will still be looking like Peter Pan's uncle.

'Sammy, it's a large site,' said Rachel, 'and since the council's considering granting a change of use to any prospective developer –'

'Change of use?'

'Yes, at the moment, use is confined to a garage, as before,' said Rachel. 'We should build a garage?'

'Count me out of garages,' said Sammy, 'except for what I sometimes need in the way of petrol.'

'Then we should do some quick thinking,' said Rachel. 'The site's almost on our doorstep.'

'Our thinking has to relate to the right kind of development,' said Boots, 'and how much capital we'll need to cover cost of purchase, cost of drawing up plans, and cost of building. Any ideas?'

'Wait till I've knocked a hole in me head,' said Sammy.

'To see what comes out?' said Rachel.

'If it's me brains,' said Sammy, 'don't let them get away. Push them back in. I need them. Besides, I've had 'em all my life, and they're among me best friends.'

'Nor have they ever let you down,' said Rachel.

'Granted,' said Sammy.

'Daniel will be back here tomorrow,' said Boots, 'so I suggest he and Tim join us in a board meeting tomorrow afternoon. After all, if we go for purchase and development, it'll mean handing them a full-time workload.'

'You think it'll be too much for them?' said Rachel.

'Not a bit,' said Boots. 'They did an excellent job of handling everything connected with the building of our Bethnal Green factory.'

'And they've got Paul as a highly valuable assistant now,' said Sammy. 'That lad was wasting his talents with the Labour Party. Which reminds me, how's Phoebe getting on upstairs with the book-keepers? It's her first day.'

'She has a chair, a desk and some paperwork,' said Boots. 'I fancy that's enough for a fair start.'

'Bless the girl,' said Sammy fondly. 'All right, then, phone your dad, Rachel, and tell him we'll consider making an offer. See if he knows the asking price.'

'A pleasure, Sammy,' said Rachel.

'Hope so,' said Sammy. 'Well, I'd better get back to me desk and do some work. Carry on, Rachel.'

Chapter Thirteen

CID men from Scotland Yard, called in by the police of Bloomsbury, weren't ready to leave the flat until midway through the afternoon. It had been a gruesome task, disinterring the three bodies and going through their clothes in an attempt to find anything that would identify them.

Nothing had come to light. Their limp suits, reduced by rats, not only revealed empty pockets, but an absence of labels. Their shoes were English-made in Northampton. So were those of thousands of other people.

The bodies had now been removed and a minute forensic examination was to be conducted consequent on the discovery that all three men had been shot. The CID men did not need to advise Miss Peebles to find alternative accommodation for the time being. Miss Peebles was already packing her belongings with the intention of departing for ever from the place. The policemen asked her to keep in touch with them, since they would like to interview her again.

Mr George Fisher, the landlord, having received a phone call from Miss Peebles, arrived while the CID men were still present. They were waiting for him. He was horrified by events, and responded to all questions by assuring the policemen he had no knowledge whatever of the victims or what had happened to them.

'Who was the previous tenant, sir?'

'A lady by the name of Katje Galicia.'

'How'd you spell that, sir?'

Mr Fisher spelled it out.

'She was foreign,' he said.

'What nationality?'

'I believe she was a Russian refugee, but I can't be certain. She never discussed her background with me.'

'Before she left, did she make any complaint to you about a smell?'

'No. There wasn't a smell. When I showed Miss Peebles over the flat, there was no cause for any complaint, which I'm sure she'll confirm.'

'Yes, I can confirm that,' said Miss Peebles. 'I've already mentioned there was no smell at all until a week or so ago.'

'The victims have been dead for months,' said one CID man, 'and the triple murder could have happened while this woman Galicia was still the tenant. What kind of a woman was she, Mr Fisher?'

'Middle-aged and very pleasant,' said Mr Fisher.

'Exactly when did she give up her tenancy?'

'Fourth of June.'

'Do you know where she lives now, sir?'

'I've no idea.'

'Didn't she leave any forwarding address for letters that might have arrived after she left?'

'She said she'd send it to me, but didn't. At least, I never received it.'

There were more questions, more answers, before the CID men finally departed. Mr Fisher then apologized sincerely to Miss Peebles for the ghastly discovery.

'Not your fault,' said Miss Peebles, 'but I've a suspicion the answer lies with the foreign woman, the one you thought was a Russian refugee.'

'It was only a thought,' said Mr Fisher, a portly man who, at this moment, seemed to have shrunk a little. His brow was creased with worry.

'I think the police consider her suspicious,' said Miss Peebles.

'So do I, now,' said Mr Fisher, 'and when the hounds of the press get to know of these murders, I'll lose all the other tenants and won't have a hope in hell of any future ones.'

'And I must tell you, Mr Fisher, I feel so ill that I'm going now. I'll be staying with a friend until I find a new flat.'

'Let me have your phone number.'

'Yes. I'll write it down for you.'

The news broke on the six o'clock broadcast.

Lieutenant General Kersch heard it. He also heard that the bodies had been discovered in a Bloomsbury flat. Three of them. He called in an assistant.

'You heard?'

'Yes, Comrade General.'

'So?'

'The location, a Bloomsbury apartment. The suspect, Katje Galicia.'

'Our suspect. Go to the apartment she occupied

and find out if it's definitely where the bodies were discovered.'

'At once, Comrade General.'

'Use your credentials as a Soviet journalist with a natural interest in a terrible murder.'

'I'll take my notepad.'

'You'll be an idiot if you don't.'

The officer returned an hour later to confirm that the apartment in question was definitely the one that had known Katje Galicia as a tenant.

'Yes, definitely, Comrade General.'

'That's so, is it?' said Kersch. 'Well, there's been more news. The police are looking for a woman of that name.'

'Will you advise them that we know her?'

'I'd be an idiot myself if I did,' said Kersch.

When Paul arrived home from work, he found Lulu in the living room, moving chairs about.

'What's going on?' he asked, dotting her lips with a kiss.

'Oh, I'm having a conference this evening with several Labour activists,' said Lulu, placing some kind of agenda on each chair.

'What for?' asked Paul.

'To discuss how to put new life into the Party's election campaign,' said Lulu.

'There's no election coming up,' said Paul.

'That's the point,' said Lulu. 'There's nothing of importance going on among activists. There should be. We intend to liven things up in South London, and get the press interested.'

'Oh, me gawd,' said Paul, 'not with marches and

demonstrations and the Red Flag again.'

'It's sad you're losing your enthusiasm,' said Lulu. 'That's what comes of working for a capitalist. I'm having to campaign for both of us.'

'And am I having to wait for my supper?' asked Paul.

'Oh, you can get supper,' said Lulu. 'It's your turn, anyway.'

'My turn's coming up a bit too often,' said Paul. 'What've we got lined up?'

'Some corned beef from Kennedy's,' said Lulu.

'Again?'

'You like corned beef.'

'Not six times a week.'

'Don't exaggerate,' said Lulu, 'just please me by doing the meal. I've had a tiring day at headquarters.'

'It's time the agent upped your wages,' said Paul. 'You'd get more working locally as a shorthand typist.'

'My work for the Party is a labour of love, you know that,' said Lulu. 'Paul, you're not complaining, are you?'

'Not now,' said Paul, 'but I might tomorrow. Oh, well, san fairy.' He went to the kitchen to start the supper, thinking a political marriage had its drawbacks. It was denting his Socialist armour and making him perverse in his attitude. If things didn't change, he might have to talk seriously to Lulu. As it was, Grandma Finch was so disapproving of husbands letting wives go out to work that she was likely to drop in one day and do some serious talking herself. She'd mentioned she might call to see what kind of a place they'd got. It was about time, of course, that he invited her and Grandpa Finch for Sunday tea. The presence of Grandpa would keep Grandma's disapproval at a moderate level.

He put supper on the kitchen table later. Corned beef, mashed potatoes, sliced tomatoes and runner beans. He and Lulu ate it while making conversation. Lulu said she'd bought some cider to give to their guests. Paul said they weren't his guests. Lulu said she'd like it if he could be helpful instead of grumpy.

'Grumpy?' said Paul. 'Me?'

'Well, yes, love,' said Lulu. 'Very grumpy.'

'I think I'll go to bed with a headache after supper,' said Paul.

'No, you won't,' said Lulu. 'I want you to be nice and to join the discussion.'

'I might not be on the same wavelength as you and your activists,' said Paul.

'Oh, I'd like you to raise any contentious points that come to your notice,' said Lulu. 'Arguments about aims and proposals can be stimulating. And you're interesting when you're argumentative. You make your points with good logic.'

'I might get short of logic if your activists turn up singing "The Red Flag",' said Paul.

As it turned out, the activists arrived in a bunch at eight o'clock and in orderly fashion. There were five young women and two young men. The young women were of the earnest breed, and plainly dressed. The young men were sober and thoughtful, wearing suits. Lulu welcomed them and introduced them to Paul. One young woman said, 'I've heard about you.'

'We all have,' chorused the other young women.

'You're Lulu's champion,' said the first young woman. 'It's great to know a husband can be his wife's chief support in politics. Mind, I don't believe in marriage myself. It gets in the way of a woman's chief interests.'

That was how Lulu used to talk, thought Paul.

'What are a woman's chief interests?' he asked.

'Mine are to help the development of a social structure that will do away with poverty and class friction.'

'Socialism?' said Paul.

'What else?'

'I'm in favour,' said Paul, 'as long as the structure doesn't fall apart.'

'Why should it once our Labour Party is our permanently established government?'

'This is going to be a jolly evening,' said Paul.

It wasn't quite like that. Everyone talked at once, across each other, and in conflict with each other. Lulu, in the chair, kept asking for order and for each person to be heard without interruption. But the earnest young women and the two intense young men were each of the opinion that his or her voice should be heard at all times. They all aired their own views on the best way a Labour government could eliminate the monarchy, render the Conservatives superfluous and deliver perfect Socialism to the workers. Since, despite the conflicting moments, their views all coincided, Paul thought one voice could speak for the lot, except that there'd be a never-ending discussion on whose voice it should be.

He made himself heard.

'Hold your horses,' he said loudly. No-one took any notice. 'Lulu,' he said, 'shut them up.'

'Order!' exclaimed Lulu.

Silence fell for the first time since eight o'clock.

'Listen,' said Paul, 'you're not talking about Socialism, you're all talking about a Communist republic. For your information, the workers themselves won't wear it. They all know too much about the downtrodden Russian people. Lulu's dad, the MP for Southwark, will tell you so.'

'Who's that bloke?' asked one of the young men of no-one in particular.

'Lulu's husband,' said one of the earnest ladies.

'I wondered what he was doing here. Lulu's actually married to him?'

'Didn't you get that when she introduced him?'

'I thought she was joking. She's really married? Poor woman.'

'Ronald, shut up,' said Lulu.

'Mr Chairman,' said Paul to Lulu, 'ask for a vote on whether or not a Socialist structure, as defined at this meeting, should be on speaking terms with a Communist republic.'

'The question isn't called for,' said a young man.

'Throw him out,' said the other bloke.

'We can't. He lives here.'

'Well, ask him to sit on the stairs, out of the way.'

'If you don't come to order,' said Lulu, 'you'll be thrown out yourselves. Paul has got citations for his past leadership of the Young Socialists. Concentrate on what we're here for. To exchange ideas for a lengthy campaign.'

That sparked a new flush of voluble enthusiasms. After a while, someone said, 'Where's your husband, Lulu?'

'Where are you, Paul?' called Lulu.

'In the kitchen eating biscuits and reading an Agatha Christie whodunnit,' called Paul.

'Man, he's a dissenter,' said someone.

Cider gurgled as glasses were filled from bottles. The conference became noisier. Lulu chucked them all out at ten o'clock, having decided that enthusiasm was a bit of a disaster, that a crowded living room was the wrong kind of venue.

Paul was making a bedtime drink of Horlicks for Lulu and himself.

'I'm sorry about all the noise,' said Lulu

'Hope it didn't disturb our neighbours,' said Paul. Their neighbours next door were a young couple like themselves, but didn't go in for politics, except for voting Conservative, a disappointment to Lulu. 'One ought to consider neighbours and what they might think.'

'Paul, that's a middle-class attitude,' said Lulu.

'Well, Brixton's got all kinds,' said Paul, 'including ladies of the entertainments profession.'

'Oh, you mean the kind of unfortunate women who've become the victims of capitalist oppression,' said Lulu. 'It's forced them into their unhappy lives.'

'Well, I met one the other night when you were studying Karl Marx and I was coming back from your dad's place,' said Paul.

'You did what?'

'Gave her a light for her cigarette,' said Paul. 'She didn't look unhappy or oppressed to me. In fact, she was as jolly as a dolly, and said she'd be chuffed to oblige me for a half-price fee.'

'Objection!' cried Lulu.

'To what?' asked Paul.

'To you encouraging a Brixton floozie to make you an offer,' said Lulu.

'A Brixton whatter?' said Paul.

'Floozie,' said Lulu. 'Don't you know that's what Americans call them?'

'Well, no, I've never been there,' said Paul.

'You should do serious and informative reading and leave silly detective novels alone,' said Lulu. 'Now, about this encounter of yours –'

'About the half-price offer?' said Paul. 'Oh, I turned it down.'

'Oh, you did, did you?' said Lulu. 'Well, thanks for being so considerate of your wife's feelings.'

'I told her some other time, maybe,' said Paul. 'Well, Socialists have got to be kind to victims of capitalist oppression.'

Lulu stared at him. He winked. She shrieked and went for him, and they had a stand-up set-to in the kitchen. Lulu won. Paul tripped and fell over. Lulu trod on him.

Still, they made it up later, and Lulu promised not to hold any more conferences in their semi-detached.

'Good-oh,' said Paul, 'that'll save me ducking out and going in search of Gloria.'

'Gloria?'

'Yes, the jolly dolly in the entertainments

profession, the one who'll oblige me for a half-price fee,' said Paul.

'You stinker, that's not funny,' said Lulu, but her acceptance of their neighbours' right not to be disturbed saved him from being beaten noisily to death.

Chapter Fourteen

Tuesday.

Scotland Yard's CID officers were examining the necessity of tracing a woman by the name of Katje Galicia. She was not listed on any files or records. They interviewed Mr Fisher again, and received from him a very helpful and detailed description of the lady. They made arrangements to circulate copies of a drawing, and to contact Immigration at ports. Meanwhile, officers began to ask questions of existing tenants of the Bloomsbury house, and of people living close by.

At home, Chinese Lady was busy with her housework. She had recently celebrated her seventy-seventh birthday with a family party, but was as active as ever. More than once Sir Edwin had suggested she might like to have a daily help, only to be informed that not until she was chronic with old age would she ask for assistance around the house.

Sir Edwin was in his study, reading the morning newspaper, his attention wholly fixed on the front-page report of the triple murder in Bloomsbury. The report included an announcement that the police wished to trace a previous occupant of the flat in question, a woman by the name of Katje Galicia.

Sir Edwin mused. Katje Galicia was the Polish woman he had first met during Polish army manoeuvres just before the war, and who had re-appeared in his life some months ago. She proved to be a worry and a bother to him by threatening to expose his German background to his family, unless he gave her the names of British agents active during and after the war. But at a moment when his worry was at a peak, she disappeared as unexpectedly as she had arrived. He'd received a goodbye letter from her, a letter couched in warm and friendly terms.

He had no doubt that she'd left the country, perhaps to return to Poland. Now, apparently, she was a possible suspect in the case of this triple murder, the bodies having been found in the flat she'd been renting.

How could a woman murder three men and bury their bodies in her flat, and all without disturbing other tenants?

What should he do? He thought about it, picked up the phone and put a call through to an old colleague, George Coleman, now sixty but so invaluable to British Security that he was presently the head of a department in MI6.

Sir Edwin spoke at length to him.

'Well, good of you to call me, Edwin old friend,' said George. 'Information noted. You feel sure Katje Galicia left the country?'

'Very sure,' said Sir Edwin, his study door closed.

'Well, of course, I know we have a file on her, a Polish army officer before the war, an agent for the

140

post-war Polish Republic and recently attached to the Soviet KGB. If I remember right, the file records your meeting with her at those pre-war manoeuvres.'

'I'm aware of that,' said Sir Edwin.

'How does retirement suit you, Edwin?'

'I laze about very enjoyably.'

'I hope I'll do the same when my time comes,' said George.

'What will you do about this information I've just given you?' asked Sir Edwin.

'Oh, keep it under my hat,' said George.

'You'll do nothing?' said Sir Edwin.

'Nothing,' said George. 'Edwin, old friend, the last thing this department will ever do is bring you out into the open. We owe you too much, so does the country. Whoever these three murdered men are, and I fancy they'll turn out to be the Russian agents Katje Galicia mentioned to you, the case is in the hands of the CID. It's their responsibility to find her.'

'That's your opinion?'

'It's my firm intention to leave all matters to the CID,' said George. 'Live your lazy life, Edwin. You deserve it. And give my warm regards to Lady Finch. Thanks again for phoning. So long, ease your worried brow.'

Sir Edwin was in excellent spirits when he and Chinese Lady were enjoying their mid-morning coffee, so much so that he agreed to accompany her on her shopping round, something he always tried to avoid.

At the Foreign Office, Bobby Somers received a call from the Soviet Press Bureau of London.

'Good morning, Mr Somers.' The English was guttural. 'Kersch here.'

'Good morning, Mr Kersch.' Bobby had heard from this gentleman before, in connection with three missing Bureau journalists. One took Russian journalists with a pinch of salt, of course. 'What can I do for you?'

'I would like you to arrange for me to view the bodies of the three murdered men found in a Bloomsbury apartment yesterday, hah?'

'Good God,' said Bobby, 'you suspect they might be your missing journalists?'

'I suspect that very much.'

'Well, of course, there's no reason why our Home Office should refuse your request,' said Bobby. 'Leave it with me and I'll phone you back.'

'Ah, good. Good. Thank you.'

'By the way,' said Bobby, 'would any of your missing men have known the woman the police are trying to trace?'

'Woman?'

'Her name's Katje Galicia, according to my newspaper.'

'There is no woman of that name on our staff, Mr Somers.'

'I see,' said Bobby, aware of the ambiguity of the answer. 'Well, I'll get back to you sometime today about permission to view the bodies.'

'Thank you.'

Bobby had a word with his department chief, Sir Ainsley Woodbourne.

'So the head of the Soviet Press Bureau wants to take a look at the bodies, does he?' said Sir Ainsley.

'What have we got, then? Dirty political work in the wilds of Bloomsbury?'

'It's dirty work on someone's part,' said Bobby.

'CIA agents, perhaps?'

'Do we know if the Russians took out any American agents prior to this triple murder?' asked Bobby.

'A tit for tat?' said Sir Ainsley. 'I don't know, and neither do you. Not our province. But MI6 might be informative.'

'Shall I find out?' asked Bobby.

'I think not,' said Sir Ainsley, 'they'll accuse us of poking our noses into affairs exclusively their own. Let's wait for the one o'clock news, and see what's developed. By then, the woman Katje Galicia might have been traced.'

'And with her, the key to the mystery?' said Bobby.

'Perhaps, but still not our province,' said Sir Ainsley. 'I'll contact the Home Office and arrange for them to permit our – um – friend at the Soviet Press Bureau to view the bodies. You can get back to him sometime this afternoon, and let him know. If he's grateful enough to deliver a couple of tins of caviar, we'll have one each.'

'Sounds fair,' said Bobby, entirely unaware that if anyone at all could tell the police something about the movements of Katje Galicia around the estimated time of the murders, Grandpa Finch could.

At the Camberwell Green offices of Adams Enterprises Ltd, Daniel returned to his desk following his time in Boston.

'What-ho,' said his cousin Tim, Boots's son. 'Glad to see you back. What've you brought me, a hamburger?'

'Several,' said Daniel, 'but we ate them on the plane coming home.'

'Well, come round with Patsy sometime and tell Felicity and me about America,' said Tim.

'Will do,' said Daniel. 'How's everything here?'

'Jammed up,' said Tim, 'I've been one-handed for a fortnight, except for some help from Paul. Listen, I heard from your dad that you've got some interesting snapshots.'

'Yes, of a Boston supermarket,' said Daniel.

'What's that, an American version of Petticoat Lane?'

'Not quite,' said Daniel. 'It's an eye-opener.'

'So's Marlene Dietrich,' said Tim. 'She's appearing at the London Palladium next week.'

'Hard luck,' said Daniel, who knew that as it would mean nothing to Felicity, Tim wouldn't go without her.

'There's a board meeting this morning,' said Tim. 'Rachel, our dads, and you and me. It'll be about possible purchase and development of a large site in Camberwell, so tighten your braces and button your jacket.'

'A large site in Camberwell?' said Daniel.

'That tickles you?' said Tim.

'Considerably,' said Daniel, sounding like Sammy, his dad.

Jennifer was at school, Maggie Forbes was doing the housework, and Felicity was about to go shopping. Maggie would go with her. Felicity was always happy to get out and about, to feel fresh air on her face and to know there was space around her. The house was limiting, especially at times when restlessness tugged at her.

In the hall, she felt for her warm-lined raincoat, found it and lifted it from its peg. In front of her, the hallstand mirror glittered with silvery light. It was a mirror she knew was there, but it had never been her friend.

Something happened, something that made her stiffen and then tremble. Out of her damned blackness appeared the blurred mistiness of her own face. Misty eyes, misty forehead, misty chin and a mistily puce mouth. Trembles turned into vibrations. Oh, the angels, there it was, the reflection of her own face, and it stayed as a visual if misty certainty, for a full minute before slowly fading. It had not been clear enough for her to decide if her looks had changed for the worse now that she was thirty-two, but what did that matter? A mirror had spoken for her at last.

'Maggie!'

Maggie came running.

'Mrs Adams?'

'Maggie, is this hallstand mirror cracked?'

'Cracked, mum?'

'Yes, is it?'

'No, mum.'

'What d'you see in it?'

Maggie took a look.

'Just me face, which could do with a bit of improving,' she said. 'Well, I'm never going to be like Margaret Lockwood, the film star. She's lovely.'

'There's nothing wrong with the mirror, then?'

Maggie looked at her mistress, and at the eyes that could not see.

'Beg pardon, mum, but what makes you ask a question like that?'

'Because, Maggie, if the mirror isn't playing up, I think I've just glimpsed my own face.'

'Oh, Mrs Adams, it's started to happen again?' Maggie was in the know about past moments and about the fact that they'd been absent lately.

'Yes, Maggie, it's started to happen again. Come along, leave the housework, put your hat and coat on and we'll walk to the shops.'

'Oh, Lor', d'you think you ought to?' said Maggie. 'Wouldn't it be best to sit and rest your eyes?'

'No,' said Felicity, 'let's take them out into the open air. I feel they want light.'

'Oh, bless us, d'you really feel that, mum?'

'Definitely,' said Felicity.

So she and her faithful housemaid went walking to the shops, Maggie holding her arm, guiding her and protecting her from the aggressive trees that lined the pavements of the roads and avenues in this residential area of South-East London. Felicity had never used a white stick. She considered it a gruesome advertisement of her disability, and in any case, neither Tim nor Maggie ever allowed her to go out on her own, never mind her complaint that such fussiness made her the equivalent of a dependent old woman.

Maggie marvelled at the spring in the step of her mistress. She was walking so confidently. But Maggie had to steer her occasionally, and did so with care and affection. She thought Felicity a brave and lovely woman. She herself was plump and a little plain, but she was not discontented. She saw her future always in relation to this family, and the master, in fact, had recently asked her to think about a living-in arrangement.

Felicity did her shopping almost blithely, making payments from the coins in her purse. She knew farthings, halfpennies and pennies by touch, as she did with the silver coins, a tiddler (threepenny bit), a tanner (sixpence), a bob (shilling), a florin (two shillings) and a half-crown (two shillings and sixpence).

The shopkeepers in Herne Hill knew her very well, and gave her kind but unpatronizing attention.

As today.

'Butter, Mrs Adams? Well, I can always recommend Danish.'

'Mr Hicks, you know I won't buy Danish, although I've nothing against the Danes. Don't most of us own a smidgeon of Danish blood from the time of Alfred the Great?'

'Well, I'm sure you'd know, Mrs Adams.'

'The Danish Vikings swamped us, Mr Hicks, and helped to build our nation. All the same, as usual, I'll take the best English or New Zealand butter. We owe New Zealand.'

'I won't argue with that, Mrs Adams.'

'Good. Say New Zealand, then. What a lovely morning, isn't it?'

In the butcher's shop.

'Lamb chops, Mrs Adams? Yes, fresh from Wales, and as pink as a – um –'

'Don't say baby's bottom, Mr Richards, not in

front of Maggie. I don't mind myself, but Maggie's a well brought-up girl.'

Maggie giggled.

'Well, Mrs Adams, let me say our Welsh lamb, as ever, is as tender as you could wish.'

'I'm proud of the Welsh for their lamb and their leeks, Mr Richards. Four chops, please.'

'That'll be – let's see – seven and fourpence according to weight, and eight coupons according to regulations, Mrs Adams.'

'Eight? Regulations? What a swine. The war's been over for years, and we're supposed to be among the victors. The French lost, but don't you know they can now buy more meat than we can?'

Maggie smiled. Mrs Adams was in fine form this morning.

'Mrs Adams,' said the elderly butcher sadly, 'I don't know much about the Frenchies, only ever having been as far as the Isle of Wight, but I do know I still only get limited supplies from my wholesaler, which means I still have to limit my customers, which is upsetting to me.'

'My hairy commandos never thought they were spilling their blood for the cause of upsetting our family butchers, Mr Richards. I'd like to mount my chariot of fire and puncture the Minister with my burning arrows.'

'Well, I'm a God-fearing man, Mrs Adams, but I wouldn't stand in your way.'

'That's the stuff,' said Felicity.

'My word, mum,' said Maggie, as they left the shop, 'you didn't half let yourself go, like.'

'Oh, there's spring in the air, Maggie.'

'It's the beginning of autumn, mum.'

'Well, something's making me feel drunk, and it's not autumn,' said Felicity.

'It's what that mirror's done for you,' said Maggie. 'Wait till you tell Mr Adams, he's going to be that pleased for you.'

'Step lively, Maggie,' said Felicity, she herself carrying the shopping basket. 'Hello, what's that?'

'It's the post office pillar box, mum,' said Maggie, taking a firmer hold of her mistress's arm, 'and you sort of hit it with the basket.'

'Oh, well, let's go in and buy some stamps,' said Felicity. 'That'll make the pillar box feel the biff was accidental. An injured pillar box that felt it was done on purpose might not accept our letters, or if it did it might chew them up.'

'Mrs Adams, you're a real laugh this morning,' said Maggie.

'Better than being a moody old washout,' said Felicity.

Chapter Fifteen

The snapshots of the Boston supermarket were passing from hand to hand around the boardroom table, with Daniel answering questions.

'Daniel, you say supermarkets are food stores?' enquired Rachel.

'Yes, mainly,' said Daniel, 'but you can buy kitchen utensils in this one, as well as magazines and newspapers.'

Interior snapshots provided views of fully-stocked shelves and special displays.

'There's a proposition here, I'll say that much,' observed Sammy thoughtfully.

'There is if we buy the Camberwell site you've mentioned,' said Daniel.

'So what we'd get is a store where housewives could buy all their groceries in the one place instead of going from shop to shop, is that it?' said Boots.

'That's it, Dad,' said Tim.

'It's a certain winner,' said Daniel.

'It would cost a fortune to build and stock,' said Rachel.

'Well, we want the site for development, and we've made Symons, the owner, an offer,' said Sammy.

'He's considering it, which means he's going to ask us to up it. But we didn't have a supermarket in mind for development. Now it looks like we might have, although I'm not sure we can lay out a fortune, Rachel. We've got a healthy bank balance, but a fortune? Ladies and gents, we'd have to raise one.'

'It could be worth the risk,' said Daniel.

'Yes, it could,' smiled Rachel. 'But regarding a supermarket development, shall we first find out the approximate cost of the whole venture?'

'Very sensible,' said Boots, 'but we're up against time. What comes first is to make sure we acquire the site, and if we dither about the price, we may be beaten to it by some other developer.'

'Increase our offer, Pa, if that'll clinch it,' said Daniel.

'We can raise our offer if we must, Sammy,' urged Rachel.

'Well,' said Sammy, still thoughtful.

'You've got reservations, Sammy?' said Boots.

'Some,' said Sammy.

'That's not like you, Uncle Sammy,' said Tim.

'There's planning permission to think about,' said Sammy.

'True,' said Boots, 'planning permission for an American-style supermarket.'

'Boots, the council's willing now to grant a change of use from a garage,' said Rachel.

'I think Sammy's wondering, as I am, if the council will be in favour of a large store that might rob local grocers and greengrocers of most of their customers,' said Boots.

'But competition's the lifeblood of private enterprise,' said Tim.

'And death in some cases to small businesses,' said Boots.

'Come on, Pa,' said Daniel to his dad, 'you're in favour, aren't you?'

'I've got to hand it to Boots,' said Sammy, 'his thoughts coincide with mine, which means will we get planning permission for a supermarket?'

'If we don't, Sammy, should we worry?' said Rachel. 'We consider a different development.'

'All right,' said Sammy, 'show hands, all those who are voting for the firm to up the offer for the site now and immediate, as is called for.'

All hands went up.

'Motion carried, I think,' said Boots. 'Fair enough. Ownership of the site is the first priority. When that happens, we decide how to proceed.'

'Uncle Boots,' said Daniel, 'we're going to be in real money with a supermarket, you've got my guarantee.'

'Well, wrap it up in a couple of warm woollen blankets, Daniel old lad,' said Boots. 'Guarantees can catch cold in the winter.'

'Boots, d'you have serious doubts?' said Rachel.

'No, not Boots, he doesn't believe in getting serious,' grinned Sammy, 'that's just his education talking. And anyway, let's respect his thinking equipment. He's got his share of that, or he wouldn't have made general in the army.'

'Colonel,' smiled Rachel.

'No difference, not unless colonels have got more stripes than generals,' said Sammy.

'Gongs, Pa,' said Daniel, 'and generals—'

'So all right, they can all play in a brass band,' said Sammy. 'Right, then, meeting over. Rachel, do me a favour. Phone Mr Symons, the site owner, and make an appointment for you and me to see him on the quick. Person-to-person stuff always pays profitable dividends. And if I can't make him sing, you will. Wear your fur hat and a fancy jumper.' Tim and Daniel yelled with laughter. Boots smiled. Rachel rolled her eyes. 'Pardon me,' said Sammy, 'but did I say something?'

'Nothing that didn't make sense,' said Boots.

'Did it make sense?' asked Rachel.

'A fur hat and a fancy jumper? It made sense to me,' said Boots, 'and I think it will to Mr Symons.'

'I think I'll go and blush unseen,' said Rachel, 'and make the phone call as soon as I've recovered.' But she was laughing as she left the boardroom. Her life was bound up with the Adams family, and she loved it. Especially as Boots and Sammy assured her that as the mother-in-law of Edward, husband of her daughter Leah, she was one of them.

Mr Symons proved very agreeable to a meeting, as long as he wasn't kept waiting, so Rachel fixed it for the following day. Sammy expressed pleasure.

'But I shan't wear a fur hat and jumper,' said Rachel.

'Why not?' said Sammy.

'Why not? My life,' said Rachel, 'I shall need a skirt as well, won't I?'

'I pass,' said Sammy.

Mr Greenberg phoned a little later.

'Sammy my friend,' he said, 'ain't life happy?'

'Over the top sometimes,' said Sammy.

'Vell, is it over the top, Sammy, to tell you Michal

has found for Susie a handsome barometer in a valnut frame?'

'It's certain sure you're Susie's friend for life, Eli old cock, and give my regards to Michal. What's the damage, by the way?'

'Vhy, Sammy, vould I charge you vhen it's for Susie?' said Mr Greenberg. 'It's a present, Sammy.'

'Well, I appreciate that, Eli,' said Sammy, 'but fair's fair. I asked and you've obliged, and I can't remember when you haven't. So how much?'

'Say a silver florin, Sammy?'

Since that was as good as giving the item away, Sammy said, 'Plus a fiver for delivery charges if Michal or Jacob will drop it in at my office?'

'A pleasure, Sammy. You're a fair man.'

'By the way, don't mind me asking, Eli, but does the barometer work?'

'It's in front of my eyes, Sammy, and it's promising fine veather. Vhat could be vorking better?'

'Only a Rolls-Royce engine,' said Sammy.

Anneliese Bruck, an elegant figure in a stylish navy blue costume and a light blue toque hat, having followed directions from Major Gibbs on how to reach South London, emerged from Lough-borough Junction railway station, Camberwell. There she made enquiries of a fellow passenger, a genial old bloke who, having been told she wished to get to the centre of South London, informed her that Camberwell Green was as good as anywhere. A bus would get her there, he said, and the obliging old codger walked with her to the right bus stop. She smiled and thanked him.

'It's a pleasure, love,' he said.

Love? Did he know what he was saying? And what should she say in return? Sir, this is so sudden?

Off he went, and at the bus stop Anneliese was aware of a broad thoroughfare and large Victorian houses on either side, houses she thought typical of London. Along came a bus. She boarded it, and when the conductor approached her for her fare, she asked a question.

'Does this bus go to Camberwell Green, if you please?'

The conductor, a cheerful young bloke who didn't have the same complaints about life or chilblains as a lot of old folk, looked at her. Well, here's a bit of all right, he thought.

'Believe me, lady,' he said, 'if we don't get there it'll be because me driver's lost his way.'

'Lost his way?'

'Fred's a bit short-sighted, y'know.'

'That I can't believe,' said Anneliese.

'Just joking, lady. He'll get us there.'

'Could you let me know when we do?'

'I'll tip you the wink, don't you worry, but I'll have to charge you a tuppence for yer ticket.'

'How much is that?'

'Two pennies, and I hope you ain't going to give me four 'apennies or eight farthings. We get our share of saucy kids, y'know.'

'I see.' Anneliese smiled. It made the young conductor feel as if his late old granny had left him a hundred quid instead of her stuffed parrot. 'I'm sure I have two pennies,' said his classy passenger, opening her purse. She extracted the two coins, and in return for them was given a clipped ticket.

'There we are, love,' said the conductor.

Love? That again? Londoners, she thought, were kind but familiar.

The bus, travelling down the long course of Coldharbour Lane, gave her a view of the Victorian brick and stone dwellings on either side. Yes, it was typical of London, in her opinion. After several minutes, and two stops to allow passengers to alight or board, the road converged with Denmark Hill, and from there rumbled on towards a busy junction. It crossed the junction and stopped at Camberwell Green.

'Camberwell Green, Camberwell Green!' bawled the conductor. Anneliese followed several passengers to the platform. The conductor gave her a smile. 'Here we are, lady,' he said, 'Camberwell Green. Mind how you go.'

'Thank you,' said Anneliese.

'Any time, love, any time,' he said, and Anneliese alighted, smiling. The bus moved off, and from the pavement she saw a small oasis of green grass surrounded by railings. She recognized it as the green she had seen on the day when Colonel Lucas was driving through London to the Old Vic.

She began to walk in the direction Colonel Lucas had taken, her mind fixed on finding living accommodation, preferably a three-room apartment, called a flat by the British. She found herself in the bustle of Camberwell Road, where a number of single-storey shops were dwarfed by three-storey houses built behind them. The houses were reached by alleyways between blocks of these shops. Anneliese wondered if any of them had rooms to let. Major Gibbs, her English brother-in-law, had

156

told her to look in the windows of newsagents' shops. Newsagents, he said, rented out their window spaces to people who had something to sell, like a pram, a bike, or some such item, and advertised it on a plain postcard. 'You'll find some cards offer rooms at very affordable rents,' he said.

Anneliese decided, first of all, that she didn't want to live amid the bustle and noise of a main road. She must investigate the character of residential roads and streets, and hope to find a quieter environment. She turned left into Wyndham Road, and saw at once it was very mixed. Some houses looked well enough, others looked neglected or in need of repair. She thought this a possible result of the war, and that nothing so far had been done about it. She turned and made her way back to the main road. Two coloured immigrants were walking along, broad-faced West Indians, a man and a woman. They looked at her. Her sister had told her the UK was now accepting immigrants from the West Indies. She essayed a friendly smile. They responded with teeth-gleaming beams, as if delighted to be noticed.

'Good morning,' said Anneliese as she passed them. She was, after all, an immigrant herself. She re-entered the main road and saw a newsagent's shop a little way ahead, and when she reached it, sure enough there were cards in the window. One offered a concertina for three and sixpence, another a child's large teddy bear for two shillings, and a third a stamp collection for seven shillings and sixpence. Addresses were given in all instances.

Anneliese inspected the cards one by one, looking for what she wanted. Her eyes alighted on a scrawled advertisement for a flat in Ruskin Street at a pound a week.

'Well, I'm sure that's very good value,' she murmured to herself. She entered the shop, waiting until the plump proprietress had finished serving a customer, then asked if she could be told where Ruskin Street was.

'Ruskin Street, ducky? It's second on the left from here. You after that flat?'

'I should like to look at it,' said Anneliese.

The proprietress studied her.

'I'm not sure it'll suit you, dearie.'

'Oh? Why not?'

'Well, there's not too many amenities, but go and look at it and see what you think.'

In response to such friendliness, Anneliese bought a fashion magazine, thanked the woman and left. She found Ruskin Street, again typically Victorian, and knocked on the door of number 17. A beefy woman with a round red face answered the knock. Her blouse was of an indeterminate colour, her skirt a dowdy brown. But she was cheerful in her greeting.

''Ello, what can I do yer for?'

'Good morning,' said Anneliese, 'I believe you have a flat to let.'

'Well, so I 'ave, so I 'ave. Come in, come in, and I'll take you up.'

Anneliese entered the passage. The wallpaper was dark with age, and the stairs in front of her were covered with linoleum that could have first known the light of day while Queen Victoria was still alive. She followed the large lady up the stairs all the way to the top floor, the lady wheezing a bit, but delivering cheerful comments about what a nice flat it was.

It turned out to be three small rooms as bare as Mother Hubbard's cupboard, except for an untidy heap of old newspapers in one. No bathroom, no amenities of any kind. The large lady confided happy information to the effect that the loo and handbasin were on the first floor.

Anneliese, quite certain the flat was not for her, said, 'Oh, I didn't realize it was unfurnished.'

'Oh, you can get a few sticks of furniture down at Mason's, where they sell good second-hand stuff very cheap,' said the large lady.

'If you'll excuse me, I don't think I want to do that,' said Anneliese.

The large lady gave her a new look.

''Ere, you a foreigner?'

'I'm from West Germany.'

'Well, that's foreign, ain't it? That's more foreign than anywhere. Be off with you. Go on, 'oppit. We don't want no Germans 'ere. I wouldn't 'ave climbed all them stairs if I'd known.'

'I'm sorry you feel like that,' said Anneliese, and departed with good grace, descending the stairs effortlessly, while the large lady followed very much like a lumbering elephant, wheezing with an abundant chestful of indignation.

Chapter Sixteen

Anneliese escaped from the house to the hoarse strains of umbrage. She resumed her walk along the main road, and spotting another newsagent's shop on the other side, she waited until traffic had cleared, then crossed. She studied the window cards. One offered a flat, and she noted it was furnished. The rent was twenty-five shillings a week, the address, 118 Camberwell Road.

This was Camberwell Road. Anneliese put aside her misgivings about noise and bustle, and went looking for number 118. She found it. It was one of those large houses erected in an area behind shops. She reached it through an alleyway. It was three-storeyed, with a basement and a small flight of steps up to the central front door. The forecourt was quite spacious, and two dustbins stood at the corner of the house. Curtains looked clean, and the front door looked approachable.

She knocked. It took some time for the door to open and reveal a lanky man with untidy dark hair, agreeable looks and a suggestion of a five o'clock shadow. He was dressed in an old navy blue jersey and blue slacks. He stared at her, his brown eyes reflecting distinct approval.

'Well, well,' he said, 'an artist's model, I presume?'

'An artist's model?' said Anneliese. 'I'm afraid you're mistaken. I've called about the flat you're advertising.'

He picked up her light accent.

'Dear lady,' he said, 'whoever you are and wherever you're from, you're very welcome. The card was only put in the newsagent's window this morning. I hope such a quick response means a lucky day for me. Do me the pleasure of stepping in and I'll show you what's on offer.'

'A moment,' said Anneliese, still conscious of the large lady's unfriendly comments. 'I must tell you I'm from West Germany.'

'Are you?' he said, apparently unbothered by the disclosure. 'I'm from Chipping Norton myself.'

'Chipping Norton?' said Anneliese, stepping into a square hall.

'Don't let it alarm you, I've grown out of it. Harry Stevens. How'd you do?'

'I'm Anneliese Bruck, Mr Stevens.' She spelled her surname.

'Um – frau or fraulein?' he enquired.

'Fraulein, but Miss now I'm in England.'

'Well, delighted to meet you, Miss Bruck,' said Mr Harry Stevens, 'and I hope you'll like the flat. Frankly, I could do with the rent money. I write short stories for magazines, which works out at only about five a year, so I'm struggling to stay solvent and to keep my daughter dressed and fed.'

'And are you struggling to keep your wife dressed and fed too?'

'That's a painful reminder that I lost her during

161

the war, a victim of a flying bomb in 1945, while I was serving in the navy.'

'Oh, I'm sorry,' said Anneliese.

'No hard feelings, Miss Bruck, you had your own casualties.'

'It was that kind of war,' said Anneliese, relieved to find he was easy to talk to.

'It's all over now,' said Mr Stevens, 'so let's forget it, what d'you say?'

'We can at least not talk about it,' said Anneliese.

'That's the stuff,' said Mr Stevens, thinking her unusually striking in both looks and voice. 'Come on, let me take you up to the flat. It's on the first floor.'

'Thank you,' said Anneliese, liking him but well prepared to reserve judgement on what he was about to show her, although the square hall was a great improvement on anything she had seen in the house in Ruskin Street.

The stairs were carpeted, and if the carpet was in a threadbare condition, there was a sense of diligent housework about the place. The first-floor landing shone with light from a window. Anneliese favoured light, very much so, since she remembered so much darkness during the last year of the war. Sometimes the only light came from buildings ablaze with fire from an air raid. The RAF and American air force bombers had been merciless.

For the next minute or so she experienced something happily different from that which had confronted her in the grimy house of the large woman. Simple pleasure. The flat on offer here consisted of an airy bedroom, comfortable living room, cosy kitchen and a very welcome bathroom

with toilet. The furniture, including that of the bedroom, was quite attractive, and there was a table and
reading lamp on each side of the double bed, a
boon to Anneliese, for books kept her company on
the nights when she found it difficult to fall asleep.
The kitchen was small, yes, but fully equipped,
although it was obvious that nothing was new.

'Sorry to press you, but what's your verdict?'
asked Mr Stevens.

'Yes, I like it, very much,' she said, feeling sure
that such a flat would not stay vacant for long.
'Everything looks well cared for.'

Mr Stevens smiled.

'You can thank my daughter for that,' he said.
'She's my housekeeper, financial manager and
sergeant major. Have you ever been ordered about
by a twelve-year-old sergeant major?'

'Your daughter?' said Anneliese.

'Cindy,' said Mr Stevens, with another smile.

'She's only twelve and does all your housework?'

'Most of it, and she also takes care of what money
I earn from scraping a living. I write well-known
short stories of London life. That is, well known to
Cindy and my agent. I don't get as many accep-
tances as I'd like. I could find a job as a well-paid
bricklayer in this age of development and re-
development, but I wouldn't be as happy as I am
now. I'm waiting, of course, to become rich and
famous.' Mr Stevens laughed at the possibility.
'Look, I still don't want to press you, Miss Bruck, but
is it possible you'll take this flat?'

'I should like to very much,' said Anneliese,
'especially as the house is quieter than I thought it
might be.'

'The traffic noises don't intrude too much,' said Mr Stevens. 'Did you say you'd take the flat?'

'I'd like to move in on Saturday, Mr Stevens.' That was when she was due to end her stay with her sister and brother-in-law. 'Would Saturday be convenient for you?'

'Convenient? A fine old pleasure, believe me.'

'Shall I pay a month's rent in advance?'

'Shall you? You're offering to? What a delightful young lady you are.'

'Not quite a young lady, Mr Stevens.' Her precise English was a fascination, her blue eyes magical. Well, they were at this moment to hard-up Harry Stevens. 'At twenty-five shillings a week, a month's rent would be five pounds, yes?'

Her command of the nature of British currency was as efficient as her command of the language.

'Are you going to offer me that amount in advance, Miss Bruck?'

'I wish to be sure of the apartment,' said Anneliese, 'to have your promise that I can move in on Saturday.'

'Miss Bruck, if I could promise you the moon as well, I would,' said Harry fervently.

'How kind,' smiled Anneliese, 'but it's the rooms I would like, not the moon.'

'Yours, on my honour,' said Harry, a man of forty with little idea of how to make the best use of his limited income. As he had said, Cindy, his daughter, did the budgeting. Fortunately, the house was his, left to him by his wife, who had inherited it from her parents. But it was Cindy who made sure there was enough money available to pay the costs of rates, gas and electricity. 'Move in on Saturday, by all means, Cindy and I will be delighted.'

'Thank you, Mr Stevens,' said Anneliese, and produced a crisp white fiver from her handbag. 'There,' she said, and gave it to him.

'Well, on my soul,' said Harry, 'that's noble of you. Now Cindy can pay the milkman, the newsagent and the grocer. Let's see, don't you need a signed lease in exchange for this fiver?'

'Mr Stevens, if you will give me your word as an English gentleman that I can stay indefinitely as your tenant, that will be good enough for me. One can still trust an English gentleman, I hope? That hasn't changed for the worse, has it?'

'God knows, so much else has,' said Harry. 'Look here, you shall have a rent book at least. I'll get one, make it out, include some kind of tenancy guarantee and sign it.'

'Thank you, Mr Stevens. Where is your daughter, by the way?'

'At school. She'll be home at teatime.'

'I look forward to meeting her,' said Anneliese. 'Oh, and where do you write your stories?'

'Oh, I've turned a top-floor room into a study to keep the sound of my typewriter away from the ground-floor flat where Cindy and I exist,' said Harry. 'There's a skylight up there. I'll show you when you move in – wait a moment, can I offer you coffee?'

'Thank you, but no,' said Anneliese, 'it's nearly lunchtime and I must go. I'll see you on Saturday.' She smiled. 'Take care of the rent advance.'

'Oh, Cindy will pounce on that,' said Harry, 'and perhaps give me a bob or two for myself.' He laughed. Anneliese thought him – what was the word? Bohemian, yes, like the artists and writers of Paris, who could handle their paintbrushes but were always careless about money. So they were always broke. 'Let me see you down to the door,' said Harry.

He accompanied her down the stairs to the front door, shook her hand warmly and said goodbye to her.

'Goodbye, Mr Stevens, and thank you again,' she said.

'A pleasure, believe me,' said Harry, and watched her descend the steps and walk to the alleyway. Fascinating, he thought, absolutely fascinating. If I were a rich man, damned if I wouldn't throw my hat in the ring.

But why, I wonder, has she chosen to come here from Germany? And to live in a flat in Camberwell? I place her in Belgravia, among the nobs.

Let's see, what was I doing before she arrived?

Anneliese, emerging from the alleyway, began to walk back to Camberwell Green. She also began to wonder if she had not been too impulsive. Perhaps she should have asked for a day to think it over. But no, the apartment was too appealing, its situation perfect if she succeeded in securing a nursing post in a London hospital this side of the river.

Reaching the Green, she thought about a light lunch. If she frequently had a strange feeling that she was in harmony with English people, she was not sure she was going to like English food once she had left her sister's home. It was reputed to be stodgy and overcooked. On the other hand,

German meals in normal times weren't complete without mounds of potatoes.

She spotted a restaurant called Lyons. She hesitated, then went in. It had quite a welcoming atmosphere, with a large number of tables and a waitress service. It was half-full of people. She chose a vacant table and sat down. People looked, drawn by her stylish appearance. She studied the menu. The offerings were light and simple. A waitress came up, pad and pencil at the ready.

'What can I get you, madam?'

'I would like your poached egg on toast, please,' said Anneliese.

'With a slice of grilled bacon?' tempted the waitress.

'Oh, yes, thank you,' said Anneliese. If there was one thing she had taken to it was an English breakfast of eggs and bacon, which Brigid served regularly. 'And a cup of coffee to follow, please.'

Well, here's a proper lady, thought the waitress, and as polite as anything.

'Won't be a tick, madam,' she said, and moved to an adjacent table to attend to the wants of a young, pleasant-faced man. Paul Adams, enjoying his lunch break from the offices of Adams Enterprises, ordered eggs and bacon, and a bread roll with butter.

'You and your eggs,' smiled the waitress, 'you'll turn into a chicken one day.'

'You'll know when,' said Paul, 'it'll be the day I come in squawking, and with my feathers flying. Who's the lady?'

'A lot more polite than you are,' said the waitress, and off she went with the orders.

Paul made a covert study of the well-dressed woman, so different from the usual run of Lyons customers. Lulu's dress sense was improving rapidly, but had a long way to go to level up with this fair woman's stylish perfection. Only Aunt Polly, and perhaps cousin Rosie, could have matched her.

Anneliese looked around. The restaurant buzzed with conversation. A little laughter was heard at some tables. A visitor to her family home before the war had said that in an English restaurant or on an English train, the atmosphere was one of a strained and awkward silence. The English, he said, travelled and dined gloomily. No-one spoke to anyone else. Well, that isn't the case here, thought Anneliese. She caught the eye of the young man. He seemed very interested in her. Paul smiled, a slightly guilty smile for staring. Much to his surprise, his smile was returned, but not in any guilty fashion.

Since she had chosen to live among the people of South London, Anneliese was resolved not to be found wanting. If she was reserved, perhaps just as reserved as the English, she had never been aloof or unapproachable.

Now she said, 'Good morning.'

'Same to you,' said Paul, an extrovert, 'except it's now afternoon.'

'Young man,' said Anneliese, 'you are splitting hairs.'

'Shall I come and share your table?' offered Paul, keen to talk to her.

'Thank you, but I think not,' said Anneliese, suspecting he was actually trying to pick her up. Not that he was objectionable. He was a young man of healthy and pleasing looks. However, some conventions had to be observed.

The waitress returned with her order, and placed it before her.

'There we are, madam, hope you enjoy it.'

'Thank you,' said Anneliese.

The waitress crossed to Paul and gave him his lunch.

'Good-oh,' he said, 'I'm in serious need of sustenance.'

'When aren't you?' said the waitress, and departed smiling.

For the next several minutes, Anneliese Bruck of Berlin enjoyed her lunch in fairly close proximity to Paul Adams, cousin of Tim Adams, once a wounded British prisoner of war in the care of German doctors and herself as his nurse.

Paul could not help being intrigued by this striking woman. He had noted her slight accent. He did not, however, make any further attempt to engage her in conversation. He was not the kind of young man to make an idiotic nuisance of himself. He respected the woman's reservations. He left when he had finished his snack lunch, but couldn't help giving her a goodbye smile as he passed her table. Again she returned his smile.

And that was that. He paid his bill at the counter and departed, having left a tip.

Anneliese would have lost all reservations had she known who he was.

Chapter Seventeen

'Hello, yes, yes?' The growling, guttural voice sounded like that of a man whose short fuse was about to blow.

'Somers of the Foreign Office here, Mr Kersch,' said Bobby.

'Ah, Mr Somers,' said Kersch, changing from a growl to a gruffness. 'Yes, what have you to tell me, hah?'

'It concerns your request to view the bodies of the murdered men,' said Bobby. It was mid-afternoon. The BBC announcer delivering the one o'clock news had informed the listening public that the mystery woman, Katje Galicia, had not yet been traced, that the identities of the murdered men were still not known, and that Scotland Yard was pursuing a broad range of inquiries. 'Mr Kersch, I'm able to let you know our Home Office has instructed the police to allow you to visit the mortuary. In fact, the police will send a car to pick you up at four this afternoon, if that's suitable.'

'Good, yes, very good, Mr Somers,' said Kersch. 'I will, of course, have an assistant with me.'

A bodyguard, thought Bobby with an inward smile, to prevent Scotland Yard from abducting him. Russians were suspicious of the smallest gesture offered by any official of the Western Powers.

'An assistant? Yes, of course, Mr Kersch,' he said.

'No-one will be offended if we travel in my own car and follow the police car?' said Kersch.

'I shan't be offended in the least,' said Bobby, 'nor will our Foreign Minister. I hope your viewing of the bodies will resolve your worries.' Bobby could be very much the civil servant in these kinds of circumstances. When he recounted little incidents to his French wife Helene in his civil servant's voice, she fell about hysterical with laughter.

'Thank you, Mr Somers, I am grateful,' said Kersch, but he failed to hint that a gift of caviar might arrive at the Foreign Office.

It was a little after four when the bodies of the three murdered men were laid out at the mortuary to allow the head of London's Soviet Press Bureau to inspect them. Accompanied by an assistant, a handsome, keen-eyed Ukrainian, he took his time to dwell on the hideously disfigured faces of the victims.

Eventually, with a decisive shake of his head, he said to a Home Office official in thickly accented English, 'No, I recognize none of them. Despite decay, I can definitely say they were never members of my Bureau. But may the law catch and hang their murderers. Thank you. Goodbye.'

In the car going back to their offices, the assistant said, 'I could swear myself, Comrade General, that one was Bukov, and another was Alexandrov.'

'I know that, you idiot,' said Kersch, 'but it was

not something to tell these English decadents. They'd want to know why it was necessary to send a team of three Bureau journalists on a news-gathering mission. It would make them suspect that news wasn't the objective, and that could lead to the expulsion of all our present members. You know what that would mean, don't you?'

'Siberia.'

'Or worse. Let Scotland Yard rot in its investigation of the murder of men they can't identify. They will never find Katje Galicia, the only person who could help them. She's too cursed clever. But we'll find her. She's the one who liquidated Bukov and the others, I'm certain. When we do lay our hands on her, she'll scream for a whole month before she dies.'

Katje Galicia, however, was a long way off. She was in Vermont, USA, with her son, the man who had shot and killed the three KGB officers. He was working as a hospital doctor, and she was making herself very agreeable to an elderly American businessman who also happened to be a widower and a millionaire. She was living under the name of Olga Kuschka, and her passport identified her as Latvian.

She was a clever woman indeed.

'Well, I'm blessed,' said Cindy Stevens, on arrival home from school. 'You've really let the flat already?'

'Didn't I just say so?' said her father.

'You managed all by yourself?' said Cindy, an earnest young lady of twelve years. Slim and neat in her school uniform, with her light brown hair dressed in pigtails, she was precocious in her self-assurance and in her tendency to be bossy.

'I didn't need help,' said Harry, 'the lady was charming.'

'Did you give your hair a brushing before she arrived?' asked Cindy.

'I didn't know she was coming, she simply arrived and knocked,' said Harry.

'And your hair was like it is now, all mussed up?' said Cindy. Harry applied a hand to his hair and brushed it with his fingers. 'Oh, well never mind now, Dad, if you've let the flat I'm pleased with you.'

'It's let all right,' said Harry, 'I'm in receipt of a month's rent in advance.'

'A month's?' said Cindy. 'That's five pounds. Dad, where is it?'

'Here,' said Harry, and dug a hand into his hip pocket. 'No, here,' he said and dug a hand into his trousers pocket. He produced a folded white fiver.

'Hand it over,' said Cindy, and took it from him.

'I could do with a few bob myself,' he said.

'Well, as you managed to let the flat, I'll let you have something when I've paid our grocer and got change from him,' said Cindy.

'Kind of you,' said Harry.

'Oh, you're not a bad old dad,' said Cindy, 'just a bit casual and absent-minded. Now, what's the lady like?'

'Let's see now.' Harry mused. 'Pretty aristocratic,' he said.

'What?' said Cindy.

'Quite striking.'

'Aristocratic and striking? Daddy, people like that don't live in Camberwell. We're all homely and hard-working.'

'And I think she said she was German,' said Harry. 'Yes, I'm sure she did.'

'German? German?' Cindy looked astonished.

'Or was it French?' Harry mused again. 'No, German, definitely.'

'Dad, what have you done?' gasped Cindy. 'There'll be some people who'll throw rotten cabbages at her. And there might be some who'll chuck bricks at our windows.'

'I'll be sorry for anyone who does silly things like that,' said Harry. 'She's a delightful woman.'

'Well, I hope she is,' said Cindy. She thought. 'P'raps we could say she's French. What's her name?'

'What was it now?'

'Oh, come on, Daddy, wake up.'

'I made a note of it somewhere, for a rent book,' said Harry. 'Yes, got it. Bruck.'

'Brook?'

'No, a German Bruck. Miss Bruck.' He spelled it out for Cindy, as Anneliese had for him.

'Well, we won't say she's German. No, best if we don't. What's her English like?' Cindy was thorough about details, whereas her dad was casual.

'Faultless,' said Harry.

'Oh, good,' said Cindy. 'We'll tell busybodies she's Miss Brook. Well, there's more busybodies in Camberwell than anywhere. We'll let them think she's from Wimbledon, which is posher than here.'

'No, that won't do, pet,' said Harry, 'she doesn't sound like anyone from Wimbledon.'

'All right, we'll stick to her being French, then,' said Cindy, 'and you can tell me more about her later. I'll dash off now and pay the grocer and butcher, and get this fiver changed. Oh, have you been to the newsagent's and asked for the card to be taken out of the window?'

'It slipped my mind,' said Harry.

'Oh, well, I'll tell him,' said Cindy. 'You peel the potatoes for supper while I'm gone.'

'Cindy, I'm trying to put the finishing touches to a story.'

'All right, do it, and then peel the spuds,' said Cindy.

'Very good, Sergeant Major,' said Harry.

'Don't be cheeky,' said Cindy, and out she went from their ground-floor living quarters.

'What's this?' asked Mr Godfrey, the butcher.

'A five-pound note,' said Cindy.

'Well, I never did,' said a lady customer, having a good look, 'I ain't seen one of them since me old dad died and we found four under 'is mattress.'

'Cindy, you sure it's not a dud?' said the butcher, holding the fiver up to the light.

'Oh, come on, Mr Godfrey,' said Cindy, 'me dad's a writer, not a forger.'

'Well, this here fiver's a work of art, if you know what I mean,' said the butcher.

'Oh, I know all right,' said Cindy, 'and when I tell me dad he'll probably sue you.'

Mr Godfrey chuckled.

'You're all right, girlie,' he said, 'and so's this here fiver, I bet. And nor won't I ask where your dad got it from.'

'Oh, much obliged, I'm sure,' said Cindy.

A sum of seventeen shillings and fivepence was owed to the butcher, so she received change amounting to four pounds, two and sevenpence. Feeling rich, off she went to the grocer's shop, where the proprietor, Mr Topping, received her with a smile, even if her dad did owe him over ten bob. Cindy was a well-known character among all the shopkeepers. They saw her as an engaging Miss Madam.

'Well, well, Cindy,' said Mr Topping, 'you're paying off all your owings at one go? Bless me if I ain't joyful. Would you like a quarter-pound packet of me best Lyons tea?'

'Not half, if it's for free,' said Cindy.

'Well, would you mind if I charged just sixpence?'

'But that's the normal price,' said Cindy.

'Still, you can have it on tick.'

'No, I don't want to run up more owings,' said Cindy, 'and I don't want any expensive tea, just the fivepenny packet. Expensive groceries could ruin me dad. And me as well.'

'How is yer dad?'

'Oh, up in the air,' said Cindy.

She paid for the tea and for the owings, which cost her ten shillings and ninepence. Then she went along to the newsagent and asked him to take the card out of the window because the flat was let.

'That's quick,' said the newsagent. 'Who's he let it to?'

'A French lady,' said Cindy. 'From Wimbledon,' she added.

'Wimbledon?'

'Yes, where her French ancestors lived,' said Cindy.

'Well, I never,' said the newsagent, 'how did she come to— That's it, Henry Robbins, talk to yerself.'

Cindy had vanished with a swish of her school skirt and a whisk of her pigtails.

Scotland Yard's top men weren't inclined to accept the denial by the head of the Soviet Press Bureau that the murdered men were known to him. The fact that three members of his Bureau had disappeared about the same time as the murder was too much of a coincidence.

They asked the Home Office for permission to contact the Soviet Embassy.

'For what reason?'

'To ask if the dental records for the three missing Russian journalists could be sent from Moscow.'

'Ah.'

'It's one way of confirming whether or not they can be linked with these corpses.'

'Ah, yes. I'll let you know.'

'Daddy! Daddy!' Jennifer rushed to meet her father when she heard him arriving home from work. 'What d'you think!'

'I think I see you, little puss,' said Tim, closing the front door. 'What's exciting you?'

'Mummy.'

'Has she promised you a ride on an elephant, then?'

'No, she's seen herself!' Jennifer's exclamation mark positively made itself heard. 'In this mirror.' She pointed to the hallstand mirror.

'She did what?'

'She saw herself! She said so!'

'Steady, angel.'

'But she did, Daddy, she did, she wouldn't have said so if she hadn't.'

'Where is she?'

'In the kitchen with Maggie. They've done apple pie for our supper. Mummy said it's your favourite sweet.'

Tim chucked his hat at the hallstand and made for the kitchen, where Felicity and Maggie were preparing supper.

'I heard you arrive, Tim, it sounded noisy,' said Felicity.

'Only with Jennifer's help.'

'Come and join the party,' said Felicity.

Tim wrapped his arms around her, and her body communicated the vibrations of a woman high on hope.

'What's this story about the hallstand mirror?' he asked.

'It did something for me at last,' said Felicity, 'it showed me what I look like. It was all a bit misty, so I wonder, was it being kind? I mean, exactly what do I look like?'

'Same as ever,' said Tim, delighted by the news.

'Daddy, you have to tell her what the same as ever is,' said Jennifer.

'A knockout,' said Tim. 'It really happened, did it, Puss?'

'Not all that clearly, but yes, it happened,' said Felicity, 'and d'you mind putting me down? You've got my feet off the floor. Well, almost.'

Tim released his happy wife, stood back and searched her eyes. Her face was slightly flushed.

'Felicity, are you a little delirious?' he said.

'A lot more than a little, Tim,' she said.

'Mr Adams, your wife's been like that all day,' said Maggie, 'there's just no stopping her.'

'Yes, and ever since I came home from school as well,' said Jennifer. 'She did a dance with me all round the kitchen. Daddy, isn't it wonderful? I mean, Mummy's really going to be able to see one day, isn't she?'

'When that day arrives, little girl, we'll treat you to a ride on two elephants – one at a time,' said Tim, who was thinking of the possibility of corneal grafts if Sir Charles Morgan eventually decided the condition was promising enough. Tim had his own hopes, but he had begun to wonder if Felicity's sight would really come back without some kind of treatment. Sir Charles had mentioned there was no operation he could perform at present. But in time, perhaps, he would change his mind.

'Daddy, I'm not bothered about elephants,' said Jennifer.

'Good,' said Tim, 'elephants can be a big bother. Now, let's celebrate. Pop out and bring back a bottle of champagne, little puss.'

'Mr Adams, Jennifer couldn't do that,' said Maggie.

'Well, a bottle of fizzy lemonade, then,' said Tim.

'Oh, dear,' said Jennifer, 'I think Daddy's being a bit dirilous himself.'

'Never mind about champagne or fizzy lemonade,' said Felicity, 'we already have something to help us celebrate.'

'What's that?' asked Tim.

'Bramley apple pie,' said Felicity.

'With custard,' said Jennifer.

'Who could ask for more?' said Tim.

'You didn't, did you?' said Mrs Brigid Gibbs to her sister.

'Why not?' said Anneliese.

'You gave five pounds to a stranger?'

'Yes, to secure my tenancy,' said Anneliese. 'He was a charming man, a gentleman, and by the time we had settled the matter we were no longer strangers.'

'He's a writer of short stories, you say?' said Brigid.

'I rather feel he's typically so,' smiled Anneliese. 'His mind seems mainly occupied by his work and not by worldly matters. He has a twelve-year-old daughter who looks after him and the housework – oh, and apparently manages his finances, such as they are. He's a widower.' Anneliese had one of her sober moments. 'His wife was killed by a rocket bomb.'

'Did you tell him our English grandmother was killed during an air raid by the RAF?' asked Brigid.

'No,' said Anneliese. 'He admitted we had our own casualties. Oh, when I told him I was from Germany, he just smiled and said he was from a place called Chipping Norton. That was a welcome reaction after my experience with someone else.' And Anneliese recounted how a certain large woman drove her from her house with a torrent of insults.

'There are always people who won't forgive us,'

said Brigid. 'So, you're moving to South London on Saturday?'

'That was the agreement we reached,' said Anneliese.

'Well, I hope you haven't made a mistake,' said Brigid.

'If I can secure a post at a London hospital, I feel I can begin a new life quite happily,' said Anneliese.

'And you've given up any possibility of tracing the British commando you knew at Benghazi?'

'There's simply no chance of that,' said Anneliese.

'Well, to be frank,' said Brigid, 'I did feel the whole idea was rather absurd.'

Chapter Eighteen

'Now you'll be all right while I'm at school?' said young Miss Cindy Stevens to her dad the following morning.

'Young lady, I usually do manage to get through the day,' said Harry.

'Let me see your socks,' said Cindy. Harry pulled his trouser legs up. 'Now look at that,' said Cindy.

'At what?'

'You're wearing odd socks again,' said Cindy. 'Sometimes, Dad, I just don't know what I'm going to do with you.'

'How about a few bob from the fiver you changed at the shops yesterday?' suggested Harry.

'I've put two shillings in the cocoa tin,' said Cindy, 'but mind you don't spend them a bit reckless.'

'Now listen, miss, among other things, I need some new typewriter ribbons and some quarto paper,' said Harry.

'Well, make a quick list and I'll get them for you on my way home from school,' said Cindy.

'I've a feeling,' said Harry, 'that my life's not my own.' But he made a list, gave it to Cindy, and off she went, as lively as the proverbial cricket.

'Oh, the two bob in the cocoa tin,' she called back

from the front door, 'you can have that for pocket money, Dad.'

'My gratitude is overwhelming,' said Harry.

'But like I said, don't spend it all at once.'

'That'll be the day,' said Harry.

Later that morning, Rosie's husband arrived at the Croydon Labour Exchange. The place had a welcoming air, the current Government-inspired approach being to make unemployed persons feel they mattered. Matthew had to wait for an interview with one of the assistants, and eventually found himself sitting at a table opposite a helpful woman.

'Now, what kind of work are you looking for?' she asked kindly.

'None for myself,' said Matthew, and went on to explain he was after two people, preferably a married couple, who could assist in the running of a poultry farm at Woldingham.

'Woldingham?'

'Yes, it's a few miles from here, I know,' said Matthew, 'but there's an annexe. They can live in, and won't be asked to pay rent. Would you have a married couple on your books?'

The assistant consulted her file. She extracted a card.

'Well, count yourself lucky, Mr Chapman,' she said. 'We do have a married couple listed, a couple who would prefer to work together. A Mr and Mrs Robinson. Shall I ask them to call on you for an interview?'

'I'll need to talk to them, of course, and to determine if they're suitable,' said Matthew. 'And

I'll pay their train fare. It's only fifteen minutes from East Croydon station to Woldingham.'

'I must say, Mr Chapman, we don't get many Croydon people looking for farm work, especially as the council is planning a future of major development, but give me the full address of your farm.'

Matthew gave it, together with the phone number, and was told he'd be informed about date and time of interview.

'Well, thanks,' he said, 'and as they say down in Dorset, "A helping hand is worth a bob, when it be concerning a likely job."'

'But Woldingham isn't in Dorset, Mr Chapman.'

'No, but I were once,' said Matthew in Dorset dialect.

What a charming man, thought the lady official as he left, and that thought intensified when the next applicant turned out to be a known layabout whose fixed idea of an acceptable job was that of a waiter with guaranteed tips of ten untaxable quid a week and no overtime.

'We still have nothing like that to offer you, Mr Porter.'

'I'll have to stay on the dole, then.'

'In Russia, Mr Porter, you'd be compelled into work, probably as a street cleaner.'

'Well, I ain't in Russia, and I ain't going to emigrate there, either. I'll stick to me dole till you come up with a waiter's job with guaranteed—'

'Yes, we know of the conditions you lay down, Mr Porter, and we can't compel you into other work. Good morning.'

*   *   *

The Home Office applied to the Soviet Embassy for co-operation in the matter of the triple murder. Could the dental records of the three missing Russian journalists of the Soviet Press Bureau be sent from Moscow for inspection by Scotland Yard?

'We'll let you know.'

'Thank you. Your help will be appreciated.'

'Of course. We'll let you know.'

Sammy popped into Boots's office at midday.

'Just back from seeing Mr Symons, old mate,' he said. 'Rachel did her stuff in a right royal get-up with frills.'

'I presume you mean she performed,' said Boots. 'Exactly how, and what was the result?'

'Give over,' said Sammy, 'you don't think she did the cancan, do you?'

'What, then?'

'She just sat there, smiling and looking like a box of cream chocolates and putting in a nifty word now and again,' said Sammy. 'Poor old Manny Symons could hardly keep a grip on the extra percentage he was after, but he did, although it was a strain on his tonsils. Anyway, the site's ours, Boots, he'll sign the contract.'

'And you're keen on a supermarket development?' said Boots.

Sammy said the property company would at least apply for planning permission. If that was granted, he said, then he'd get Tim and Daniel, with an architect, to come up with a suitable design and the full cost of the project. He'd be in favour, he said, if the cost didn't ruin the firm, which he was afraid it might.

'Well, today's building costs ain't exactly modest, y'know, Boots.'

'I do know,' said Boots.

'You could build a semi-detached house in Norbury for three hundred quid before the war,' said Sammy. 'It 'ud be near to eight hundred now, taking in price of the plot. So what's the erection of a whacking great stocked-up supermarket going to cost on top of nearly two thousand quid we're having to pay for the site?'

'A fortune,' said Boots.

'I've got a few thousand personal quids in the bank,' said Sammy, 'and so have you, I daresay. But we ain't rich, Boots, not by today's standards.'

'If I know you, Sammy,' said Boots, 'you don't favour a bank loan.'

'Not on your life,' said Sammy, 'not at the interest they charge. On top of that,' he said, 'they'll be breathing down our necks all the time, even when we're in our private beds.' 'With our private wives?' said Boots. 'That as well,' said Sammy. 'Banks you owe money to wouldn't think twice about getting in bed with you and your trouble and strife, just in case you were whispering to her about doing a bunk to Monte Carlo with your spare pocket money. No, Boots old cock, we raise the capital ourselves, us and the firm. If we can't, we'll opt for a more affordable development. Mind, I think Daniel's right, I think a supermarket could be a winner. So does Susie.'

'And I think myself that Daniel and Tim see it as the best part of their business future,' said Boots.

'Well, you and me, Boots, and Tommy, have probably had our best days in the business,' said

Sammy. 'We've got to think about moving aside.'

'You'll be seventy before you take your first side-ways step,' said Boots.

'Oh, well, I've still got me facilities,' said Sammy.

'Faculties,' said Boots.

'Fortunately, them as well,' said Sammy.

'A supermarket,' murmured Polly that evening.

'Yes, it's still the major topic at the office,' said Boots.

'It's a leap into the unknown,' said Polly, 'and there are large holes in the unknown.'

'I asked my English teacher if she knew what supermarkets were,' said Gemma, 'and she told me she'd never heard of them.'

'I didn't ask anybody,' said James.

'Why didn't you?' demanded Gemma.

'It didn't occur to me,' said James.

'Mummy, that boy of yours is getting too smart for my good,' said Gemma.

'Are you, James?' asked Boots.

'I'm not all that smart,' said James. 'I need help.'

'What kind of help?' asked Polly, who had switched off the television set in favour of family conversation. She had a growing suspicion that television could render families mute, which was not a fate she desired for her nearest and dearest. 'Yes, what kind of help, James?'

'I think Cathy Davidson wants to marry me,' said James.

'Crikey,' said Gemma, 'now he's gone from being smart to being cuckoo.'

'Would you care to repeat what you said, James?' asked Boots.

187

'Yes,' said James, 'I think Cathy Davidson wants to marry me.'

'I forbid it,' said Polly, 'I forbid it now, today, tomorrow, next week or any time in the future. And I believe, James, I've had to say that kind of thing before.'

Gemma giggled.

Cathy Davidson was the eleven-year-old daughter of Mrs Anastasia Davidson, a lady whose grandparents were Russian. It was generally agreed by Polly and her family that the lady's Russian tendencies were of a dangerous kind. Well, she had her eye on Boots, which Polly considered not only dangerous but a bloody cheek. So whenever said lady called, and she called on any kind of pretext, Polly ordered James and Gemma to pull up the castle drawbridge, load their muskets, man the barricades, and fill up the parapet barrels with boiling oil. She also ordered Boots to hide himself in the dungeon.

She had actually been heard to cry, 'She's here, she's at the door! Don't let her in! James, arm yourself! Gemma, hide your father!'

Or something like that. It was all a glorious act, of course, and suited Polly down to the ground. Gemma had hysterics, James grinned, and Boots turned never a hair. It would end with Polly answering the door and informing the lady that whatever she had come for wasn't available. Or words to that effect.

Some months ago, the lady's daughter Cathy had taken to waiting for James after school and getting him to walk her home. James, the easy-going son of his dad, fell in with her wants, but experienced the surprise of his life two days ago, when the pretty young miss asked if he was going to give her a present on her next birthday, and if he was she'd like a ring.

'A ring, Cathy?'

'Well, I'll be twelve next birthday,' said Cathy.

'Oh, I'll buy you a present, of course,' said James, 'say a box of chocolates if my Uncle Sammy's business friends include a geezer who can come up with a pound box.' Pound boxes of chocolates were still 'under-the-counter' items. That is, still part of post-war shortages.

'Oh, no, not chocolates,' said Cathy, 'they're not the same as a ring, and don't mean as much.'

'Why, what kind of a ring d'you have in mind, then?' asked James, walking her through a leafy Dulwich avenue to her home.

'Oh, you know,' said Cathy.

'Well, I've an idea I might know if I were old enough,' said James, 'but I've got a few years to go first.'

'It needn't be expensive,' said Cathy, 'just the kind I could be proud of when I show it to my friends.'

'Wait a moment,' said James, 'are you talking about a romantic ring? I'm definitely not old enough for that.'

'Oh, it could just sort of represent a promise,' said Cathy, who, at only eleven, was madly in love.

'Blow me,' said James, who wasn't, 'you don't make promises at our age.' He was coming up to twelve himself, but already had his dad's firm features, and precocious girls were watching his development while studying their own.

'Still,' said Cathy, 'we do like each other, don't we?'

'Well, of course,' said James, 'but I still think a box of chocolates would be best for your birthday.'

Now, he was putting to his family his belief that Cathy wanted to marry him, and his mum was virtually saying only over her dead body.

'I don't think we need to worry about tomorrow or next week,' said Boots. 'In fact, I don't think we need to worry at all.'

'Listen, old bean,' said Polly, 'you're in the happy state of never worrying about anything. Have you considered what it would be like if we became related by marriage to Anastasia Davidson, the Russian female spider? She'd eat me at the wedding breakfast, and have you at bedtime. That—' She stopped. The doorknocker had sounded. 'My God, she's here. Jam the door, James. Open fire, Gemma. Get under the piano, Boots, there's no time to lock you in the larder.'

The caller, however, was a neighbour, asking if her cat had found its way into the house.

'No, I'm sorry, we haven't noticed it,' said Polly who, in answering the door herself, was mentally equipped to do battle, but not with this harmless neighbour.

'Oh, my apologies for disturbing you, Mrs Adams.'

'We'll keep an eye open for your cat,' said Polly. 'We're always on the lookout, anyway, for wandering feline creatures.' Especially those that reach our door in the guise of Russian female spiders, she thought.

In bed that night, she mentioned to Boots that if

he ever gave the slightest encouragement to Mrs Davidson, she'd do him a serious injury. Boots asked what form the injury would take. Polly said two broken legs.

'The lady's a joke, and so's that threat,' murmured Boots.

'It's no joke, it's a promise,' said Polly. 'As for young Cathy, in another three or four years she'll be thinking about seducing James.'

'We can guard against that,' said Boots, switching off the bedside light.

'How?' asked Polly.

'We'll dress him in armour,' said Boots, 'the kind that won't yield to Cathy's can-opener.'

That tickled Polly.

'You old love,' she said, 'you're the best thing that ever happened to me and the twins.'

'Accept a return compliment,' said Boots.

They fell asleep, content as always with each other.

Chapter Nineteen

Just before Flossie, their daily maid, put breakfast on the table for Polly and her family the following morning, Boots glanced at the daily paper. The Bloomsbury murder was still front-page news. He hadn't taken any great interest in the crime, apart from thinking there were always some monsters existing among millions of decent citizens.

For the first time, he saw the name of a woman the police wished to interview.

Katje Galicia.

His memory stirred into life, and he remembered a strange incident of months ago, when Chinese Lady and Sir Edwin had been away on holiday, and he had gone to check that everything was in order at their house. He had disturbed two intruders, two uglies, who had covered him with a revolver and demanded information about a woman called Katje Galicia, insisting that he knew her. They called him Finch, which pointed to the obvious fact that while they knew of his stepfather, they had never met him. By their accent, he placed them as Russian. They became increasingly menacing. However, he managed to outwit them, and to call the police. They were taken away under arrest. Since then he had heard nothing, and had told his stepfather only that there'd been an intended burglary.

Katje Galicia. There it was, the name, in the front-page report. What the devil should he do? Let sleeping dogs lie, as he had in respect of the incident of two ugly intruders?

'Breakfast, Mr Adams, breakfast,' called Flossie, 'it's on the table.'

'Come on, Daddy,' called Gemma, 'what're you doing?'

'Bringing the paper in,' said Boots, entering the kitchen, which owned a windowed dining area.

'I forbid it to be read at the table,' said Polly.

'Crikey, Mummy, you're doing a lot of forbidding lately,' said Gemma.

'Someone has to keep this family civilized,' said Polly.

'And what d'you have to do, Dad?' asked James.

'Listen to your mother,' said Boots. And let more sleeping dogs lie, he thought. No sensible man would help to uncover a nest of vipers that might poison the peace and quiet of his stepfather's well-earned retirement.

'Oh, we all have to listen to Mummy,' said Gemma, enjoying her egg and bacon. Stepsister Rosie kept the family supplied with fresh eggs, and the grocer supplied bacon. In addition, cousin David often supplied a joint of beef, which was always delivered by his Italian farmhand, Enrico Cellino, cousin Paula's husband. 'Of course, I don't mind.'

'Nor you shouldn't,' said Flossie, filling a large teapot from a boiling kettle. 'Your mother's a sensible lady.'

Polly glanced at Boots, and made a little face. Boots smiled, knowing better than anyone that his still-vivacious wife rated sensible women as dull as plain suet pudding.

At her home in Bow, East London, Clare Roper was enjoying her own breakfast. With her dad already on his way to work, she was talking to her mum about Jimmy and his family and relatives.

'I suppose with all the money they've got as fact'ry owners, they live a bit posh, do they?' said her mum.

'Oh, no,' said Clare. 'They've got nice houses and gardens, but they're not posh, they're just like us mostly.'

'Don't they have servants?' asked Mrs Roper.

'Servants?' said Clare. 'Mum, of course they don't, they ain't— they're not what's called landed gentry.' She hadn't yet been to the homes of Tim and Felicity, and Boots and Polly. 'They've all come up from hardship in Walworth. Grandma and Grandpa have told me that lots of times.'

'I can't say Jimmy talks like any Walworth boy,' said Mrs Roper.

'Mum, you can't call Jimmy a boy,' said Clare. 'He's a young man and smashing, I still can't hardly believe sometimes that he's going to marry me.'

'Now then, Clare love, don't put yourself down,' said Mrs Roper, 'Jimmy's lucky to get a lovely girl like you. When you're Sunday-dressed, it wouldn't surprise me if one of the royal dukes didn't fancy you.'

'I don't want to be fancied by any duke,' said Clare, 'I just want to be Mrs Jimmy Adams.'

'You sure his family don't have servants?' said her

194

mum. 'I would if me and your dad had their kind of money.'

'Mum, people don't have servants like they used to in the old days,' said Clare, who had no idea that at this moment Jimmy's Uncle Boots and his family were eating a breakfast prepared and served up by their daily maid.

Arriving for her day's work at the factory, she popped first into Jimmy's office. He was always early at his desk.

'What-ho, queen of my heart,' he said, 'come to give my day a thrilling start, have you? All right, close the door and park yourself on my lap and we'll see what your legs look like this morning. Wrinkled stockings will be fined five bob.'

'Oh, you daft thing,' said Clare, but she swooped, leaned over his desk and planted a loving kiss on his lips.

'What's that for specially?' asked Jimmy.

'Oh, just because you're you and not a royal duke,' said Clare.

'A royal duke?' .

'Just something me mum thought up – well, she said that in me Sunday best I'd be a royal duke's fancy.'

'You tell your mum you're my everyday fancy, and not to put ideas into your head about bumping into dukes in Hyde Park,' said Jimmy.

'Doing what? Oh, as if I would,' said Clare. 'Listen, do any of your families have servants?'

'Only Uncle Boots and Aunt Polly, because Aunt Polly's a bit upper-class,' said Jimmy, 'and only cousin Tim and Felicity, because Felicity's blind.'

'Oh, it's a shame about Felicity, but me mum guessed right that some of you might have servants, which is a real surprise to me,' said Clare. 'Jimmy, we're not going to have one, are we?'

'Why, would you like a butler, then?' said Jimmy.

'A butler? Me? What would I do with a butler?'

'Well, he could answer the door for you,' said Jimmy.

'You get dafter,' said Clare, 'but you're still a smashing feller.' She never kept her feelings to herself when having a chat or some earnest talk with Jimmy. 'Well, I'd best get to the switchboard.'

She made her way to the general office, and said good morning to the girls there. They responded in casual fashion. She knew they still didn't like the fact that she was going to marry the boss's son. She noticed her comfortable switchboard chair had been changed for a plain one. She didn't say anything, and sat down.

The chair collapsed under her, and she sprawled.

'What a clumsy cow,' said one girl.

'It's her fat bum,' said Sally, who had once been the friendliest of the girls.

Clare picked herself up and straightened her skirt. Her right elbow felt bruised.

'Who did that?' she asked. 'Who changed my chair for this one?'

'What one? Oh, that one. It was all right till you sat on it.'

Clare didn't pursue the matter. She phoned the maintenance foreman and he brought her a replacement chair, taking away the one now reduced to matchwood, a grin on his face. The switchboard pinged, and she attended to the first call of the day. Thereafter she was busy. She did not intend, in any case, to make an issue of spite, to run to Jimmy with a complaint and cause a real flare-up in the general office.

She had the spirit and the stamina to hold out until Easter, and to keep her bruised elbow to herself. Jimmy would have given her full marks had he known.

However, Mister Tommy called in with paper-work for the girls, and the first thing he noticed was the absence of the switchboard chair. It had a padded seat and back for the comfort of the operator, who was tied to the switchboard all day, whereas the other girls moved about to fish files from cabinets or to take dictation.

'Clare, what's happened to your chair?' he asked.

'Oh, I think the office char moved it somewhere, Mister Tommy,' said Clare.

'Well, I'll get someone to find it,' said Tommy, presently caught up in the family debate on a super-market development. Sammy had spoken to him, and Tommy let him know he wasn't all that much in favour of what it would cost.

He distributed the paperwork among the girls and left in busy fashion.

Sally, looking uncomfortable, said, 'Sorry, Clare. I know where the chair is, I'll get it for you.'

This gesture improved the atmosphere, much to Clare's relief. She was a fighter by instinct, but preferred to be cheerful and friendly.

During the day she kept thinking, oh, help, imagine me marrying into a family that's got servants, it's nearly like me marrying a duke.

*   *   *

From her office, Miss Stella Peebles phoned Mr Fisher.

'Hello?' said her ex-landlord.

'Miss Peebles here.'

'Hell,' said Mr Fisher, 'if you're going to remind me of that murder, let me tell you it's not necessary, I'm stuck with the worry day and night.'

'Mr Fisher,' said Miss Peebles, 'I've something on my mind that might be important.'

'Christ,' said Mr Fisher, 'more important than three murdered men?'

'Do listen,' said Miss Peebles. It had occurred to her only ten minutes ago, she said, that before she moved into the ground-floor flat, he had shown her over it. But on arrival they had found five men there, five strange men, one of whom in a foreign accent had mistaken her for some woman with a very un-English name. Could Mr Fisher remember that name?

'I remember the incident,' said Mr Fisher, 'but damned if I can remember the name.'

'Could it have been the name of the woman the police are looking for? Here in my newspaper it's spelt as Katje Galicia.'

'My God, yes, now I think about it, that could have been the name,' said Mr Fisher.

'Telephone Scotland Yard,' said Miss Peebles.

'Curses, I'll have to,' said Mr Fisher.

'Let them know what those five men looked like.'

'Christ,' said Mr Fisher again, 'are you suggesting three of them might be the discovered corpses?'

'No, I'm not suggesting it,' said Miss Peebles, 'I'm just hinting at the possibility.'

'Well, I'll mention that hint to Scotland Yard.'

Scotland Yard took the call with interest, and the conversation was lengthy. But when Mr Fisher mentioned that Miss Peebles thought three of the five men might be the murdered ones, the CID officer taking the call pointed out it was almost certain the murder had taken place before Katje Galicia vacated the flat.

Following this phone conversation, two senior CID officers made a positive move. They called on MI6 to ask if anything was known of a woman by the name of Katje Galicia.

'Katje Galicia?'

'Yes.'

'What is her nationality, do you know?'

'We suspect her to be Russian, and to be implicated in this triple murder. Your help is requested.'

'Much of our information is classified.'

'This is an inquiry into a triple murder. Do you or don't you have any information on Katje Galicia?'

'A moment, please.'

The following interval resulted in the CID officers being presented to Mr George Coleman, who took their inquiries in hand with helpful politeness. He was able to produce a file and to inform the policemen that Katje Galicia was a Polish woman, known to have been an officer in her country's pre-war army and to presently be an agent of the Polish Republic. She was also known to have been in England for several months before disappearing. At no time, however, did her activities come under suspicion.

The only really helpful aspect of this information

was that the missing woman was Polish. As for the possibility that she was engaged in espionage, well, every capital on both sides of the Iron Curtain was infested with agents, something endemic to the Cold War. What Scotland Yard really wanted was some clue as to Katje Galicia's present whereabouts. Mr Coleman said his department, regrettably, had completely lost track of her. However, he was able to confirm the known description of the lady.

The CID officers could only hope for a response from a shipping port or an airport.

'Matthew!' Rosie was calling, her warm voice carrying quite a note of music through the crisp autumn air.

Matthew and Jonathan were inspecting the sheep for a sign that their winter coats of wool were developing, and the lambs for a sign that they were ready for market. Emma always refused to take part in this kind of inspection. It made her feel, she said, that the lambs were on trial for their lives, and that she was judge, prosecutor and jury.

'Matt, Rosie's calling,' said Jonathan.

Rosie's voice sang again from outside the farmhouse.

'Jonathan!'

'Is it me or you exactly?' said Matthew.

'Matthew! Jonathan!'

'Now we know, it's both of us,' said Jonathan, and up they went, passing the extensive wired-off chicken run on the way.

'Jonathan,' said Rosie, 'Emma wants to talk to you.'

'Right,' said Jonathan and entered the house.

'And who wants to talk to me?' asked Matthew.

'I do,' said Rosie, 'but it's nothing to make you start running, it's simply that a lady from the Labour Exchange has just phoned to tell us the applicants for work will be at the station at ten thirty tomorrow, and would we pick them up. A Mr and Mrs Robinson.'

'Well, damn fine, Rosie, I'll pick them up.'

'There, what a handy man you are, Matt, and so obliging.'

'Down in Dorset—'

'No, spare me,' said Rosie, 'we've been down in Dorset so often I've got hay in my hair as well as chicken feathers.'

'Ah, well, they do say—'

'Tell me tonight,' said Rosie, and escaped, laughing.

In the living room of the farmhouse, Emma was confiding something to Jonathan.

'Emma, are you sure?' he asked.

'Quite sure,' said Emma, 'Dr Dimmock has just confirmed it.'

'Well, aren't that a knockout?' said Jonathan. 'Another toddler?'

'Not before time,' said Emma, 'considering Jessie's nearly seven.'

'Emma, blowed if you aren't my best girl, and more,' said Jonathan.

'Blowed if I'm not,' said Emma. 'I'm seven weeks on the way.'

'Which tells me we did the right thing in deciding to move back home,' said Jonathan, 'even if it'll be a bit painful leaving Rosie and Matt.'

'Oh, they understand,' said Emma. 'Jonathan,

we'll be able to give our children much more time.'

'And maybe have more time for each other,' said Jonathan.

'And we'll see more of our parents,' said Emma, thinking of her dad, whose hardening arteries were a source of worry to her mum.

'It'll be a new beginning, Emma, that it will,' said Jonathan.

'That it will, Jonathan,' said Emma.

Emma wasn't the only one happily expectant. Down in Kent, Sammy and Susie's elder daughter, Bess, was six months pregnant, and her American husband, Jeremy, was fussing her.

Daniel had been down to see his sister, taking Patsy and the children with him.

Now, at home, he was asking Patsy if she thought Bess was doing a bit too much on the farm, considering it was her first pregnancy.

'Daniel, Bess can do everything she normally does,' said Patsy. 'Don't you know African women often work in the fields right up to delivery time?'

'And what are their husbands doing?' asked Daniel.

'Probably drinking coconut milk laced with jungle juice,' said Patsy.

'I'll ring Jeremy and tell him to try some of that the day Bess is admitted to the maternity ward,' said Daniel. 'It's a strain on a husband, y'know, walking up and down and waiting.'

'Oh, sure,' said Patsy. 'And tell Jeremy to save some of the juice for his mother. She'll be coming over, and Bess told me she's a fusspot too.'

'Well, she and Jeremy will find out together what

coconut milk and jungle juice can do for an expect-
ant dad and an expectant grandma,' said Daniel.
'Incidentally, where would they get the ingredients,
I wonder? Sainsbury's?'

'No, you kook, in Africa,' said Patsy.

'Well, Jeremy could make an appointment to see
Dr Livingstone, I presume,' said Daniel.

Patsy laughed. Her English fun guy was still cute,
still the kind of husband who gave her happy feelings as his wife. She was completely attuned to life
in the UK, and even proud that this old country
really was emerging from the doldrums, with the
young people creating a new culture, that of
modern music allied to bright fashion. It was as
if the young were determined to put the ravages
of war far behind them, to develop this new kind of
music, and to lead the way in fashion. Girls looked
delightful in their flared skirts and stiff net petti-
coats, a fashion beginning to take on all over the
country, making Daniel's fashion-conscious dad a
happy man, even if he still thought jeans only fit for
American cowboys. His comments about them
tickled Patsy, and Daniel too.

'Daniel, you're sweet,' she said.

'Sugary?' said Daniel.

'No, cute,' said Patsy, who knew he was against
that label.

'Might I point out I'm a two-legged bloke and not
a teddy bear?' he said.

'But, Daniel, you're my teddy bear, you sure are,'
said Patsy.

'That's a fact, is it?' said Daniel.

'Sure is,' said Patsy, 'but when you keep your
promise to take me and the children to the London

Zoo, watch out for the lions. They eat teddy bears.'

'Patsy?'

'Yes, Daniel?'

'You're cute, you sure are,' said Daniel, who knew she was against him talking like a cowboy.

Chapter Twenty

'Hello, hello, Phoebe?'

'Yes, it's me,' said Phoebe that evening, 'who are you?'

'Philip, who else?'

'Philip, why do you keep ringing me?'

'Because I like chatting to you.'

'I suppose you realize people are beginning to talk,' said Phoebe.

'What people?'

'Well, people who get to know, of course,' said Phoebe.

'Like your mum and dad?' said Philip.

'Yes, and my brother Jimmy,' said Phoebe, 'and my Uncle Boots and Aunt Polly.'

'How do they get to know?'

'I tell them,' said Phoebe. 'And then there's Jimmy's fiancée, Clare, she's known for weeks.'

'Do they all talk about us in whispers?' asked Philip, whose sergeant instructor had almost written him off as a hopeless example of a lovelorn cadet.

'Not my mum and dad,' said Phoebe, 'they're very frank, and they're wondering what you're up to.'

'Tell them I'm an admirer of their youngest daughter,' said Philip, 'and that I'll be home this weekend to take her dancing.'

'Well, I won't be able to see you Saturday afternoon,' said Phoebe, 'I'm going to our Brixton shop with Mum to buy some new clothes.'

'Buy something dizzy and I'll photograph you on Sunday,' said Philip.

'Are you talking about a pin-up photograph again?'

'Not half,' said Philip.

'And where will you photograph me?' asked Phoebe.

'In your garden shed?'

'You'll be lucky.'

'Well, fellers can get lucky some days,' said Philip.

'What d'you think of bikinis?' asked Phoebe.

'Bikinis?'

'Yes, these new two-piece swimsuits.'

'They wouldn't suit me,' said Philip. 'Here, you're not thinking of buying one, are you?'

'Suppose I did?' said Phoebe.

'I'd go cross-eyed.'

'Don't worry,' said Phoebe, 'my dad says over his dead body will I be allowed to wear three fig leaves.'

Over the phone, Philip yelled with laughter.

An official at the Soviet Embassy advised Scotland Yard that the required dental records of the three missing Bureau journalists were being forwarded by Moscow. Scotland Yard expressed thanks.

Lieutenant General Kersch permitted himself a sour smile when told of Moscow's co-operation. He doubted if the records would turn out to be the right ones. Moscow no more wanted a Scotland Yard investigation into the activities of the missing men than the Soviet Embassy did.

Friday morning.

Matthew, having picked up Mr and Mrs Robinson at Woldingham station, drove them to the poultry farm. Rosie came up from scattering meal for the chickens to meet the couple. She stopped and blinked. The Robinsons were West Indians, the man broad and sturdy, his wife bountiful. Both looked about forty.

'My wife,' said Matt, a bit of a grin lurking.

'My, I sure am tickled,' said Mrs Hortense Robinson, beaming at Rosie and then happily eyeing the broad vistas of green.

'I'm mighty pleased to meet you, ma'am,' said Mr Joe Robinson, glancing shyly at Rosie.

Rosie, accepting she was momentarily flummoxed, glanced at Matt, who responded with a quizzical look. It told her he'd been flummoxed himself when meeting the couple at the station.

'Well, it's nice of you and your wife to come all this way, Mr Robinson,' she said.

'It wasn't no bother, ma'am,' said Mr Robinson.

'Let's go into the house and do our talking over coffee,' said Rosie. 'Would you both like coffee?'

'Sure would, Miz Chapman,' beamed Mrs Robinson. 'Joe, now you mind you wipe your boots first.'

'I'll mind,' said Mr Robinson.

Matt was coming to a quick conclusion that here were a hard-working couple who were willing to please. Rosie, leading the way into the kitchen by the back door, had a feeling that surprise was going to be the least of her impressions.

Mrs Robinson, looking around, said, 'Lordy, I never did see a more handsome kitchen, Miz Chapman, nor did Joe. Ain't that right, Joe?'

'You never been righter, old lady,' said Joe.

'Sit yourselves down,' said Matt, 'and we'll talk.'

Rosie had the coffee pot ready, and she served four steaming cups, with a jug of hot milk and a bowl of sugar. Mrs Robinson fluttered a bit without losing her beam, and Joe let quick smiles come and go.

Matt asked if they knew anything about poultry farms, and bountiful Hortense said they sure did, that she and Joe had reared hundreds of chickens way back in Antigua, but it was a poor living, seeing most people there had their own chickens scratching around their back yards. Rosie asked about egg production.

'Why, Miz Chapman, wasn't there eggs Joe and me tooken to hotels and suchlike?' said Hortense.

'But not paid fair for them,' said Joe. 'I ain't given to complaining like a babe that's not been fed, Mr Chapman, but Hortense and me lived very poor, so when the chance came to come to the island of our Queen, we jumped at it like rabbits with a monkey on their tails.'

'Joe and me, we knows chickens too right, Miz Chapman,' said Hortense.

'And how to make fine layers of 'em,' said Joe. 'You got cockerels, and Hortense and me knows how to tickle 'em good. Then there's chicks aplenty.'

Rosie and Matt found themselves impressed by these two likeable people from the West Indies.

Their eagerness to be taken on was visible.

Rosie said, 'Let my husband show you the farm. There are sheep and lambs as well as hundreds of Rhode Island Reds.'

'Ah, them's the best,' said Joe. 'Don't get disease, don't get ornery, don't fight each other. Hortense and me, we'll be mighty glad to look around, Mr Chapman.'

So Matt took them around, introducing them to Emma and Jonathan, who were grading eggs in the large shed adapted to that purpose. Matt explained that Emma and Jonathan were leaving in two weeks, and it was for this reason that he and Mrs Chapman were looking for new hands. Hortense and Joe said they were ready and willing to be taken on, and Matt escorted them to the chicken compound, leaving Emma and Jonathan looking at each other.

'Did I actually see what I saw?' asked Emma.

'They're coming in every week,' said Jonathan.

'Immigrants from the West Indies?' said Emma.

'Seems so,' said Jonathan.

'Did Matt know he and Rosie were going to interview two of them?' asked Emma.

'I don't recollect him saying so,' said Jonathan.

'Will they fit in, Jonathan?'

'Well, we fitted in, Emma.'

'Yes, but we only came from south-east London, not the West Indies,' said Emma.

'It's up to Rosie and Matt to take a chance on them,' said Jonathan. 'Emma, look at this batch of eggs, all double yolkers, I reckon.'

'I reckon too, Jonathan,' said Emma. 'Put them in the trays for the hotel in Reigate.'

As a final gesture, Rosie and Matt showed the

agreeable applicants the live-in quarters, the annexe, an attractive abode with all essential amenities. Hortense stared, Joe rolled his eyes.

'Miz Chapman,' said Hortense, 'Joe and me, we live in one room down by West Croydon, and this, Lordy, it's a palace, ain't it, Joe?'

'It sure is,' said Joe.

Matt and Rosie took them back into the house, then had a confidential exchange with each other.

'Have we got a problem or a cure?' asked Matt.

'You mean do we make up our minds now, one way or the other?' said Rosie.

'I think they could be good workers, especially as they aren't novices,' said Matt, 'but I'm not sure we should make our minds up right now.'

'Let's give ourselves the weekend to think it over,' said Rosie.

'On account of them being black?' said Matt.

'It was a surprise, I admit, when I first saw them, but I hope we won't hold their colour against them,' said Rosie. 'I simply wonder if they'll find themselves able to adapt. Don't you see, Matt, there aren't any of their own people around.'

'That's true, and we have to consider it, so yes, we'll think it over,' said Matt, and they rejoined the applicants. Matt told them that he'd let the Labour Exchange know on Monday if he and his wife would take them on. If so, their employment would commence Monday fortnight at three pounds a week each and free lodging. Eggs would be given to them, and the occasional chicken.

'Well, thank you kindly, Mr Chapman,' beamed Hortense. 'Joe and me, we're rightly disposed to wait and hope.'

'We've been treated fair,' said Joe.

Matt drove them back to the station, where he reimbursed them for the cost of their train fare. He shook hands with them and said goodbye. Hortense said what a pleasure it had been to meet him and his lady wife. Joe echoed the sentiment.

When Matt returned to the farm, Rosie said that during the time he'd been away, she'd come to the conclusion there was no real reason why they couldn't employ the Robinsons. Matt said that was a fair comment.

'But let's give it the weekend, Rosie, and see if we're positive by Monday.'

'Matt old soldier, my thoughts exactly at this moment,' said Rosie.

Aunt Victoria had moved in with Tommy and Vi, and was happy with her rooms, comfortably furnished. She had brought several items of her own, as well as a trunkful of mementoes. She was touched by the inclusion of a gifted television set, which Tommy thought would divert her enough to keep her from making too many demands on Vi's time.

Vi, so equable, would put up with her mum's possessiveness and make no complaint. But she had her own interests, inside and outside the home, and Tommy knew he had to get the arrangement on the right footing as soon as possible, or it wouldn't work. Fortunately, Vi's mum was more amenable than formerly, and he quickly got her interested in various TV programmes. In fact, after only three or four days, he reckoned she was on the way to turning into an addict.

He spoke to Vi.

'I think it's going to work, Vi.'

'It's working at the moment, Tommy, she hasn't had a single grumble about anything.'

'I don't meself see all that much of her, except at breakfast and supper.'

'Oh, I see a little more of her than that during the day,' said Vi, 'but so I should.'

'Well, she's your mum, Vi, and we never meant for the arrangement to make just a lodger of her,' said Tommy.

'Having her has taken worry off our minds,' said Vi.

'Only right to have her, Vi, only right,' said Tommy.

Saturday afternoon.

Anneliese had moved into her flat, having been driven to Camberwell by her brother-in-law. Major Gibbs had met the owner of the house, Harry Stevens, inspected the flat and approved it, although he was not sure if Anneliese would fit in with the environment and its cockney population. While noted for being good-natured, cockneys also had a reputation for being noisy, especially when disgorging from their pubs after closing time on Saturday nights. And if old-time knees-ups were a fading ritual, they were still occasionally performed by women who'd had a drop or two.

Major Gibbs pointed this out to Anneliese, who immediately said that anyone who had known how Russians and Himmler's SS could behave, would find London cockneys cultured by comparison.

'Well, I like 'em myself,' said Major Gibbs,

'they're tough and down to earth, and the men have made names for themselves on every battlefield from Waterloo to Arnhem. Good luck, Anne. Brigid and I will keep in touch with you. Don't forget to come and spend some weekends with us, and we'll definitely expect you for Christmas. And let us know when you secure a hospital post.'

'Yes, of course,' said Anneliese.

'Good,' said Major Gibbs, who thought her in poise, character and experience well qualified to become a matron. 'Oh, and your landlord, Stevens, seems a decent chap. You should be able to get on with him as his tenant.'

Anneliese smiled.

'Oh, I think I could always get on with decent chaps, John.'

'Well, you're a survivor, Anne, and that'll always see you through any crises in your new way of life,' said Major Gibbs. 'Goodbye for the time being.'

The moment he left, Anneliese began to unpack her two large suitcases.

'Excuse me?'

Anneliese looked up. At the open door of the bedroom stood a slim young girl in a neat dress, hair fashioned into twin pigtails that reminded her of the indoctrinated girls of Hitler's time. Aged ten, even nine, they were all drilled and marshalled into huge square formations on great fields.

'Oh, hello,' she said, 'could you be Mr Stevens's daughter Cindy?'

'Yes, I'm Cindy, I've just come back from the shops and I said to Daddy we ought to offer you a cup of tea. So he put the kettle on and he ought to be filling the pot by now.'

'Thank you, Cindy, yes, I would like a cup,' smiled Anneliese. 'No sugar, please.'

'All right, Miss Bruck,' said Cindy, who was studying this lady tenant with curiosity and interest, 'I'll go and make sure Daddy hasn't forgotten. You'll have to excuse him if he's bit absent-minded at times, he's always got some plot for a story on his mind. I won't be long.' Off she went, a quick and busy little girl.

She found her father downstairs in their kitchen. He was in the act of filling the teapot.

'What did she say, would she like a cup?' he asked.

'Yes, but with no sugar,' said Cindy. 'Crikey, Daddy, she's ever so posh and elegant.' She drew out the last syllable, turning it into 'ghaaant'.

'Did you catch her accent?' asked Harry, as Cindy set out cups and saucers.

'Yes, but it's only slight,' said Cindy, 'and I'm sure no-one would think she's German, so we needn't say so. I'm pleased with you for letting her have the flat, I think she's nice.'

'So I'm in your good books?' said Harry.

'Daddy, you're always in my good books,' said Cindy, 'and sometimes a bit more than other times.' She stirred the pot with a spoon, let the contents settle and then filled the cups through a strainer. 'Have you done the rent book?'

'Yes, all done and signed,' said Harry.

'Lummy, you're really awake,' said Cindy. 'I'll take the book up with the tea.'

Anneliese was hanging clothes in the wardrobe when Cindy reappeared with the tea.

'Thank you, Cindy, how kind.'

'Oh, that's all right,' said Cindy, studying the lady

afresh. My, she did look ever so elegant. 'And here's your rent book. Daddy's filled it in and written down and signed what he says is a guarantee.'

'Give him my thanks,' said Anneliese.

'Yes, I will,' said Cindy, disappearing only to return. 'Oh, if you want any shopping done today, I could do it for you as you're busy unpacking.'

Here's a quaint and helpful young girl, thought Anneliese.

'Thank you, Cindy, but I'd like to do that for myself,' she said. 'I must get to know the shops.'

'Yes, that's ever so sensible,' said Cindy, and down she went to tell her father that the lady really was nice. 'But remember, we've got to make that advance rent last for a month.'

'Well, you've got most of it,' said Harry, 'I've only got a few bob.'

'Yes, and mind you don't spend it reckless,' said Cindy. 'And I've just thought, you ought to buy a bunch of flowers for the lady.'

'Eh?' said Harry.

'I don't know what she must think that you didn't give her some when she arrived,' said Cindy, 'and I don't know why I didn't think of it myself. It's all this worry, I suppose.'

'What worry?' asked Harry, as they sat drinking tea.

'About us being poverty-stricken,' said Cindy, frowning.

'We're not exactly poverty-stricken,' said Harry, 'I'm still earning a bit.'

'But you haven't had a new suit for ages,' said Cindy. 'What clothes you do have are falling to pieces.'

'Still, we've got enough to eat, drink and be merry,' said Harry. 'And listen, I've a plot for a new short story.'

'Well, you'd best tell me,' said Cindy.

Harry described the plot, which involved the murder of the wife of a CID officer. His superintendent allows him to take charge of the investigation, and the climax arrives when it's discovered he murdered her himself for the sin of adultery.

'So what d'you think, little lady?'

'Daddy, I don't like you writing about adultery, it's not nice, and it shouldn't be allowed,' said Cindy, now Miss Prim and Proper.

'Well, not something to be encouraged, no,' said Harry, 'but we're only talking about a story.'

'But instead of adultery, couldn't you say she's done a lot of shoplifting?' suggested Cindy.

'Would any bloke murder his wife for that?' asked Harry.

'Well, a strict-minded policeman might,' said Cindy.

'I've got my doubts,' said Harry, 'but I'll think about it.'

'Yes, all right,' said Cindy. 'I've got to go to the shops again.'

Chapter Twenty-One

Anneliese, out shopping herself later, found that the shopkeepers were a friendly and helpful breed. A very polite one looked as if he was thinking of bowing to her. That was due to her aristocratic look, which drew glances from customers.

And whispers, such as, 'Blimey, where did she come from, not off a Billingsgate fish barrer, I bet.'

'Buckingham Palace, more like. Here, she ain't Princess Marina, is she?'

Princess Marina, Duchess of Kent, was the elegant Greek widow of the Duke of Kent, killed in a plane crash during the Second World War.

Anneliese shopped in a leisurely way that helped her to decide which shops she preferred, finally returning to the flat with a laden bag. She was in her kitchen, stowing her groceries in the larder, when Harry appeared at the open door.

'Oh, hello, Mr Stevens,' she said.

Harry held a vase containing half a dozen bronze chrysanthemums in one hand while using the other to tidy his hair, which on this occasion wasn't necessary. Anneliese smiled at the gesture, that of a man not sure of his appearance.

'Permit me,' he said. Cindy, in going out to the

shops again, had done so just to get the flowers, for which she had paid the bargain price of ninepence. She put them in the vase and told him to present them to their lady tenant. Harry had asked why she couldn't present them herself, and Cindy had said the lady would like it best from him. You sure? Of course, said Cindy, and don't drop the vase going up the stairs.

Anneliese, accepting the vase, smiled and said, 'How very kind, Mr Stevens. Thank you. Do come in for a moment.'

Harry entered the kitchen, glanced around and decided it already had a homely, busy look.

'Settling in, Miss Bruck?' he said, watching her as she placed the vase on the window sill above the sink. The light caught the blooms.

'Yes, indeed I am, Mr Stevens, and I've also found some shops I like.'

'They're a good bunch of obliging blokes, the shopkeepers,' said Harry, 'and they'll always knock a penny off a bill if you're hard up.'

'Well, if I'm down to my last shilling one day, I'll ask for that concession,' said Anneliese.

'Yes, do that. Cindy and I get down to our last six-pence at times,' said Harry, and Anneliese thought what a natural and homely man he was.

'And what does Cindy do when that happens?' she asked.

'Gives me a talking-to,' said Harry, 'then goes out to shop on tick.'

'On tick?' said Anneliese. Despite her excellent knowledge of the English language, some euphemisms eluded her, and so did certain colloquialisms. 'What does on tick mean?'

'Running up bills that you settle when you can afford to,' said Harry.

'Shopkeepers allow Cindy to do that?' said Anneliese,

'If they didn't, they'd get a talking-to themselves,' said Harry. 'Well, I'm delighted you're settling in, Miss Bruck. Now I'd better do some scribbling.'

'You're working on a story?'

'I'm working on a plot,' said Harry.

'Short-story plots have a surprise ending, don't they?' said Anneliese.

'Can I take up a few more minutes of your time to get your opinion of this one?' asked Harry, still fascinated by his striking lady tenant.

'I'd be happy to hear it,' said Anneliese.

Harry gave her the same outline he'd given Cindy, around the murder of a CID officer's wife and the investigation leading to the unexpected discovery that the detective himself was the guilty man.

'What d'you think, Miss Bruck?' Harry often discussed plots with his irrepressible daughter, but this was the first time he'd confided in an adult. One had to be careful about airing a storyline, for it could be pinched.

'Excellent,' said Anneliese.

'You think so?'

'Yes. Go and write the story, Mr Stevens.'

'Right,' said Harry. 'I've got my notebook of scribbles somewhere. Your opinion, Miss Bruck, has given me a lift.'

'Self-confidence can be a great help, Mr Stevens, and thank you again for the flowers,' said Anneliese, smiling to herself as he left. But she closed the door firmly, feeling she must discourage anything in the nature of regular visits.

'Well, what did she say?' asked Cindy.

'She said we were very kind.'

'Crikey, she must've said more than that,' protested Cindy, 'you've been up there for years.'

'Years?'

'Ages,' said Cindy.

'Oh, we had a pleasant chat,' said Harry, 'and she's settling in nicely. But listen, you and me shouldn't poke our noses in too often. We've got to respect her privacy.'

'But we've got to let her see we don't mind that she's German,' said Cindy. 'Underneath, she might be trembling a bit about that.'

'She might be what?'

'Well, sort of on tenterhooks,' said Cindy. 'I can't remember the war meself, but I do know it finished up with no-one liking the Germans.'

'Well, for all that, I like Miss Bruck,' said Harry.

'So do I,' said Cindy, 'and we ought to let her know she doesn't have to be on tenterhooks with us.'

'We'll tell her nothing of the kind, you imp,' said Harry. 'Now, where did I put my scribbling pad?'

'Only on the table in front of your eyes,' said Cindy.

'I'm going barmy in my old age,' said Harry.

'Daddy, you're not old, you're only forty, and some people are sort of nicer when they're a bit barmy,' said Cindy.

'I'm flattered,' said Harry.

'Oh, that's all right,' said the imp.

*　　*　　*

Phoebe was dancing the evening away with Philip, the skirt of her bright buttercup-yellow dress swinging and swishing. The band, new and unknown, was a bit of all right, with a guitarist, a flautist and a honky-tonk piano. Modern bands were given to experimenting with instruments in a growing need to produce the kind of music hitherto unknown. They were the beginners of a trend that was to find fame and wild popularity in time.

Young people swirled around, separating from partners to freely express their rhythms while facing each other, then latching on to jive or swing together.

Phoebe, separating from Philip, lost him to an interceding girl in a state of excitement.

'Let's go, man,' she cried exultantly, 'you've got the legs. Go, go.'

Phoebe fought her way back.

'Do you mind?' she said.

'Push off,' said the female interloper.

'Where's your manners?' demanded Phoebe.

'Me mum's minding them.'

'Hoppit,' said Phoebe, and since the interloper looked ready to square up to her, Philip brought his heart-throb out of the danger zone.

'Now, Phoebe—'

'Listen,' said Phoebe, 'if my dad knew you were bringing me to dance halls, he'd tell you never to darken our doorstep again, even if you are his grandson.'

'I'm not his grandson, saucy pussycat.'

'Well, you're some relative of his,' said Phoebe, jigging, 'and I don't want him to feel ashamed of you. You didn't fancy that hideous girl, did you?'

'She just popped up in front of my eyes,' said Philip, swinging to Phoebe's jigging, at which moment up came a good-looking youth with a quiff.

'I've lost me bird,' he said to Philip. 'Could I borrow yours for a couple of hours, pal?'

'D'you mind if I keep her to myself?' said Philip.

'Well, if you want to be greedy –'

'It's not that,' said Philip, 'it's just that she's special.'

'Fair comment, mate, but I still think you're a bit greedy.'

'Look,' said Philip, 'you're getting in the way of the music, so do me a favour and get lost.'

That settled the issue.

'So I'm special, am I?' said Phoebe.

'Well, your mum thinks so, and so does your dad,' said Philip, picking up the rhythm again, 'and so do I.'

'Oh, in that case, you can give me a kiss when we say goodnight,' said Phoebe.

Which invitation Philip accepted, of course, when they eventually arrived at her front door. After a few minutes and several kisses, Phoebe went a little dramatic.

'Stop,' she said, 'd'you want to make me faint?'

'Didn't you nearly faint once before?' asked Philip.

'It wouldn't surprise me,' said Phoebe. 'I'm a girl, not a boxer.'

'Who wants to kiss a flat-faced boxer?'

'His flat-faced girlfriend, I expect,' said Phoebe. 'Still, you'd better come in and say hello to Mum and Dad, and I'll ask Mum to get you a cold drink.'

'Cold?' said Philip. The night was hardly warm.

'Yes, to cool you down,' said Phoebe. 'Look how you've crumpled my dress.'

'But you're wearing a coat,' said Philip.

'Yes, and that's crumpled too,' said Phoebe. 'By the way, I'm not going to show you my new swimsuit that Mum bought for me at our Brixton shop this afternoon.'

'OK,' said Philip, 'I'll wait till you're wearing it and I've got my camera handy. You in a swimsuit, I can hardly wait.'

'I think,' said Phoebe, opening the front door with her key, 'I think I'll ask Mum to put ice in your cold drink.'

'Why?'

'You've gone all flushed,' said Phoebe.

Sunday afternoon.

Chinese Lady and Sir Edwin were entertaining Lizzy and Ned to tea. Lizzy and Ned were among Chinese Lady's favourite Sunday tea guests.

The phone rang just when she was about to put the kettle on. Sir Edwin, answering the call, found Bobby on the line.

'What can I do for you, Bobby?'

'I managed to get hold of that book you wanted,' said Bobby, 'the original 1934 edition of *Shelley and Byron* by Isabel Clarke. Found it in a Charing Cross Road bookshop during my lunch hour.'

'Bobby, I'm delighted,' said Sir Edwin.

'I meant to let you have it yesterday,' said Bobby, 'but it slipped my mind. Helene says if my mind starts slipping too often, she'll bang my head. She will too. It's her French verve. Anyway, she'll call on you tomorrow and let you have it.'

'You must allow me to pay for it, Bobby.'

'Do me a favour, and consider it a well-deserved present,' said Bobby. 'By the way, any opinions on the triple murder in Bloomsbury?'

'Why do you ask?'

'Oh, your years working for the Government must have given you some idea of what goes on in a cloak-and-dagger world,' said Bobby.

'Is it a cloak-and-dagger murder?' asked Sir Edwin.

'The Soviet Press Bureau is interested,' said Bobby. 'That's in confidence.'

'In that case, Bobby, the victims are probably Russian agents,' said Sir Edwin.

'If it's discovered they are, balloons will go up,' said Bobby. 'My dad's with you, isn't he?'

'Yes, he and your mother,' said Sir Edwin.

'How's he looking?' asked Bobby. 'Yesterday, I thought he looked a bit peaky.'

'I assure you, he's not looking peaky now,' said Sir Edwin, 'he's in the mood to enjoy an old-fashioned Sunday tea.'

'One of Grandma's specials?' said Bobby.

'You can rely on that, Bobby.'

'Edwin? Edwin?' Chinese Lady was calling. 'The kettle's boiling.'

'I heard that,' said Bobby, a smile in his voice. 'Give her my love, and tell Dad to enjoy his tea. So long, Grandpa.'

'My felicitations, Bobby, and my grateful thanks for finding that book.'

*   *   *

Monday.

'I don't believe it.' Detective Inspector Crouch of Scotland Yard's CID was disgusted, bitter and sceptical. None of the dental records sent by Moscow matched the teeth of any of the corpses.

'Could be the records of any three Russkies,' said Detective Sergeant Ambrose.

'Let's call on the gentleman in charge of the Soviet Press Bureau.'

'Kersch, sir?'

'That's the fellow.'

Lieutenant General Kersch, known to British Intelligence by his KGB title, but not to Scotland Yard, received them politely.

'How can I help?' he asked, big and formidable.

'Mr Kersch,' said Inspector Crouch, 'we received from Moscow the dental records we asked for.'

'Moscow is always ready to help Scotland Yard,' said Kersch.

'The help in this case leads us nowhere,' said Inspector Crouch. 'None of the records can be identified with the teeth of your missing journalists.'

'Ah, so?' Kersch raised a bushy eyebrow. 'What is your conclusion, then?'

'Our first conclusion is that the murdered men aren't your missing journalists. Our second conclusion is that perhaps Moscow made a mistake and sent the wrong records.'

'I can inform you, Inspector, that Moscow does not make mistakes.'

'Who are we referring to, Mr Kersch? Your diplomatic services or your security people?'

Kersch rumbled deep in his brawny throat.

'I am a journalist and therefore unable to answer that question,' he said. 'Did you make your request for the dental records through the Soviet Embassy?'

'Yes.'

'Then you must ask that question of the Embassy, Inspector.'

'Allow me to ask another,' said the inspector. 'When you saw the bodies, were you absolutely positive you could not identify them?'

'Positive? Yes.'

'Yet not one of your missing journalists has been found?'

'So?'

'It's very odd, isn't it?'

'I agree, yes,' said Kersch, 'and I hope your investigation into the murder of the unknown men will take in a successful search for our missing journalists. Thank you, Inspector.'

Leaving the building, the CID officers entered their car.

Inspector Crouch then said, 'I'm damn sure his three journalists have been found.'

'Meaning, of course, that they were found under those Bloomsbury floorboards,' said Sergeant Ambrose.

'I'm also sure Kersch knows it,' said the inspector, 'so what's he up to?'

'He's the head of the Bureau,' said Sergeant Ambrose, 'and we know how the top brass of any Soviet organization deal with defectors. If three of Kersch's staff were suspected of asking for asylum, then –'

'They'd have been sent back to Moscow for elimination,' said the inspector.

'It's a fishy case that needs quick cracking, sir.'

'So does the Iron Curtain, Sergeant. That's where these kind of skulduggeries originate.'

Chapter Twenty-Two

Cindy was at school. Anneliese wanted some information. Hearing the faint clicking of a typewriter from a room on the second floor, she climbed the stairs. She knocked on the door, which was slightly ajar.

'Mr Stevens?'

'Who's that?' The voice carried above the clicking.

Anneliese, wondering who else it could be but herself, said, 'Miss Bruck.'

'Oh, yes, come in, Miss Bruck.'

She pushed the door wide and stepped in. The room was furnished frugally with just a desk and its chair, an old leather-upholstered armchair and a wastepaper basket. There was, however, a corner cupboard. Its door was open, its shelves containing a mixture of files, boxes of quarto writing paper, and odds and ends of stationery. Harry was sitting at the desk, on which stood a typewriter. There was a sheet of paper in the machine and he was silently reading from it, his lips moving. He wore a white shirt, a plain blue pullover and grey trousers. His thick hair was fairly tidy for once.

'So sorry to disturb you, Mr Stevens –'

'Oh, come in, Miss Bruck,' he said again, and turned his head. He came to. 'Hello,' he said.

'I'm disturbing you,' said Anneliese.

'Certainly not,' said Harry. He pushed his chair back and came to his feet. 'You're welcome to command my attention any time.'

'I really don't wish to command your attention, Mr Stevens, only to ask you if there's a laundry near here.'

'A laundry?' Harry thought. 'Let's see – oh, yes. Turn right out of the house and it's about fifty yards up towards the Green.'

'Thank you,' said Anneliese, impeccable in a dark grey costume and white shirt-blouse, 'I only wanted to know if there was one in the area. Are you busy putting together the story you mentioned?'

Harry smiled.

'If you need a laundry, I need some earnings,' he said.

'Yes, of course,' said Anneliese, and turned to go.

'I'm about to make myself a cup of coffee,' said Harry, looking at his old gunmetal wristwatch. 'Would you like a cup?'

'How kind,' said Anneliese, 'but I have to go out.'

'Sure?' said Harry.

'Quite sure,' said Anneliese. 'I have an appointment at the London offices of the Royal College of Nursing.'

'Come again?' said Harry.

'I'm a nurse, Mr Stevens, and hoping to be taken on by a London hospital, but first I believe I have to be approved by the Royal College of Nursing.'

'Well, knock me down with a paper bag,' said Harry, 'that's the surprise of my life.'

'Why?'

'God knows, it just is,' said Harry.

Anneliese smiled and left.

Matthew phoned the Croydon Labour Exchange and informed them that he had decided to take on Mr and Mrs Robinson two weeks from today. The official thanked him and said the Robinsons would be advised accordingly. What would they be paid? Three pounds a week each and free lodging, said Matt.

'Well,' said Rosie when he put the phone down, 'now all we have to do is to see how well they work and if they can fit in.'

'Yes, that's all,' said Matt. 'But all might fall apart if they land us with headaches.'

Felicity was on one of her frequent shopping expeditions with faithful Maggie. It typified her constant desire to get out and about. Even if only one grocery item was required, it became a good enough reason to walk to the shop in question, in company with her caring housemaid. Maggie was now living in and very happy with the arrangement, especially as her master and mistress, and their little girl, all made her feel like one of the family.

What Felicity wanted from the grocer today was, at Maggie's prompting, at least half a pound of Cheddar cheese.

'Good morning, Mrs Adams,' said Mr Hicks, the grocer, 'how are we today?'

'On this side of your counter, we're fine,' said Felicity. 'How are you on your side, Mr Hicks?' She had never seen his counter, of course, or the grocer himself, but she had come to feel the one and the other were friends.

'I can't grumble, no, I can't,' said Mr Hicks, who truly felt that in comparison with the disability of this blind lady, he was considerably well off. 'What can I get you, Mrs Adams?'

'Just some of your best Cheddar cheese,' said Felicity. 'A pound, if possible.'

'Ah,' said Mr Hicks. Cheese was still not too plentiful, any more than butter was, or dairy cream. 'A pound, Mrs Adams?'

'If it's not too much to ask for,' said Maggie.

'Would twelve ounces be enough?' suggested Mr Hicks, dropping his voice a little because of the arrival of another customer.

'That's a very acceptable compromise,' said Felicity.

Mr Hicks placed a large section of Cheddar on the cheese board, and used the traditional wire to cut off a good-looking wedge.

Felicity drew a sudden breath. Before her eyes appeared an unmistakable if misty vision of a shining white marble counter and the cloudy image of moving hands. Hypnotized by the vision, she stared and drew a deeper breath. Maggie, always alert to whatever might be affecting her mistress, noticed her tense concentration.

Mr Hicks, weighing the cut portion of cheese, saw the scales record a weight of a little over twelve ounces. He placed it on a sheet of greaseproof paper, reached under his counter and with a dexterous sleight-of-hand gesture, produced a small white cardboard carton of Cornish cream from an iced tray, which he quickly wrapped up with the cheese. He glanced briefly at Maggie. She nodded in happy and appreciative assent of the grocer's deft performance. It was known as an 'under-the-counter' shenanigan, a favour granted to prized customers.

Mr Hicks, placing the packet in a paper bag, said, 'Here we are, Mrs Adams.'

With the images fading, Felicity took the purchase and put it into her shopping bag. Mr Hicks delivered the total price of the cheese and cream in low tones unheard by the other customer, and Maggie watched as Felicity opened her handbag, found her purse, extracted it and felt for coins. Her fingers were trembling. Maggie didn't say anything, and neither did she offer any help. It was always understood that Felicity would be her own help in manageable matters.

She gave Mr Hicks the right amount of coins, thanked him and left the shop in company with Maggie.

'Maggie,' she said, 'who has the cheese?'

'You have, mum,' said Maggie, 'you put it in your shopping bag, and there's a carton of Cornish cream as well.'

'Really? What a lovely man Mr Hicks is,' said Felicity, spring in her step as on another occasion.

'Excuse me, mum,' said Maggie, 'but did something happen at the counter?'

'Not half, Maggie old dear,' said Felicity, her irreplaceable home help and guide arm in arm with her. 'Tell me, does Mr Hicks have a ring on his finger?'

'Yes, a plain silver one,' said Maggie.

'I thought that was what I glimpsed.'

'You saw his ring, mum, you saw it?' Maggie went open-mouthed and wide-eyed.

'I saw his counter and his hands, and something I thought was a ring,' said Felicity, high on adrenalin.

'Oh, me gawd,' breathed Maggie, 'I can't hardly believe it. Did you see his hands all clear, like?'

'Not clearly, Maggie, but through a faint mist, as on the occasion when I saw my face in the hallstand mirror,' said Felicity.

'Oh, ain't that really hopeful?' said Maggie. 'Steady now, mum, you're trying to walk all over the place.'

'Hang on, then,' said Felicity, 'I'm giddy.'

Compulsively, she phoned Tim at his office as soon as she was home. The switchboard girl put her through.

'Hello, Tim Adams here.'

'And here it's me,' said Felicity.

'Felicity, are you in trouble?'

'No, just giddy,' said Felicity. 'Darling, I had to talk to you.' And she told him of the happening in the grocer's shop. Tim said these incidents were beginning to make a happy man of him, so Felicity said he could easily imagine what they were doing to her. She hadn't been able to resist phoning him about this latest one.

'Next time, Puss, hang onto it,' said Tim.

'Oh, yes?' said Felicity. 'How do I do that?'

'Use your will power,' said Tim, 'it's been your best friend and mine from the time you spent your first week in the hospital at Farnham.'

'Oh, I've willed my eyes many times to hang onto what I've been seeing,' said Felicity, 'but as I've failed, perhaps my will power needs recharging.'

'We'll discuss,' said Tim.

'By the way,' said Felicity, 'there'll be fresh fruit and real Cornish cream for a sweet this evening. Mr Hicks produced a carton from under his counter.'

'What a way to run a shop,' said Tim, 'but everybody's doing it, and I'm all in favour of real Cornish cream and a banana. Look, I've got to ring off in a moment. Daniel and I have an appointment with a representative of the council's planning committee about the possibility of arranging an appointment with the full committee.'

'Good grief,' said Felicity, 'you've an appointment to make another appointment?'

'That's the way it goes with local government these days,' said Tim. The immediate post-war Labour government had extended the responsibilities of councils, compelling them to employ more administrative staff. Accordingly, bureaucracy was getting in the way of quick decisions.

'Go to it, then,' said Felicity. 'Any ex-commando should be able to knock holes in bureaucrats.'

'Sammy and Boots tell me it's not so easy, that they're all made of foam rubber,' said Tim. 'See you later.'

They said goodbye and rang off.

A few minutes later, Tim and Daniel sallied forth to keep their appointment.

'Before we can officially consider your application for planning permission, you must submit two copies of your architect's comprehensive blueprints, together with equally comprehensive details of all that the development entails,' said Mr Birdswell, a council official. 'You realize, of course, that a – um – supermarket is entirely unknown to our planning committee, and must be studied with exceptional care and diligence.'

'Of course,' said Tim. 'We've brought all that you've just mentioned, and which you also mentioned in your letter.' He placed a thick folder on the council official's desk. Mr Birdswell, handsome in a severe way, as if critical of himself, glanced at the folder without opening it.

'When does the planning committee next meet?' asked Daniel.

'We are always conducting meetings for the purpose of examining planning applications, Mr Adams. That is, weekly on Wednesdays.'

'You'll pass our application to your committee?' said Tim.

'In time, in time,' said Mr Birdswell.

'Could you give us an idea of how much time?' asked Daniel.

'I'm not in a position to be specific, only to advise you that in due course you'll be notified when you can attend a preliminary meeting of the committee.'

'We'd very much appreciate a quick notification,' said Daniel.

'You'll understand, of course, that you must await your turn,' said Mr Birdswell, 'but we'll do our best to facilitate matters. I'm pleased to have had this opportunity to meet you. Thank you for coming.'

On their way back to the offices, Daniel said he had a feeling they'd be lucky if they met the committee before the New Year.

'If we haven't been notified by the end of October,' said Tim, 'we'll try to arrange for some

November the Fifth's firecrackers to be smuggled in and placed under Birdswell's chair.'

'You can have that job,' said Daniel, 'you're the expert on commando tactics.'

Lulu, who had called in to see her doctor on her way home from work, left the surgery a relieved woman. She had thought she was pregnant, but she wasn't.

Paul, already home, was waiting for her.

'What's the result, Lulu love?' he asked, giving her a kiss.

'False alarm, thank goodness,' said Lulu.

'Thank goodness? What's that mean?'

'Paul, we can't afford a baby,' said Lulu.

'Yes, we can,' said Paul, 'and I thought you were happy about the prospect.'

'Yes, until it occurred to me today that we can't afford the time to look after a child,' said Lulu. 'We're both working, we both need our jobs. And you know I've got hopes that mine will help me qualify as a candidate for an election.'

'Ruddy hell,' said Paul, 'you're still on that old trail. Lulu, your life has changed, and so's mine. We're set for raising a family.'

'But what about my career?' asked Lulu, spectacles nicely in place, sweater and skirt nicely in favour of her figure.

'You've been so quiet about that lately that I thought you were coming down to earth,' said Paul.

'Paul, you're entitled to your career with your capitalist family's firm,' said Lulu. 'I'm entitled to my career as a possible Labour Party MP.'

'That's not a career,' said Paul, 'that's pie in the sky.'

'Some pies in the sky are reachable,' said Lulu.

'Come here,' said Paul.

'What for?' asked Lulu.

'I'm going to smack your bottom for not being an expectant mum,' said Paul.

'That's it, fall back on that old male stuff,' said Lulu. 'But watch it, Tarzan. The war might be over, but you could still get wounded— Paul, don't you dare!'

He was after her. She fled. He caught her up and grabbed her. She twisted around in his arms, and her spectacles slipped to the end of her nose. That gave her such a comical look that his good nature surfaced.

'All right, crisis over,' he said, 'but I'm going to have a serious talk in bed with you tonight. In bed is when you listen to me.'

'Paul, I'll look forward to it,' said Lulu, adjusting her glasses. 'We could have a really serious talk about the Party's most worthwhile MPs. Like Ernie Bevin, George Lansbury and Herbert Morrison. Think what Herbert Morrison did for the workers when he ran the London County Council. He—'

'Shut up,' said Paul.

'You're not still shirty, are you?'

'No, long-suffering,' said Paul, 'so let's give politics a rest until a General Election comes up. Right now, you can start preparing supper.'

'Excuse me, but—'

'No buts, it's your turn,' said Paul.

'You sure?'

'You bet I am, so don't get cheeky,' said Paul. 'Remember my rights are equal to yours. So put your apron on and get cracking.'

'What a brute,' said Lulu.

'You're right,' said Paul, 'feel my muscles.'

Chapter Twenty-Three

Cindy, home from school, found her dad upstairs at his typewriter.

'Crikey, you still doing your story?' she said.

'Still at it, Cindy.'

'I can tell that,' said Cindy, 'your hair's all mussed up. As usual.'

'Creating a masterpiece, I'll have you know, is head-scratching,' said Harry. 'Unless you're a genius. Then you create with your eyes shut and no headaches.' He glanced at his young daughter. She looked sweet in her school uniform of white shirt-blouse, striped tie and pleated brown skirt. 'Enjoyed some good schooling today, pet?'

'Oh, rapturous, except Miss Finney had got the blues,' said Cindy.

'Ragtime blues?' said Harry.

'Ragtime? What's ragtime?' asked Cindy.

'Pre-war,' said Harry.

'Well, she'd got some blues,' said Cindy. 'I expect she's been disappointed in love.'

'Rotten for a woman of forty,' said Harry, 'but she's still got time to find an acceptable bloke, she's still a fine figure of a woman.'

'Well, you're not going to be the bloke,' said

Cindy. 'I don't want her as a stepmum, she smells of camphorated oil in the winter.'

'Probably got a weak bosom,' said Harry.

'What?'

'A weak chest,' said Harry.

'Well, I don't want you getting near it,' said Cindy. 'When are you going to finish that story?' She knew her dad always took time to complete one. He'd finish a manuscript, read it, then write it all over again, and not once, either. And even now, his wastepaper basket was stuffed up with pages he'd discarded.

'I think it'll be finished in a couple of days,' said Harry.

'Then let's hope it'll earn us some lolly,' said Cindy. 'Would you like a cup of tea and a fruit bun?'

'Not half, you sweet girl,' said Harry. Cindy had made the fruit buns herself, and he thought what a treasured wife she would be to some man some day.

'I'll put the kettle on,' said Cindy, moving to the door. 'Oh, is the lady in? I could ask her if she'd like a cup.'

'She's up in town,' said Harry.

'What's she gone there for?'

'She said – let's see, what was it? Something about – oh, yes, she's a nurse and wants to get approval for work in a London hospital.'

'She's a French nurse?' said Cindy.

'German,' said Harry.

'Now, Daddy, you know we agreed to say she's French in case some silly people started throwing stones at our windows,' said Cindy.

'Yes, but you and I know she's German,' said Harry.

'Daddy, that's just between you and me,' said Cindy. 'Crikey, I never thought of her as a nurse, more like a German duchess. Well, if you get flu, she'll be able to look after you and get your temperature down.'

'If I get ministration from Miss Bruck,' said Harry, 'my temperature will go up.'

Cindy, knowledgeable, giggled.

'Daddy, you're funny sometimes,' she said, and went down to put the kettle on.

Cindy, of course, was a lot older than her years. She was pretty sure, for instance, that whenever her dad was due to visit the school with other parents, Miss Finney did her best to get really close to him. Miss Finney fancied Harry, Cindy was pretty sure of that too, so she made a habit of standing between them whenever necessary. That protected her dad from meeting up with Miss Finney's proud bosom. Well, some women would say that kind of contact was as good as a proposal of marriage, and Cindy knew her dad was so easy-going he might fall for it, even if he didn't want to.

Anneliese arrived back at five thirty. Cindy, about to prepare supper for herself and her dad, heard the opening of the front door and emerged from the kitchen into the hall.

'Oh, hello,' she said, apron-clad.

'Hello, Cindy,' smiled Anneliese.

'Daddy said you're a nurse.'

'So I am,' said Anneliese, 'although I haven't worked as one for some years.'

'Daddy said you went up to town to get approved.' Cindy was fascinated by the thought of this aristocratic-looking woman ministering to the sick.

'Yes, so I did, Cindy, and so I am now,' said Anneliese, smiling again. Her interview had been prolonged, the examination of her professional documents, her recorded experiences and her work permit all very thorough, the questions numerous and searching. Yes, it was true, she had nursed wounded British prisoners of war, including a very outstanding British commando. She gave his name and rank. Why do you remember him particularly? Simply because he was the kind of patient one doesn't easily forget, she said.

Eventually, after a long-drawn-out afternoon, she was informed that her German nursing qualifications had substance in Britain. Was she willing to accept a post with the National Health Service, which was in need of fully qualified and experienced nurses? Yes. Then you will hear from us.

Accordingly, her pleasure was visible as she stood in the hall with Cindy.

'Oh, goodness,' said Harry's versatile daughter, 'are you going to do nursing in one of our hospitals, Miss Bruck?'

'That,' said Anneliese, 'is why I'm here in London.'

'Wow,' said Cindy. She thought. 'Did the people you saw mind that you're French?'

'French?' said Anneliese.

'I mean German,' said Cindy, pinking a little at her mistake.

'They were interested in my background, of course,' said Anneliese, 'but no-one took offence and I left without bruises.'

'Oh, good,' said Cindy. 'I think you're ever so

nice. Shall I make you a cup of tea? Daddy's upstairs still writing his story, and you should see his wastepaper basket, it's stuffed with pages he's chucked away.'

'Cindy, I would love a cup of tea,' said Anneliese.

'Would you really?' Cindy looked delighted. 'I'll make it and bring it up. Then I'll start cooking the sausages Daddy and me's having for our supper. He likes grilled sausages, they'll tear him away from his old typewriter.'

'Cindy, how good you are to your father,' said Anneliese, and made her way up to the living room of her flat. She took off her hat, sat down in an armchair to relax, and opened up the newspaper she had bought, the *Evening Standard*. She glanced only briefly at the front-page report on Communist atrocities against the British in Malaya. She always felt it was Hitler's war against the Soviet Union that had provoked a rise in worldwide Communism and set in motion a war against capitalism.

She turned pages, looking for what she hoped would be information on London entertainments. She found the right page and began to absorb herself in theatre billings.

It wasn't long before Cindy knocked on the door.

'Miss Bruck, I've brought your tea.'

'Come in, Cindy.'

In the girl came, carrying the cup and saucer, which she placed on a little table beside the armchair.

'Thank you, Cindy.'

'Oh, that's all right, Daddy always says a cup of tea perks us up,' said Cindy. 'Now I'd best get on with our supper.'

Out she went, leaving the door open. Anneliese heard her go upstairs. Sipping the hot tea, which did perk one up in a more definite way than coffee, voices reached her ears.

'Yes, Daddy, but you ought to go down and tell her you're pleased to hear she's going to work at a London hospital.'

'No, I didn't ought to, pet, we mustn't keep intruding or we'll get to be nuisances. If she's happy about her prospects, then I'm happy for her.'

'But, Daddy, she doesn't have anyone to talk to except us.'

'Well, if she gets in need of visitors, perhaps she'll let us know, Cindy. Otherwise, let's respect her privacy.'

Anneliese put her cup and saucer down, came to her feet and closed the door. That shut out the voices, but she did hear Cindy going downstairs moments later.

She returned to her evening paper. She made a note of theatres offering the kind of productions that appealed to her. After half an hour of very pleasant relaxation, she went to her kitchen to examine the larder and fridge, and to decide what she would like for her own supper.

She heard Cindy call from below.

'Ready, Daddy, so come on down.'

'Coming, Cindy.'

Harry's vibrant tones sang through the house.

Anneliese heard him coming down. She thought he hesitated for a moment on the landing before resuming his descent. She supposed the hesitation meant he had thought about saying hello to her, only to decide to take his own advice and avoid being a nuisance.

Strangely, she wouldn't have minded.

The inquest by jury on the three dead men had returned a verdict of murder of persons so far unknown by a person or persons unknown, which was no help to anyone. Scotland Yard's CID officers were getting nowhere. They hadn't any kind of clue or lead to work on. They were in a blind alley and were likely to remain there unless the victims could be identified. Each one must have had relatives of some kind, but none had come forward to report that a son, a husband or a brother had gone missing.

That pointed, of course, to the growing belief of the police that the victims really were the three missing members of the Soviet Press Bureau, something denied by Kersch, head of the Bureau. Nor did the Soviet Embassy offer help. Its officials were blank-faced in response to inquiries.

As for shipping ports and airports, none could offer any information on a woman called Katje Galicia. Had the inquiries related to a certain Olga Kuschka and her son Pyotr Kuschka, holding Latvian passports, there would have been a response from London Airport.

Thursday.

Anneliese, an orderly woman by nature and training, was making a little collection of her jewellery, some of which she had inherited from her mother. She wished to get a valuation from a jeweller and then to have it insured. There were pearl necklaces, gold bracelets, sparkling diamond brooches, cameo brooches and other items. She had rarely worn any of them during her war years as a nurse, and never during the immediate post-war years in West Berlin, when the shattered city was the stark hunting ground of desperate people. Since her arrival in England she had felt safe enough to adorn herself lightly with one thing or another. All the same, London undoubtedly had its share of thieves and burglars.

She placed the collection in a leather handbag, put on her hat and coat, and left the house. Cindy was at school and Mr Stevens out. Neither had intruded on her for the last day or so.

Having spotted a jeweller's shop in Camberwell Road on her shopping expeditions, she made her way there. The nameboard above the window read 'Morrison's, Jewellers, Est. 1898'. It was a small shop, and the proprietor, a large handsome man of dark visage, was serving a lady who wanted an ornamental christening spoon of silver. Anneliese waited until the purchase was made, then advanced to the counter, which was lined with glass containers displaying all kinds of jewellery, ranging from the cheap to the expensive.

'Good morning,' she said.

'Ah, good morning, madam,' smiled the jeweller, Mr Morrison.

'Do you do valuations for insurance?' asked Anneliese.

'Happily, madam, happily, and such service for only one per cent.' Mr Morrison had a lisp. Anneliese took another look at him, at his dark liquid eyes and his engaging smile. A Jew? Yes, she was sure of it, and the certainty revived the hideous memories of Himmler's concentration camps for a fleeting second.

'Then would you be so kind as to value these for me?' She opened the leather handbag and held it up for Mr Morrison to inspect the contents.

'If you please?' he said. She let him have the bag, and he carefully spilled the items onto a large square of black velvet. Against the black, silver gleamed, gold glowed and tiny diamonds sparkled. Mr Morrison studied the collection with professional interest touched by keen speculation. 'Why, madam, what do I have here?'

'My personal jewellery,' said Anneliese.

'I will make a careful valuation of everything,' said Mr Morrison, taking up a silver and diamond brooch quite lovingly. He inspected the back of it. 'Ah, from Aachen's of Dresden, I see.'

'Yes, much of it is of German origin,' said Anneliese, wondering how he would react. He looked at her. He hadn't failed to pick up her slight accent. Now he took note of her colouring and her blue eyes.

'Madam is – ?'

'Yes, I am German,' said Anneliese.

Mr Morrison, impressed by her frankness and the directness of her clear eyes, said, 'I have no objection to giving you a valuation for insurance. Allow me to itemize everything and to give you a receipt. You will be able to call again in two days, on Saturday?'

'Yes,' said Anneliese.

'Your name, please?'

247

'Miss Anneliese Bruck. B-r-u-c-k.'

'German, yes,' said Mr Morrison, and to her surprise, he smiled. 'In this country, most people take other people as they find them. There are exceptions, of course.'

'You mean prejudice exists among some English people?'

'Among some of all peoples.'

'Well, I live here now,' said Anneliese, 'and I'm sure I shall find out which kind of English people have prejudices.'

'If I may speak frankly, you will have to understand, in your case, that it isn't prejudice but anger and disgust,' said Mr Morrison.

'I do understand,' said Anneliese, 'I've seen so much of what caused it.'

'Photographs of the concentration camps?'

'No, the camps themselves,' said Anneliese.

Mr Morrison sighed.

'Why did God allow it, Miss Bruck?'

'Can any of us answer that question?' said Anneliese.

Mr Morrison gave her another look. She seemed composed, but there was a darkness in her eyes. He judged her to have memories she would rather forget.

'Allow me a few moments,' he said, and began to write down a description of each piece of jewellery on a sheet of headed notepaper. When he had finished, and the items were all back in the leather bag, he handed the paper to Anneliese. She glanced at it. It was a signed receipt, the signature J. Morrison.

'Thank you, Mr Morrison, I'll call again on

Saturday morning,' she said, placing the receipt in her handbag.

'My pleasure, Miss Bruck,' said Mr Morrison, and came out from behind his counter to see her to the door. He opened it for her. She stepped out, only to be bumped by a quick-moving man.

'Oh, sorry, missus, it's me legs trying to run off with me,' he said with a friendly grin.

'We all— oh!' Anneliese expelled an angry cry as a hand yanked at her handbag.

'Give it 'ere, yer bleedin' cow!' hissed the bag-snatcher.

Mr Morrison, large but a good mover, issued from the shop and dealt the man a huge thump between his shoulder blades. He let go of the hand-bag and went tumbling. He righted himself before he hit the pavement and ran, knocking pedestrians aside.

'I must apologize for some of Camberwell's people,' said Mr Morrison. 'Are you all right, Miss Bruck?'

'Quite all right, and thank you, Mr Morrison,' said Anneliese. 'My handbag is something I can't afford to lose. Yes, thank you very much.'

'My pleasure,' said Mr Morrison, thinking her a remarkably composed woman.

'Goodbye until Saturday,' said Anneliese, going on her way and avoiding the stares of the curious onlookers.

Walking back to her flat, she thought about the fact that Mr Morrison, a Jew, had foiled the bag-snatcher in a swift and determined way. How ironic, how splendid. The thought again brought back the all too active memories of the war, but this time they were of her years as a German army nurse. That led to reflections on her time in the hospital at Benghazi and then, inevitably, to the British commando officer, Lieutenant Tim Adams, a man who had always had his place among her happier memories. Yes, there were happier moments to remember, those that related to the part she herself had played in the successful recovery of badly wounded soldiers.

Had Lieutenant Adams survived? Was it possible he was still alive? If so, where was he? She had something of his, which she would like to return to him.

Chapter Twenty-Four

Boots's office phone pealed. He picked it up.

'Hello?'

'Mr Adams, there's a call for you, from a solicitor,' said the switchboard girl.

'Solicitor?' said Boots. 'What's he after, a fee?'

'He just said he'd like to talk to you, it's a Mr Duncan.'

'Duncan?' said Boots. 'I've a feeling that that name is familiar. Put him through, Gillian.'

The caller was connected, and in a quiet and pleasant voice made himself known as the senior partner of Duncan, Gibbons and Mayberry of Winchester.

'My apologies for disturbing you at your business, Mr Adams, but you may remember I had occasion to contact you several years ago.'

'So you did, Mr Duncan,' said Boots. The occasion had been brought about by the death of Elsie Chivers, a neighbour he had known during the family's years in Walworth. 'You dealt with Miss Chivers's will.'

'Quite so, Mr Adams. She left everything to you, which, apart from a few trinkets, came down to all that was in her bank account, some three hundred pounds.'

'So what's come up?' asked Boots, who had special memories of Elsie Chivers. 'Has there been a mistake? Does the bank want it back?'

'Not at all, Mr Adams, not at all,' said Mr Duncan. 'What I have to tell you is that Herr Meister, a lawyer from West Germany, is over here on business, representing a manufacturing company negotiating a contract for imports of metal from a British firm. He's overseeing terms of the contract in company with one of the German firm's directors. Germans are very thorough about most things, including the printed word. While here, Herr Meister has instructions to also act for the executors of the will of a landowner called Fredrik Lansberg, the deceased husband of Miss Chivers.'

'I see.' Boots was silent for a moment. He knew that Elsie Chivers, during her unsettled time in Germany, had married a man called Lansberg, a semi-invalid to whom she had been more of a nurse than a wife. It was after his death, in the early 1920s, that she made plans to return to England.

'As you and I know, Mr Adams, Miss Chivers rarely used her married name,' said Mr Duncan, 'and indeed, until her death I was unaware she'd been married. Then, of course, her papers, including her passport, revealed the information.'

'If I'm right,' said Boots, 'there was nothing of importance concerning her German husband. Exactly how well did you know her?'

'Only through the nursing home in which she was confined because of ill health,' said Mr Duncan. Boots knew it was more than that. She had been a mentally disturbed woman. 'I was asked by the Superintendent there if I'd call and draw up her will.'

'Yes, I remember now,' said Boots, 'but what is her dead husband's will to do with me?'

'Mr Adams, Miss Chivers left everything she owned to you,' said Mr Duncan, 'and it now seems that that is a little more than a few trinkets and some three hundred pounds.'

'What is meant by a little more, Mr Duncan?'

'It seems, Mr Adams, that you stand to inherit the estate of the late Fredrik Lansberg,' said Mr Duncan.

'Good God,' said Boots.

'Is it possible for me to come and see you at your home, so that I can explain in detail on behalf of Herr Meister, who is too busy himself?'

'Yes, come and see me, Mr Duncan.'

'Could you possibly make it sometime this week?'

'Yes, come to lunch on Saturday,' said Boots, 'arriving at twelve noon, say. Will that suit you?'

'That will suit me very well.'

'Fine,' said Boots and gave his address to the solicitor, together with details of how to get there from Winchester.

When he put the phone down, his thoughts were all directed at Elsie Chivers, a gentle lady whose life had been one of sadness and tragedy. She had lived with her widowed and possessive mother only a few doors away from his family in Walworth. Mrs Chivers seemed to hate her gentle-natured daughter, and Elsie had suffered years of spite and humiliation at her hands. Mrs Chivers's ill-nature was so legendary that the street kids called her The

Witch. In 1914, a little while after Boots had enlisted in the army, she was found dead in her bed, her throat cut. Elsie, accused of the murder of her mother, stood trial at the Old Bailey, but was found not guilty. Boots, himself a witness, produced evidence that went a long way towards convincing the jury of her innocence.

After a light midday lunch, Anneliese went shopping in the East Street market. She had an urge to discover every aspect of life in this area of South London. She found herself mingling with its housewives amid all the hustle and bustle of a street market. The stallholders were hearty and persuasive.

'Come on, ladies, try me bananas – pure gold, I tell yer, which ain't been touched by human 'and till yer start peeling 'em. Here y'ar, missus, one and tuppence a bunch of five.'

Anneliese bought a bunch. The stallholder dropped it into her large shopping bag, took the money and told her if he hadn't got a wife and four kids, he'd offer to take her to Butlin's Holiday Camp for a gorblimey wild week.

'How kind,' said Anneliese.

'Be a pleasure, love, I tell yer.'

At another stall, she listened to more sales talk.

'Roll up, me darlings, I got fresh-picked Bramleys at sevenpence a pound – here, lady, give yer old man and yer kids a treat of apple pie and they'll love yer for ever.'

'Five pounds, please,' said Anneliese, who had lately come to terms with Imperial measurement.

'Coming up, me darling,' said the stallholder. He

weighed the fruit and tipped it into her shopping bag, the large apples descending with little muffled thumps. The stallholder, looking at her, said, 'Strike a light.'

'Excuse me?' said Anneliese.

'You on the stage, might I ask?' enquired the impressed stallholder.

'No, but do I look as if I am?' smiled Anneliese.

'Not half. Knock spots off the Palladium gals, you would. Well, five pounds of them pippins is two and eleven, lady.'

'Two shillings and elevenpence, yes?'

'That's the ticket, missus. Ta.' He received three shillings and gave her a penny change. His eyes followed her as she left to merge with the crowds of shoppers.

' 'Ere, come on, wake up, Charlie Chaplin, and give me six of them Bramleys for apple dumplings,' said the next customer.

'I'm with yer, lady.'

'But the other one tickled yer fancy, did she?'

'Bit of all right, she was.'

From other stalls, Anneliese bought potatoes, cabbage, onions, leeks, oranges and two large bunches of black Hamburg grapes. Everything, except the grapes, was tipped breezily into her shopping bag, making it bulge with produce. The grapes were placed in a carrier bag for which she paid threepence. Such bags cost a mere penny before the war. Then she began to make her way out of the market, feeling quite exhilarated.

Her heavy shopping bag bumped a buxom woman.

' 'Ere, watch it, dearie.'

'So sorry,' said Anneliese.

'That's all right, love, no harm done, only it ain't what I'd do meself, carry a bag of coals down the market this time of the day.'

'I'll remember that,' said Anneliese, and went on her way with extra care. She lugged her heavy shopping bag back home. The house was still quiet, and her footsteps echoed as she climbed the stairs to her apartment.

Harry returned from his outing at ten to three. Anneliese heard him entering the house, which at once seemed to bring life back to it. She waited five minutes, then went down to see him, carrying a paper bag containing a bunch of the Hamburg grapes.

'Mr Stevens?'

'Tally-ho,' called Harry from the kitchen. 'I'm back from the chase and making myself a pot of tea. Come in, Miss Bruck.'

Anneliese showed herself. Shades of Olympus, thought Harry in Homeric terms, enter a goddess in shining raiment. She was wearing a loose-waisted honey-coloured dress that reached to just below her knees. In appreciation, he bowed from the waist, his unbuttoned overcoat flapping.

'What is that for, Mr Stevens?'

'I'm paying homage,' said Harry.

'Homage?'

'Yes, to my treasured tenant.'

Anneliese laughed.

'Treasured?' she said. 'Is that because I paid a month's rent in advance?'

'I won't say that wasn't welcome, it was, believe me,' said Harry, 'but what I meant was that Cindy and I are glad to have you around.'

'Thank you,' said Anneliese. 'I came down to let you know I bought some grapes in the market.'

'You've discovered the market?' said Harry.

'Yes, and found it a very cheerful place, with excellent prices,' said Anneliese. 'I bought some grapes among other things, but far too many. Would you and Cindy like to have these?' She placed the bag on the kitchen table. Harry opened it up and took a look.

'Well, aren't you a lovely lady?' he said, his smile laden with warmth. 'Black grapes, by jingo, talk of goddesses bringing gifts.'

'Goddesses?'

'That's my feeble writer's imagination falling over itself,' said Harry.

Anneliese laughed again.

'I don't call that feeble, Mr Stevens, and may I point out your kettle's boiling its head off?'

'Is it?' said Harry. 'Oh, so it is.' He took it up and filled the teapot. 'Would you like a cup while you're here?'

'Thank you, Mr Stevens, I would,' said Anneliese, surprising herself.

'Good-oh,' said Harry, and put cups, saucers, sugar bowl, milk jug, slop bowl and teapot on a tray. He regarded the tray, and looked triumphant that everything necessary was there. 'Let's have it in the living room,' he said. 'More comfortable there.' He led the way, and Anneliese followed him into a room that did indeed look comfortable. Armchairs, cushions, little tables, velvet curtains and warm colours were all inviting, and everything, she noted, looked as if Cindy regularly dusted and polished. The fireplace was handsome, the fire laid, and ornaments decorated the mantelpiece. There was a radio on a sideboard, but no television was visible. Cindy would have told her they couldn't afford one.

Harry offered her an armchair with a table beside it, and she seated herself. He milked the cups, put a tea-strainer on one, took up the teapot and poured. Out from the spout came a stream of hot, clear water.

'Eh?' said Harry.

Anneliese wanted to laugh again.

'Isn't it usual to put the tea in first?' she said.

'It's what normal people do,' said Harry. 'I'm one of the others. But hold on, don't go away, I'll try again.' Out he went, taking the teapot with him. There was still plenty of hot water in the large kettle. He boiled it up again, emptied the teapot of its cooling water, and put in tea from the caddy. When he rejoined his tenant, he was smiling but apologetic.

'Don't apologize, Mr Stevens,' said Anneliese, 'we all have our moments.'

'I have more than most,' said Harry. He emptied the diluted milk from one cup into the slop basin, and put in a new dash. He poured. This time the spout issued hot golden tea. 'Well, look at that,' he said, 'it's tea. Sugar, Miss Bruck?'

'No sugar, thank you,' said Anneliese, and took the cup and saucer he proffered. Harry filled a cup for himself, added just a little sugar, and sat down.

'Well, that's one absent-minded mistake made good, I hope,' he said.

'Oh, it's very good,' said Anneliese, sipping. 'Mr Stevens, are you cold?'

'No, are you?' said Harry. 'Shall I put a match to the fire?'

'I'm quite warm, thank you,' said Anneliese, 'I simply wondered why you're still wearing your overcoat.'

'My overcoat? Am I? Crazy crickets, so I am.' Harry looked at her. She looked at him. She laughed. Harry laughed. They both laughed. 'Now you know what a prize clown I am,' said Harry. He stood up, slipped his coat off and sat down again. Anneliese was still laughing. 'Don't get hysterics,' he said, 'they're catching.'

'Oh, I'm sorry, Mr Stevens, but you're so funny,' she said.

'Is that good?' asked Harry.

'Oh, much better than merely good,' said Anneliese, thinking of SS men who considered that being amusing was to break the window of a Jewish shop with the proprietor's head.

Harry, changing the subject, asked her if she liked the East Street market. Very much, said Anneliese, the people and the stallholders were most friendly, and she'd been called ducky, darling, dearie, love, missus and lady. Harry said it was always like that down the market. What was it like in Berlin markets?

'Push and shove,' said Anneliese.

'Same as ours,' said Harry. 'By the way, I went up to town to hand my short story to my agent. I waited while she read it. She liked it so much that she's going to touch the magazine publishers for a much larger fee than usual.'

'I don't think I've a right to ask what a much larger fee would be,' said Anneliese, enjoying her tea.

'Say two hundred quid?' said Harry, slightly dazzled by her shining legs. 'That would keep Cindy and me going for quite a while. But it'll be a lot less than two hundred, of course.'

'I wish you luck, but I thought you were going to let me read the story when it was ready,' said Anneliese.

'Did I promise that?' said Harry. 'Hell, I think I did, but when I finished it last night, after any amount of rewriting, I had an urge to deliver it to my agent this morning. Tell you what, I'll let you have a copy of the magazine when it comes out, and you can read it then. How's that?'

'I'll be delighted,' said Anneliese. She finished her tea and came to her feet. 'Thank you for being so kind, Mr Stevens, but I must go now.'

'Well, it's been a pleasure, tea and a chat,' said Harry, getting up and seeing her to the door. She smiled and made her way upstairs. What a remarkable woman, thought Harry, moves like a duchess, speaks English like one, plants herself in the middle of cockney Camberwell, and goes down the market as if it's an everyday event for her. She's got to have some fancy bloke somewhere. No, not fancy, far more likely to be a six-foot Guards officer with a title, especially as from what she's told me, she's probably off SS goons for life. Well, good luck to her, she's cool but she's a charmer.

* * *

When Cindy arrived home from school and was shown the large bunch of grapes gifted by Miss Bruck, her eyes sparkled.

'Oh, fab,' she said, and helped herself to some. 'Well, that proves one thing.'

'Which is?' said Harry.

'She likes you.'

'I hope she likes both of us,' said Harry.

'I think I'd best go up and thank her,' said Cindy.

'For liking us?' said Harry.

'No, for the grapes,' said Cindy.

'Stay here,' said Harry, 'I've already spelled out our appreciation. Who's peeling the potatoes for supper?'

'You are,' said Cindy, 'you promised, so's I could do my homework. Oh, how did you get on with your short story?'

'I think it's as good as sold.'

'Oh, fab,' said Cindy, 'that proves another thing.'

'And what's this one?' asked Harry.

'You're not just a man who wears odd socks,' said Cindy.

Chapter Twenty-Five

'What?' said Polly, a few minutes after Boots had arrived home from his work. 'What did you say?'

'A Winchester solicitor, Mr Duncan, is coming to lunch on Saturday,' said Boots. 'The twins will be at Rosie's poultry farm for the day, clucking with the chickens, so there'll be just the two of us to entertain Mr Duncan. I'm relying on you to play the charming hostess, and on Flossie to lay on a handsome lunch.' Flossie Cuthbert of Peckham was still Polly's domestic jewel as her daily maid and cook.

'Hold on, you old hustler,' said Polly, looking lissom in a slenderizing dress of peachy silk crêpe, 'I want to hear more than the fact that we've got a solicitor from Winchester coming to lunch. Give.'

'Where are the twins at the moment?' asked Boots.

'In the study,' said Polly, 'and doing what they usually do at this time of day. Their homework. It keeps them out of Flossie's way while she's cooking dinner.'

'Right,' said Boots. 'You sit down, Polly, and I'll mix you a gin and tonic, and pour myself a finger of Scotch. Then I'll tell you why I've invited Mr Duncan to lunch.'

'The offer of a gin and tonic is a nice touch,' said Polly, 'but does it tell me I'm going to need it? That is, have you done something so frightful that we're going to be dispossessed by a solicitor acting for some injured party?'

'Nothing like that,' said Boots, attending to the drinks. 'If we were, I certainly wouldn't have invited him to lunch.' He smiled. Polly's little theatrical moments were all part of her endearing qualities. While she wasn't as domesticated as Emily had been, and still not much of a cook, she was always responsive, always a vital companion and a surprisingly equable mother.

Seated with her, he gave her the details of his conversation with Mr Duncan. If his recounting commanded all her attention, it also aroused her curiosity about a woman she had never known. Accordingly, it wasn't what was going to follow from a meeting with Mr Duncan that evoked her first comments, it was Boots's relationship with the late Elsie Chivers.

'You mentioned the lady some years ago, old scout, at the time of her death, but you discouraged questions about her. So I thought, of course, that you'd been her lover. I know it happened before I met you, but—'

'I was never her lover, Polly,' said Boots. 'She was a neighbour of our family, and we all had an affection for her, a very gentle woman.' If, as he had suspected many times, there was one moment when she gave in to an uncontrollable surge of hatred for her dreadful mother, that suspicion was to remain his alone. Lizzy, Tommy, Sammy and Chinese Lady had always been happily content with the jury's verdict of not guilty, but because the murder and the trial had been so unpleasant, and the crime remained unsolved, out of affection for the memory of Elsie Chivers they never talked about her at any length.

'But to leave you everything she had must have meant you were special to her,' said Polly.

'Everything she had at her death amounted, you remember, to a little over three hundred pounds,' said Boots, letting the uplifting quality of the whisky linger on his palate.

'But there was her late husband's will, the one Mr Duncan mentioned to you,' said Polly.

'When I last spoke to her, a few days before she died, I think she'd forgotten she was ever married,' said Boots. He had told Polly certain facts about Elsie, but had never mentioned the murder of her mother. He had assured Elsie that by his silence she could rest in peace. 'Certainly, I'm positive there was nothing on her mind concerning her husband's will and what it might have meant.'

'Well, I suppose we shall find out exactly what it does mean over lunch on Saturday,' said Polly. 'If another three hundred pounds, will you deposit it in the twins' savings accounts?'

'Either that, or put it towards a new fur coat for you,' said Boots.

'You old darling,' said Polly, 'I think you're still fond of me.'

'Much more than I am of Anastasia Davidson,' said Boots.

Lieutenant General Kersch had received a signal from Moscow, recalling him. He knew what that meant. Despite his high rank he was to be interrogated in connection with his failure to find Katje Galicia and to discover who had eliminated the three missing officers and why. Nor had he or his staff located an associate of Katje Galicia, a man or a woman called Finch.

There was no room in the KGB for failures. That was something he also knew.

Cindy was listening to gramophone records being played on the radio. The programme had just broadcast a song by an American vocalist called Nat King Cole. He had a kind of melodious, caressing voice. Now a recorded number by the highly popular Frank Sinatra was pleasing her ears. Older girls at her school talked about how he sent them swoony, which Cindy thought about as soppy as a wet hankie.

Harry was scribbling outlines of a new short-story plot. He was always searching for new storylines with a punch. He could never afford to rest on his laurels.

The Frank Sinatra record finished, and was followed by some boring old crooner's number. So Cindy took the opportunity to say, 'Dad, you working on another short story?'

'Well, that's the way it goes, pet,' said Harry.

'You wouldn't have to keep thinking up new plots if you wrote a book,' said Cindy.

'A novel, you mean? Sounds great,' said Harry, 'but it could take me a year and what would we live on until it was published? And that's assuming it would be. As it is, I do earn some lolly for the occasional short story.'

'Well, I don't know where it all goes to,' said Cindy.

'You should do,' said Harry, 'you're our money-minder.'

'Yes, but it still dribbles away,' said Cindy.

'You've got something left of our lodger's advance, haven't you?' said Harry.

'Yes, some of it,' said Cindy, 'don't forgot we had to settle shop bills.'

'Sorry about our money problems, Cindy love,' said Harry.

'Oh, dear, I suppose there's just not enough of it,' said Cindy. 'If you wrote a novel, you could earn lots more.'

'Something like *Murder at the Vicarage*, à la Agatha Christie?' suggested Harry.

'Crikey, a thriller?' said Cindy.

'With lots of bodies?' said Harry.

'How many would a lot be?' asked Cindy.

'Say one in every room and two on the doorstep?' said Harry.

'Daddy, you sure that's not too much of a lot?' said Cindy.

'Well, say one in the conservatory, one in the vicar's study, and one under the grand piano,' said Harry.

'Yes, all right,' said Cindy. The programme of records finishing, she switched the radio off. 'Now you can think up the storyline.'

'And decide on whodunnit,' said Harry.

'Daddy, I'm serious,' said Cindy. 'I mean, you could get famous and rich. Mind, I don't know if that wouldn't make Miss Finney so excited she'd come after you.'

'I'd be stuck between being famous and being collared, you think?' said Harry.

'Well, if Miss Finney collared you—' Cindy was stopped by a knock on the living-room door and the sound of Miss Bruck's voice.

'Mr Stevens?'

Harry came to his feet, walked to the door and opened it. The fair goddess smiled at him, and fateful images of Miss Finney vanished into limbo.

'Oh, hello,' he said. He looked homely and comfortable in his old sweater and slacks, and Anneliese looked heavenly in an Oxford blue sweater and a cream-coloured pencil skirt. That is, heavenly to Harry's optics.

'So sorry to interrupt your evening, Mr Stevens, but I wondered if I could talk to you about a telephone for the apartment,' said Anneliese.

'Telephone?' said Harry. 'Well, I daresay – come in, Miss Bruck, and we can do some talking.'

Anneliese entered.

'Hello, Cindy,' she said.

'Oh, hello, Miss Bruck,' said Cindy, coming to her feet. 'Ever so nice to see you.' In grown-up fashion, she added, 'Come and sit down.'

'Thank you,' said Anneliese, and Cindy indicated one of the fireside armchairs. The fire was alight, the evening being chilly. Anneliese sat down. 'You see, Mr Stevens,' she said, 'I think I shall need a phone. Among other things, it would keep me in touch with my sister at Aldershot. I'd pay for all costs of installation, of course, and all charges, but I rather think I need your permission as owner of the house.'

'Granted,' said Harry.

'You've no objections?'

'I can't think of a single one,' said Harry. 'I'll pop out to a public phone in the morning, ring the local GPO manager and get it all arranged.'

'Well, thank you, Mr Stevens, how kind.'

'Oh, Daddy was born kind,' said Cindy. 'Of course, I wasn't there at the time, but his mum, my grandma, told me so, and she ought to know, don't you think?'

'That's Cindy having a flight of fancy,' smiled Harry.

'We all have those at times,' said Anneliese.

'Daddy's just had one,' said Cindy, 'about a plot for a novel.'

'A novel?' said Anneliese.

'Yes, one that would make him rich and famous,' said Cindy.

'Another flight of fancy,' said Harry.

'He's going to call it *Murder at the Vicarage*,' said Cindy, 'with bodies all over the place.'

'A murder mystery?' said Anneliese.

'It's Cindy's idea, that I should write a novel,' said Harry, 'but as I told her, it could take me a year and I'd earn nothing in that time. We'd end up on bread and water, which wouldn't be much of a life for a growing girl.'

'I see,' said Anneliese. 'Well, I think you should still give it thought, Mr Stevens, even if you do come down to bread and water. But would that happen while you're receiving rent from me?'

'There you are, Daddy, we'd still have some money every week,' said Cindy.

'But could I write a novel, I wonder?' mused Harry.

'You should try,' said Anneliese. 'Oh, by the way, I've a little problem. My kitchen sink tap is leaking.'

'Sounds as if you've got a worn washer,' said Harry.

'Can you tell me where I can hire a plumber?' asked Anneliese.

'No need for that,' said Harry, 'I'll do it for you.'

'You can do plumbing?' said Anneliese.

'Not comprehensively,' said Harry, 'but I can change a washer. No trouble at all. I've got a little box of washers, if I can find it, and tools for the job if I can remember where they are.'

Anneliese laughed. Harry Stevens was a very human man.

'You'll have to excuse Daddy being a bit forgetful,' said Cindy.

'Oh, we all have forgetful moments, Cindy,' said Anneliese.

'Daddy, you can do it now,' said Cindy.

'Do what now?' asked Harry.

'Change the washer, of course,' said Cindy. She looked at Anneliese and rolled her eyes. Anneliese smiled.

Harry proved he had a useful practical side. He found a new washer and tools, and went up with Anneliese to her flat. She watched while he opened up the closed compartment under her kitchen sink, turned off the water supply to her tap, then removed the housing with an adjustable spanner to expose the worn washer.

'There we are, it's on its last legs,' he said. He took it off, replaced it with the new one and put the housing back on, tightening it with the spanner. Then he turned on the supply and tried the tap.

The water gushed. He turned the tap off and waited. There was no leak.

'Mr Stevens, how clever of you,' said Anneliese. 'I'm very impressed.'

'Nothing to it,' said Harry. 'If you'd asked me to fit you a new hot water system, the story would have been different.'

'I'm only aware you've stopped the tap leaking,' said Anneliese. 'Thank you very much.'

'You're welcome,' said Harry.

When he rejoined Cindy, she asked how he'd got on. Harry said the tap was now a non-leaking one.

'Was Miss Bruck pleased?'

'She said she was.'

'Oh, good,' said Cindy, 'we don't want her to leave or we'd stop getting her rent.'

'Cindy, there's more to life than rent,' said Harry.

'Not when you're hard up and the cupboard's all bare,' said Cindy.

'Cue for a plot,' said Harry.

'No, you've got one,' said Cindy. '*Murder at the Vicarage*, which is going to make you rich and famous.'

'If so,' said Harry, 'keep it dark from Miss Finney.'

After breakfast on Saturday morning, Cindy had to remind her father twice that he'd promised Miss Bruck to go out and ring the GPO about having a phone put in for her. So out he went to a public phone box. When he came back he was able to inform Miss Bruck that the GPO would do the job on Monday. Anneliese thanked him and said what a kind and helpful gentleman he was. Harry said the nearest he'd come to being a gentleman was when his grammar-school education earned him a wartime commission as a lieutenant in the Navy. His captain addressed the officers collectively as gentlemen.

'On my return to civvy street,' said Harry, 'I reverted to being just another bloke.'

Anneliese laughed. It had been over ten years since laughter had come easily to her. It was doing so now.

'Mr Stevens, gentlemen are born, not made,' she said.

'I was born in Chipping Norton, a little market town in Oxfordshire,' said Harry.

'So?' said Anneliese.

'I can recollect only being called a born tearaway.'

'What is a born tearaway?' asked Anneliese.

'A perishing young rip,' said Harry.

'Rip?'

'Rascal,' smiled Harry.

'And now you're just another bloke?' said Anneliese, returning his smile.

'You could say so,' said Harry.

'Mr Stevens, you're far too modest.'

'Look here,' said Harry, 'if it's not too personal a question, haven't you ever been married?'

'Oh, there was a German SS officer once,' said Anneliese quite readily, 'but he was killed during the German advance on Paris in 1940. So we never married.'

'I'm sorry,' said Harry.

'Don't be,' said Anneliese. 'Had he lived we

should have violently disagreed towards the end of the war. He was a dedicated Nazi, I was a disillusioned one, very much so.'

'I see,' said Harry. 'Well, I'll take myself up to my desk now, and type up some of my notes.'

'For a novel?' said Anneliese.

'For some kind of plot,' said Harry.

Anneliese felt her apartment was a little too quiet after he'd gone. Such a human man was very pleasant company.

Later, she collected her jewellery from Mr Morrison, together with his written valuation, which told her that the whole was well worth insuring. She paid him his one per cent fee, thanking him for his service. He was courteous and kind in his manner, yet she felt there was just a little undercurrent that suggested he was not too comfortable, after all, about the fact that she was German. It was as if he had thought that over.

She supposed she must expect such reactions in some people, especially Jews.

Chapter Twenty-Six

Flossie Cuthbert, invaluable in Polly's kitchen, prepared the Saturday lunch with the visitor in mind. Flossie, nearing thirty now, was happy in her work and, naturally domesticated, she particularly enjoyed cooking. Usually, she served a light lunch for herself and Polly at midday, and dinner for the family in the evenings. She worked from eight in the morning until half past six in the evening, and from eight until two on Saturdays. Her hours were long, but her employers paid her generously. Hers was a labour of love, for she adored Polly and the twins, and had a crush on Boots.

It meant that Polly's only real kitchen work on weekdays was to attend to the washing-up of the dinner things. Boots helped her with that and so, occasionally, did the twins. It was on Saturday evenings and every Sunday that Polly's limited talents as a cook were tested, but Boots and the twins kept their peace about such things as the occasional burnt offerings. Polly was too entertaining as a wife, and too endearing as a mother, for husband or twins to suggest she should attend cookery classes.

Having consulted with Flossie about the Saturday lunch, Polly agreed that an oxtail casserole, a hot and succulent winter dish, followed by apple turnovers and custard sauce, would surely be to the visitor's liking. Flossie secured the off-ration oxtail from the butcher.

Mr Duncan arrived punctually at noon. Middle-aged, bespectacled and dressed in sober grey, he looked typical of his profession. However, his demeanour was pleasant, and on being introduced to Polly, he gave her an old-fashioned bow in acknowledgement of her sex and elegance.

With the twins out for the day, Boots served aperitifs in the lounge that provided a view of the well-kept garden. He and Polly, both capable of creating the right kind of atmosphere, encouraged the solicitor to talk about the reason for his visit.

'Ah, yes, a long story, according to all that I heard from Herr Meister, the German lawyer,' said Mr Duncan, and began to explain in detail. When Herr Lansberg, the husband of Elsie Chivers, died sometime after the end of the Great War, his will showed he had left everything to her. How wise she had been to ask the executors to appoint an administrator for the estate, particularly as the latter turned out to be a man both honest and efficient.

There came the time when Herr Lansberg's widow, the late Elsie Chivers, disappeared. Every effort was made to trace her during the years up to the beginning of the Second World War, the executors resisting the attempts of the local Gauleiter to claim the estate for the benefit of the Nazi Party when Hitler came to power.

'That, according to Herr Meister, meant for the benefit of the Gauleiter and his family,' said Mr Duncan. 'The political corruption of the time—'

'I beg we won't discuss politics,' said Polly, but with a sweet smile.

'Quite so,' said Mr Duncan, and resumed his account of all that Herr Meister had told him. The circumstances of the Second World War brought inquiries to an end. The administrator, however, continued to run the estate and its farm, although his workforce was gradually reduced to women and elderly men. Everything suffered badly during the last year of the conflict. A thousand boots every day trod and trampled the fields, the farm, and every floor of the grand house and outbuildings. First German boots, and then Russian. Livestock had been slaughtered. To make matters worse, the Russian advance into Germany resulted in foreign slave workers escaping the shackles of German factories, and these starving and desperate people had swarmed over the estate.

However, the administrator, then fifty years old and still conscientious, began the post-war work of pulling the estate together with the aid of new and old workers, although occupation of the zone by the Russians did not make things too easy.

'Herr Meister was sorry to hear—' Mr Duncan was interrupted by the sound of the lunch gong, or rather, by Flossie beating a frying pan with a large spoon. Polly did not believe in gongs. They belonged, she always said, to great houses or grand mansions. Anywhere else, they were pretentious affectations. Polly had no affectations herself, and if some people thought her upper-class voice was a sign of snootiness, that was their mistake. She was always quite happy to have Flossie shout from the kitchen, 'Dinner's coming up, Mrs Adams.'

But Flossie had said that as the visitor was a professional gent, she wasn't going to shout, that there ought to be a gong. Polly said she was certainly not going to buy one, and that Flossie could simply show herself and announce lunch. No, it ought to be a gong, insisted Flossie.

Hence the metallic sound of a large spoon thumping a frying pan.

It made Polly roll her eyes. It made Boots smile.

'I think lunch is ready, Mr Duncan,' said Polly. She was at her best in her styled coiffure and a ruby dress fastened at the neck with a silver brooch. She was becoming sensitive about what her years – fifty-seven of them – might be doing to her slim neck.

Flossie, in a white lace-edged front over a navy blue dress, began serving as soon as they were all seated. She started with toasted shrimps in a creamy fish sauce. Imaginative menus often made Boots think of the plain but nourishing meals Chinese Lady had served up in his young days. Starters were an unknown factor among Walworth families then, and would, in any case, have been an unaffordable luxury.

Mr Duncan, enjoying the shrimps, returned to the subject in hand.

'Did both of you know Miss Chivers?' he asked.

'My husband alone had the pleasure,' said Polly.

Mr Duncan said that Herr Meister, acting for the estate's executors, had been sorry to hear that Frau Lansberg had died. As her late husband's lawyer, he had met her several times, and found her a natural gentlewoman. Her death meant it was her own will that was now the main legal factor.

At which point, Flossie, forgetting herself, reverted to custom and called from the kitchen.

'Casserole coming up, Mrs Adams.'

In she came with the steaming cauldron. Mr Duncan caught the aroma and it made a happy man of him.

Over this main course, Mr Duncan said that some years after the war, when the estate was in far better order, the executors had renewed their attempts to locate Miss Chivers. While these attempts were unsuccessful, they did at least discover from a reliable source that she had returned to England as long ago as the 1920s. So a notice of inquiry was placed in English newspapers concerning the present whereabouts of Frau Elsie Lansberg, formerly Elsie Chivers of Walworth, London.

'The advertisement was brought to my attention, Mr Adams, and I replied to it.'

'And that brought you into contact with the German lawyer?' said Boots.

'Indeed it did, Mr Adams, and I was the first to notify Herr Meister of the fact that the unfortunate lady had died nine years ago. I was also able to tell him that by the terms of her will, everything she owned was left to you. He then requested me to let you know what this meant.'

'Exactly what does it mean?' asked Boots, and Polly thought he was hardly an example of excited anticipation. But then, when had he ever departed from his casual and whimsical self? Well, yes, there had been occasions, but this wasn't one of them.

'Yes, do tell,' she said, 'I'm all agog myself.'

'Mr Adams,' said Mr Duncan, 'by the aforesaid terms, you are now the owner of the late Herr Lansberg's estate near Altenburg, south of Leipzig.

The area, I understand, is predominantly agricultural, and the estate comprises a large amount of parkland, a working farm, a mansion and an excellent bank balance. Herr Meister wishes you to know you have much to thank the executors and the administrator for. They have persisted in carrying out their obligations through many difficult years. The whole estate is now yours.'

'I'm staggered,' said Boots. You don't look it, old turnip, thought Polly. 'What exactly does all this amount to?' asked Boots.

'The executors have calculated that the present worth of the estate is, in sterling, one hundred thousand pounds minimum,' said Mr Duncan.

Polly emitted a soft whistle.

'Good God,' said Boots, and thought of Elsie Chivers and the mere three hundred pounds she had in the bank at the time of her death. And just prior to her death, when he was with her, she had said not one word about her late husband's estate or his will. It had been totally out of her mind. She had been haunted by the worst moments of her past, by the murder of her mother and the fact that she had thrown in her lot with Edwin Finch, a German espionage agent at the time.

'I'm sure, of course, that you need to think about the matter,' said Mr Duncan, 'but at this moment, do you feel you might wish to take over the estate?'

'It's in the Russian zone?' said Polly.

'That, perhaps, is not the best of circumstances,' said Mr Duncan, whose enjoyment of the meal was not distracting him from the subject in hand. 'But I understand there's no serious interference with private life.'

'Even so,' said Polly, 'any attempt by my husband to put himself within a hundred miles of a Russian-occupied sector of Germany will be met with all the force at my command. Cricket bats, iron pokers and garden forks. Ye gods, when I think of what the Russians do and have done to each other, and to other people, I tell myself the Red Terror of Bolshevism is still alive and kicking. Boots, you may have inherited an estate in Germany, but you're certainly not going there.'

'We'll discuss,' said Boots.

'Herr Meister, I'm sure, will be happy for you to think it over,' said Mr Duncan, 'although he would like to know how you intend to act before he returns to Altenburg next week. That is, whether you'll take the estate over or give instructions to sell it, when, of course, the proceeds would be yours, less what expenses will have been incurred up to the day of the sale.'

'Well, let's leave it at that until Monday,' said Boots, 'by which time my wife and I will have come to a decision. I'll then phone you.'

'Excellent,' said Mr Duncan, and from then on the lunch proceeded more informally to its finish. The solicitor, when leaving, thanked Polly and Boots for their hospitality, and asked for his compliments to be given to the cook.

'Well, dear old sport,' said Polly, when she and Boots were doing the washing-up, Flossie having departed, 'what are you going to tell me?'

'About this will?' said Boots. 'In the first place do I want such a bequest, one that originated from a man who'll only ever be a phantom figure to me?'

'But in the second place,' said Polly, 'it's come directly to you from Elsie Chivers. In the third place, since I'll never allow you to go anywhere near the estate, you must consider selling it.'

'Do we need the money?' mused Boots, drying the dishes Polly was passing to him.

'I don't,' said Polly. 'There's nothing I want that I don't already have – no, wait. Yes, except a washing-up machine. Haven't I read that Americans already have them?'

'I think they call them dishwashers,' said Boots.

'I don't care what they're called,' said Polly. 'Tell Sammy to import some and to mark one down for us. Now, what were you going to say about this prospective windfall?'

'I'm thinking of the administrator, the man who kept everything going all through the Thirties and the war, and has put the estate back into working order,' said Boots. 'He deserves to have it far more than I do.'

'Flying cuckoos,' said Polly, 'I wasn't suggesting you should give it away.'

'There's some serious thinking to be done,' said Boots.

'Well, keep me informed, old love,' said Polly.

Later, they were in the garden, the day being crisp and bright after the rain of yesterday. In the vegetable plot at the top of the garden, Polly's now famous runner beans were looking tired, foliage drooping and remaining beans hardening.

'Winter's coming,' she murmured.

'Is it coming to us?' asked Boots.

'To us?' said Polly. 'What d'you mean?'

'We're on the way to sixty, Polly,' said Boots.

'God, don't remind me of that frightful prospect,' said Polly. 'I never wanted to be forty, even less did I want to be fifty, and sixty I regard with horror.'

'Be of good cheer, dear girl, you won't look it, yours is the secret of the eternal flapper,' smiled Boots. 'All the same, the old order's changing, Polly, and the younger ones are coming into their own.'

'Our younger ones?' said Polly.

'The twins?' said Boots. 'No, not their generation. I mean Daniel and Patsy, Tim and Felicity, Edward and Leah, Emma and Jonathan, Paul and Lulu –'

'Don't list them all,' said Polly, 'it's too overwhelming. Great fires of London, you're not talking about retiring, are you?'

'Not a bit,' said Boots, and put an arm around her shoulders as they traversed the garden paths. 'But Tim, Daniel and Paul are playing progressively more important parts at the offices, and Sammy's delegating.'

'Sammy?' said Polly.

'His major interest is our fashions side,' said Boots, 'although he's keeping an eye on what's happening about the prospective supermarket. Even so, he's handed all negotiations over to Tim and Daniel. Only two days ago, when we were having a pub lunch together, he said that when our lot retired—'

'Our lot?'

'Tommy, me and himself. That when that happened, we could rest easy about the future of the business, that it'll belong to our sons and daughters, our nieces and nephews.'

'Good grief,' said Polly, 'is Sammy's electric circuit wearing out?'

'Not yet,' said Boots, 'and he'll still be keeping an eye on the overheads when he's ninety. Did I mention the supermarket?'

'Yes, and that Tim and Daniel are handling all the negotiations,' said Polly.

'Well, as you know,' said Boots, 'we think the cost is going to be prohibitive. We could give our ready capital a boost of, say, fifty thousand pounds.'

'Fifty thousand?' said Polly. 'And from where is that to come, old clever clogs?'

'From the sale of this German estate,' said Boots. 'When I phone Mr Duncan on Monday I'll ask him if the administrator would like to buy it himself, and if so could he raise fifty thousand pounds to do so.'

'But it's worth a minimum of a hundred thousand,' said Polly.

'That's where the administrator would get his deserved reward,' said Boots.

'But could he raise fifty thousand?' asked Polly.

'Any bank would loan him the money if it meant he would have the estate as his security,' said Boots.

'Well, you old darling,' said Polly, 'you're a Samaritan and a smartypants all rolled into one.'

'Smartypants?' Boots laughed. 'You've been listening to Patsy.'

'Yes, isn't she a sweetie?' said Polly.

Chapter Twenty-Seven

Chinese Lady and Sir Edwin drove to Woldingham
to have lunch with Rosie, Matthew, Emma,
Jonathan and their children. It might have been a
roast chicken lunch, but wasn't, for the poultry farm
partnership had gone well beyond dining on their
hens. Rosie served what she knew was a favourite
with her grandparents, sweet lamb chops.

How healthy Rosie looked, thought Chinese
Lady, her complexion coloured to golden-brown by
the open air. And at thirty-eight, she was still a
beautiful woman, with a never-changing love of life
and family. The whole family, not just her own. It
was no wonder Boots had a special affection for his
adopted daughter, right from the time when, as a
lonely little girl of five, neglected by her selfish
mother, she had longed to be loved and cared for.

However, Chinese Lady could hardly believe her
ears when Rosie, during some talk about Emma and
Jonathan leaving, said a West Indian couple were
going to take their places.

'West Indians, Rosie?'

'Immigrants from the West Indies, Grandma,'
smiled Rosie.

'Well, I can't hardly believe it,' said Chinese Lady.

'Don't they grow bananas out there? And coconuts and things?'

'Whatever they grow, Maisie,' said Sir Edwin, 'it doesn't pay very well. So there's a steady trickle arriving here in the hope of finding a better life.'

'Our winters might be hard on them,' observed Jonathan.

'Oh, Mr and Mrs Robinson looked to me as if snow would make them laugh,' said Emma.

'It doesn't make the hens laugh,' said Jonathan, 'they can't get at the worms. Durned if they don't sulk.'

'And sulky birds don't lay so well,' said Matt.

'And don't make snowballs, either,' said eleven-year-old Giles, dark like his father.

'Well, I must ask, Rosie,' said Chinese Lady, 'could people that grow bananas look after chickens?'

'The Robinsons can, Grandma,' said Rosie, 'they've brought up chickens of their own all their lives.'

'And perhaps the occasional banana,' said Matt, winking at ten-year-old Emily.

'Mummy, could they grow some for us?' asked Emily. 'I like bananas.'

'I like shrimps and winkles, like Grandma gives us when we have Sunday tea with her and Grandpa,' said Giles.

'Bless the boy,' said Chinese Lady, then added dubiously, 'I just don't know about West Indians, Matthew.'

'About whether they'd like shrimps and winkles?' smiled Matt.

'Oh, I was hardly thinking of inviting them to

Sunday tea,' said Chinese Lady, 'it's always a family thing.'

'What's a family thing, Mummy?' asked Jessie, nearly seven.

'A little get-together of mums, dads, kiddies and grandparents, like this,' said Emma.

'The cock's crowing,' said Giles importantly. In the beamed dining room of the farmhouse, the sound of the strutting bird was clearly heard.

'What's it making that noise for?' asked Chinese Lady, a townie all her life.

'Grandma, it's telling us some of the hens have laid,' said Emily. 'Well, that's what I always think.'

'Lord,' said Chinese Lady, 'what chickens can do, would you believe.'

'Amazing,' smiled Sir Edwin.

When he and Chinese Lady departed for home sometime after lunch, Rosie and Matt presented them with a dressed chicken and a box containing new-laid eggs. Chinese Lady said she didn't know how to thank them.

'Grandma dear,' said Rosie, 'take them home with our love.'

On the way, Chinese Lady referred to the West Indians who were going to take the place of Emma and Jonathan. Did Edwin feel it would be safe?

'Safe, Maisie?'

'Well, I mean, won't black people be a bit frightening to Giles and Emily?'

'Only if they practise voodoo,' said Sir Edwin.

'Lord above,' breathed Chinese Lady, 'what's whodo?'

'Voodoo.'

'Yes, what's that?'

'A witch doctor's ritual.'

'Edwin, are you trying to give me palpitations?' asked Chinese Lady as they motored into Warlingham, from where the urban development of outer London began.

'I trust not, Maisie. I don't think the country is importing witch doctors. Be assured of that.'

'I just don't know,' said Chinese Lady, shaking her head, 'I just don't know.'

Sir Edwin smiled. The world was becoming wide open, but to his Victorian-born wife it would always remain happily unknown, apart from her awareness that it was full of foreigners. In any case, it was her steadfast belief that nothing of interest or importance ever happened outside the United Kingdom. Of course, there were exceptional occasions, but these only produced people who should never have been born, like Lenin the Bolshevik and Hitler the Hun.

'Edwin, we'll have a nice cup of tea when we get home,' she said.

'As ever, Maisie, I look forward to it,' said Sir Edwin, who always considered he had made the best moves of his life in defecting to Britain and in marrying this Walworth-born woman of unchanging values and fixed beliefs. Gibraltar was no firmer rock than Boots's resolute mother.

That evening, Anneliese took a bus to the West End's theatreland to see a highly popular American musical, *South Pacific*, starring Mary Martin. Anneliese was a serious theatre-goer in the main, but she'd lately felt in the mood for something totally light-hearted. She was thawing out, she knew that. The reason, she supposed, was this total change of country and environment, this quite stimulating existence among the down-to-earth people of South London. It represented an almost intoxicating release from all that she had hated since the time when she first began to realize Himmler was a monster, that there were no heroes in his SS, only subordinate monsters.

The thawing-out had begun on the day Colonel Lucas had shown her the Old Vic Theatre. That had been an adventure, an excitement. Now the thawing-out process was being hastened by her days in the house of Harry Stevens and Cindy, two people who, however hard up they were, owned a natural kindness and lived their lives as if each day was a happy harbinger of the next.

She could often hear them. They never closed doors.

'Daddy, for goodness' sake, you'll lose your head next.'

'Well, I need a new one, anyway.'

'I think Miss Finney likes your old one best.'

'I'll stick with what I've got, then, if that'll make her happy.'

Who was Miss Finney? Mr Stevens's lady friend? Well, as a very pleasant man he would appeal to more than one kind of woman. He had said he came from a small market town in Oxfordshire. Oxfordshire. He would know Oxford.

She would love to see that ancient university city one day.

Clare was staying with Jimmy and his family for the weekend, so that evening he took her to the cinema to see a Cary Grant movie. They enjoyed it and when they left, Jimmy asked Clare if she fancied some fish and chips.

'Crikey, not half,' said Clare.

So he took her to the fried-fish shop, where she asked for plaice and chips, and he had rock salmon and chips. They put salt and vinegar on, and ate the repast out of the newspaper wrapping while strolling to the bus stop near Camberwell Green. Clare, a born cockney, thought it simply great, eating fish and chips with Jimmy. It showed that as the boss's son, he didn't have any side.

Later, on the bus taking them to his home, she said how much she'd enjoyed the evening, that the film had been great, especially as she had a bit of a crush on Cary Grant. Jimmy asked if he was second best to that suave Hollywood star.

'No, course not,' said Clare. 'You're me best bloke ever, Jimmy.'

'I'm chuffed, then,' said Jimmy. 'Tell me, is your bottom drawer full up yet?'

'Well, I don't know,' breathed Clare, 'd'you think I'm going to talk about me bottom drawer on a bus?'

'What about a whisper or two?' asked Jimmy.

'I should say not,' said Clare, 'and, anyway, I'm not supposed to talk about it to me intended.'

'Who's he?' asked Jimmy.

'Stop asking daft questions,' said Clare.

'You can still whisper if your bottom drawer's full up yet,' said Jimmy.

'Well, if you must know,' whispered Clare, 'I've started a second.'

'With frillies?' whispered Jimmy.

'Jimmy, you're thinking sexy.'

'Well, it's a nice change from thinking about old Mother Hubbard and her forty kids,' said Jimmy.

It was late when they reached his home, so late that Susie, Sammy and Phoebe were all abed. So the young lovers had the lounge and its sumptuous settee to themselves. So, of course, they kissed like lovers, which sent Clare dizzy. Caresses followed, exciting her. Oh, I'll go under in a minute, she thought. But she stayed afloat, although only just.

'Oh, help – Jimmy, me dress – me blushes.'

'I can see your dress, I can't see any blushes,' said Jimmy.

Clare issued another protest.

'Oh, look at me legs!'

'I am looking,' said Jimmy happily. 'Permission to tell you they're sexy?'

'Sexy?' said Clare, tugging at her dress. 'Me legs? Are they really?'

'Totally,' said Jimmy, 'let's have another look.'

'Jimmy!'

Still, it wasn't actually too blushmaking, and as always whenever she had a date with Jimmy, she was wearing her very best nylons, and when a girl had legs as good-looking as hers, she didn't want them to go unnoticed by her best bloke ever.

Kisses became very disturbing.

'You darling,' said Jimmy, breaking off.

'Jimmy, oh, Lor', you're making me feel I want to take all me clothes off,' gasped Clare.

'Wow,' said Jimmy, 'is that what fish and chips do to you?'

'No, it's what you're doing to me right now,' said Clare. 'Jimmy, if we don't stop I'll get to be a fallen woman.'

Jimmy clapped a hand over his mouth to muffle a shout of laughter. He knew Clare regarded herself as modern, and to hear her say something that belonged to a Victorian melodrama was a yell.

'All right, Clare love,' he said, 'we'll go up to bed now.'

'Yes, we'd best,' said Clare, rearranging her dress.

'Yours or mine?' said Jimmy, straight of face.

'What? Yours or mine? Oh, you're wicked.'

'You're sexy,' said Jimmy, 'and that's my problem as the son of my Christian mother.'

'But is it a nice problem?' asked Clare.

'I tell you one thing, you darling,' said Jimmy, 'I don't want to let go of it.'

'Jimmy, I like being in love.'

'So do I,' said Jimmy, 'especially with you, Clare.'

They went up to their rooms then in the quiet of the house, leaving the dangerous moment to commit suicide on the settee. Well, in a manner of speaking, as it were.

Anneliese arrived back from her theatre visit at eleven. Cindy was in bed, but lights were on, and as she climbed the stairs she heard the faint clicking sound of Mr Stevens's typewriter. She guessed he was lost in another creative spell. She smiled to herself, and continued her ascent. His workroom door was open.

'Mr Stevens?'

'Hello there?'

She entered the room. He was seated at his desk in just an open-necked white shirt and dark blue trousers, pullover on the floor, as if a thing of unimportance. But he looked like a man comfortable with himself and with life.

'You're still working, Mr Stevens?'

'Got to, y'know,' said Harry. 'Have to earn a regular crust for Cindy and myself.'

'May I ask what you're writing?'

'Frankly, I'm not sure,' said Harry. 'That is, I'm not sure if it's going to be another short story or my first attempt at a novel. Accordingly, you're looking at a mixed-up bloke. It's about two people who meet on a night train from London to Scotland. A man and a woman. He's a psychopath and so is she, but neither knows it of the other. She's a beauty and he's a charmer. She decides she's going to kill him with a long sharp knife before the train reaches Edinburgh. He makes up his mind he's going to strangle her and chuck her body out of the window. They have a compartment to themselves, d'you see?'

'*Wunderbar!*' exclaimed Anneliese in German.

'Eh?' said Harry.

'Thrilling,' said Anneliese.

'D'you think so, Miss Bruck?'

'Surely a plot like that would make a novel as easily as it would a short story,' said Anneliese.

'Perhaps it would if I could spin it out and give the reader cause to gradually suspect the protagonists aren't what they seem to be, an attractive man and a stunning woman getting to know each other,' said Harry. 'Without, of course, suspecting they're psychopaths. As it is, I'm struggling along not sure which it's going to be. What a curse that I can't make up my mind.'

'Throw the short-story idea away,' said Annelise, 'concentrate on creating an exciting novel.'

'What a splendid woman you are,' said Harry, 'what a privilege to have you as a tenant. Did you enjoy the theatre?'

'Very much,' said Anneliese, her light accent fascinating her landlord. 'I'm not a great lover of musicals, but *South Pacific* was a delight.'

'Isn't that the musical that's given us a really rousing song?' said Harry. 'I think it's called "There's Nothing Like a Dame". I've heard it on the radio.'

'Yes, that's the one, Mr Stevens,' smiled Anneliese.

'Well, there's nothing like a woman, either,' said Harry, who might be absent-minded when putting his socks on, but had a clear conviction that a woman could do far more for a man's well-being than a hot-water bottle or a new overcoat. He'd married Pamela, his late wife, in 1935, when he was twenty-two, and in the few years they'd had together before a flying bomb blew her off the face of the earth, he had known only the best aspects of marriage. He wondered what it would do for a man who took this German woman as a wife. Her wealth of fair hair, her expressive blue eyes, her poise and her elegance, all made her a pleasure to behold. He supposed she'd gone to the theatre with an escort. He didn't ask, however. He was curious, yes, but knew it was none of his business. 'Nothing like a woman, either,' he said again, with a smile.

'What does that mean?' asked Anneliese.

'That life can't do without women,' said Harry.

'It can't do without men, either,' said Anneliese. 'That is, some men.' Her eyes darkened.

'Are you thinking there are others, like those of Himmler's SS?' asked Harry.

'Yes, and the fact that there were far too many of them on both sides of the Eastern border,' said Anneliese. 'Goodnight, Mr Stevens.' Those abrupt words accompanied a departure just as abrupt, and Harry heard her go down to her flat. He supposed he shouldn't have mentioned Himmler or the SS. Perhaps her hatred was due to a sickening experience at the hands of some SS drunks. But would even SS drunks have degraded a German army nurse?

Drunken Russian soldiers from the other side of the Eastern border would. The tales of the rape of Berlin girls and women by Stalin's victorious troops were known throughout Europe.

God, he thought, could that have happened to Anneliese Bruck, so proud a woman? The possibility put him off any further writing, and he went to bed after a brief while. But he lay still thinking about her, and it was some time before he fell asleep.

Chapter Twenty-Eight

Sunday morning, early.

Cindy was at the open front door, putting an empty milk bottle on the step, when the curly-haired paperboy arrived with the *Sunday Express*.

'Watcher, Cindy,' he said. He was fourteen, freckled and grinning.

'Oh, it's you, Billy Riddle,' said Cindy, taking the paper from him.

'It's Biddle, if yer don't mind,' said Billy.

'Well, all right, good morning and goodbye,' said Cindy.

'I'm thinking of coming after you, in a couple of years or so,' said Billy. 'You'll be grown a bit by then, and I'll be ready to take yer round the Serpentine on Sundays.'

'Crikey, what a thrill,' said Cindy. 'Hoppit.'

'Wait a bit,' said Billy, 'you heard the latest news?'

'What latest news?' asked Cindy.

'Well, in a Walworth Road pub last night, according to me dad,' said Billy, 'some bloke went up to some other bloke, stared him straight in 'is eyeballs and accused him of being an SS bleeder – excuse me French – that worked at one of them German concentration camps, although me dad said he looked more respectable than our insurance man, which is saying a lot.'

'You're making it up,' said Cindy.

'No, I ain't, me dad told me, and he was there, wasn't he?' said Billy. 'Oh, yus, and then this first bloke chucked 'is glass of beer all over the other bloke. Up he jumped, sort of drowning in beer, and left the pub at a gallop, and the first bloke went after 'im, hollering for the coppers. Talk about lively, me dad said he'd 'ave paid to see it. Well, so long, Cindy, see yer.'

Off he went on his delivery round. Cindy closed the door and returned to the kitchen, where she finished preparing the breakfast of cereal and toast.

She called in clear ringing tones.

'Daddy! Breakfast!'

'I'm here,' said Harry, entering the kitchen in his white shirt and blue trousers. His hair was brushed and he smelled of Pear's soap. Cindy's petite nose twitched. She liked the smell. She gave him a kiss on his fresh-shaven chin.

'Good morning, Daddy.'

'To what do I owe this greeting?' smiled Harry.

'Well, you look nice,' said Cindy, 'and you're going to write a novel and make us rich.' She placed a small jug of milk on the table as Harry sat down. They both liked milk on their rice crispies. 'Oh, there's your Sunday paper. Billy Riddle brought it and said he's going to take me round the Serpentine when I'm older.'

'He'll be older himself by then,' said Harry, 'and a regular terror, so don't go anywhere near the Serpentine with him.'

'D'you know what else he said?'

'No, I wasn't there,' said Harry, as they ate their cereal.

So Cindy told him about the incident in the pub.

'D'you believe it?' she asked.

'It could be true, pet,' said Harry. The Western Powers had been conducting searches for German war criminals since the end of the conflict. It was estimated that thousands had escaped, changing their identities to live inconspicuously in various countries throughout the world. Some had been traced and extradited to face trial. How many remained at large was an unknown quantity.

'You mean the bloke that had beer thrown over him really could have been a German?' said Cindy, who, although she'd been too young during the war to understand what was going on, now knew terrible things had taken place. 'A real German?'

'A German war criminal,' said Harry soberly.

'Crikey, Miss Bruck couldn't be one, could she?' asked Cindy breathlessly.

'That's something I'll never believe,' said Harry. 'She hasn't hidden anything about herself, she frankly admitted she was German, and she looks us straight in the eye. She hates all those Germans who committed atrocities, which you'd expect of a nurse.'

'Well, I think she's nice,' said Cindy, 'but I still don't think we ought to tell people she's German. It's best to say she's French.'

'Have it your way, pet,' said Harry.

A little later, when breakfast had finished, Harry was doing the washing-up like a helpful old dad, and Cindy, inspecting the contents of the larder, was trying to decide what to cook for Sunday dinner.

'Daddy, we've only got some rashers of bacon and some slices of cold ham,' she said. 'But they'd best be eaten. Now, if you were rich we could have a fridge and keep our food in it. And we could always have a roast joint on Sundays.'

'Lord, Cindy love, we are up against it, aren't we?' said Harry. 'But we do have twenty-five bob a week from Miss Bruck, and there aren't many Sundays when we don't have a joint, so we're not that skimped.'

'No, but I'm making sure we've always got shillings in my purse,' said Cindy. 'We've just got to think of the times when I've only been able to scrape farthings out of it.'

Harry smiled. Things had never been as desperate as that, but Cindy could dramatize like a housewife on her beam ends. The main trouble, of course, was the indeterminate time between a payment for one short story and payment for the next. It was those intervals that brought about the scrimping and scraping days, but somehow Cindy always managed to put something on the table and to persuade the shopkeepers to give tick. Cindy was so like her mother, just as caring and industrious. She was also a bright and intelligent girl.

'Well, you've got more than a few farthings at the moment, Cindy.'

'Yes, but when are you going to get paid for your short story?' asked Cindy.

'Well, I've signed the contract, Cindy, for a fee of a hundred pounds –'

'Daddy, you said it might be two hundred.'

'I think I got carried away,' said Harry. 'Anyway, my agent's promised me she'll suck an advance of fifty pounds out of the publishers any moment.'

'Fifty pounds?' said Cindy. 'Bless me socks, Daddy, we will be rich. Well, for a while we will. Can we go to the park this afternoon?'

The October day was pleasant, and quite balmy after a cold and sometimes wet spell.

'Of course, Cindy pet,' said Harry. Cindy loved walking in Ruskin Park, and went there often with a friend or with himself. 'Some fresh air will liven us up, and blow some of my cobwebs away, eh?'

'We might meet that nice man again,' said Cindy. A couple of months ago she'd been in the park with Cecily Chase, her best friend. She'd tripped and sprained her ankle. A young man, out with his girl-friend, came to her assistance. She simply couldn't put her foot to the ground, so he carried her to the casualty department of King's College Hospital, from where Cecily ran to fetch Harry, and it was Harry who carried Cindy home after treatment. Cindy was full of praise for the young man, making him sound heroic.

'Well, yes, he might be there this afternoon,' said Harry.

'What was his name?' asked Cindy. 'He told it to you, didn't he?'

'I think so,' said Harry. 'Yes, I think he did, but blowed if I can remember.'

'Crikey, your brainbox, Dad, it needs dusting,' said Cindy, shaking her head in doleful recognition of his mind always being a bit far away.

'Half a mo,' said Harry. 'Was it Haddon? No, I don't think so. Still, I'll remember it sometime.'

'Yes, when your head's out in the fresh air,' said Cindy.

A little later, she went to see her friend Cecily for an hour, saying she'd be back well in time to do the Sunday dinner. Harry went up to do some writing.

At fifteen minutes to eleven, Anneliese, having heard his typewriter going, knocked on his door.

'Mr Stevens?'

'Ahoy there, Miss Bruck, step in,' said Harry.

In she came, a delight in a turquoise blue New Look dress of shortened length. Shortened lengths made the fashion more acceptable these days. The full-length version was rapidly losing its appeal. Young women now felt it aged their appearance, with which fashion-conscious Sammy Adams fully agreed.

'Good morning, Mr Stevens, so sorry to disturb you,' said Anneliese, 'but I heard Cindy go out some time ago, and as I've just brewed some coffee, I wondered if you would like a cup.'

'Coffee?' said Harry vaguely.

Anneliese smiled.

'It's mid-morning, Mr Stevens.'

'Is it? Yes, I suppose it must be.' Harry, living with the development of his storyline, was time-confused. 'Coffee, did you say? Well, that's an irresistible offer. Thanks very much.'

'I'll fetch it,' said Anneliese, and did, on a tray with a little jug of warm milk and a bowl of sugar. She placed it on his desk.

'You're lighting up my life,' he said.

'I'm sure you don't mean that, Mr Stevens.'

Harry, now clearer of mind, knew that was a

warning note. Don't get too close. Again he thought that perhaps she'd suffered a frightful experience, perhaps the kind that had put her off all men for the rest of her life. It was eight years since the war had ended, but there were still horrors being uncovered.

'Oh, just a little comment, Miss Bruck, to let you know how much I appreciate the coffee,' he said as lightly as he could.

'A little return for your kindness, Mr Stevens,' said Anneliese. 'The day is quite lovely, isn't it? I shall go for a long walk this afternoon.'

'Have you seen our local park?' asked Harry, lightly sugaring his coffee.

'Park?'

'Yes, Ruskin Park. It's a little way past Camberwell Green. It's delightful for a stroll compared to a walk along the main road, especially on a Sunday afternoon. Cindy and I are going there after dinner.'

'Are you?'

'It's Cindy's favourite Sunday pastime.'

'I see.' Anneliese hesitated, then said, 'Perhaps you and Cindy would show me where it is.'

'You'd like to walk there with us?' said Harry.

'Would you mind?'

'Not in the least,' said Harry, 'you'd be very welcome. Say about two this afternoon?'

'Yes, thank you, Mr Stevens.' The thought of an afternoon stroll around a London park had caught hold of Anneliese. She smiled and left Harry to his coffee and his creative hour.

Some while after Cindy was back, Harry joined her in the kitchen and told her that their tenant was going to be with them on their excursion. His daughter's eyes opened wide.

'Well, imagine that,' she breathed.

'It's not a sensation,' said Harry, 'is it?'

'Well, not a sensation, not actually,' said Cindy, who had a bacon, ham and creamed potato pie ready to bake in the oven, with peppered sliced tomatoes on top. It was a recipe of her late mother's, and she was skilled enough to see it through. 'More like – well, a sort of occasion. Daddy, you'll have to put your best suit on.'

'Will I?' said Harry. 'Have I got one?'

'Yes, your grey one,' said Cindy.

'That suit,' said Harry, 'is almost as old as I am.'

'But you still look nice in it,' said Cindy. 'I bet Miss Bruck will look fab, so you've got to look a bit smart yourself. Crikey, fancy her coming with us. Are you thrilled?'

'Cautious,' said Harry.

'Cautious?' said Cindy.

'About her footsteps,' said Harry. 'Suppose she trips and sprains her own ankle? Who's going to carry her to hospital?

Cindy giggled.

'Daddy, you're ever so funny sometimes.'

'There's nothing funny about our lady lodger spraining her ankle in Ruskin Park,' said Harry.

At half past two they were there, in the park, the afternoon balmy with mellow sunshine, the grass moistly green, the paths smooth and tidy, the vista a pleasure to the eye.

Cindy was between Miss Bruck and her dad, her pretty Sunday frock complemented by a round light brown hat, worn only on the Sabbath. Harry was pleasantly attired in his grey suit and a dark grey trilby. Anneliese wore her turquoise blue dress and a summery white hat.

'It really is very nice here,' she said.

'I thought you might like it,' said Harry.

'London has many parks, I believe,' said Anneliese.

'Dozens,' said Harry. 'You've heard of Hyde Park, I imagine.'

'Hyde Park?' said Anneliese. 'Yes, of course, Mr Stevens.'

Bless me, thought Cindy, why are they talking so stuffy?

There were people everywhere, people of all generations. Jimmy Adams was strolling with Clare. The park was a favourite with Clare. Modern she might be, though not as much as Lulu, but she saw her times with Jimmy in this tranquil environment as romantic. They strolled hand in hand, Clare thinking she'd nearly lost her head on the settee last night.

'How are the girls treating you now?' asked Jimmy. He'd come to suspect there were occasions when they gave Clare a hard time. She had never said so, nor would she, so the question gave her pause for thought.

'Oh, they're all right, Jimmy,' she said, 'I get on fine with them. Except –' She emitted a little laugh.

'Except what?' said Jimmy.

'Well, I think they'd all like to marry you, so –'

'All of 'em?' said Jimmy. 'I'm in line for a harem? I don't think my mother would stand for that, and I know Grandma Finch wouldn't. Of course, if it did

302

come to pass, as they say, you'd be my number one.'

'Oh, honoured, I'm sure,' said Clare. 'I was going to say that because they'd all like to marry you, they're a bit jealous of me. But they're all right, honest.'

Three people were approaching, a very attractive woman, an easy-limbed man and a young girl.

'Daddy, look,' exclaimed the young girl, 'there he is, the nice young man.'

'So it is,' said Harry. 'At least, I think it is.'

They met on the path, the young couple and the threesome.

'Hello, mister,' said Cindy.

Everyone stopped.

'Hello,' said Jimmy.

'Don't you remember me?' said Cindy, never backward. 'That time I sprained my ankle?'

'Well, well,' smiled Jimmy, 'so there you are again.' He looked at Harry, remembering him as the girl's father. Harry smiled. 'How is she these days, Mr Stevens?'

'Cindy? Lively as a jumping bean,' said Harry.

'And yourself and your wife?' said Jimmy, always inclined to be friendly.

'Pardon?' said Harry. 'Oh, this lady is Miss Bruck, renting a flat in my house, and Cindy and I are introducing her to the park.' He remembered the young man's name then. 'Miss Bruck, this is Mr Adams. He came to Cindy's rescue when she sprained her ankle here a couple of months ago.'

'Then it's a pleasure to meet you, Mr Adams,' said Anneliese.

'Meet my fiancée as well,' said Jimmy. 'Clare Roper.'

'Hello,' said Clare, who thought the woman highly posh.

'Hello,' said Anneliese.

A little chat ensued, and then they parted, Harry going on with Cindy and Anneliese.

'Mr Stevens,' said Anneliese after a few moments, 'is Adams a common English name?'

'It's not uncommon,' said Harry.

Anneliese glanced back at the sauntering couple.

'I once nursed a wounded British officer called Adams,' she said. 'It's too much to expect that that young man might be related, isn't it?'

'My own name isn't uncommon,' said Harry, 'but as far as I know I'm only related to family members in Chipping Norton.'

'Miss Bruck,' said Cindy, 'did you really nurse a British soldier?'

'Yes, Cindy, I did,' said Anneliese. 'A fine young man, a badly wounded prisoner of war.'

'Oh, fab,' said Cindy.

'Fab?' said Anneliese, enjoying the park, the sunshine and the balmy afternoon.

'Short for fabulous,' said Harry, conscious of people glancing at the elegant German woman.

'Hardly fabulous, Mr Stevens.'

'You'll have to argue that with Cindy,' said Harry.

'I am not going to argue with anyone on such a peaceful day as this,' said Anneliese, 'and I'm delighted with the park.'

They strolled on.

Chapter Twenty-Nine

The first thing Lulu received when she arrived for her work at the Labour Party's headquarters on Monday morning was two weeks' notice, due, said the constituency agent regretfully, to a new limit on overheads. Lulu responded indignantly, saying it was abominable for the Party to put one of its most faithful activists on the dole. Not only should it not be allowed, but it was totally against every principle of Socialism. The agent said not to get so upset, and Lulu said well, she was upset, very, and that her dad, the local MP, wouldn't like it a bit. Unfortunately, said the agent, her dad was suffering himself from the limitation on expenses, as were all other Labour MPs. Funds were tight, and that was the plain truth.

'Well, the plain truth ought to be measured for a coffin,' said Lulu.

'Now, Lulu, as a first-class copy typist, there's no reason why you can't get a job, say at the Town Hall, or with a private firm.'

'A private firm's capitalist,' said Lulu, 'so if you'll give me time off I'll go down to the Town Hall now.'

'Of course,' said the agent.

So down she went to the Town Hall on the corner of Larcom Street, only to be advised to apply again in six months' time. Meanwhile, they would put her name on a list and get in touch with her if a post fell vacant before then.

Lulu was left with having to tell Paul she'd be out of work in two weeks. If he said never mind, Lulu love, go on the dole until you get fixed up, she'd hit him.

Two engineers from the GPO called at Harry's house at nine thirty, and Harry introduced them to the applicant, Miss Bruck. Anneliese was asked to sign documents before the men began work. She did so, and they said how lucky she was that an established telegraph pole was only a short distance away on this side of the road. It meant that with a bit more luck the phone would be in place by tomorrow.

'Well, thank you,' said Anneliese, 'that will be excellent.'

'Our pleasure, miss,' said one man. 'I'm George, and me mate's Dave. He'd like to ask you a question.'

'Yes?' said Anneliese.

'Any tea going, miss?' said Dave.

That was Anneliese's first encounter with the tea-drinking British working man and trade unionist.

Boots phoned Mr Duncan, as promised, and spoke to him about the estate at Altenburg in West Germany. Yes, it could be sold, preferably to the administrator if he could raise fifty thousand pounds.

'I beg your pardon, Mr Adams?'

'My wife and I decided we can't take the estate over ourselves,' said Boots. 'Or, rather, we've no wish to, and we both feel first refusal should be the privilege of the administrator. Does he have a family?'

'Indeed, yes,' said Mr Duncan. 'Herr Meister, during the long conversation I had with him, informed me there was a wife, two daughters and a son.'

'Then perhaps the son might like to step in when his father retires,' said Boots.

'You have thought this over, obviously, Mr Adams,' said Mr Duncan, 'but do you realize that an offer of fifty thousand for an estate worth a minimum of one hundred thousand is hardly fair to yourself?'

'It's fair to the administrator, I hope,' said Boots, 'and I'm suggesting that if he needs a loan for the purchase, his bank would or should gladly give it to him. Will you act for me in this matter, and through Herr Meister? If so, I'd be obliged.'

'Mr Adams, it will be a pleasure,' said Mr Duncan. 'I'm to take it that your decision to sell at fifty thousand is firm and definite?'

'Irrevocable,' said Boots, smiling to himself. Polly had used that word. My decision is irrevocable, she had said, and so is yours, old top, or I'll refuse to let Flossie iron your shirts. 'Yes, it has to be sold, Mr Duncan, to the administrator.'

'Very well, Mr Adams.'

'Sammy?'

'I'm all ears, old mate,' said Sammy, looking up from his desk.

'Regarding the capital needed for constructing and equipping the proposed supermarket,' said Boots.

'Listen,' said Sammy, 'I ain't too fond of my own

brother reminding me of what's going to be a shocking pain to me. I was telling Susie that what we might have to lay out could be so hurtful I'll need an anna-something.'

'Anaesthetic?' said Boots.

'That's it,' said Sammy. 'I admire you for being able to say it, but could you spell it as well?'

'Yes, if asked,' said Boots.

'Monday's my day for asking daft questions,' said Sammy. 'All right, say what you've got to about capital for the supermarket.'

'It's a long story, but I'll cut it to the bone,' said Boots, and put Sammy in the picture about Elsie Chivers's will and her German husband's will. Then he spoke of how he would end up with fifty thousand pounds. 'That, Sammy, can be added to what we can raise from the firm.'

'I'm dreaming,' said Sammy.

'It was fairly unbelievable to me at the time, Sammy.'

'You'll invest fifty thousand?' said Sammy.

'Why not?'

Sammy mused.

'Poor old Elsie Chivers,' he said, 'how did she come to marry a German geezer?'

'One of those things, Sammy,' said Boots guardedly. 'Everything was all over the place at the end of the Great War.'

'D'you remember the murder trial?' said Sammy.

'I do my best not to remember,' said Boots.

'But you did your stuff, chum,' said Sammy. 'It strikes me, if you don't mind me saying so, that you must have been the bloke Elsie most fancied, or she wouldn't have left everything to you.'

'She was years older than me, Sammy.'

'Boots, you can never tell with women.'

'True, Sammy, you can't.'

'They're not like us, y'know.'

'Let's be thankful for that,' said Boots, and went to tell Tim and Daniel of the unexpected windfall that would add to the capital available for the supermarket project. They were delighted. Tim, however, echoed Sammy's assumption.

'The lady must have fancied you, Dad.'

'Answer your phone,' said Boots, and left before anything more could be wormed out of him.

Elsie Chivers and his memories of her were his own and always likely to remain so, as were certain things he knew about his stepfather.

Failing identification of the three murdered men, Scotland Yard was unable to make headway. A halt was called to the investigation, and all notes were filed along with other unsolved cases. The Yard, in effect, was throwing the case at the Soviet Press Bureau, since the investigating officers were convinced that the three victims were the Bureau's own men, despite denials.

The head of the Bureau, Kersch, was presently on his way back to Moscow to face interrogation. Katje Galicia and her son were enjoying life in Vermont, USA, and Sir Edwin Finch was an untroubled man.

'Paul?'

'Hi, Lulu,' said Paul, greeting her arrival home with a warm and friendly kiss. 'Excuse my apron, but I'm at the kitchen sink peeling potatoes.'

'Oh, your pleasure, I'm sure,' said Lulu, her spectacles dark with a frown. 'I've had a lousy day myself.'

'Why? Has some weedy Tory creep with only half a mind chucked a bomb at Headquarters?'

'If you're trying to be funny, it won't work,' said Lulu.

'What's up?' asked Paul.

'I've been given two weeks' notice.'

'Eh? What?'

'I'm glad you find it hard to believe,' said Lulu. 'I'm livid with incredulity.'

'It does seem rotten,' said Paul, 'you've always been a great worker.'

'Two of us are having to go,' said Lulu.

'That's hard luck for both of you,' said Paul. But he wasn't surprised. He'd always thought Headquarters overstaffed, that its paid employees did more talking than working. Of course, their political enthusiasm inspired their heady discussions, but someone had probably taken note. And Lulu, as far as he knew, had been last in and accordingly first to go, even if her dad was the constituency's MP. Also, she was often prime mover in a talking bout. 'Well, cheer up, Lulu. You'll—'

'Don't tell me to cheer up,' said Lulu. 'It's infantile. We need what I earn.'

'We can manage,' said Paul.

'Well, you can speak, of course, from a platform of self-satisfaction,' said Lulu.

'Hold on,' said Paul, 'it wasn't me that fired you. Lulu, what's happened to your fighting self? You're sagging. Stand up straight and put your chest out. You've got the kind of chest that looks proud and happy when it's standing out, and I should know.'

'That's it, kill me with funnies,' said Lulu.

'You'll soon get another job,' said Paul. 'Tell you what, I'll talk to Uncle Sammy. The business has any amount of employees and varied work. Shop manageresses, shop assistants, factory hands, typists, shorthand typists, lady bookkeepers – Sammy's daughter Phoebe has just started in our bookkeeping department – machinists, telephone girls—'

'Stop,' commanded Lulu.

'What for?' asked Paul.

'Your family firm is a typical example of expanding capitalism,' said Lulu. 'Believe me, the last thing I'll ever do is betray my Socialist principles by working for that kind of outfit.'

'Lulu, be practical,' said Paul. 'Private enterprise can live side by side with Socialism, and it's never going to be nationalized, unless the electorate votes the Communist Party and the *Daily Worker* into power.'

'Shut up,' said Lulu.

'Lulu, you've asked for this,' said Paul. He swooped, placed one arm around her back, and the other arm behind her knees. He lifted her. Lulu kicked and yelled. 'Quiet,' said Paul, 'think of the neighbours.' He carried her into the living room, sat down on the settee, turned her struggling body over and laid her face down across his knees.

Lulu kicked.

'You wouldn't dare!' she gasped.

Paul administered a smack on her bottom. It wasn't much more than a playful smack, but Lulu yelled that she'd kill him.

'Next time,' said Paul, 'it'll be a dozen smacks instead of only one.'

Lulu rolled off his lap onto the floor, hair tumbling, glasses slipping, skirt any-old-how and eyes smouldering. She looked up at him.

'You swine,' she said.

'I know,' said Paul, 'when's the divorce going to happen?'

'You mean when do I chop your big fat head off,' said Lulu, straightening her glasses. 'Listen, King Kong, when d'you think your dad could find me a typist's job?'

'Lulu?'

'Well, all right, I've got to have some job,' said Lulu. 'To help with the outgoings. Otherwise we wouldn't be equal.'

Paul laughed and joined her on the carpet.

'Come here, Mrs Equal,' he said, loosening her skirt.

'Oh, my God, no, not on the carpet,' gasped Lulu.

'There's a first time for everything,' said Paul.

'Well, for God's sake, take that silly apron off, then,' said Lulu.

Paul had a word with his Uncle Sammy at the offices the next morning.

'Stone the crows,' said Sammy, 'Lulu's got the sack and wants a job here?'

'That's it, Uncle Sammy,' said Paul.

'Well, she's family, of course,' said Sammy, 'but is she still a red-hot Socialist?'

'I can't tell a porkie, Uncle Sammy, she's heart and soul for the Labour Party,' said Paul. 'But she's

312

a conscientious worker, and won't let her politics interfere with the job.'

'I've got to be sure of that,' said Sammy. 'I don't want to come in one morning and find all me staff singing "The Red Flag" and asking to form a trade union. I'm not against trade unions, except I don't want one walking about in these offices.'

'I promise you,' said Paul.

'You're on top of Lulu, are you, me lad?'

Paul coughed.

'Could you rephrase that, Uncle Sammy?'

'I mean, who's wearing the trousers?'

'Well, I'll be frank,' said Paul, 'it's been a struggle, a long one, but I can now confidently say I'm in command.'

'Sounds all right,' said Sammy, 'but Lulu might just be lying low. As I mentioned to your Uncle Boots yesterday, women ain't the same as men. You've got to watch them and their funny ideas about who's in charge. I should know. Still, as I said, Lulu's family, so I'll tell you what I'll do, I'll give her a job doing some typing for the property company and helping out in the shop the rest of the time. How's that?'

'Good on you, Uncle Sammy, I'll tell her.'

'And tell her if she'll go to evening classes and learn shorthand, I'll promote her.'

'Right,' said Paul.

'What?' asked Lulu that evening. 'Help out in the shop when I'm not typing, and go to evening classes?'

'You'll get to be a first-class shorthand typist,' said Paul.

313

'No, I won't,' said Lulu.

'Yes, you will,' said Paul.

'It'll turn me middle class for sure,' said Lulu. 'It'll scar me for life. Could I endure a fate like that? You know me, so I ask you, could I?'

'Easily,' said Paul, 'you're a tough cookie, Lulu. You might get to feel a bit ill while you're turning middle class, but you'd survive, especially as I'll always be around to nurse you through any illness.'

'You and your funnies,' said Lulu.

'Lulu, d'you know you're getting to look nicer every day?' said Paul with a meaningful smile.

'If you're thinking about that carpet again, forget it,' said Lulu. 'Still, about the job, I'll take it.'

'Good girl,' said Paul. 'Oh, one thing, don't form a trade union, or it'll be Uncle Sammy who'll fall ill.'

Lulu gave him a look. Her spectacles glinted, her mouth twitched and she laughed.

'I think your Uncle Sammy's afraid of modern women,' she said.

'So am I,' said Paul, 'but I'm fighting it.'

Annabelle spoke to her husband.

'Nick, I suppose you realize Philip is getting thick with Phoebe.'

'I realize he's a bit smitten,' said Nick. 'Still, who can blame him? He'd have to go a long way to spot any girl prettier than Phoebe.'

'Nick, they're cousins,' said Annabelle.

'Not first cousins or anything like it,' said Nick, 'they're not really related, except by adoption.'

'All the same –'

'They're young and they're enjoying life,' said

314

Nick. 'Let's leave 'em to it. I sometimes wish we could have our young years all over again. Thinking back, Annabelle, talk about fun and games. What a sexpot you were, and a teasing one as well.'

'Nick Harrison, I was never like that,' said Annabelle. 'Was I?'

'You bet you were,' said Nick. 'I wonder if Philip thinks Phoebe is?'

'Nick, she's only sixteen.'

'I know,' said Nick, 'and Philip's only seventeen. That's what I mean, this is the springtime of their lives, and they're enjoying it.'

'Well, I hope it doesn't go to their heads,' said Annabelle. 'Things are changing, and young people stay out much later at night than we used to, and aren't very modest in their behaviour.'

'Oh, I don't know,' said Nick, 'I can remember—'

'Well, don't,' said Annabelle, 'it might make you talk about it in front of Linda and Philip.'

'There was that time when – let's see, when –' Nick inserted a pause.

'When what?' asked Annabelle.

'I've forgotten,' said Nick.

Chapter Thirty

Time was going by, as time always did.

Much to her satisfaction, Anneliese received an official letter that enabled her to apply directly to the Matron of King's College Hospital for a post. The Matron, formidable in her high majesty but receptive in her interest, examined the German woman's documents, including her work permit, with a keen and discriminating eye, took in verbal details of her extensive experiences as a German army nurse and advised her, at the end of the interview, that there was a post available in casualty. For a nurse who had dealt with wounded soldiers of war, many of them emergency cases, no doubt, casualty would be a suitable beginning, would it not?

'Yes, indeed,' said Anneliese, 'and I'm sure I shan't disapoint you.'

Matron regarded her with eyes that did not lack a human touch. She liked the composure of the woman, her faultless English, and what could only be interpreted as the self-assurance of a very experienced professional.

'I think we can safely say this hospital will be glad to have you, Miss Bruck.'

'I am glad, Matron, to be here,' said Anneliese.

'England was the home of my grandmother.'

'Is that why your English is so good?'

'Yes,' said Anneliese, 'my sister and I are both bilingual.'

'Splendid,' said Matron.

'Mr Stevens?' Anneliese, arriving back from her interview, found her landlord in his kitchen.

'Hello there,' said Harry. His relationship with his tenant was on mutually acceptable terms. While he did not know the exact details of her traumatic times, he understood the obvious, that they had made her disinclined to let people get too close. He and Cindy met up with her occasionally. That is, they bumped into her sometimes, but didn't otherwise make contact with her, even though Cindy was progressively more interested in her.

'Mr Stevens, am I interrupting?' she asked now.

'Not a bit,' said Harry, 'I'm just getting myself a light lunch.'

'Lunch?' said Anneliese. 'Mr Stevens, it's past two thirty.'

'Is it?' said Harry. 'I wondered why I was feeling peckish.'

'I had a light lunch myself at the Camberwell Green teashop, and that was nearly two hours ago, since when I've been shopping,' said Anneliese. 'Mr Stevens, you must take better care of yourself whenever Cindy is at school.'

'Oh, well, ups and downs, and bits and pieces, that's life, Miss Bruck,' said Harry airily.

'You'll get ulcers,' said Anneliese.

'Oh, I grew a tough stomach in the navy,' said Harry.

Anneliese smiled.

'So did our U-boat crews,' she said. 'Mr Stevens, I'm happy to tell you I've secured a post in the casualty department of King's College Hospital.'

'Whacko,' said Harry, 'that's a winner. It's only half a mile from here. Congratulations.'

'Thank you,' said Anneliese. 'I shall be starting on Monday. Day duties. Now I must phone my sister and tell her the news.' Her telephone had been installed. She smiled again. 'I must also leave you to get on with your late lunch.'

That's all very well, thought Harry, as he broke an egg into the hot water of the poaching pan, but what's lunch compared to my feelings? My feelings are the very devil, and doing me no good at all. He made a face at the rapidly poaching egg, then remembered to slip a slice of bread in the toaster.

He was a philosophical man, however, and knowing that nothing could ever come of his feelings, he ate his simple meal of poached egg on toast without letting frustration do a wrecking job on his appetite.

There was always Cindy. At least she'd be with him for six or seven more years, say, before she was married. Could any man have known a more treasured daughter? She'd been born in 1941, on a day when his ship, on convoy duty in the bitter and treacherous waters of the Atlantic, had destroyed a U-boat with a ferocious barrage of depth charges. On periodical home leaves he had come to know his infant daughter, and to appreciate fully the caring qualities of his wife, Pamela, a London girl.

Well, he had lost Pamela, and so Cindy and his writing filled his life. He simply wished he did not have to compete with a million other authors who wrote short stories for magazines. Then perhaps his income would be on a steady basis, not an erratic one.

What was it Cindy had asked him to do before she left for school? He thought. Oh, yes, one of the usual chores. Peel the potatoes and prepare the sprouts. He decided to do that now, before he forgot. Potential plots were forever lurking in his mind, plots that weren't always winners, and rejections still punctured his pride. His agent didn't earn much commission from him, but she stuck with him on the grounds, she said, that one day she was sure he'd come up with an international winner.

He was peeling potatoes when Miss Bruck reappeared.

'Mr Stevens, would you care to share a pot of tea with me?'

'A pot of tea?'

'Freshly brewed,' said Anneliese, and there it was, on a tray, the pot, the cups and saucers, milk, sugar and two small plates, with two slices of fruit cake resting on the top one.

'What can I say, except you're a brick,' said Harry.

'A brick?' said Anneliese.

'A euphemism, meaning a good and kind person.'

'Oh, yes, I think I've heard my English brother-in-law use the word,' said Anneliese, 'but how did that meaning originate?'

'Search me,' said Harry. 'Lost in the mists of a Victorian building site on a foggy day, perhaps. Sit down, Miss Bruck.'

They sat down opposite each other at the kitchen

table, and Anneliese poured the golden tea, with a slice of lemon for herself this time, and milk for Harry. The fruit cake, she said, had been bought at a baker's shop in the main road, and she hoped it would prove eatable. Harry said he knew the baker's shop, and that their bread, cakes and pastries were first-class. He did not, however, say that Cindy baked their own cakes, usually at weekends, and that, accordingly, she didn't allow his hard-earned money to be spent on shop goodies.

As it was, the baker's cake was very good, the tea excellent, and he listened while Anneliese spoke about this new beginning to her life, that of a nurse at the local hospital. Harry thought she was speaking to herself as much as to him, rather as if she was mapping out her future to her satisfaction.

Cindy, arriving home from school, blinked at the sight of her dad and the lady lodger sort of living it up at the kitchen table.

'Oh, hello,' she said.

'Hello, Cindy,' smiled Anneliese, rising. 'Your father and I have been sharing a pot of tea, and I'm just going.'

'Oh, you don't have to go because of me,' said Cindy.

'I must, I have things to do,' said Anneliese, putting cups and saucers back on the tray. She picked up the tray, smiled and said, 'Thank you for your time, Mr Stevens.'

'Oh, the thanks are all mine,' said Harry, and with a smile for Cindy, she departed.

'Well, fancy that, you spending the afternoon in here with her,' said Cindy.

'Not the whole afternoon, just an hour,' said Harry.

'Still, like I told you before, she must like you,' said Cindy.

'It means nothing, pet,' said Harry. 'Oh, by the way, on Monday she's taking up a nursing post in King's College Hospital.'

'Wow,' said Cindy, 'won't she look fab in her uniform?'

'Don't all nurses?' smiled Harry.

'I bet one of the doctors will fall in love with her,' said Cindy.

'Perhaps they all will,' said Harry.

'Crikey, that'll be something,' said Cindy. 'Look, here's a letter for you. I picked it up off the mat. It must've come by the afternoon post, and you didn't notice, of course.'

'Hope I'm not getting old before my time,' said Harry, slitting the envelope and extracting the letter. A cheque fluttered. He looked at it and the letter. His agent had sent him payment of his short-story advance, less ten per cent commission. 'Well, what about this, Cindy, forty-five quid,' he said.

'Crumbs, we're rich!' exclaimed Cindy. 'Well, for a month we are. Just draw out ten pounds at a time.'

'Can you spare me a few bob for myself?' asked Harry.

'I'll see,' said Cindy. She looked at the sink and shook her head. 'Daddy, you haven't finished doing the potatoes and sprouts.'

'Well, d'you see, Miss Bruck invited me to share a pot of tea with her,' said Harry, 'and I didn't feel I should say no.'

'Oh, that's all right,' said Cindy, 'you can invite her back sometime, in her nurse's uniform.'

'We'll see,' said Harry. 'I'll finish the spuds and sprouts now.'

'And I'll do my homework,' said Cindy. 'Daddy, where's that cheque?'

'Here,' said Harry, and searched the table. No cheque.

'Look in your pocket,' said Cindy.

It was in the hip pocket of his trousers, folded. He handed it to Cindy with a grin. She said she'd look after it until tomorrow, when she'd let him have it back so that he could bank it in the morning and draw ten pounds a few days later.

'Very good, m'lady,' said Harry.

'Don't be cheeky,' said Cindy.

Harry ruffled her hair and resumed his appointment with the potatoes and sprouts.

They were very rich by Saturday, because their tenant handed them another month's rent in advance. Harry said a weekly rent would be OK. Anneliese said she was happy to pay month by month, since the apartment was so pleasant and comfortable. Was Mr Stevens happy about that himself?

'Delighted, and so will Cindy be,' said Harry, who had received the money at his desk. She handed him her rent book and he made the entry.

'Thank you,' said Anneliese. 'You have a very sweet daughter, Mr Stevens.'

'Believe me, I know that,' said Harry.

'Are you making progress with your novel?'

'Struggling progress,' said Harry. 'I'm hoping

when I go to bed each night to wake up and find the creative spark of a genius is firing my engine. Then the sweat and struggle will be a thing of the past.'

'Well, I shall try to do you a good turn,' said Anneliese.

'How?' asked Harry.

'Each night when I go to bed myself, I shall pray for that to happen to you,' said Anneliese.

'It could work,' said Harry, 'if you're on speaking terms with the Almighty.'

Anneliese laughed.

Harry was sure the echoes were still floating softly around his typewriter minutes after she'd gone. That was his writer's imagination, of course.

That gave him an idea for another short story. A country house, and a certain room where soft echoes of a lady's laughter were heard at night.

No, corny and done before, many times. Still, perhaps he could give it a new touch.

Meanwhile, it pleased him that his lovely lady tenant was finding it easier to laugh. Possibly, her scars were beginning to heal.

Bobby and Helene were working in his dad's garden, as they did most Saturday mornings. It took the heavier work off Ned's hands, and Lizzy was grateful for that. Ned was having to cope with the problems of his hardening arteries.

The children being in the house with their paternal grandparents, Helene said, 'Bobby, your papa is looking so well.'

'Yes, a lot better,' said Bobby, trimming the edge of the lawn with long-handled shears, 'and I'm delighted for the old lad. He's earned a long and happy retirement. By the way, what're your thoughts on Felicity?'

'Ah, isn't it wonderful that she has these moments when she can detect things?' said Helene, digging up dead runner-bean plants. 'Everyone has much hope for her.'

'Tim's not sure,' said Bobby, then, 'ouch!'

'Bobby?' Helene looked up.

'I think I've just sheared my right foot off.'

'Bobby!'

'No, it's OK,' said Bobby. 'I missed. But it was a close shave.'

Helene lifted her eyes to the sky like a woman asking Someone Above to give her patience.

'It is impossible,' she said.

'What is?' asked Bobby.

'That after all these years you are still an idiot,' said Helene. 'But what did you mean, Tim isn't sure?'

'He's not sure any miracle's going to happen to Felicity,' said Bobby, clipping away. 'He says her moments of vision are always blurred or misty, that she never has a clear sight of anything. She says so herself, but it doesn't stop her thinking she'll see an object clearly one day. Tim thinks it should be happening now. Well, occasionally.'

'Bobby, *chéri*, we must all remain hopeful,' said Helene. 'Without hope, Felicity will get so depressed, yes, and so will Tim.'

'I know they will,' said Bobby soberly.

'Life can be cruel,' said Helene, 'as it was for those poor men murdered in London. How strange that no-one has even identified them, and that the police cannot find the murderers.'

'It's a mystery,' said Bobby, who could have said that in Whitehall the general assumption was that the answer lay with the Soviet Press Bureau, but that the Bureau wouldn't play. 'But my mind's more on Dad and Felicity than who did the deed.'

'We must be positive for both of them, not gloomy,' said Helene.

'I'll follow that line, my French hen.'

'Ah, now you think I'm a bird?'

'Let's say a dolly bird with French feathers.'

'Well, you are a cuckoo, then.'

They laughed at each other.

'Mama! Papa!' Estelle, their daughter, nearly seven, was calling from the kitchen door. 'You've got to come and have coffee now, and you're not to keep Grandma waiting.'

'What a woman,' said Bobby, 'she's giving orders already.'

As Tim and Felicity entered their bedroom that night, Felicity said, 'The light's on. Tim, the light's on.'

'I've just switched it on,' said Tim. 'Are you telling me you can see it? Or what can you see?'

'A glow,' said Felicity.

'Not the light itself?' said Tim.

'No, but a distinct glow,' said Felicity.

'Distinct?' said Tim. 'Do you mean clear?'

'No, not clear and sharp, just a glow, Tim.'

'All the same, that's one more reason for hope,' said Tim, 'so try hanging onto it, as you've tried before.'

Felicity stood quietly for a while, Tim with his arm around her.

'It's fading now,' she said.

Determined not to be discouraging, Tim said, 'It's still one more reason for hope, so keep hanging on, Puss.'

'I'm hanging on every day, Tim,' said Felicity.

'The first time something does come through clear and sharp,' said Tim, 'we'll make an appointment for you to see Sir Charles Morgan again.'

'It won't be long, Tim, I'm sure it won't,' said Felicity.

Chapter Thirty-One

Monday arrived, so did rain and so did a letter for the Adams Property Company Ltd.

Tim opened it, read it, showed it to Daniel, and together they went to see Sammy.

'What's up?' asked Sammy.

'The council's planning committee has turned us down,' said Tim.

'Without even inviting us to a meeting,' said Daniel.

Sammy took the letter, leaned back in his chair and read it. In effect, it said that under no circumstances would the planning committee consider or sanction the proposed supermarket development. Such a development would mean the inevitable closure of all food shops in the neighbourhood, and indeed, many objections had already been officially lodged by shopkeepers. Adams Properties had made their own points in their application, and these had been noted, but the council could not grant permission or entertain an appeal.

'Well, we could go to law, of course,' said Sammy.

'And how much would that cost?' asked Daniel.

'Lawyers' fees in a case like this couldn't be estimated without all of us having fatal fits,' said

327

Sammy. 'So even if we won, what good would that do? We'd all be dead, and our bank manager wouldn't feel so well, either.'

'We're not going to fight?' said Tim.

'Look at it this way,' said Sammy. 'This planning committee's ahead of us. They can see heavy competition forcing the closure of grocers, greengrocers and suchlike, places where their grannies and our grannies have done their shopping since Waterloo. Did we win Waterloo, by the way?'

'Wellington and the Prussians did,' said Tim.

'Well, don't tell Bobby's Helene,' said Sammy. 'She's French. No, I'm sorry, fellers, but we're not going to appeal. We'll wait till next year and make a new application.'

'A year's a long time in my young life,' said Daniel.

'It's just a passing hour or so at my age,' said Sammy. 'Blind O'Reilly, every year's running away from me at a gallop. I'll be old by next week.'

'Then what are we going to do with the site?' asked Tim. 'Let it stand vacant for a year and more?'

'I don't like the sound of that,' said Sammy. 'I'll talk to your dad. He was willing to weigh in with fifty thousand smackers, and if it's not going to be used, we don't want him giving it to some old ladies' home, not if it could still be useful to the business. After all, it's a loving bequest from the late Elsie Chivers that was.'

'Loving bequest?' said Tim. He smiled. 'Does that mean my dad sent roses to her on Valentine's Day?'

'Well, let's face it,' said Sammy, 'women have always fancied your dad, but you can take it from me, Tim, your mother – our Emily – and your high-class stepma never had to worry about Elsie Chivers.' He rubbed his chin. 'Boots ain't that kind, anyway, and your grandma brought him up to see that he wasn't. I'll go and talk to him.'

'Something on your mind, Sammy?' said Boots, when his brother walked in.

'Something that's put Daniel and Tim in gloomy street,' said Sammy, and handed Boots the letter. Boots read it. Rachel came in.

'Sammy,' she said, 'do I see a frown?'

'Rachel, what you see is me face wearing a headache,' said Sammy.

'What for a headache?' asked Rachel, and she was shown the letter too. 'My life,' she said, 'we should weep?'

'It's stopped Tim and Daniel in their tracks,' said Sammy. 'And there's Boots about to have fifty thou going spare. So what do we do? Leave the site sitting empty?'

'The site, Sammy,' said Boots, 'is close to public transport and shops, so a three-storey block of modern flats at reasonable rents would be my bet. You made a great job of developing the old Southwark Brewery site, and Tim and Daniel did a first-class piece of work in selling the flats off. The planning committee could hardly turn down a housing development, and no shopkeeper's going to object, since it'll mean extra customers.'

'Much better than not developing the site, Sammy,' said Rachel.

'Don't I know it?' said Sammy. 'I'm in favour, and you can believe me when I tell you I did have me doubts about getting planning permission for this American supermarket. Right, I'll get Tim and Daniel to draft a new application.'

'Hold your horses, Sammy,' said Boots. 'Let's give Tim and Daniel the chance to come up with some suggestions of their own, rather than plonk ours in their laps. They need a challenge after this set-back. If they decide on some kind of housing development off their own bat, then we can pool all suggestions for discussion, and see what the consensus is.'

'Half a mo,' said Sammy cautiously, 'is that some-thing to do with counting the population?'

'No, Sammy, it's an agreement arrived at by general consent,' said Rachel.

'Talk about what education has done for you and Boots,' said Sammy. 'I'd like to have been educated myself.'

'Oh, you're educated, Sammy,' smiled Rachel, 'far more than any old Etonian.'

'In that case, I'll go and talk educated to Tim and Daniel,' said Sammy, 'and encourage 'em to start thinking. Much obliged, Boots.'

'You're welcome, Sammy,' said Boots.

'And you'll hold the fifty thou in reserve?'

'I will when I get it,' said Boots.

'I'm touched, old soldier,' said Sammy, and off he went to talk to Tim and Daniel.

'Boots,' said Rachel, 'when I first came to know Sammy and you and your family, I also came to know Elsie Chivers.'

'A charming lady,' said Boots, taking up a letter from his morning mail.

'With a frightening mother,' said Rachel.

'Water long under the bridge now, Rachel,' said Boots.

'Yes,' said Rachel, but quite prepared to believe Elsie Chivers had been in love with him. 'Yes, Boots, water long gone now.'

And Boots thought how strange it was that Elsie Chivers or events relating to her had cropped up so frequently in his life.

Anneliese spent her first week working in casualty, and in that time proved herself an invaluable member of the emergencies team. She was back in the profession almost as if she had never left it. And as to how she looked in her cap, cape and uniform, Harry could only guess, for it was kept at the hospital. She changed into it when she arrived and out of it when her duties were over. She was very friendly whenever they bumped into each other, and he thought her return to a nursing career was good for her. He noted she took a bath every evening on her return.

One evening, quite late, when Cindy was in bed, she came up to Harry's workroom.

'Mr Stevens?'

'Enter, Miss Nightingale.'

Anneliese showed herself. She was in a warm white towelling robe, girdled, her fair hair quite fluffy. She's had a shampoo, thought Harry. She looked delightfully informal.

'Why do you call me that?' she asked, smiling.

'Oh, Florence Nightingale and all that,' said Harry.

'I see.' She smiled again. 'Are you busy?'

'Still struggling,' said Harry, 'but I think I can see my way ahead now.'

'Good,' said Anneliese. 'I'm going to make a hot drink. Would you like one? It's the drink my English grandmother called a hot toddy.'

'I know,' said Harry, 'spirits, sugar and hot water. If you're inviting me to partake, well, that's very nice of you. I'll come and get it, shall I?'

'No, stay with your typewriter and I'll bring it up,' said Anneliese. She did so after a few minutes, and since she also brought a glass for herself, Harry supposed she was going to keep him company for a while.

'This is very welcome,' he said. 'Is it whisky-based?'

'Brandy, with brown sugar,' said Anneliese, perching herself against his desk and looking down at him as he sniffed the aroma of the drink.

'Well, good luck, Miss Bruck,' he said.

'Good health,' said Anneliese, clinking glasses with him.

They drank to each other, with Harry thinking how relaxed she was.

'You look pleased with life at the moment,' he said. 'How are you finding things at the hospital?'

'Everything is as I hoped,' she said. 'The hospital is splendid, the doctors, specialists and nursing staff so very good.'

'And the casualties you've had to deal with?' said Harry.

'Varied, as you would expect. Some serious, some not so serious. As to yourself, Mr Stevens, you work too hard, you must relax more.'

'Am I listening to a nurse, Nurse Bruck?'

'It's Sister Bruck.'

'Sister? Already?'

'Matron gave me that rank at the start,' said Anneliese, 'but I'm not on duty now, Mr Stevens. How is your story coming? Is it to be definitely a novel?'

'Between you, you and Cindy have convinced me to take the plunge,' said Harry, 'and if I go under, pull me out and do a professional resuscitation job on me. That's if you're around at the time.'

'Wear a lifebelt, Mr Stevens, and take no chances,' smiled Anneliese, as they enjoyed their toddies. 'How are the psychopaths?'

'Driving me mad,' said Harry. 'How does one get into the mind of such a person? I've been reading a lengthy book on Jack the Ripper, surely the world's number one psychopath.'

'No, Mr Stevens,' said Anneliese, 'Jack the Ripper comes a very poor second to Himmler. Or to Stalin. You may believe that. I do hope in researching the minds of psychopaths, you won't be affected. You are a very nice man, and should stay so.'

'Well, certainly, I'll do what I can not to turn into another Himmler,' said Harry.

'You don't mind my talking to you? I'm not keeping you too much from your writing?'

'This is a welcome break,' smiled Harry.

'Mr Stevens, I believe you said you came from Oxfordshire. Do you know Oxford?'

'Like the back of my hand,' said Harry.

'And can you drive a car?' asked Anneliese.

'I can,' said Harry, 'but I don't own one. Can't afford to.' If he splashed out on anything whenever

333

a short-story payment arrived, it was clothes for Cindy. She loved clothes, even at only twelve.

'If I hired a car one Sunday,' said Anneliese, 'would you care to drive me to Oxford? I'd love to see it, with you and Cindy.'

'Miss Bruck?' Harry was registering surprise.

'I really would,' said Anneliese.

'Well, my word,' said Harry, 'you'd like a day out in Oxford with Cindy and me?'

'Am I being presumptuous?'

'Presumptuous?' said Harry. 'Not a bit. But Oxford at this time of the year, with the students in residence and absorbed in their tutorials, means we wouldn't be able to visit the colleges, as tourists are allowed to at vacation times. An Easter vacation time would be preferable. Could you wait until then?'

'In this new life of mine,' said Anneliese, 'I have time to wait and I'm happy to.'

'Fine,' said Harry. The lady's mellowing, he thought. She looked a dream in that white robe. And what's she wearing under it, I wonder? Not very much, that's my guess. Steady, man, keep your imagination on a pure level. Pure? I'm kidding myself.

'Mr Stevens?'

'Have I said something?'

'No, but you are looking at me as if you're researching my mind. I assure you, whatever dark secrets I may have, they aren't those of a psychopath.'

'Perish the thought,' said Harry. 'Was I looking?'

'Yes, as if you were trying to find something sensational about me,' said Anneliese.

Sensational wasn't the word, thought Harry. Bewitching was the right adjective.

'Oh, it was probably due to a writer's interest in people,' he said. 'We build up some of our characters around men and women we meet.'

Anneliese laughed.

'You are thinking of putting me into a story?' she said.

'It could happen,' said Harry.

'Then, if so, treat me sympathetically,' said Anneliese. She finished her drink. 'I really must go now, I've taken up far too much of your time.'

'Not at all,' said Harry, 'and there's no need –'

'No, I must leave you to yourself now,' said Anneliese.

'Thanks for the hot toddy, and for your company,' said Harry, opting for politeness. Well, he was taking care not to let his feelings run away with him.

'Goodnight,' smiled Anneliese, and took herself down to her apartment, along with the empty glasses.

Mr and Mrs Robinson, immigrants from the West Indies, had begun their work for Rosie and Matthew at the poultry farm, and if they needed to be taught how to handle the sheep, they needed no instructions on how to look after egg-laying chickens or how to grade the eggs. They were cheerful, willing and talkative, and used their own kind of hen language when chatting to the chickens. Nor did they quail at the oncoming chill of winter. They wrapped themselves up in overcoats and pulled on thick woollen hats.

Major Gorringe, a near neighbour and a brisk, whisky-complexioned retired old soldier, called one afternoon and buttonholed Rosie in her kitchen.

'I say, Rosie old gel,' he said, 'have to tell you Mildred had a fright yesterday.' Mildred was his wife.

'I'm sorry to hear that,' said Rosie, 'did she bump into a fox?'

'Eh?'

'One of our ravenous specimens?' said Rosie.

'No, nothing like that,' said Major Gorringe. 'Any fox that came face to face with Mildred would wish it hadn't. Fact is, when she was in the village store yesterday, damned if she didn't spot two darkies. Made her feel she was in the wilds of the Congo. The shopkeeper told her they were working for you and Matt, and Mildred's got the wind up about going out at night.'

'Coincidentally, so have Joe and Hortense,' smiled Rosie.

'Who?'

'Joe and Hortense, our West Indian workers,' said Rosie. 'The area's strange to them. No buses, no crowds, no markets, no people of their own kind, and so they're a little scared of what might be going on here at night.'

'Well, I'm damned,' said Major Gorringe, 'never heard such tosh, Rosie. This is a place of peace and quiet. Nothing fishy happens here at night.'

'I'll tell them that, Major,' said Rosie. She smiled. 'Will you tell Mildred?'

'Eh? Ah, I see, yes, got to convince her she won't be murdered in her bed,' said Major Gorringe. 'Sensitive woman, you know, Rosie, what? Are your darkies temporary?'

'Permanent, if they prove satisfactory,' said Rosie.

'Well, damn me,' said Major Gorringe, 'how are they managing?'

'Oh, without fuss,' said Rosie. 'They buy and cook their own food and live in the annexe.'

'Have to tell Mildred that.' Major Gorringe grinned. 'Don't want her thinking she's going to be boiled and eaten, eh?' He departed chortling.

Rosie busied herself for the next few minutes, then opened the kitchen window, rang a little brass bell and called.

'Matt – Hortense – Joe! Coffee time!'

'Coming, Rosie,' called Matt. He was talking to Joe about the profusion of rabbits, and Hortense was in the shed, grading a bushel of new-laid eggs.

'Mista Chapman,' said Joe, as he and Matt walked across the field towards the farmhouse, 'why don't you buy a ferret?'

'We had one a few years back,' said Matt, 'but the damn thing left half-eaten rabbits all over the place, and that brought in a legion of foxes.'

'Mista Chapman, you git yourself a real smart ferret,' said Joe, 'and I'll teach it to kill rabbits and bring 'em to hand.'

'You can do that trick?' said Matt.

'I sure can, boss,' said Joe.

'Well, we'll give it a go,' said Matt, 'and every rabbit the ferret lands at your feet intact, you and Hortense can have. For eating or selling.'

'Mista Chapman, Hortense and me, we've got ourselves a fine life here,' said Joe, 'and I'm thanking you.'

'You think you can cope with the winter?' said Matt.

337

'Well, it ain't gonna worry me at night,' said Joe, 'there ain't no woman warmer in bed than Hortense.'

Hortense, large, bouncy and beaming, joined them from the shed and they entered the farmhouse kitchen together, to be greeted by the aroma of hot coffee and a smiling Rosie.

Hortense and Joe felt happy, even if people did give them curious looks when they were out shopping.

Chapter Thirty-Two

'What's happening now?' asked Patsy of Daniel on his arrival home one evening.

'Well, nothing much, except that here I am after a long day's work,' said Daniel.

'Not that, you goof,' said Patsy, 'I mean what's happening with the new plans for that site?'

'We've decided to apply for permission to build a three-storey block of flats at economical rents that'll still give us a fair return by way of income,' said Daniel. 'The rents have to be inviting, since it's a working-class area.'

'Oh, great,' said Patsy, 'now I can stop worrying, and so can the children.'

'Worrying about what?' asked Daniel.

'About you doing your own worrying and losing your hair,' said Patsy.

'Come again?' said Daniel.

'Daniel, I don't want a bald guy for my husband,' said Patsy, 'and the children don't want a bald father.'

'Great pumpkins,' said Daniel, 'am I losing my hair, then?'

'Not yet,' said Patsy, 'but all this worry about no

supermarket and what to do with the site, it's been showing, and I've been looking for the first signs of hair loss.'

'It's all still there,' said Daniel.

'There's been none on your hairbrush?' said Patsy.

'None,' said Daniel. 'Listen, I don't come from a bald line of ancestors, and in any case, Grandma Finch wouldn't stand for any of us going bald. Every hair on my head is in place, got it?'

'Now, Daniel, don't lose your cool,' said Patsy. 'It's great that you and Tim have come to a decision with your pa and Uncle Boots, and I'll tell Arabella and Andrew they're not going to have a bald father.'

'If you keep on like this,' said Daniel, 'I'll be telling them in five minutes that they've got a bald mother. I'll scalp you, you monkey.'

'That's my guy,' said Patsy, and gave him a kiss and ran a hand through his hair. 'Oh, great,' she said, 'but I think you need a trim, honey.'

Daniel fell about.

However, the satisfying fact was that the property company had made up its collective mind to apply for new planning permission, and Sammy had said a consensus was acceptable at a board meeting, even if it was a bit educated.

Lulu was now working for the Adams family firm, a capitalist enterprise, the while waiting for her dad to point her at an inspiring job in the Houses of Parliament. To wit, as a member of one of the secretarial teams attached to Labour MPs. That could mean the first real step towards the ultimate goal, that of becoming an MP herself.

Paul was pretty sure that if she did reach giddy heights, he'd have to take a back seat. She'd been strong on politics ever since he'd first known her, and politics would be her first love as an MP. Well, he'd have to be philosophical about that, especially as she'd always been straight with him. She had never hidden her ambitions, she'd been frank and consistent. He'd have to go along with her.

However, for the time being she was an employee of the family firm, and taking the work in her stride. She was also taking note of conditions and of how private enterprise operated. If she thought she might find Adams Enterprises treating their staff as slave labour, or at least with a heavy hand, she was compelled to revise her opinion. Nobody had any real grumbles or any passionate desire to join a trade union, and the general office girls, in effect, avowed a death-or-glory devotion to their bosses. Indeed, Marjorie Trapper, a shorthand typist, declared that if there was any day when Mr Adams senior (Boots) didn't call her in for dictation, it was a day of gloom.

'What pathetic piffle,' said Lulu. 'You can't think about him like that. He's married, and you're dating someone yourself, so you said yesterday.'

'Oh, I never think about awkward things like that when Mr Adams is giving me dictation,' said Marjorie. 'They get in the way of dreams.'

'Become a Labour Party supporter,' said Lulu. 'Then you'd forget all that rubbish.'

'What, and let Mr Sammy down?' said Marjorie. 'He'd stop my bonuses.'

'You get bonuses?' said Lulu.

'Yes, we all do, twice a year,' said Marjorie.

So that's why they're devoted, thought Lulu. Wait a minute, Paul's never told me about bonuses. She saw him now and again during their days at the office, and the swine got her rag out and her glasses steamed up by insisting on calling her Mrs Adams. That, he said, was to let the staff know their relationship was strictly on business lines from nine until five thirty. Talk about how men could send women barmy with their drivel.

'Paul,' she said to him at home, 'you never told me you get bonuses.'

'I'll get one at Christmas,' said Paul, 'and another in June. Everyone gets bonuses, in the offices, in the shop below, in the dress shops and in the factory. You'll get yours as long as you don't talk out loud about the advantages of Socialism.'

Lulu's spectacles took on a glint of suspicion.

'It's bribery of the workers,' she declared.

'Bribery for what purpose?' asked Paul.

'To stop them joining trade unions,' said Lulu.

'Do what?' said Paul.

'I'm convinced,' said Lulu. 'And I'm standing by my conviction.'

'You're standing on one leg, then,' said Paul. 'Listen, don't you like your job?'

'It's a bit trivial,' said Lulu.

'It's never a bad move, starting at the bottom,' said Paul.

'Well, I don't intend to stay there long,' said Lulu.

'You're a real tiger,' said Paul. 'By the way, whose turn is it to get the supper?'

'Yours,' said Lulu.

'Just testing you,' said Paul, 'and you've come up with a fib. It's your turn.'

'You sure?'

'Positive,' said Paul.

'Oh, all right,' said Lulu. Then, 'Let's do it together.'

'Sounds chummy,' said Paul. 'OK, together, then.'

'Now you can give me a kiss,' said Lulu.

'Later,' said Paul, 'then I'll have time to give you a lot more than a kiss.'

'Suffering cats,' said Lulu, 'is there no escape for a woman?'

One evening, Anneliese came down to speak to Harry and Cindy. They were in the living room, seated at a fireside table and playing the card game of crib. Cindy loved such moments with her dad, they represented a cosy togetherness.

'Mr Stevens, I'm sorry to interrupt –'

'No need for sorrow, Miss Bruck,' said Harry, rising, 'we're pleased to see you.'

'Ever so,' said Cindy, progressively fascinated by their striking lodger.

'I wonder,' said Anneliese, as elegant as ever in her turquoise blue dress, 'would you and your father like to see the musical *South Pacific* in the West End?'

'Crikey,' breathed Cindy, 'would we, Daddy?'

'Isn't that the musical you saw some time ago?' asked Harry of Anneliese.

'Yes,' said Anneliese, 'and I enjoyed it so much that I'd love to see it again. I have a half-day at the hospital next Saturday, so I thought the after-noon matinee would be suitable for Cindy. I've just phoned the box office, and they've reserved the seats, providing they receive my cheque before Saturday. Would you both like to come?'

'Miss Bruck,' said Harry, 'that's a lovely gesture, but you must allow me to pay for the tickets.'

'No, no, Mr Stevens, thank you, but please let it be my privilege,' said Anneliese. 'It's settled, yes?'

'I'll buy the interval drinks,' said Harry.

'Good,' said Anneliese. 'What card game are you and Cindy playing?'

'Crib,' said Harry, 'and I owe Cindy nine peanuts so far.'

'Crib?' said Anneliese. 'Cribbage? I know that game. My English grandmother taught it to my sister and myself.'

'I'm getting the feeling that your English grand-mother was quite a character,' said Harry.

'Yes, she was,' smiled Anneliese.

'Would you care to join Cindy and me in a three-handed game?' asked Harry.

'May I?'

'Oh, yes, come on, Miss Bruck,' said Cindy.

So Anneliese sat down with them at the fireside table and they played the three-handed game for an hour. Cindy was impulsive in her play, Harry dashing, Anneliese shrewd in her technique, but extrovert in her mood.

It was an hour of recreational pleasure, and when Anneliese finally returned to her apartment, Cindy looked at her dad with a cheeky smile.

'Fancy that,' she said.

'Fancy what?' said Harry.

'Treating us to the theatre and playing crib with you,' said Cindy.

'With us,' said Harry.

'Oh, just with you, really,' said Cindy.

'Stop trying to make something of nothing,' said Harry. 'It's your bedtime, so hoppit.'

'Sweet dreams, Daddy.'

'Goodnight, minx.'

At lunchtime the following day, Boots and Ned were enjoying time together in the pub opposite the Camberwell offices. Ned had taken a leisurely walk to the pub from Denmark Hill, Lizzy having said the fresh air would do him good as long as he didn't exert himself. He and Boots had been close friends since before the First World War, and it was a pleasure to meet for a drink and a pub sandwich. Boots was on old and mild, Ned favouring a dark Guinness, and the sandwiches were of fresh ham and biting mustard.

Boots thought Ned was looking better. There were times when his mouth had a slightly blue tint, an indication of his heart trouble. Today, he certainly seemed relaxed, his conversation of an easy kind.

'I tell you, Boots, life's a picnic today compared to what it was like in the Twenties and Thirties.'

'Age of the flappers,' said Boots.

'Stockings and pink garters,' said Ned with a grin. 'You're not the only one who remembers. But it was tough for older people with families to bring up, wages criminally low and kids making do with farthings for pocket money, if anything at all. Let's see, isn't Socialism and fair do's for the workers what Paul's wife believes in?'

'Lulu?' Boots smiled. 'From what Sammy tells me, Lulu's main regret is that she was born too late to help Lenin launch the Russian Revolution.'

'Well, what does that point to?' said Ned. 'That she's going to light Russian fireworks in the bosom of the family?'

'She'll be lucky to get any firework within ten yards of Chinese Lady's bosom,' said Boots. 'And even if she does, she'll find she's up against an automatic rejection system.'

'I don't think Lizzy would favour that kind of comment on her mother,' said Ned, but with another grin.

'You can tell Lizzy I'm proud of our old lady's bosom,' said Boots. 'It did wonders for me as an infant. Well, whatever life was like in our early days, Ned, the years since have been well worthwhile.'

'Leaving out six years fighting loudmouth Hitler,' said Ned.

Boots mused on the point.

'It was well worthwhile, Ned, the effort of getting rid of him,' he said, 'even if it did cost a hell of a lot of blood, toil, tears and sweat.'

'As per Churchill the prophet,' said Ned. 'But Hitler's war cost you Emily. Between ourselves, and with nothing against Polly, d'you ever miss her?'

'Emily? I think about her, yes, of course I do.' Boots's response was on an easy level. A little smile of reminiscence touched his lips. 'Emily was the girl next door, and of the kind one doesn't forget.'

'A character in the family's book,' said Ned.

'Very true,' said Boots, 'and I believe Lizzy felt I let Emily down when I married Polly.'

'Oh, you can take it from me, Boots, Lizzy forgot all that years ago,' said Ned. 'She likes Polly. Who couldn't? On top of that, who couldn't admire her for all she did as an ambulance driver in the Kaiser's war?'

'I'll ask her to show you her album of photographs of her time in France and Flanders when you and Lizzy next call,' said Boots. 'By the way, do Bobby and Helene still turn up most Saturday mornings to keep your garden going?'

'They do,' said Ned, 'and it gives Lizzy a chance to fuss the children. As for the gardening, Bobby and Helene helped me grow some very welcome vegetables and sackfuls of runner beans. How were yours?'

'Polly's?' said Boots. 'She picks sackfuls of her own every year and takes them to one of her mother's orphanages. I think the orphans will turn green in time.' He finished his beer, and Ned finished his Guinness. It had given him colour. Boots thought he was a tough old nut at nearly fifty-nine. He was fighting his hardening arteries as well as he'd fought all the years of coping with his artificial leg. 'How d'you feel these days, Ned?' Boots asked the question casually. He knew Ned didn't like people to fuss.

'How do I feel? Like a two-year-old,' said Ned.

'Right, let's get going, then,' said Boots, 'it's time I was back at my desk.'

'I'll come across the road with you and say hello to Sammy and the others,' said Ned.

Boots paid the bill, and they left the pub, crossing the road to the firm's offices. They climbed the stairs at the side of the shop that represented Sammy's first venture into the realms of real business. Boots stopped on the landing.

'Take it easy, Ned,' he said.

'Oh, a few stairs aren't a problem,' said Ned.

'Good,' said Boots. 'Well, go and say hello to Sammy and the others. Take your time and I'll run you home when you're ready.'

'I'll accept the lift,' said Ned, and made his way to Sammy's office. He found Rachel there.

'Ned? Hello,' said Rachel, giving him a velvety smile, 'long time no see.'

'That's my hard luck,' said Ned, 'you're always worth a look, Rachel. Right, Sammy?'

'I concur, don't I?' said Sammy. 'Rachel's a female woman, which is a pleasure to a bloke who keeps seeing women wearing trousers. Beats me, women wanting to look like men. Men ain't much to look at, in any case. Enjoy your pub pint with Boots, did you, Ned?'

'Just the job,' said Ned, and spent several minutes chatting with Sammy and Rachel, mostly about how the business was doing, a favourite topic with Sammy. Then he went to see his nephews, Tim and Daniel, in the office they shared. Ned had a soft spot for these two.

'What-ho, Uncle Ned,' said Daniel.

'Welcome to the den,' said Tim.

'Just thought I'd look in and see if you're in control of your overheads,' smiled Ned.

'We'd get the order of Uncle Sammy's boot if we weren't,' said Tim.

'I've got to admit it,' said Daniel, 'my old man slips on a special boot for that kind of action. What's brought you here, Uncle Ned?'

'I've just had an extended pub lunch with Boots across the way,' said Ned, 'so I thought I'd pop in and see who's working and who's doing cross-words.'

'Be our guest,' said Tim.

Ned had a very pleasant chat with his nephews, both of whom thought him a resilient old soldier with his tin leg. Tim noticed a slightly pinched look to his mouth, but that was the only sign of his heart condition.

The phone rang. Daniel took the call.

'I'd better get back now,' said Ned to Tim. 'Your dad's giving me a lift.'

'I'll fetch him,' said Tim. He left the office, Ned following to wait in the corridor. Tim, reappearing, said, 'There's a buyer with Dad, so I'll run you home.'

'Thanks, Tim, but I can get a bus,' said Ned.

'You could, but you're not going to. Come on, I've got the keys of Dad's car, and it's parked outside.'

Ned descended the stairs with Tim, taking them slowly. Boots's Riley was alongside the kerb. He and Tim seated themselves. Tim started the engine.

'It's a long way to Tipperary,' said Ned.

'Tipperary? That's a long time ago,' said Tim, wondering what had brought to Ned's mind the old song of the Great War. As he slipped into gear, he heard a sudden little sound, like a hiccough cut short. He glanced to his left. His uncle's head had slumped to the dashboard, his body was limp and his face a whitish-grey. Tim went into neutral gear.

'Ned? Uncle Ned?'

He put his hand under his uncle's chin, lifted his head and turned it. His face was waxen and nerveless, his mouth loose, his eyes closed, and his breathing faint. Christ, thought Tim, he's either having a heart attack or a stroke. He hesitated only a second or two before making up his mind what to do and where to go. He drove fast to King's College Hospital, not more than a minute away. On arrival there, response from the casualty department was immediate, and Ned, still unconscious, was stretchered through to the intensive care unit after only one quick minute of examination.

Tim, alarmed, wanted to follow, but was asked by a nurse to stay in the casualty waiting room. He waited, but not patiently. The only person there, he walked up and down, worrying about Ned and what he might have to tell Aunt Lizzy. His years as a commando had taught him how to make quick and definite decisions, but at this moment he was unsure of himself. Should he find a phone and call Aunt Lizzy? Was she entitled to be here at such a time? Yes, perhaps she was, but if Uncle Ned was on his way out, it would almost certainly happen before she got here. No, better to wait and perhaps be able to give her the kind of information that, hopefully, wouldn't relate to a death certificate. Well, should he phone Boots, then, his sound and reliable pa? No, there was nothing even he could do.

So he waited and waited, worry increasing. Not until nearly half an hour had passed did someone come to see him, by which time he really was expecting the worst.

Chapter Thirty-Three

She entered the waiting room, a nursing sister immaculate in her cap and uniform.

'Mr—?'

Tim turned to face her.

'I'm—' Just that came out, just a brief second of time flitted, and then his eyes opened wide and his firm mouth gaped.

Anneliese stared. Recognition was instant and mutual, even though eleven eventful years had passed since that last day in the German-run hospital at Benghazi. They were both older, yes, but neither had changed to any real extent. She was still a blue-eyed, perfect-looking German woman, he still strong-featured and fine-looking.

To Tim, she was the well-remembered epitome of the wartime nursing profession at its most caring and determined, despite the fact that, because he represented the enemy, she was always naturally inclined to keep her distance.

To Anneliese, he was an emotional reminder, like some German wounded she had nursed, of the best kind of soldier, the kind whose courage and dignity were far removed from the nightmarish brutality of Himmler's SS.

She was finding this moment of reunion unbelievable. Tim was finding it incredible, so much so that he thought he was dreaming.

Anneliese was the first to speak.

'Lieutenant Adams, is this happening?'

'Lieutenant Bruck, I could ask the same question of you,' said Tim, who might have mentioned he finished up as a captain. But what was the point?

'I did not know the world was as small as this,' she said.

'Small?' said Tim. 'It seems to me at this moment that it's shrunk so much that everyone everywhere will soon be bumping into everyone elsewhere.' He took a few steps forward. 'God knows how you came to be here, in this hospital, but let me say it's a delight to see you again. Salutations, Anneliese Bruck.' He took both her hands and delivered a kiss on her cheek. Anneliese accepted it, but with the slightest of flushes.

'I'm so pleased you survived,' she said, 'so very pleased.'

'I think we need to talk, for I'd certainly like to know how a German army nurse finished up here,' said Tim. 'But not now.' He became urgent. 'If you've come to tell me how Mr Somers is, tell me now. He's my dear old Uncle Ned.'

'Dr Hardy, who's attending him, Mr Adams, asked me to be frank and to tell you Mr Somers has suffered a stroke,' said Anneliese.

'Oh, hell, I suspected that,' said Tim. 'What else do you have to say?'

'That Dr Hardy isn't diagnosing it as fatal,' said Anneliese. 'Mr Somers has lost control of his speech and a facial nerve for the moment, but we're confident he'll recover, given complete rest and the necessary treatment.'

'You're sure?' said Tim.

'Optimistic,' said Anneliese.

'How optimistic?' Tim was pressing.

'Dr Hardy is very optimistic, Mr Adams—'

'Tim. We aren't strangers, Anneliese.'

'No.' Anneliese smiled. 'Dr Hardy feels he can be more definite in his opinions tomorrow.'

'But can he say at this moment that if my uncle recovers he won't be left handicapped?' asked Tim.

'Given time and the right treatment, there should be no serious consequences,' said Anneliese.

'Should be?' said Tim. 'You mean might be?'

'Tomorrow,' said Anneliese, 'the diagnosis will be more definite. Tim?' She spoke his name gently. 'You can be hopeful, believe me.'

'He's a fine old chap,' said Tim, 'a Great War veteran with a tin leg.'

'I know,' said Anneliese. 'We have his medical record. He's had several consultations here about his heart condition. That was before I joined the staff some weeks ago. But no visitors today, please, although his wife will be allowed just to look in on him for a moment, if she wishes.' Anneliese's professional air had a sympathetic warmth to it. She was still in wonder at coming face to face with Tim. How extraordinary life could be.

'I see,' said Tim. 'What would you advise me to say to his wife?'

'You could tell her all I've told you,' said Anneliese, 'that she can expect recovery, although we aren't sure at this moment how long it will take.'

'Well, that's a lot better than I was expecting,'

said Tim. He gave her an affectionate look. 'But if you're not the last word in the unexpected, who is?'

'I share your feelings,' said Anneliese. She smiled. She had a little more time to spare. 'If you were able to call again tomorrow, I'll give you something that belongs to you.'

'What on earth can that be?' asked Tim, anxious now to phone Aunt Lizzy.

'Your beret,' said Anneliese. 'You left it behind on the day you escaped your escort. It came into my possession, and I've kept it ever since.'

'Why?'

Anneliese smiled again.

'My dear man –'

'That sounds very English.'

'Yes. My paternal grandmother was English. About your beret, you must know that many fighting soldiers keep mementoes and souvenirs of war. So do some nurses. But there, Tim, if you visit again tomorrow, I'll give you back your commando beret. Oh, one more thing, then I must go. I know your wife was blinded in an air raid. May I ask how she is now?'

'Still blind,' said Tim, 'but coping as well as she always has. How the devil did you know? No, never mind, I hope you and I will be able to talk at length to each other sometime, but not now. You must be busy, and I need to call Uncle Ned's wife. Is there a phone I could use?'

'Come with me,' said Anneliese.

'Sister Bruck?' A nurse from casualty was calling. 'Sister Bruck, you're wanted.'

'A moment,' called Anneliese. She showed Tim

into an empty consulting room, and left him to make his phone call while she hastened to the casualty unit.

Lizzy was getting cross. Boots should have brought Ned home ages ago. She hadn't minded the two of them dallying a bit at the pub, talking, of course, about old times, but they must have been there over two hours by now, nattering away. And men talked about gossiping women. She eventually decided to call the pub, before vexation turned into worry. At that point her phone rang.

'Hello, is that you, Ned?'

'No, it's Tim, Aunt Lizzy.'

'Tim?' said Lizzy.

'Yes.' Tim braced himself. 'I'm at King's College Hospital.'

'What? Have you had an accident, then? Shouldn't you be phoning your father?'

'Aunt Lizzy, it's about Uncle Ned.' Tim knew he couldn't make light of the matter. 'Aunt Lizzy, I'm afraid he's had a stroke.'

'Oh, my God,' said Lizzy.

'Don't panic, he's going to recover.' Tim explained exactly what had happened, and what he had been told, while Lizzy gripped the phone tightly and tried to steady herself. 'I'm going to phone Pa at the office, then I'll come and drive you to the hospital. You'll be allowed just to look in on Uncle Ned—'

'Just to look in?' said Lizzy. 'He must be worse than you say, then.'

'No, not according to the message I received from the doctor,' said Tim. 'It's just that Uncle

355

Ned's going to take time to recover. You make yourself a hot cup of tea and wait for me. I won't be long.'

'Tim, are you sure he's going to be all right?'

'I was told we could be optimistic,' said Tim, and Lizzy was reminded of other times when optimism was called for. 'Don't worry too much, just wait for me.'

He phoned his father. Boots listened.

'Say no more, Tim old lad, go ahead,' he said. 'You've got the car, anyway. I'll walk up to the hospital.'

'Sorry, Pa, the order is no visitors today, except for Aunt Lizzy. I'll talk to you later, when I get back to the office.'

'Well, you know how I feel about your Uncle Ned,' said Boots, 'so do me a favour and find out when I can visit, will you?'

'Of course. Must go now.'

Tim hoped to see Anneliese when he and Lizzy arrived at the hospital, but she was busy in casualty. However, a nurse took Lizzy to the intensive care unit, and she was allowed to look in on Ned. He was attached to a machine registering his heartbeats. Asleep, he looked pale, drawn, very still and loose-mouthed. Lizzy, of course, felt deeply upset. Her sons and daughters were all dear to her, but Ned was the man who had taken her out of sooty Walworth and given her all she had ever dreamed of as a growing girl. A house in a leafy avenue, a house with a bath and a garden, and a life of happily sharing with him the ups and downs of bringing up a family. This wasn't the first time his heart condition had given her shock and worry, but she had never seen him looking as ill as he did now.

Dr Hardy, a cardiologist, intercepted her as she left the intensive care ward. He assured her they had been able to treat Ned in good time, that his constitution was of the kind that would help him recover, although the diagnosis could be more definite tomorrow.

'Oh, do everything you can for him,' begged Lizzy.

'Be assured, Mrs Somers. Come in again tomorrow.'

'Oh, I will,' said Lizzy, 'with my eldest son.' Bobby, she knew, would certainly want to be with her.

The afternoon was well advanced by the time Tim finally arrived back at the office to give Boots and the others the full story of Ned's crisis. They all took it in soberly, but it was only to Boots that Tim subsequently spoke of his extraordinary encounter with Anneliese Bruck, the German army nurse who had done so much to help him recover from the serious wounds he had sustained during a commando night raid on a German strongpost in the desert.

'Can you believe it, Dad old soldier, that when this noble angel of mercy walked in, I found myself staring at that German army nurse, Lieutenant Bruck?'

'I can believe it if you say so,' said Boots. 'And what are you saying, that she was your very own angel of mercy?'

'You've heard me talk about her,' said Tim.

'It's a strange world,' said Boots.

'You can say that again, ten times over,' said Tim. 'By the way, you can look in on Uncle Ned tomorrow. Aunt Lizzy will be going with Bobby in the morning. It'll have to be the afternoon for you and me.'

'You want to visit again, Tim?'

'We'll only be allowed a few moments,' said Tim, 'and while there, I have to see Anneliese Bruck again.'

'For any special reason?' asked Boots.

'Yes, she has a beret of mine, one I left behind on the day I escaped,' said Tim. 'She wants to return it to me.'

'Now I know for sure that truth is stranger than fiction,' said Boots. 'I think I'd better phone Bobby.'

By evening, most people in the families emanating from Chinese Lady knew that Ned was hospitalized. The grapevine had been working overtime on telephones. Bobby and Helene were with Lizzy. So were Edward and Leah, Emma and Jonathan, and Annabelle and Nick. Annabelle complained that it was very high-handed of the hospital not to allow visits by her dad's nearest and dearest until tomorrow.

'Uncle Boots let me know about that when he phoned me at my office,' said Bobby. 'If you want to argue the matter with him, Annabelle, you can, but count me out.'

'Well, it's very upsetting,' said Annabelle.

'Of course it's upsetting,' said Bobby, 'but Dad's obviously so ill at the moment that any visitor could only stand and stare. And get in the way of the medical team. I'll drive Mum there tomorrow morning.'

Lizzy was in her kitchen at the moment, with Leah and Helene. She was insisting on making a large pot of tea for everyone. She needed to be doing something, she said.

'Anyway,' said Annabelle, 'if Dad has to stay in hospital for ages, who's going to look after Mum?'

'Look after her?' said Emma.

'Look after Mum?' echoed Edward.

'We can't leave her on her own,' said Annabelle. 'Nick and I think we should have her.'

'I haven't said so,' commented Nick. Annabelle was becoming a bit bossy. That was a fact, and young Linda was complaining that her mum was getting after her about all sorts of things.

Bobby knew his mother was the last kind of woman who'd want to be looked after while she still had life and breath. So he said, 'Wait till she's in a wheelchair.'

'The day when Emma's mum is in a wheelchair,' said Jonathan, 'will be the day when I'm ninety.'

'I wouldn't argue with that,' said Bobby.

Polly had poured Boots a pick-me-up in the form of a neat whisky.

'Buck up, old love,' she said, 'Ned will pull through. You said so yourself.'

'I had that from Tim,' said Boots. 'Polly, poor old Ned, he was in fine form all through lunch, so much so that he insisted on coming across to the offices with me to say hello to everyone. I wonder now, was he close to a breakdown without knowing it, and did climbing those stairs set it off?'

'Perhaps,' said Polly, 'but don't blame yourself.'

'Incidentally, Polly, let me tell you who informed Tim of Ned's condition.'

'I presume the doctor,' said Polly.

'No, not the doctor,' said Boots. 'You remember all Tim has told us of his hospitalization as a wounded prisoner of war?'

'Yes, and I well remember him making a great thing of how much he owed to his German army nurse,' said Polly.

'That German army nurse is now working at King's College Hospital,' said Boots. 'She was Tim's informant on Ned's condition.'

'What?' said Polly. 'No, that's fantasy, old bean, fantasy, it has to be.'

'Not according to Tim,' said Boots. 'While we're all concerned about Ned, I can't help feeling something remarkable has happened outside of that. Pay attention, Polly.'

'Dear man, I can't wait to hear more,' said Polly.

Unbelievably, said Boots, Tim had not only come face to face with his erstwhile German army nurse, but she had told him she had something that belonged to him. Polly asked what something? His commando beret, said Boots, which Tim had left behind on the day he escaped. The nurse, Anneliese Bruck, had kept it ever since as a souvenir of a time she considered eventful and memorable.

'Memorable?' said Polly. 'Memorable? Now I'm picturing a wartime headline. "Beautiful German army nurse falls in love with wounded British commando".'

'Your imagination, Polly, fascinates me,' said Boots.

'It's feasible,' said Polly.

'Let me tell you one more thing,' said Boots. 'The lady wishes to return the beret to Tim, and has promised to do so tomorrow.'

'Sainted aunts,' said Polly, 'I can't keep up with this kind of stuff.'

'Try,' said Boots.

'Give me some help, then,' said Polly. 'Make it a gin and tonic. Then we'll drink to wartime memories and Ned's prospects of recovery.'

Meanwhile, Tim had conveyed to Felicity details of the astonishing materialization of Anneliese Bruck. Felicity, of course, had known of the German woman for years, but she found it hard to believe the reunion was accidental. A thought struck her.

'She's been following you, Tim.'

'Following me?'

'Obviously. With your beret in her nurse's kit-bag.'

'Kitbag?'

'That's my guess.'

'So she's been following me with her kitbag for how long – over eleven years?' said Tim. 'Sounds highly improbable to me, Puss.'

Felicity, of course, had come to the same conclusion as Polly, and that induced her to say, 'Love turns some women into hunters.'

'You mean that if I get to meet her again at the hospital tomorrow, I'll be trapped and bagged?' said Tim.

'You would be, if it weren't for unchangeable circumstances,' said Felicity.

'What circumstances are those?' asked Tim.

'Tiger, you've already been bagged,' said Felicity. 'By me. So if she points a German shotgun at you, tell her where she can stuff it.'

'Without forgetting you're a lady, would you mind telling me where?' asked Tim.

'In her kitbag,' said Felicity. 'So forget everything except finding out how your Uncle Ned is coming along.'

Tim smiled. Through all her years of blindness, Felicity had gamely refused to give in to self-pity. She was a natural leg-puller. He'd seen her as a jolly-hockey-sticks type when he'd first met her as an ATS subaltern at Troon. She was more sophisticated now, but still a typical leg-puller at times.

'You're a sweet woman, Puss.'

'I'm a trusting one,' said Felicity. 'If I weren't, I'd never let you have this second reunion with Annie Whatsername. By the way, if they do let you see your Uncle Ned tomorrow, give him my love.'

'I will,' said Tim. 'Incidentally, have you had any bright moments today?'

'Any flashes of light?' said Felicity. 'Not today, lover.'

The last one had been two days ago. They were still happening regularly. Tim was waiting for one that was clear and sharp, even if it only lasted a few seconds.

Chapter Thirty-Four

Anneliese, arriving home from the hospital, went straight to her wardrobe, and from its high shelf she pulled clear the green beret of a British commando. It was wrapped in tissue paper.

Life did have its impossible moments, its violent or unimaginable twists and turns. Had she ever thought, during that day when the staff of the Benghazi hospital were evacuating the town in the face of the British advance, that over eleven years later she would be living here amid the cockneys of Camberwell? And that she would come face to face with the wounded British commando she had come to care for? That was the most impossible of moments, yet it had happened.

She took her usual bath and lay musing.

Afterwards, she prepared a light meal for herself. Her daily lunch at the hospital was sufficient to eliminate the need for a substantial evening meal.

As she ate, she heard the now very familiar sounds of Harry Stevens and Cindy making life a laugh for each other. Cindy's voice rang high at times, as now. 'Daddy, oh, now look what you haven't done.'

What, I wonder, hasn't he done? Anneliese smiled to herself.

Later, hearing his typewriter going, she went up to
see him. As usual his door was open. She had come
to feel he never closed it simply because it would
shut him off from Cindy.

'Mr Stevens?'

'Heigh-ho,' said Harry, 'happy to see you, Miss
Bruck. How's your day been at the hospital?'

'Oh, a typical education,' said Anneliese.

'Education?' said Harry.

'On how mankind persists in doing itself grisly
injuries,' said Anneliese. 'Except for one gentleman
who was struck down through no fault of his fellow
men, and was close to cardiac arrest when he was
brought in.'

'What the hell's cardiac arrest?' asked Harry.

'Heart failure,' said Anneliese.

'But they don't call it that any more?'

'No, not often.'

'How is the gentleman now?'

'He's doing – what is the English phrase now? Yes,
as well as can be expected. He has the right kind of
constitution to help his recovery.'

'Well, I don't know him, but I wish him the best
of luck,' said Harry.

'I'm sure he'd thank you for that,' said Anneliese.
She smiled. 'Mr Stevens, I'm going to be inquisitive.'

'Are you?' said Harry, smiling back at her. 'What
about? My own constitution?'

'I'm sure your constitution is excellent,' said
Anneliese. 'It's your novel I'm inquisitive about.'

'Well, I hope inquisitive means interested,' said
Harry.

Anneliese regarded him with visible good

humour. Here was a man refreshingly different from Hitler's fanatics, the destroyers of Germany. Harry Stevens, she thought, was a man of unfailing good nature, who did not seem to feel the challenges of life had to be met with fanatical zeal. Doggedness, yes, that was his métier, not death or glory. He had a natural preference for a quiet and simple existence, and for being a kind and indulgent father to his delightful daughter.

'Mr Stevens, have you finished the first chapter?' she asked.

'Of this novel?'

'Yes.'

'I'm light-headed,' said Harry.

'Are you?' said Anneliese. 'Why?'

'I've actually just reached the finish of the third chapter,' said Harry, 'and that includes any amount of rewriting.'

'Well, that's splendid, isn't it?' said Anneliese, with sincerity.

'As good old Euclid said, that has to be proved,' observed Harry.

'Mr Stevens, would it be impertinent of me to ask if I may read those finished chapters?'

'Impertinent?' said Harry. 'Good heavens, no. But I've got reservations.'

'About what, Mr Stevens?'

'I speak, Miss Bruck, as an author with a limited faith in his outpourings.'

'Oh, dear,' murmured Anneliese.

'I agree, fully,' said Harry. 'In fact, I'd go so far as to say, "Oh, hell, get a steady job with an insurance company, Harry Stevens." However.'

'Yes?' said Anneliese.

'If you're sure you'd like to read these chapters, I'll risk it,' said Harry.

'I would like to, very much,' said Anneliese.

'I call that courageous,' said Harry, modesty uppermost. He picked up a wad of completed pages, and handed it to his tenant. 'By the way, be a sport,' he said.

'A sport?' said Anneliese.

'Yes, keep them in page-number order,' said Harry.

'Yes, of course,' said Anneliese.

Cindy called from down below.

'Daddy? I'm going to bed now.'

'Right, pet,' called Harry. 'I'll come down and tuck you in.'

'Daddy, I'm twelve years old, not six.'

'Oh sorry, Cindy love, I forgot.'

Up from below came Cindy's parting shot.

'You'll forget your head next.'

A little grin brightened Harry's well-kept teeth.

'It's a lovely life,' he said to Anneliese.

'You're to be envied, Mr Stevens,' she said. 'Now I shall do some interesting reading.'

'You hope,' said Harry.

Anneliese smiled and returned to her flat, taking the three chapters with her.

She made herself a drink, settled down in her fireside armchair and began reading. On a table sat the green beret, newly brushed.

Boots received a communication from Mr Duncan the following morning, advising him that the administrator had agreed to purchase the estate for fifty thousand pounds. Would Mr Adams accord-

ingly sign the enclosed documents that would allow
negotiations for the sale and purchase to proceed
further?

'I'll deal with these at the office, Polly,' he said,
having shown her the letter.

'Yes, I know what you want to do first,' said Polly.
The twins were on their way to school. 'You want to
phone the hospital and get a bulletin on Ned.'

'Yes, I'd like to,' said Boots.

The bulletin was encouraging, the patient
conscious and stable. Sammy, advised of this by
Boots, said that was going to make his day a lot
happier. Good old Ned, he said, was a family heirloom.

'Heirloom, Sammy?'

'Sort of, Boots. What's the word?'

'Bequeathed?'

'That's it, bequeathed to Lizzy by his late mum
and dad. If you get me.'

'I get you, Sammy.'

Lizzy and Bobby were allowed to see the patient at
eleven. A nurse was making one of her periodical
checks of the machine that registered his heartbeat.
Ned was awake, but looked wan and disorientated.
However, after a little while, he not only recognized
his wife and son, he managed to issue a few stum-
bling words from lips still slightly slack. The words
were incoherent, but a sign that his vocal cords were
struggling to improve. Lizzy gave him a smile, said
some affectionate words, and lightly patted his
blanket.

'Keep going, Dad,' said Bobby.

They were not encouraged to stay long, but were assured by Dr Hardy that the patient had every chance of recovering. The pertinent question was how long would it take? Lizzy said she didn't mind how long, providing it would work.

'He does need extended rest and treatment,' said Dr Hardy.

'Well, all I ask,' said Lizzy, 'is that we can have him back home when the time's right.'

'I think, yes, I think I can promise you that, Mrs Somers,' said Dr Hardy.

'Thanks for all you're doing for him,' said Bobby.

On their way out they passed a nursing sister. Anneliese Bruck gave them a smile, although she did not know who they were any more than they knew her.

Boots and Tim arrived in the afternoon. They were allowed to look in on Ned for a few moments and no more than that. He was asleep and not to be disturbed. Then they went to reception and asked if they could see Sister Bruck.

The receptionist took their names, made enquiries and informed them that Sister Bruck was busy in casualty. She would not be available for some while.

'If you'd care to wait – ?'

'We'll wait,' said Tim.

It was forty minutes before Sister Bruck entered the waiting room. Depending from her shoulder by its long strap was a large white handbag. Boots and Tim came to their feet. Anneliese smiled. She had time to spare. It was her afternoon break, although an emergency might cut it short.

'Good afternoon, gentlemen,' she said, her composure and her perfect English equalling those of a well-brought-up native of these shores. 'I'm so sorry to have kept you waiting.'

'Don't mention it,' said Tim. 'Anneliese, this is my father, once Colonel Robert Adams, now a civilian like me, but fairly important to his family and his business. Pa old soldier, this is Anneliese Bruck, once my Benghazi nurse and my guardian angel. She never forgot my daily intake of salt tablets.'

'So you're his saviour, are you?' said Boots.

'Mr Adams, your son had many absurd moments then, and has now had another,' said Anneliese. She and Boots regarded each other with natural interest. She recognised him at once, and her blue eyes reflected new astonishment. Because of her cap and uniform, Boots for the moment was only aware he might perhaps have seen her before today. 'I simply cannot believe this,' said Anneliese.

'What can't you believe?' asked Tim.

'I met your father many weeks ago,' said Anneliese. 'Mr Adams, don't you remember that?'

Boots took a keener look at this classical German blonde. Memory stirred.

'Well, I'm damned,' he said.

'I hope not,' said Anneliese. 'You were introduced to me outside your house. I was with your daughter Eloise and her husband, Colonel Lucas, friends of my sister and her husband.'

'Good God, so you were,' said Boots.

369

'Great balls of fire,' said Tim, 'what have we got now? Another head-blowing example of a shrinking world?'

They all looked at each other. Tim showed a huge grin. Boots's lurking smile surfaced. Anneliese's lips twitched and she laughed. It was infectious enough to catch on.

Then for long minutes it was all quick words of fact, reminiscence, and cementing friendship, Anneliese eventually reaching the moment when she extracted Tim's commando beret from her handbag. It was folded and wrapped in tissue paper. She gave it to Tim. He unwrapped it, and there it was, a souvenir of Benghazi, the war in the Western Desert, and a German army nurse who had an English grandmother.

'Now what do I say?' he asked.

'Thank you?' suggested Boots.

'That doesn't quite tell the whole story,' said Tim, and Anneliese thought him very much his father's son. They were both fine-looking men, with the same kind of deep grey eyes, although the father's left one seemed a little darker than the right. She diagnosed impaired sight. Was that the result of a war wound?

'Anneliese,' said Tim, 'you must meet my wife and daughter one day soon.'

'You must invite me, then,' said Anneliese. 'Have you and your father seen Mr Somers?'

'We were allowed a short time with him,' said Tim, 'and it seems he's slowly improving.'

'I'm very glad,' said Anneliese. 'I really must go now, my afternoon break is up. How very nice to have met both of you again, and how grateful I am that life can be kind enough to give us moments to treasure. Some events are forgettable, some are always remembered. Goodbye now.'

'Only for the time being,' said Tim.

'It's been a great pleasure,' said Boots.

They shook hands with her and left.

Chapter Thirty-Five

Friday evening.

Anneliese was ready to return the first three chapters of Harry's novel. They had absorbed her. The first chapter dealt with the progressive build-up to a frightful murder, that of a psychiatrist. Harry had defined clearly the victim's character and his method of dealing with patients, while making a shadowy and anonymous figure of the would-be murderer. His description of the eventual act itself was quite chilling.

The second chapter featured a scenario at Euston station, where a night train to Scotland awaited passengers. Harry had drawn interesting little cameos of people arriving and boarding, creating an atmosphere of anticipation. He gave prominent attention to a man and a woman arriving separately, the man boarding first, to thread his way along the full length of the corridor until he reached the final coach and found an empty compartment. The woman followed five minutes later, entering the compartment from the platform, and there they were, together and eyeing each other with interest. Anneliese assumed they were the principal protagonists, the psychopaths.

In the third chapter Harry dealt with how they fell into easy and fluent conversation as soon as the train clattered its way out of the station, heading north into the dark night. Anneliese thought he made a success of pointing up the man as a charming sophisticate, the woman as a quite exquisite creature of vivacious appeal, with a winning and infectious smile. The chapter ended as they entered the dining car together, with the train running at speed through the night.

Perhaps the only criticism she could make was that Harry overdid the dialogue, but she could leave it to his agent to comment on that.

She did not return the chapters until Cindy was in bed. She heard Harry calling from the kitchen.

'All quiet below decks, pet?'

'Daddy, I'm nearly asleep.' Cindy's bedroom door was open.

'Oh, carry on, bo'sun.'

Anneliese, on her landing, heard him cross to Cindy's bedroom. She heard him murmur something, then the sound of a closing door and his return to the kitchen.

Ten minutes later, down she went. She knocked lightly on the kitchen door, ajar.

'Mr Stevens?' she said quietly.

'Come in, Miss Bruck.'

In she went. He was seated at the table, enjoying a mug of tea. He wore a thick unbuttoned woollen shirt and light-coloured winter corduroys. If his thick hair needed brushing, it did not spoil the picture of a man at peace with life and his little world.

'Good evening, Mr Stevens,' she said.

'Greetings, m'lady, like a cup of tea?' smiled Harry.

'Thank you, but no,' said Anneliese.

'Sure? Hello, what's that you're clasping to your— what's that you're holding?' Harry avoided 'boz' in the nick of time.

'The first three chapters of your novel,' said Anneliese.

'Well, come and sit down,' said Harry, 'and give me your verdict. I order you to pull no punches.'

Anneliese seated herself opposite him and placed the typescript on the table.

'Harry –'

'I like that,' said Harry.

'Good. Then you must call me Anneliese. Harry, I enjoyed these chapters very much, you really have created interest, anticipation and suspense.'

'All that?' said Harry, regarding her with glimmering eyes. Damned if she wasn't wearing that soft white robe again, the robe that made an utterly fetching woman of her and reduced him to hopelessness. 'Interest, anticipation and suspense, all three?'

'Harry, it's really very good, and you must finish the whole novel, and then let your agent see it.'

'I'll have to be sweet to her,' said Harry, 'she earns very little commission from me at the moment.'

'You must finish it,' insisted Anneliese. 'Now I want to ask you a very important question.'

'Such as am I going to increase your rent? Never, Miss Bruck –'

'Anneliese.'

'That's a lovely name,' said Harry helplessly.

'Is it?' Anneliese smiled. 'Harry, are you in love with me?'

'No,' said Harry, panicking.

'I think you are.'

'Why do you think so?'

'Because of the way you look at me, and sometimes the way you won't look at me. As now.'

'I've got something in my eye,' said Harry, blinking.

'I'm sure you haven't. Harry?'

'Let's talk about German sausage,' said Harry. 'I've heard it's famous for flavour. I've never sampled it myself, but—'

'Harry, look at me,' said Anneliese. Harry sighed and looked at her. 'Now,' she said, 'if you love me, why don't you ask me to marry you?'

'Marry you?'

'Yes, why don't you?'

Harry drew a breath.

'In the first place, you can't be serious – '

'But I am.'

'In the second place, I don't have a bean, just a few quid in the bank, and Cindy's got her eye on that for bills and housekeeping. In the third place, you're fit for a prince, not an old Chipping Norton bloke like me.'

'I don't want a prince, Harry, I want a kind and affectionate man who would never dream of shooting old women or murdering innocent boys.'

'That,' said Harry, 'was the work of the depraved, and you shouldn't let your memories torment you so much.'

'Harry, I want you to marry me,' said Anneliese.

'Jesus help me,' said Harry, 'you're undermining

my common sense and my resolution. Anneliese, what could I give you? I don't even have a job, only some vague prospects as a writer.'

'I have enough for both of us, and even more,' said Anneliese, composure unfaltering. It represented determination. 'My sister and I inherited a small fortune when Mama died. My share was transferred from a German bank to a Farnham bank only a week after I arrived, and has since been transferred to a bank here, in Camberwell Road. So what is there to worry about?'

'A hell of a lot,' said Harry. 'We'd all be living off your money, and that's out. Out, Anneliese, out.'

'Very well, I'll give it all away,' said Anneliese.

'All your money?'

'Yes. I would rather have you as my husband and Cindy as my daughter than money in a bank.'

'You don't know what you're talking about,' said Harry, as desperate as the last man aboard a sinking ship.

'I at least know exactly what I want,' said Anneliese. 'Harry, you are going to marry me, do you understand?'

'No,' said Harry, 'I'll fight it, day and night, so help me God.'

'It will do you no good, for I shall win,' said Anneliese. 'Harry, I love you, do you at least understand that?'

'What?'

'So marry me,' said Anneliese. 'You have nothing, you say, but you have yourself and that is worth more to me than anything else I can think of. I live here among London's cockneys, and they call me "love" and "dearie". But in Russia and Germany, I have known cruelty beyond all forgiveness, I have seen stacked bodies of murdered people, and roadsides littered with men, women and children who have died of cold and starvation. I have known Russians almost on my heels, and that, Harry, is terrifying.'

Harry was silent for a moment, then he said, 'Tell me, were you ever a victim of rape?'

'No, Harry, I escaped Stalin's barbarians when I reached Berlin, when they were only a short distance behind our medical team. We all kept going until we stumbled into the safety of the American lines.'

'Thank God for that,' said Harry.

'If I had suffered in that way,' said Anneliese, 'would it have made you see me differently?'

'It would only have increased my feelings for you,' said Harry.

'And you would have married me?'

'Like a shot,' said Harry, 'but not out of pity.'

'So why won't you marry me now?'

'I've told you.' Harry almost groaned. 'I definitely need help. Anneliese, fetch a doctor.'

'My dear man, you don't need a doctor,' murmured Anneliese, 'you have me.'

'I'm still trying to fight that,' said Harry. 'May I ask you a personal question?'

'Please do,' said Anneliese.

'What are you wearing under that robe?'

'Only myself.'

'God, I'm done for,' said Harry, and went down with the ship.

'You will marry me, then?'

'I could have stayed afloat,' said Harry, 'but I

forgot to wear a lifebelt. God knows what Cindy will say when I tell her I'm going to marry you.'

'She may surprise you,' said Anneliese. 'Harry, please arrange everything concerning the marriage, and now come upstairs with me.'

'Don't tell me you're going to sit me down at my typewriter,' said Harry.

'Heavens,' said Anneliese, 'would I want to do that to a man who has just proposed to me? No, no, we shall make love as a guarantee that we belong to each other, and then I am going to look after you for the rest of my life. Harry, have you no idea how I need a man like you after knowing the worst of all kinds?'

Harry shook his head and smiled.

'All I know is that you arrived in this house like God's gift,' he said.

'So come upstairs,' said Anneliese.

Harry, his common sense defeated, thought, well, what was the point now of fighting temptation?

'Lead on, Lady Godiva,' he said.

They slept together that night, consummating their marriage in advance. Harry discovered warm, responsive beauty, and Anneliese discovered just what her new life was going to mean to her. The wonders of loving and being loved.

When Harry went to his own room early in the morning, Anneliese lay in perfect content, dismissing at last from her mind the pictures that had haunted her. They would come back, perhaps, but now there would always be Harry.

And Cindy.

*   *   *

'Daddy!'

'You're staggered?' said Harry, at breakfast with his daughter. 'So am I. But it's true.'

'True? It's utterly fab,' enthused Cindy. 'Crikey, who'd have thought it? Miss Bruck of all ladies. D'you know what Mr Topping, the grocer, calls her?'

'Tell me.'

'Queen Anne of Camberwell. He says he feels like bowing low every time she comes into his shop. Oh, wow, Daddy, aren't you proud of yourself?'

'The point is, pet, how do you feel about it?'

'About you marrying her?'

'And about her becoming your mother?'

Cindy, who could not remember her natural mother, gave the question some thought.

'Well,' she said, 'I've sometimes had a dreadful feeling it might turn out to be Miss Finney. Imagine it being our fab French lodger.'

'German.'

'Still, when you're married to her she'll be Mrs Stevens, so that's all right,' said Cindy. 'Daddy, I'm ever so happy for us.'

'I'll have to get a job, Cindy,' said Harry. 'I'm a qualified accountant, so—'

'Harry?' Anneliese appeared at the open kitchen door, dressed in hat and coat.

Harry quivered a little. Still very fresh in his mind was that night-time discovery of just how beautiful she was, and how responsive she'd been. She herself looked as composed as ever, except for the little smile parting her lips.

'Oh, there you are, Anneliese,' he said, 'I've just

been telling Cindy you're going to be her mother.'

'And do you mind, Cindy?' asked Anneliese gently.

'Oh, no,' said Cindy, 'I've just been telling Dad I had an awful feeling it might have been one of my schoolteachers, Miss Finney. She's been fancying Daddy for ages. I'm ever so glad it's going to be you.'

'Cindy, you're the dearest girl, and we shall be a very happy family,' said Anneliese. 'Harry, I'm just off to the hospital for the morning, and wanted to remind you we're all going to the theatre this afternoon.'

'Crikey, yes,' said Cindy, 'it could be a sort of celebration, couldn't it?'

'Yes, so I'll see you both later,' said Anneliese.

Harry saw her to the front door.

'I haven't come to yet,' he said, opening the door.

'Well, darling, I'm walking on air myself,' said Anneliese, 'and wondering what guided me to your house all those weeks ago.'

'A postcard in a shop window,' said Harry.

Anneliese laughed softly and kissed him warmly on his mouth. Then she walked out and down the steps towards the morning bustle of Camberwell Road, her footsteps light and quick.

Harry wondered how on earth he had come to win such a woman.

Sunday morning.

'Edwin,' said Chinese Lady, 'we must go and see Lizzy this afternoon.'

'Of course,' said Sir Edwin.

'I'm sure she's feeling a little bit better about Ned now.'

'This morning's bulletin did offer definite hope, Maisie.' Sir Edwin had just phoned Lizzy to be told improvement was taking place.

'I don't know what would become of Lizzy if anything happened to Ned,' worried Chinese Lady. 'I don't like things happening to any of the family.'

'Fortunately, my dear, we have an extraordinarily healthy brood.'

'Yes, but you never know,' said Chinese Lady, frowning. 'We'd best ask Lizzy if we can go and see Ned tomorrow, just in case.'

Sir Edwin smiled. Maisie was implying, of course, that if anything was going to happen to Ned, she ought to be there with Lizzy before it came about.

'I think we can rely on the opinion of Dr Hardy, Maisie.'

'Yes, but you never know,' said Chinese Lady again.

'Quite so, my dear, one never knows,' said Sir Edwin gently. His long and varied life had taught him that that was true of many things. Only his unchangeable Victorian wife was entirely predictable.

By Monday, Ned's improvement was continuing.

Things happened that day, though not of the kind Chinese Lady had had in mind.

Rosie and Matthew informed Hortense and Joe Robinson that they would like them to be permanent fixtures. Hortense beamed and Joe said he could now go to work on training the ferret Mista Chapman had just acquired.

A little while after Jennifer was on her way to school and Tim had left for his office, Felicity was in the kitchen with Maggie, discussing with her what shopping was needed.

'Well, ma'am, not a lot really,' said Maggie, 'except why don't we see if the fishmonger's got some nice fresh wings of skate, which everyone likes?'

'First-class idea, Maggie, let's toddle down to the shops in half an hour, say, and—' Felicity stopped. Out of the insufferable darkness appeared the misty image of a round face and a vague impression of dark eyes. A little breath escaped her, and she stared with the intensity of a woman trying to stabilize the image and make it permanent.

'Ma'am? Ma'am? You seeing something?'

'Maggie, I think I'm seeing your face.'

'Lor', me face isn't much,' said Maggie.

'It is to me,' breathed Felicity.

It was there for a full half-minute before fading.

It was one more vision, one more reason for hope.

At the garments factory, Jimmy called Clare into his office at lunchtime and gave her a silver bracelet.

'Jimmy, oh, Lor', ain't it lovely?' breathed Clare. 'But what's it for?'

'It's for you,' said Jimmy.

'No, I mean, why are you giving it to me when our wedding's not till Easter?'

'Well, I was passing a jeweller's shop one day,' said Jimmy, 'and love overcame my pocket. It's nothing to do with the wedding, it's to do with the fact that you're the girl of my dreams. I read that in one of my mum's magazines. Just a glance, and there it was at the end of a short story. Some handsome hunk, was saying it to the heroine. "You're the girl of my dreams." '

Clare laughed.

'Oh, you're me comic, Jimmy, and me friend for life.'

'Hold on,' said Jimmy, 'I'm not marrying you for friendship, I've got other ideas.'

'Oh, so have I,' said Clare, 'but I can't speak them.'

'Well, I can, as it's lunchtime,' said Jimmy. 'Come here.'

'Jimmy!' So gasped Clare moments later. 'Oh, you saucy devil.'

'How saucy?'

'Tell me again,' said Clare.

In the evening, Lulu emerged from the doctor's surgery looking a little wild-eyed. On this occasion, Paul was there, waiting for her.

'What's the verdict, Lulu?'

'It's positive this time. Positive. I'm going to have a baby.'

'Oh, little mother,' said Paul, delighted.

'Oh, hell,' said Lulu, true to form.

THE END

A SELECTED LIST OF FINE NOVELS
AVAILABLE FROM CORGI BOOKS

14451	7	KINGDOM'S DREAM	*Iris Gower*	£5.99
14895	4	NOT ALL TARTS ARE APPLE	*Pip Granger*	£5.99
14771	0	SATURDAY'S CHILD	*Ruth Hamilton*	£5.99
15045	2	THOSE IN PERIL	*Margaret Mayhew*	£5.99
14905	5	MULBERRY LANE	*Elvi Rhodes*	£5.99
14903	9	TIME OF ARRIVAL	*Susan Sallis*	£5.99
13951	3	SERGEANT JOE	*Mary Jane Staples*	£3.99
13856	8	THE PEARLY QUEEN	*Mary Jane Staples*	£3.99
13299	3	DOWN LAMBETH WAY	*Mary Jane Staples*	£5.99
13975	0	ON MOTHER BROWN'S DOORSTEP		
			Mary Jane Staples	£5.99
14106	2	THE TRAP	*Mary Jane Staples*	£4.99
14154	2	A FAMILY AFFAIR	*Mary Jane Staples*	£4.99
14230	1	MISSING PERSON	*Mary Jane Staples*	£5.99
14291	3	PRIDE OF WALWORTH	*Mary Jane Staples*	£4.99
14375	8	ECHOES OF YESTERDAY	*Mary Jane Staples*	£4.99
14418	5	THE YOUNG ONES	*Mary Jane Staples*	£5.99
14469	X	THE CAMBERWELL RAID	*Mary Jane Staples*	£4.99
14513	0	THE LAST SUMMER	*Mary Jane Staples*	£5.99
14548	3	THE GHOST OF WHITECHAPEL	*Mary Jane Staples*	£5.99
14554	8	THE FAMILY AT WAR	*Mary Jane Staples*	£5.99
14606	4	FIRE OVER LONDON	*Mary Jane Staples*	£5.99
14657	9	CHURCHILL'S PEOPLE	*Mary Jane Staples*	£5.99
14708	7	BRIGHT DAY, DARK NIGHT	*Mary Jane Staples*	£5.99
14744	3	TOMORROW IS ANOTHER DAY	*Mary Jane Staples*	£5.99
14785	0	THE WAY AHEAD	*Mary Jane Staples*	£5.99
14813	X	YEAR OF VICTORY	*Mary Jane Staples*	£5.99
14884	9	THE HOMECOMING	*Mary Jane Staples*	£5.99
14907	1	SONS AND DAUGHTERS	*Mary Jane Staples*	£5.99
14908	X	APPOINTMENT AT THE PALACE	*Mary Jane Staples*	£5.99
15046	0	CHANGING TIMES	*Mary Jane Staples*	£5.99
15031	2	THE DOORSTEP GIRLS	*Valerie Wood*	£5.99